WINGS OF FIRE

Martin Lake

For my father, George Smith, (1923–2019)

Leading Aircraftman 1808551

BOOKS BY MARTIN LAKE

Cry of the Heart

The Viking Chronicles
Wolves of War
To the Death

The Saxon Chronicles
Land of Blood and Water
Blood Enemy

The Lost King Chronicles
The Flame of Resistance
Triumph and Catastrophe
Blood of Ironside
In Search of Glory

A Love Most Dangerous
Very Like a Queen

A Dance of Pride and Peril
Outcasts
The Artful Dodger

Table of Contents

DECLARATION OF WAR

3rd September 1939

The wireless crackled into life causing the noise in the canteen to quieten a little. The voice of the announcer said, 'This is London. You will now hear a statement by the Prime Minister.'

Claire Lamb silenced some chattering girls with a look.

Neville Chamberlain's well-bred, melancholy yet emphatic voice came over the air.

'I am speaking to you from the Cabinet Room at 10 Downing Street,' he began. He sounded weary yet determined.

'This morning, the British Ambassador in Berlin handed the German Government a final note stating that, unless we heard from them by 11 o'clock that they were prepared at once to withdraw their troops from Poland, a state of war would exist between us.

'I have to tell you now that no such undertaking has been received, and that consequently this country is at war with Germany.'

Claire's hand went to her mouth. She felt dread and exhilaration all at the same time.

Chamberlain's voice continued for a little longer, explaining the reasons why the Government had taken the decision. Then his voice seemed to fade, became ghostly, the sound of a past time that had abruptly become quaint and ancient, dwindling into nothingness.

There came the sound of church bells and then a list of Government announcements.

All places of entertainment would be closed until further notice because if they were hit by a bomb large numbers would be killed or injured. People were requested not to crowd together unnecessarily in any circumstances. And then came talk of air raids, sirens and the dropping of poison gas.

Claire stared at the loudspeaker. Gosh, she thought, I'm going to be in the thick of it now. Her parents had always opposed her joining the Royal Air Force, fearing that war was around the corner. They had wanted her to stay home with them, safe and snug in the depths of Norfolk. But in the past eighteen months the only battles she'd had to fight were against over-amorous airmen. Now she might be posted to one of the airfields in the eye of the storm. They'd be worried sick.

She wasn't sure she wanted to be sent anywhere, to be honest. She was happy at Eleven Group Headquarters in Uxbridge and happy working in Air-Vice Marshal Gossage's office. Being at headquarters meant that she had a chance to shine, a chance to be noticed.

She'd been made a Company Assistant at Easter, to the great delight of her brother Jimmy who boasted to his friends that his big sister was the same rank as a Pilot Officer. She was well liked and well respected by her colleagues and her superiors. She was one of the more senior of the women plotters although she had long had her eye on a more strategic role.

Maybe the coming of war would make that more likely, she thought. After all, she was as good as any man and now the war might give have the opportunity to prove it.

She berated herself the moment she thought this. Her ambition now felt self-centred and tawdry.

She bit her lip anxiously. The country possibly faced years of conflict, just like in the Great War. Hopefully, the British Generals had learnt the lessons from those terrible years and would be able to avoid another stalemate, another bloodbath. And France did have the most powerful army in the world, an army which would surely put paid to that of Germany.

She glanced out of the window. She was less certain about the British air force, though. The Germans boasted that the RAF would be crushed within weeks by the mighty Luftwaffe. She prayed that they were wrong. She took a deep breath. Whatever happened in the next few months, she would do her very best.

She checked her watch. She needed to be in the Operations Room by noon.

She got there at five minutes to the hour. Sergeant Clover raised an eyebrow and glanced at the clock. 'The new girls have arrived ma'am. They're in the waiting room.'

Claire nodded and marched over to the room.

There were two girls there, both looking uncomfortable in their crisp new uniforms.

One leapt to her feet and saluted, the other, a very pretty girl, moved more slowly, almost as if deliberately taking her time. I'll have to watch her, Claire thought.

'Names?' she demanded.

'Betty Jones,' said the first one.

'Aircraftwoman Jones,' corrected Claire.

The girl nodded and looked crestfallen.

Claire turned to the second girl.

'Aircraftwoman Summers,' she said. She could not hide a certain tone of triumph at getting it right.

Claire stared at her for a few moments. 'And do you have a first name, Aircraftwoman Summers.'

'Yes. It's Flo. Florence'

'Florence, ma'am,' Claire said sharply. You must always say ma'am to a superior officer.'

'Even to the men? Ma'am.'

Claire's eyes narrowed with a sudden chill.

Flo gulped anxiously. She had always enjoyed giving cheek to her work superiors but now it appeared she may have gone too far and with the wrong person. She was unsure whether to hold the officer's gaze or look down. Luckily, before she made up her mind, Claire turned on her heel.

'Follow me,' she said and marched out of the room.

'That's not fair,' Flo whispered. 'She told you not to say your first name. Then she demanded mine.'

Claire pretended she hadn't heard this and smiled to herself. It was always good to keep new girls uncertain at first. To scare them even.

But then she paused in her stride. 'Did you hear Mr Chamberlain's broadcast?' she asked. 'That we're now at war with Germany?' Despite herself, she could not keep the kindness from her voice.

They shook their heads, looked astonished and then scared.

'Don't worry, Claire said. Just do your job and everything will be fine.'

Jack White whistled to himself as he listened to the broadcast. The spanner in his hand felt heavy and unwieldy suddenly and he put it back in his toolbox. Two of his uncles had died in the last war, one of them only three days before the Armistice. He felt sick inside.

Out of the corner of his eye he saw Harry Smith hurrying towards him. 'Did you hear the Prime Minister?' he called.

Jack gestured to the command hut. 'It was on the loudspeaker. The whole bloody airfield heard it.'

He stared at Harry, feeling an intense wave of concern for him. 'At least we won't be in the trenches,' he said.

'No. But we'll be in the front line.'

'You will. Not me.' Jack gave a rueful smile.

'Well, it's what I signed up for.'

Harry scanned the line of Hurricanes dotted across the field. 'I just hope they keep that warmonger Churchill out of the government. Or put him in charge of the Navy and not us.'

Jack did not answer. They had different views on Winston.

'Perhaps they'll take you back as an engineer,' Jack said.

'The RAF's spent too much money making me a pilot to allow that. Besides, becoming an engineer was only a means to an end. I only ever wanted to fly.'

But not die, Jack thought.

'Best get this kite fixed,' Harry said, tapping the wing. 'I need the practice.'

━━━

Evelyn Nash glanced at her husband. Chamberlain's speech had caused a subtle change in him. In New York he had been a witty, self-deprecating RAF aide. Now he stood more upright, more determined. There was a stern yet somehow vulnerable look on his face.

She touched him on the chest.

'What will this mean?' she asked.

'I'm a Squadron Leader, Evie. I shall be posted to some airfield somewhere.'

'Not quite the honeymoon you promised me.' She almost succeeded in making her tone sound light.

'I'm sorry, darling.' He took her in his arms and held her tight, making her feel contained and safe.

'Perhaps you should go back to America,' he said.

She pulled away from him. 'I'm not doing that, Tony. We've only been married a week.'

He started to argue, even though he knew from experience that it was a futile exercise.

'But, Evie, it will be dangerous for you here.'

'Not as dangerous as for you. Do you really think I'd let you stay here to fight Hitler on your own? Besides, what would I do in America?'

Tony's eyes flashed with a sudden thought. 'You could talk to your father's friend. The one who is friends with President Roosevelt.'

'Harry Hopkins? What would I talk about?'

'Ask him to persuade the President to come in on our side. To declare war on Germany.'

Evelyn laughed and put her hand on Tony's shoulder. 'That's what I love about the English,' she said. 'You're all so wonderfully innocent.'

Tony frowned, not understanding what she meant.

'Harry Hopkins might be keen to fight the Nazis,' she explained, 'but the American people aren't. Roosevelt knows this. Whatever he may think about the situation, he's not going to lead the country into a foreign war.'

She kissed him on the lips. 'So, you're stuck with me, buster. Whether you like it or not.'

He grinned. 'I expect I'll come to terms with it.'

―――

Rupert Buckingham looked at the cigarette in his hand. So this was it, the moment of truth; the moment he knew he had been born for.

He wondered what his father would be thinking now. Hoping that his eldest son would be a credit to him, to the family, to the country even. His father had demanded that he join the Horse Guards, just as he had done and his father and grandfather and great grandfather before him. A long line of Buckingham men taking their rightful place in the Blues.

His mouth gave a curious little turn as he recalled his father's horrified reaction when he told him he wanted to join the RAF. 'They're little better than mechanics,' he said with contempt. His view had not changed a jot over the past five years.

Buckingham gave a little snort of amusement and put the cigarette back in the packet. His father had made Lieutenant Colonel amidst the slaughter of the Great War. He would do better than that. Become Group Captain, maybe even Air Commodore or Air Vice Marshal. Why not, he thought. Why on earth not?

Frank Trent slowed to a jog. It had been a good run, he had stretched himself going to the river and back and he was satisfied at his speed. His cousin Paul Bennett hurtled past in his new Buick, tooting his horn and waving in a friendly manner. They were going downtown this evening, maybe see a movie.

He took a deep breath and walked into the house. The air seemed to vibrate and crackle. He guessed that another argument between his father and his Aunt Mildred had just taken place.

His aunt was sitting in her seat by the window, staring fixedly at her hands which clenched and unclenched ceaselessly although she seemed not to notice. His father sat by the fireplace, scanning a newspaper. It looked as if he had been there the whole morning.

'Frank's back from his run, Walter,' his aunt said.

His father flung down his paper and glared at Frank.

'Been having fun running with that boy, Jesse Owens?' he demanded. The usual attempt to rile him. He never as much as suspected that Frank admired the young black athlete.

'Plenty. Thank you.' The last words took on a tone of derision he had not really intended.

His father snorted and reached out to turn on the radio.

It crackled into life, the morning news bulletin, seemingly the only thing which interested his father anymore.

'Here is the news for Sunday 3rd September. The new Chief of Staff of the army has proposed a huge increase in army numbers. President Roosevelt has emphasised that any new soldiers will be volunteers and has ruled out conscription. He is scheduled to talk on the radio later today.'

His father shook his head in irritation.

'In foreign news, Prime Minister Chamberlain of Great Britain has announced that Britain has declared war on Germany. The Irish Free State and Spain have both declared neutrality.'

Frank stared at his aunt. Her face had gone white. Her grandfather was from England and, although she had never met any of them, she still exchanged Christmas cards with two cousins in London.

'Another European bloodbath,' Walter sneered. 'I doubt it will last as long as the Great War. Germany will soon put paid to England.' He chuckled. 'Serves them damn Limeys right.'

There was a long silence. A blackbird called from the front stoop.

'Why do you hate the British so much?' Frank asked. His father's long simmering vitriol had grown stronger over the last year.

'Haven't you read your history, boy? Haven't you heard of King George and his tyranny? About how our ancestors had to take up arms against him? Not to mention how the Limeys tricked us into going to war in 1917. Lost a lot of my pals in that war.'

'Don't talk that way,' Mildred said. 'And don't you start either, Frankie. There's enough war in the world without having it in my own living room.'

Frank muttered an apology and went into the yard.

Major Tomasz Kaczmarczyk pulled as hard as he could on the stick. If he didn't get airborne he would be a corpse.

It was the third day since the Germans had invaded. Most of the Polish Air force had been dispersed to small, secondary airstrips with limited resources. Where he was based had a runway so rough his teeth rattled as he took off. He had lost count of how many missions he had flown in that time.

His commanding officer had been killed on the second day of the invasion and he was told by telephone that he was now in charge of the Escadrille. The line must have been cut immediately after, for that had been the final communication. He would have to pursue the war as he saw fit, now.

His eyes were raw from peering at the sky, his thumb blistered from the shooting he had done. He calculated that his men had enough fuel and ammunition for only two more sorties. If they continued to be killed at the present rate, his force would be so reduced they might be able to mount three sorties.

He cleared the trees and headed west. Within minutes he saw a huge force of Messerschmitt Bf 109s heading in the direction of Warsaw. He turned towards them, heedless of the loss of fuel. If he didn't reach them, didn't fight, then the mission would be a failure.

He knew that his plane was markedly inferior to those of the Germans. But he and his men were better trained than their enemies, much better. They had already inflicted terrible defeats on German bombers and fighters. But he knew there would be few more opportunities to do so.

He led his men at breakneck speed into the German pack. The Messerschmitts were better armed and much faster but the Polish P.11 was a more manoeuvrable plane and gave better all-round vision. His men joked that it meant they could clearly recognise which Messerschmitt would kill them.

He pressed his trigger, tearing a huge gash in a German plane. It began to spiral to the earth but he had no time to see more because two Messerschmitts had turned in pursuit of him. He dodged them and then put his plane into a dizzying climb.

At five thousand metres he flipped the plane and plummeted towards the Germans. The other advantage of the P.11 was that it could dive faster than any other plane in the world. He emptied his guns as he closed, making his second kill of the day.

The rest of his men had also exhausted their ammunition and were fleeing from the action. As he approached the airstrip, he saw a thin column of black smoke rising from the rear of the field.

He made a poor landing, his exhaustion clearly taking hold. He gave a prayer of thanks that he had survived yet again. Then he looked around. Only four of the seven planes had made it back.

Wearily he climbed out of the cockpit. The senior man of the ground crew approached with a terrible look on his face.

'A German bomber spotted the strip,' he said. 'It was only one bomb but it's destroyed the last of the ammunition and much of the fuel.'

Kaczmarczyk closed his eyes, wearily. Then it was over. Everything was lost.

He took a deep breath and put his hand on the man's shoulder. 'Is there enough fuel for us to fly again?'

'Yes. But no ammunition.'

'I don't intend to fight. Not today.' He turned towards the south. 'We'll fly to Romania. And then we'll make our way to our allies in France. And, God willing, we'll beat the bastards yet.'

━━━

Air Commodore Keith Park turned off the radio and folded his arms. His gaze strayed to Air Chief Marshal Dowding who had listened to Chamberlain's address in silence, straight-backed, staring out of his office window.

Park knew better than anyone what burdens would fall upon Dowding's shoulders. On our shoulders, he realised, for as Dowding's deputy at Fighter Command, he too would be involved in the critical early decisions of the war.

Dowding was meant to have retired from the RAF in June. But at the last minute he had been informed that, because of the international situation, this would be postponed for nine months. At the time he had shown no sign of how he felt about this, one way or the other. But now Park wondered if he regretted the decision. It would be understandable if he did. He was about to find himself in the lions' den.

'Do you think our defences will hold?' Dowding murmured.

Park was alarmed to hear an uncharacteristic doubt in his commander's voice.

Dowding had fought for his system since he had become Head of Fighter Command in 1936, in fact for eighteen months before that when he had begun to support the development of radar.

Park had been involved for only a year but he had soon realised the complexities of the situation and the difficulties that Dowding had been grappling with to get it working. For him to display any doubt was truly troubling.

Dowding turned and stared at him. To Park's relief his face showed only a fierce determination. He rapped on the desk.

'No time for standing around, Park,' he said. 'We've got a battle to win.'

CONFERENCE

4th September 1939

Air Commodore Keith Park tidied the papers on his desk, got to his feet and stretched.

A silver haired Flight Lieutenant came in the room and handed him a folder marked Top Secret. 'This has just come in, sir.'

Park glanced at the contents briefly and his eyebrows rose in surprise. 'Thank you, Longley,' he said. 'Let me know if there's an update. Sir Hugh will wish to know as well.'

'Very good, sir.'

Park thrust his cap on his head and left the office.

Johnny Longley glanced at the clock. The walk from the communications office to Park's office had taken exactly two minutes but in that time he had opened the folder, read the whole document and put it back as if unseen. Nothing much got past Longley and he prided himself on it. And no one suspected this of him.

Park knocked on Air Chief Marshal Dowding's office and entered without waiting for the command to do so. Dowding did not bother looking up. There was only one person who he allowed to enter without being told to.

'Sit down, Park,' he said. He wrote a final sentence, read what he had written, crossed out a few words and signed it.

Only then did he look up at Park.

'How are things progressing?' he asked.

'Reasonably,' Park answered. He passed the folder to Dowding. 'There's been a raid on a German shipyard at Wilhelmshaven.'

Dowding seemed as surprised as Park had. 'So, first blood to us,' he said.

Dowding swiftly scanned the report. 'But by Bomber Command, unfortunately,' Park said.

'It was unfortunate for them that they lost half their planes. And with little damage to the German ships.'

'It seems they flew in too low.'

Dowding read the report again. 'This is marked Top Secret. Apart from you, has anyone seen it?'

'Johnny Longley brought it to me so, naturally, he would have read every word.'

Dowding grunted. 'He's safe enough.'

Park nodded. Longley believed that no one knew about his constant gathering of information. This was a little surprising, for Park occasionally asked him about some detail he had forgotten and Longley would put him right. As often as not, it concerned something that the Flight Lieutenant should never have known.

Dowding's telephone rang. 'The Secretary of State for Air has arrived, Park. I'd like you to stay for the meeting.'

Sir Kingsley Wood was ushered in. He was a short, portly, bespectacled man with the air of a rather thoughtful owl. He was accompanied by the Chief of the Air Staff, Sir Cyril Newall.

It was common knowledge that Dowding had been the best candidate to head the RAF but, when the time came to appoint a new man, Kingsley Wood's predecessor had given the position to the more junior and less talented Newall.

Park wondered if Wood would have made the same decision, especially now that the country was at war.

'Welcome, Sir Kingsley,' Dowding said warmly, indicating a chair. 'Sir Cyril,' he added more coolly.

Park's eyes went from Dowding to Newall. Dowding looked like a bank manager or the Headmaster of a minor public school. His nickname Stuffy suited him perfectly.

Newall, on the other hand, appeared exactly like the press would want the Marshal of the RAF to look. He was upright, well-groomed and handsome, with a faraway look in his eye. He would have suited the role in a feature film better than in life, Park thought.

'How are things with Fighter Command, Sir Hugh?' Wood asked.

'Much better, sir,' Dowding said. 'The planes are being delivered at a very good pace.'

Newall sniffed. He was an advocate of bombing campaigns and thought that the RAF should have continued to concentrate on producing heavy bombers.

Wood, however, had different ideas. The production of fighter planes was three and a half times greater than when he had taken office eighteen months earlier. Bomber production had not increased anything like as much.

'And your system, Dowding?' Wood continued. 'Are you quite happy with it?'

Dowding cleared his throat. 'Happy would be a rather optimistic term, Sir Kingsley. But the elements are in place.'

'Show me.'

Dowding got to his feet and began to chalk on a blackboard. 'Once enemy aircraft are identified by our Radio Direction and Finding stations they communicate it to Fighter Command Headquarters here.' He tapped on where he had written Bentley Priory. 'The Observer Corps verify the numbers and type of aircraft in the raid.'

'Are you happy with the Observer Corp, Dowding?' Newall asked. 'They're civilians, after all.'

'I'm a civilian,' Wood said with some asperity.

Park smiled to himself. Wood might look like a kindly country doctor but he was not a man to be crossed. He was known for getting things done and mostly he did this by diplomatic and judicious means. But, if need be, he could be determined and hard-nosed.

'The Observer Corps have exceeded my expectations,' Dowding answered Newall. He immediately turned back to the board.

'Here at Headquarters we assess the level of threat and then pass on this information to one of the three Groups which can deal best with the attack. They then use this information to decide which airfields will send squadrons to intercept.'

Newall looked unimpressed. 'But that's three links in the chain, Dowding. From the radar stations to here, to the groups and then to the airfield commanders. Surely it would be better for the radar people to communicate directly to the Command Groups or even to the airfields.'

'We've tried that in tests. We concluded that it led to a great deal of confusion. It might take a little longer but if the information comes here for my people to filter there is less chance of mishaps.'

'We don't sit on the information, sir,' Park added. 'Our latest tests show that we get it to Groups within two minutes or so.'

Newall looked unconvinced.

'And exactly what happens when the information leaves here?' Wood asked.

'Air Commodore?' Dowding said, holding out the piece of chalk.

Park got up and replaced Dowding at the board.

'One of the key improvements,' he said, 'is that the information we have is replicated exactly at the Group Headquarters and at the airfields. We have a large map of the whole country here at Bentley Priory. Groups have a similar map but only of the part of the country they are responsible for. What we plot on our maps they plot on theirs. That way, we are all singing off the same hymn sheet.'

'And at the airfields?'

'It's the same system, Sir Kingsley. They have the same map as Group does so know exactly what is going on in their airspace and nearby.'

'It still seems a long-winded process to me,' Newall said. 'Still, Fighter Command is your responsibility, Dowding, so I suppose I must leave it to you.'

Wood looked at him with narrowed eyes. 'I couldn't agree more. You've done a splendid job, Sir Hugh.'

Dowding allowed himself a rare smile.

Wood took out a handkerchief and blew his nose. He had no need to, but it bought him time to frame his more serious words.

'We have only three Groups,' he said. 'Do you think that's enough?'

Dowding nodded. '13 Group has responsibility for Scotland, Northern Ireland and the north of England. It's a large area but we don't expect it will receive much attention from the Germans as it's so far from their airfields. 12 Group has responsibility for the Midlands, East Anglia, Lincolnshire and North Wales. 11 Group has London, the south of England and Wales.'

'The southern Groups seem rather large,' Wood murmured. He looked slightly troubled but waved his hand, deciding not to say more.

'We've got good men in charge of each of the Groups,' Newall said. 'Very good men.'

'And will they obey your orders, Sir Hugh?' Wood asked. 'Obey them implicitly and without question? For that's what your system would appear to require.'

'Park's been responsible for designing how Group Commanders fit into the system,' Dowding said. 'He's best placed to answer.'

'Sir Hugh and I have discussed this at length,' Park said. 'While he will lay down the general guidelines for each day's conflict, the

Group commanders will retain tactical control. They have a closer oversight of their particular patch and will need to retain flexibility and decision making powers.'

'Patch?' Newall said. 'You make it sound like part of a local constabulary.'

'That's quite an apt analogy, sir. After all, the Nazis are no better than gangsters.'

Wood chuckled at the comment but Newall did not, wondering if Park was slyly insulting him.

'Thank you, Air Commodore,' he said. 'We mustn't keep you from your duties any longer.'

Park got to his feet, gave a crisp salute and left the office.

Newall leaned forward and spoke in a lowered voice. 'Is that fellow up to the job, Dowding? There's a question about him succumbing to stress in the last war.'

'He had fought too many combat missions over the trenches,' Dowding said in a curt tone. 'He was given a fortnight's leave, as I recall. I don't think we need to worry about Park's ability to handle stress. After all he destroyed more than a dozen German planes and damaged scores more. And there was no question about his leadership of his squadron.'

'Very well,' Newall said, although he still seemed doubtful.

Wood got to his feet. 'We must be going, Dowding,' he said. 'Thank you very much for your time.'

'My pleasure, Sir Kingsley.'

The two men left but Newall paused by the door and looked at Dowding. 'I have to say that you're doing a pretty good job, Dowding. You and Park both.'

Dowding thanked him but was unable to hide a look of surprise. Praise from an unfriendly corner was the highest praise imaginable.

PARENTS AND CHILDREN

15th September 1939

Claire Lamb took a deep breath and knocked on the door. The curtain twitched and her mother's eyes met hers. Moments later the door was thrown open by her brother Jimmy. He flung himself into her arms.

'Careful of my uniform,' she said.

'What are you doing back?' he asked, his joy immediately changing to anxiety.

'I've got three days leave. I thought I'd spend it being aggravated by my kid brother.'

She followed him into the little living room. Her father had positioned himself by the fireplace, his unlit pipe in hand. Her mother stood by the window, her hands fiddling nervously with the cords of her apron.

'What's the reason for this visit?' her father asked. 'Have you left the RAF?'

'I do hope so,' said her mother, coming forward and taking Claire's hands. 'You'll be safe with us.'

'I've not left, mum. I've got important work to do. I'm a plotter now.'

'A plotter?' her brother gasped. 'Like spies and stuff?'

She tousled his hair. 'Plotting the movements of enemy aircraft, silly.'

She fell silent, realising that talk of enemy aircraft might alarm her parents even more. 'If Hitler decides to attack, of course.'

'Why wouldn't he?' her father said. 'The Germans are trying to get their revenge because we beat them in the last war.'

Her mother put her hands to her ears. 'Don't talk of war, Henry. Don't talk of it.'

'It might not come to anything,' Claire said quickly. 'Mr Chamberlain thinks Hitler will back down now that we and France have called his bluff.'

Her mother seized on Claire's words with trembling hope, her father looked doubtful, her brother disappointed.

'I'll never get to fight,' Jimmy said, bitterly.

His father gave him a gentle clip on the head. 'Let's hope so.' He gave his son a pensive look, then glanced at Claire and straightened his shoulders.

Claire smiled brightly. 'I'm famished from the journey. How about some tea?'

'How long are you staying?' her mother asked.

'Three days. That's all I'm allowed, I'm afraid. So let's make the best of it.'

***

Frank Trent pulled on the joystick and the nose of the Piper Cub lifted gently, taking him soaring above the powerline. Every time he wondered why they had built the airstrip so close to it. There had been several incidents where inexperienced pilots had clipped the line, leading to power failures and, on a number of occasions, crashes. He wasn't sure if he was lucky or just skilful, but he'd never had any mishap.

He levelled out and swung across Smith County. He'd lived here all his life, rarely travelled far from it, at least on the ground. He had an uncle in Wichita and visited him once when he was ten but that was as far as he'd ever been. In fact, apart from the occasional foray into Nebraska, he'd rarely ventured outside Kansas. Sometimes, though, when he was flying high, he got tired of looking at the endless prairies, the patchwork of near identical farms. Then he'd find his eyes straying to the horizon. Once he's even headed west, towards Colorado and the Rocky Mountains, but his fuel gauge began to plummet and he had decided to return home. Occasionally, he thought that this decision might have been a mistake.

Smith County was smack bang in the centre of the United States. Frank liked that, liked the idea of it being central, balanced, not extreme in any manner whatsoever. He'd owned a gyroscope as a child and, as he watched it turn, he would imagine that the rest of the country was like the gyroscope's swiftly spinning wheel and Smith County the immobile axis in the centre.

To his ears, the steady thrum of the engine was like the beating of his heart. Regular, predictable, something he ignored until he noticed a sudden variation, a stutter or gasp. Then he would listen intently, hands tightening on the stick. But this was a Piper Cub and as reliable as his old bicycle.

He headed north towards the Randall holdings, amongst the largest in north Kansas. The fields glowed rich in the morning sun, acre after acre of fine wheat, golden hued and full of promise. He moved the stick gently and the plane began a slow glide downward. As he lowered the plane still further, his tongue poked out of his mouth, like a snail peering out of its shell. The wheels of the plane were only a couple of feet above the wheat now and his jaw set with concentration. He flipped a switch and the chemicals began to spray across the crops.

He loved this manoeuvre, loved the delicacy, the danger, the sheer delight.

He sprayed the field and began to make a lazy, spiralling climb. Then it happened.

Crows were nesting in trees on the eastern edge of the field and something must have panicked them for the sky in front of him suddenly filled with their darting forms. They wheeled to avoid him and he did the same.

But a couple of the birds smacked into the windscreen, one so hard it splintered the glass so he could barely see through it. Even worse, he heard the propeller shriek and then stutter to a halt. Some of the birds must have hit it.

The nose of the plane dropped a little and began to lose height. He pushed the ignition frantically but it was no use. The propeller would not turn.

Frank cursed, squinting to try to get his bearings. A hundred yards to his right he glimpsed a road and he wrenched his control stick and headed for it. Because the shattered windscreen clouded his view, he had to hazard a guess as to his altitude. But his luck held and he made it over a line of bushes. As he landed, he heard a heavy thump and screech as one of his wings ploughed into a fence. The plane spun and came to a juddering halt.

He leapt from the plane, fearful the fuel tanks may have ruptured. As he hit the ground a car braked ten yards from him and Sheriff Grover stepped out.

'This ain't no airfield,' he called.

'Get out of here,' Frank called. 'The plane might explode.'

The sheriff needed no second word, leaping into the car and throwing it into reverse. He'd gone a hundred yards when he screeched to a halt and threw open the passenger door, yelling, 'Come on son, better get in.'

Frank sprinted towards the car and fell into the seat, lurching forward as the sheriff reversed the car still further.

'That should be far enough,' Frank said.

The sheriff hit the brake and turned his gaze from Frank to the plane.

'I hope you ain't gonna make a habit of this.'

'No sir. I was hit by a flock of crows and they smashed my windscreen.'

The sheriff grunted, almost as if he didn't believe him.

'Well that plane sure can't stay in the middle of the highway. Could we push it to one side?'

'If we used your vehicle to shunt it.'

The sheriff considered this for a moment and drove back towards the plane.

Frank was allowed to telephone his cousin Paul from the sheriff's office. He arrived half an hour later in his Buick and drove to the airfield.

Henry Sutton, who owned the airfield, the plane and the crop spraying business, was remarkably sanguine when Frank told him about the crash. He'd been a pilot himself and knew that the air was a treacherous element. He organised a truck to collect the plane, clapped Frank on the shoulder and told him to go home.

'That went better than I expected,' Frank told Paul as he got into the car. 'No complaints, no recriminations. And I get the rest of the day off.'

'I'm not surprised at how old Henry acted,' Paul said, 'he can't afford to rile you. You're the best pilot in Kansas, everyone knows it.'

Frank raised an eyebrow in a sardonic manner but he was pleased at Paul's remark.

'Your pa won't be happy, though,' Paul said. 'Busted aircraft and a sheriff's record. No sir, he won't be happy.'

'When is he ever happy?' Frank said with a shrug.

'Best not tell him any lies,' Paul continued, offering Frank a cigarette. The rest of the journey involved Paul asking countless questions about the accident and Frank giving the tersest of answers.

'Pity I've got to work,' Paul said as he drew up at Frank's house. 'Otherwise I'd have taken you for a beer.'

Frank sighed wistfully and got out of the car.

He took a deep breath as he walked into the house. His Aunt Mildred immediately sensed there was something wrong, wringing the tea-towel in her hands as she hurried in from the kitchen. 'You're back early?'

He nodded and glanced at his father.

Walter Trent was in his habitual chair by the fire-place. He stared into the middle distance and, as always, Frank wondered what he was seeing. He had been a car salesman but his business had collapsed in 1932 and he hadn't worked since. His second wife, Mildred, had just about made ends meet until Frank got a job at the airfield, first as a technician and then as a pilot. Now he was the breadwinner. Or at least he had been until this morning.

'I had a crash, Mommy Mildred,' Frank said.

Her hands went to her mouth.

'I'm not hurt, not even a scratch. But the plane's pretty badly damaged. Probably salvageable though.'

His father turned his gaze from the wall to his son. 'So, Amelia Earhart has come down to earth,' he said. 'I knew it was only a matter of time.'

'I wish you wouldn't call him that,' Mildred said.

Walter gave her a sneer.

'I'm a good pilot,' Frank said.

'Then I'd hate to see a bad one.'

The silence hung in the air.

'What happened, Frankie?' his aunt asked, nervously.

'He was conceived, that's what happened,' Walter said. 'I remember the occasion well, I was drunk and his mother finally gave me what I wanted.'

'Don't talk that way,' Frank said.

'Gonna stop me?' Walter laughed mirthlessly. 'So it looks like it's back to cleaning for you, Mildred.'

'I've not lost my job,' Frank said. 'Mr Sutton knows I'm a good pilot. I'll be back at work tomorrow. You don't need to worry about money not coming in.'

His father scoffed and returned to his newspaper.

Frank gave him a withering look and marched up to his bedroom.

He sat on his bed for an hour, thinking about the accident, about his relationship with his father, about his whole life. Before today everything had seemed fine, ticking along nicely. But now something had changed. He wondered if it was the accident or the way his father had behaved towards him. But try though he might he could come up with no explanation.

But suddenly the image of his aunt's face came back to him. Of the terrible shock and fear when she had heard about the declaration of war.

'The hell the British tricked us into the last war,' he muttered to himself. Then he pulled a suitcase from the bottom of his wardrobe and began to pack some clothes.

When it grew dark, he went downstairs, leaving a note behind for his aunt. Then he left his home.

⋯

'It's good to see you, son,' Charlie Smith said. 'We'll go down the pub this evening. Show you off to my pals.' He touched the insignia on Harry's shoulder. 'A pilot, by God. Never thought I'd see that when you joined up.'

Harry grinned and touched his head. 'I've not started using Brylcreem yet. That's for the rich buggers from the posh schools.'

'Don't go getting into fights with your betters,' his mother said, sternly. 'I've told you before.'

'They're not my betters, Mum. Not your betters either. They were just born lucky.'

'You saying there's something wrong with how you were born?' Her face grew sharp, ready for an argument.

'Of course not.' He groaned inwardly. Why was there always this battle with her? Why couldn't she be happy that he was getting on in life and doing what he wanted to.

'You should have stayed as a mechanic,' she continued. 'You should have stayed at Raleigh's, like your father. Made bicycles instead of fooling around with aeroplanes.'

'If he'd done that he wouldn't have become a pilot,' his father said. 'We should be proud of him.'

Suddenly she burst into tears. 'But what if he gets killed?' she wailed.

Harry gaped in astonishment. He had never seen his proud, stern, determined mother cry before.

'What if my boy never comes home to me?'

'I will, Mum,' he muttered, 'I promise.'

'What do promises matter anymore?' She threw herself on to her chair, unable to stop her tears.

＊

'Will I like them?' Evelyn asked as they walked up to their apartment.

'I'm sure you will,' Tony said. 'Father especially. Mother, well, she takes a little more getting used to. She's rather a strong personality.'

'This is a nice area. Are we in Whitechapel?'

Tony laughed. 'No. My mother wouldn't be seen dead around there.'

I thought your father was a vicar in Whitechapel. Where Jack the Ripper prowled.'

'He assists at a church in Cable Street. Where the Black Shirts were stopped in their tracks. But they live here, quite a way from the East End.'

She glanced at the building in front of her. Like many of London's mansion blocks it was made of good quality brick with fine sash windows and many decorative features. An imposing entrance festooned with flowers greeted them.

'This is rather grand, darling.'

'Well my parents are rather grand. Father comes from a long line of churchman, the prosperous kind who ruled the church like a fiefdom. My mother is the scion of a rather ancient, proud and wealthy family. Lords of the manor in a village in Shropshire. I couldn't stand the place.'

He pressed the bell and was allowed in by a doorman.

Tony's parents lived in a large apartment on the fifth floor, overlooking an elegant garden to the rear and with a glimpse of the river to the south. The sitting room was light and spacious, with a handsome leather settee, some wingback chairs and a grandfather clock. There was an imposing bookcase on the wall opposite the window and a small wireless set beside it. It was a handsome room, if a little austere.

Tony's father was a plump, jovial man with a fine head of hair, greying around the temples. He gave his son a hug, which surprised Evelyn a little. She had never seen any man do that before.

'Welcome to our home, Evelyn,' he said. 'I'm delighted to meet you at last.' He gave her a little peck on the cheek, so gently it might have been from a butterfly.

Tony's mother was slight of build, with a long, narrow face. Her hair was cut short and she had a sharp, suspicious gaze. She was wearing a neat skirt, a starched white blouse and some pearls. Despite the fact that it was a warm day, she wore a cardigan.

She lifted her cheek towards Tony and he gave it a little kiss.

'It's high time you finally came to see us,' she said. 'When did you disembark?'

'Two weeks ago. I had to go to my unit straight away. This is the first day's leave.'

'Where is your unit? Scotland? Australia?'

He looked a little annoyed. 'No, it's Tangmere.'

'Near Chichester,' his father said, quickly, keen to change the atmosphere. 'We holidayed there in 1918 didn't we, Winifred? Antony must have been only a toddler.'

'Actually,' Tony said, 'I shouldn't have mentioned where I'm stationed. Official Secrets Act.'

His father made a show of zipping his lips. His mother gave a disdainful look.

'I suppose you'd like some tea,' she said.

'Or a sherry,' his father said. 'Or a beer?'

'It's a bit early for alcohol, don't you think?' Mrs Nash said, sharply.

'Later then,' he said, beaming at Evelyn. He seemed totally unaware that his wife had just belittled him in front of her.

It was an uncomfortable afternoon for everyone except for Tony's father. He was the life and soul of the party; pleasant, amusing and keen that everyone was happy.

Tony's mother, on the other hand, sat in virtual silence, her cool eyes scrutinising Evelyn as if she were a cat watching a little bird.

Evelyn could not decide if she most resembled an iceberg or a volcano waiting to blow. She even criticised Evelyn for referring to her husband as Mr Nash.

'He's a canon, you see. You refer to him as Canon Nash.'

I wish I had a cannon, Evelyn thought. I'd stuff you in it. But she apologised, not to him but to her.

She sighed with relief when they left.

'How did that go?' Tony asked as they walked towards the river. His voice sounded light but she could tell that he was anxious.

'Do you really want to know?'

He nodded uncertainly.

'Well in that case, it went bloody awfully. Your father was all right, quite a bundle of fun in fact. But your mother, whoa. She certainly doesn't like me.'

'She's never liked any of my girlfriends, actually.' He sighed. 'Nor my school chums, come to that.'

Evelyn raised her eyes. She wondered if his mother even liked him very much.

'We shouldn't be doing this?' Betty whispered. 'We'll get into trouble for sneaking out of the base.'

'Don't be such a baby,' Flo said. 'No one will ever know. It's my grandma's birthday and I've never missed one yet. I don't mean to do so now.'

'But why do you want me to come?'

'Because you're my best friend. In fact, from now on, I'm officially making me your sister.'

Betty smiled. The minute she had told her that she was an only child Flo had decided to take her under her wing; with a determination which brooked no argument.

They hurried towards some arches beneath a railway line. The moment they had stepped out of the Tube station they had been engulfed by the darkness of the unlit streets. Underneath the arches they couldn't see a thing. But Flo led them on without hesitation.

'How can you walk so fast?' Betty said. 'I can't even see my feet.'

'Walked along here a million times. And do you smell that? Now I know exactly where we are. It's the gents toilet. Phew.'

They came out to the street once more and now the path ahead seemed a little clearer.

'My auntie's shop,' Flo said, waving her hand to the right. Then they crossed over the road and headed to a large pub. It was completely dark because of the black-out but the sound of a badly played piano came loudly from it.

Betty hesitated in front of the door.

'What's the matter?' Flo asked.

Betty bit her bottom lip. 'I've never been in a pub before.'

Flo's mouth opened wide. 'You're kidding?'

'No. My parents are teetotaller and they'd hate the thought of me going into a pub.'

What a goody two shoes, Flo thought. She immediately chastised herself for thinking it. Poor Betty. She needed a friend. Needed a sister. She put her arm in hers.

'This is my Uncle Ted's pub, it's lovely. Come on, Betty. Let's go and see my lot.'

The pub was dense with cigarette smoke. Most of the clientele were men, a large proportion of them drinking standing up, in front of the bar and around the dartboard. The women sat at tables, with glasses of port or stout in front of them.

The biggest group of people, however, congregated around the piano. A jolly looking fat man was pounding heavily at the keyboard, his face red and running with sweat. The people around were belting out a rendition of 'Knees up Mother Brown' with more gusto than skill. Keeping in time and harmony were not concepts they had ever come across.

Suddenly the man on the piano caught a glimpse of Flo, leapt from the stool and hurried over. He wrapped her in his massive arms, bellowing with delight.

'Here's my Flo,' he cried, 'come back from the war.' Then he almost dragged her across the floor to where an elderly lady was sitting close to the piano.

'Hello Florrie,' she said.

'Happy Birthday, Nan.' Flo thrust a small bottle of lavender water into her grandmother's hands.

She opened it and dabbed a little behind her ears with delight.

'Who's your pal?' she asked.

'Betty Jones. She works with me in the WAAF. She's my best friend. Like a sister in fact.'

'Any friend of my Flo's is a friend of mine,' the fat man said. 'And you look lovely, my dear, prettier than Vivien Leigh.'

'Leave it out, Dad,' Flo said. 'You must be drunk.'

'That's the trouble when he plays the old Joanna,' a woman said, kissing her on the cheek. 'Everyone buys him drinks.'

'This is my mum,' Flo said.

'Nice to see you, love.' She stepped closer to Betty and lowered her voice. 'Do me a favour will you, and make sure Flo keeps out of trouble in the RAF. She's a bit of a rascal, always has been.'

Her father smiled and then stepped to the middle of the floor. 'Shut up you lot,' he bellowed at the top of his voice. 'My little girl Flo's come back to see us. She'll put the wind up Adolf Hitler.'

He roared with laughter and the rest of the pub cheered.

Flo went bright red but Betty had never seen her look happier.

Rupert Buckingham put the key in the lock and opened the door. Things appeared exactly as they had whenever he came back from school for the holidays. The long corridor stretching ahead of him, sparse and cold, the cloakroom on the right, the hall table which never served any function on the left, the hall clock marking off the minutes and hours.

He opened the door to the morning room. His mother was sitting at the table reading some book or other, completely engrossed. His father was sitting in the winged chair in front of the empty grate, scrutinising The Times, his indignation at whatever he was reading almost palpable.

'Hello,' Buckingham said, loudly. 'I'm home on leave.'

His mother finished the paragraph she was reading, put down her book and stared at him. 'That's nice dear.'

His father lowered his newspaper and said not a word. Then he began to fold the paper up with the utmost determination. He looked like a character in a Hollywood film, rolling up his sleeves, readying himself for a fist-fight.

His mother tilted her head a little and Rupert bent and kissed her cheek. He always marvelled at how smooth it was, like that of a woman half her age. He kept half an eye on his father.

'You're here on leave,' his father said. 'I thought there was a war on. Do your high ups allow you leave in the middle of a conflict?'

'That's exactly why we've got leave, I suspect. The lull before the storm. Jerry could attack at any moment.'

'Germans, darling,' his mother said with a tone of distaste. 'You know I don't like you using slang.'

'Garage mechanics' slang,' his father said.

Buckingham's mouth moved with a sharp and angry twist but he kept silent.

'So how long are you staying?' his mother asked.

'Two days.'

He had been given five days leave but his parents' reception made him decide he would not take all of it.

'I'll get Mrs Baxter to make up your room. When she's finished downstairs.'

'Where's Violet?' Buckingham asked. He was desperate for his sister to appear, to be able to slip away and spend time with her.

'At the stables,' his mother said. 'She won't be back for luncheon.'

Buckingham's heart sank. His parents went back to their reading.

PHONY WAR

October 1939

It was a glorious autumn but Claire Lamb was not able to enjoy it much. The two girls assigned to her, Betty Jones and Flo Summers, were proving a handful. They were supposed to be fully trained in the task of plotting the movements of attacking aircraft but Claire had serious doubts about the quality of their training.

She thought back to when she first started and recalled how difficult she had once found what was now second nature to her. The voice would come through her headphones from the radar operator, saying how many planes had been spotted, their current location, height, speed and the direction they were headed.

She would then pick up a little wooden block and slot on to it labels showing the number and height of enemy planes and the RAF squadrons sent against them. Then she used a stick to move it across the map in step with the continual barrage of information coming through her headphones. She sometimes thought that she was like a croupier in a casino but without the glamour.

And neither the radar nor the operators were infallible. She had learnt that sometimes she needed to ignore what seemed obvious from the radar and make a calculated guess about exactly where the planes were headed. It was only later on, after she had been promoted, that she found out that some of the training exercises gave deliberately sketchy information in order to test if the plotters would make such calculations. And find out how accurate they were in doing so.

'You're very good,' her commanding officer had told her the day she got her first promotion. 'Better than some of the men, even.' He had meant it as a compliment, not realising how back-handed it was. She had determined to prove his words right, more than right.

She pursed her lips as she returned her attention to the new girls' plots. Yes, she should bear in mind how difficult it was for people at first. But she could not be too lenient, could not let careless mistakes go by without pointing them out.

Betty was accurate and painstaking but too much so. Claire had been amused at first to watch her moving the blocks with avid, nervous concentration, her tongue, unbeknown to her, sticking out like a child's. But she was not working as swiftly as she should.

'You need to speed up, Jones,' Claire told her firmly after the end of another frustrating exercise. 'The Jerries would be over London while you're still showing them over Kent.'

'Sorry, ma'am,' Betty said, her face a picture of woe.

Flo was the diametrically opposite. Her hands moved as fast as even more experienced plotters but she lacked accuracy and care.

'And you're too slapdash, Summers,' Claire continued. She pointed to the latest plot she had made. 'Are these Stuka dive bombers or Messerschmitt fighters?'

'Both?' Flo said, nervously.

'They can't be both.' She crossed her arms. 'I heard the radar operator say fighters.'

'Messerschmitts, then.'

Claire took a deep breath. 'What did you do before you joined up?' she asked them both.

'I worked in the post office,' Betty said. 'My father was the postmaster. Clerical work mostly, paying out pensions and selling stamps.'

'In that case, if you made a mistake the worst you would get was an irate customer. Here, if you make a mistake, it may lead to the death of one of our airmen, many of them, perhaps. Or even to bombers getting through and dropping bombs on London.'

'Sorry ma'am.' Betty's voice was little more than a whisper.

'And you, Summers, what did you do before you joined up?'

'I worked in a betting shop in the East End. Taking bets, calculating the odds, writing them up on the boards. I enjoyed it, but everyone smoked so much. It made me cough worse than my old mum does and she smokes thirty a day.'

'So you joined the RAF for your health?' Claire made her voice as sarcastic as she could.

'No, ma'am. I wanted to see something different to Poplar.'

Claire raised her eyes to heaven. 'You're incorrigible, Summers.'

Flo beamed. 'Thank you ma'am.'

'Incorrigible isn't a compliment.'

'Oh.'

'I'll tell you later,' Betty mouthed to her.

Claire sighed. 'If you don't shape up, and smartish, I shall have to recommend that you be moved elsewhere. Typing or filing, fetching and carrying.'

She noticed the look of distress and disappointment on the girls' faces.

'All of those things are important work, of course,' she continued. 'And at least you won't have me breathing down your neck.'

'We don't mind, ma'am,' Flo said. 'We know you only want us to get better at plotting.'

Flo's enthusiasm mollified her a little.

'I certainly do.'

She glanced out of the window. 'We don't know how much longer this quiet time will last. Everyone thought that the German raids would start months ago.'

'Do you think Mr Hitler has given up, ma'am?' Betty asked.

Claire shook her head. 'I very much doubt it. He's a villain, a particularly nasty one.'

'My uncle told me that some members of the Government want us to give up,' Flo said.

Claire looked horrified and Flo stepped back, fearing she was about to slap her. 'Don't ever let me hear you saying such things again, Summers. Great Britain will never give up. Nor will the Empire. Nor will France.'

She put on her headphones. 'Now let's make doubly certain that you two don't give up.' She gestured to the training instructor to run the training tape again.

The two girls groaned but forced themselves to concentrate. Both thought this might be their last chance to prove they were up to the job.

The next hour was an agony for them. Betty felt that her fingers were made of putty as she placed the counters on to the stick. And then, no matter what she did, the stick appeared to move excruciatingly slowly. She could see in her mind's eye the pack of German bombers heading for London, see the bombs being dropped, the fires and carnage they would cause.

Flo tried to slow down, to mentally repeat what she had heard in the earphones before reacting. But she could not help herself, she moved as quickly as she always did, faster even. But now she was all butter-fingers, clumsy, careless and slapdash, with the labels slotted crazily on to the wooden block. It was a wonder they didn't fall off entirely.

At the end of the hour they bent over the map as exhausted as if they had run a marathon. They stared at each other, tears in their eyes.

They had failed. They would be shipped off to some dreary office, working on wages or sickness reports or ordering thousands of aircraft parts. Playing roles so humdrum they could weep.

They both stood to attention as Claire approached them, a more ram-rod attention than they had ever managed before. Her face looked grim.

'That was much better, ladies,' she said after a long silence. 'Much, much better.'

The girls almost collapsed on the floor. 'Thank you, ma'am,' Betty stuttered. Flo could not speak.

'Keep up the good work tomorrow,' Claire continued. 'Aim to improve even more. 08.00, sharp.'

'Could we start earlier, ma'am?' Flo asked. 'Seven o'clock perhaps.'

Claire looked at her with astonishment. 'Well goodness me. That's the first time I've heard such a request.' She heaved a sigh. 'Well I'm gorgeous enough not to need my beauty sleep so yes. 07.00 hours it is.'

The girls skipped out of the room, their faces jubilant.

Claire was just about to leave when she heard a call from the observation level above and a man gesturing for her to join him. She did not recognise him but saw that he was a senior officer so she hurried up the stairs.

He was a tall, lean man in his late forties. He gazed at her with a disconcertingly direct manner, as if he were trying to get beyond her uniform and discover the real person behind it.

'I watched how you dealt with those new girls,' he said. 'You did exactly the right thing to get them to buck up. I was very impressed with you.'

'I didn't know anyone was watching,' she said.

'A lot of officers feel that ladies aren't up to the job,' he continued, 'that they'd buckle under the pressure. I came to see if they were correct. And who better to observe than new trainees with a first-time supervisor?' He smiled. 'I doubt that even the Luftwaffe would put new girls under as much pressure as you did.'

She was surprised to find that his voice did not match his rather unnerving stare. It was pleasant and relaxed, not like how a superior officer should address someone half a dozen ranks his junior. He spoke with a slight sibilance and his voice rose at the end of every sentence as if he did not want to allow time for anyone to interrupt him. He shook her by the hand and gave what appeared almost the ghost of a bow.

'Thank you, sir.'

'Thank you, Company Assistant....?'

'Lamb, sir.'

He gave a fleeting grin and walked out of the door.

'Who was that?' she asked one of the senior officers.

'Air Commodore Park,' he said. 'Air Chief Marshal Dowding's assistant. Don't be fooled by his pleasant manner. He's as sharp as a razor blade and just as lethal.'

'I thought razor blades were meant to shave you.'

'Or cut your throat. I'm just glad he's at Headquarters and not here.'

Claire thought over their conversation. She could not agree with the officer's summation of him. She sensed that the only people he might prove lethal to were slackers and fools. And Germans, hopefully.

THE CLAYTON
KNIGHT COMMITTEE

November 1939

Frank Trent looked at the training roster for the day and groaned. It had been the same for the six weeks he'd been working at the training school. The list was made up of the newest trainees, or the most hopeless of those who had been here a while. Peter Gaunt invariably allocated these to Frank. At first he thought this was purely because the taciturn airfield owner didn't like him, which was obvious to all who saw them together.

But Gaunt had told recently him there was another reason, over and beyond this.

'You don't believe in yourself, Trent,' he said. 'Yet you're the best damned pilot in the school and a good instructor.' He left the room and paused on the threshold. 'For the record, I don't believe in you much, either. When you're on the ground, leastways.'

'I was right,' Frank said to Delaney, Gaunt's deputy. 'He can't stand me.'

'That's true; he can't. But he admires your skill - different thing altogether. But you'll get no easy ride from him. Not ever.'

Frank put his annoyance behind him as he collected the first of his trainees and headed out to the plane.

It was a challenging day. The rookies seemed to have developed extraordinary levels of clumsiness and stupidity. Perhaps their minds were on the upcoming Thanksgiving celebrations.

The weather above the Blue Ridge Mountains was beginning to look ominous during the final session of the morning. A threatening cloud bank was promising snow. He doubted he'd risk any flights after lunch.

He could sense the alarm of the young trainee in front of him.

'Don't hesitate,' Frank said. 'Show the plane that you're in charge.'

The boy nodded nervously and began the descent. The plane bucketed back and forth, partly due to the growing wind but mostly due to the youngster's dithering. Frank was just about to seize control when the wheels touched the ground. The plane bounced like a lamb in springtime but eventually slewed to a halt.

'Not as bad as it might have been,' Frank said. 'I'm cutting you some slack because of the wind. But if you land like this in good conditions I'll kick you out of the school.'

The rookie nodded, too chastened to speak.

Frank climbed from the plane and headed for the office. Snow drops began to drift in the wind.

He found Delaney talking with a stranger, a fat man in his sixties. He was well-dressed in an expensive suit and carried a new overcoat over his arm. Let's pray he doesn't want to learn to fly, Frank thought.

'This might be of interest to you, Frank,' Delaney said.

The man blinked at Frank, took a step towards him and held out his hand. It felt as flabby as it looked and as hot as blood.

'My name's Oscar Rawson.'

'Frank Trent.'

Rawson's eyes studied him with great deliberation, from head to feet. 'Mr Delaney tells me you're the best pilot here,' he said.

His eyes were piercing and Frank had the uncomfortable feeling that he was being scrutinised, weighed up and categorised.

'What do you think of the European war?' he continued.

'I don't give it that much thought, sir.' Frank paused, aware that he didn't much like this man. 'And I believe that what I think is no concern of yours.'

Rawson shrugged. 'It might be, Trent, it might be. But I'm more interested to find out if you think it's any business of yours.'

He took a deep breath, causing his double chin to wobble. 'What do you think about Adolf Hitler for example?'

Frank glanced at Delaney who grinned in reply.

'I guess I don't like the fellow,' Frank said. 'I don't like any man who throws his weight around. Any man who's a bully.' The image of his father flashed into his mind.

'Well Hitler's certainly that, Mr Trent. Certainly that.' Rawson patted his stomach as he said it, almost as if to indicate that he could throw his considerable weight around, should he choose to.

Frank's dislike of the man began to change to that of alarm.

Rawson sat down and indicated that the others should do the same. Almost as if it were his office, Frank thought.

Rawson pulled out a cigar. 'Have you heard of the Clayton Knight Committee?' he asked.

Frank shook his head although he noticed that Delaney did not.

'Mr Clayton's a New York designer,' Rawson continued. He pointed to one of the pictures on the wall. 'That's one of his advertisements. I guess you may have read comics with his pictures on the cover.'

He smiled. 'How old are you, Trent, if I may ask?'

'I'm twenty. Twenty-one in January.'

'And Mr Delaney tells me that you've been flying for what, five years? As a crop duster, mainly but with a brief stint doing acrobatics for some cowboy outfit.'

Frank swallowed. Safety legislation had put all but a handful of flying circuses out of business and those that survived did so by flouting the law and even engaging in cross border smuggling. He had left the troupe when his boss told him to take a suspicious looking package to Winnipeg.

He guessed this was the reason Rawson was questioning him. He just couldn't make his mind up which side of the law the fat man was operating on.

'But that's all history now,' Rawson continued. 'Now, back to Mr Clayton Knight. What I'm about to tell you is confidential. In fact, it probably counts as top secret in Federal terms. Do you understand, Trent? And do you understand that what I say must go no further than these four walls.' It was a command, not a question. Despite the heater in the corner, the air seemed to grow more chill.

Rawson lit his cigar before continuing.

'Clayton Trent has set up a committee with Billy Bishop, the Canadian Fighter Ace. You've heard of Billy Bishop I take it?'

Frank nodded, warily.

'Well, Mr Bishop and Mr Clayton have formed a secret committee, with the agreement of the British Government, to try to recruit American airmen to join the Royal Air Force in its fight against the German Luftwaffe.'

He was not entirely sure why, but Frank's heart leapt at these words. The thought of fighting in a war against Adolf Hitler and his thugs seemed glamorous and exciting, dangerous, daring. Yet also full of life.

'American boys fighting for the British?' said Delaney. 'I thought you said they'd be fighting for the Canadian forces.' His voice had taken on a suspicious tone.

'Yes I did,' Rawson answered. 'And technically that would be true. In fact, many of them, most of them, would remain with the

Canadian Air Force, fight in their squadrons. It's just that some might want to go to Europe directly. Fight with the RAF against the Germans.'

'With the RAF or as part of it?' Delaney demanded.

Rawson held his hands open in a gesture which implied it did not much matter.

'And what does our Government think about it?' Delaney continued. 'I hear that anyone fighting for the British will have to swear allegiance to their king.'

Rawson appeared to be wrong-footed by this question and when he answered he seemed less sure of himself than hitherto, more evasive. 'Well that's an interesting question, Mr Delaney. And the answer is being worked on even as we speak.'

He paused for a moment and licked his lips. 'It may be that boys like Frank here would only have to agree to obey Canadian Air Force regulations.'

He swung his attention to Frank. 'You'd be okay with that wouldn't you, Mr Trent?'

Frank was not used to people calling him Mr and he liked it. 'I think I would. Yes sir, I would.'

Rawson gave him a huge grin. 'Just the sort of thing to make Adolf Hitler lose sleep at night, Mr Trent. Just the thing.'

He leaned forward, as if concerned that they might be overheard, and his voice took on a conspiratorial tone. 'And, just between ourselves, I've heard on the grapevine that Mr Roosevelt has given his discreet blessing to the committee's ideas. Just between ourselves.' He tapped his nose a couple of times.

Frank was thrilled at this news although he noticed that Delaney looked far from convinced.

The three men sat in silence for a while, pondering what had been discussed.

Then Delaney turned to Frank. 'It's up to you, son. I can tell you that I won't stand in your way and I'm pretty sure that Mr Gaunt will agree to you going. But maybe your ma and pa would have a view on it.'

Frank's last discussion with his father came flying back in his mind. His hatred of the British, his glee that they might soon be defeated and overrun by the Nazis. It proved to be the clinching argument.

'I'll be twenty-one in eight weeks. I'll be my own man, then.'

Rawson got up and clapped him on the shoulder. 'And a brave man, I don't doubt.'

He reached inside his suit and gave a slim envelope to Frank.

'This is all the information you need to have about the committee, Mr Trent. And a train ticket to Regina, Saskatchewan.'

Frank looked around nervously. The place was seething with people and most of them appeared to know where they were going. Most but not all.

A dozen young men sat on the edges of benches, their eyes roving across the crowded room.

At a desk by a door sat a young woman, engrossed in paperwork. Every five minutes or so a buzzer sounded. The woman then picked up a clipboard, called a name and led a man away. By the end of an hour there were only Frank and one other man left. Neither spoke, they were too anxious.

The woman returned. 'Francis Trent,' she called, squinting at the name carefully. Frank got to his feet. She swiftly appraised him, turned on her heel and led him into an inner office.

A middle-aged officer was sitting behind a desk. He glanced at the woman who gave two little taps on her clipboard and then left.

'Sit down, sit down,' the officer said, gesturing to a chair.

Frank took a chair and hoped his nervousness wouldn't show.

'I'm Squadron Leader Green,' the man said, studying a piece of paper in front of him. 'And you must be…'

'Francis Trent.'

'Francis Trent, sir.'

Frank looked confused for a moment but then realised the officer was telling him how to respond.

'Francis Trent. Sir.'

Green looked up and gave a warm smile. 'Nice to meet you, Trent.' He lowered his voice a little. 'What do you think of the girl who brought you here?' his tone was casual.

Frank swallowed, wondering what on earth he was getting at. 'She seemed very efficient, sir.'

Green stared at him, his lips pursed thoughtfully.

'And I noticed that she tapped her clipboard when she left,' Frank added.

Green's eyes widened. 'And why do you think she might have done that?'

'I don't know, sir. Some message, perhaps.'

'Bravo. You're the first person to have noticed.' Green picked up his pen and stared at him in silence for a moment. 'And what might the message mean, do you think?'

'I don't know to be honest, sir. Perhaps a message about me.'

'Observant, honest about what you do and don't know and yet willing to hazard a guess. Goodness me, Trent, you'll be an Air Commodore before we know it.'

Frank gave a grin which he immediately hid.

'She's been observing you men while she worked,' Green explained. 'If she doesn't think a man will make the cut she does nothing. If she thinks he's worth me spending more time on him, she'll tap the clipboard, twice, as a signal. I've found her insights invaluable.'

Green bent to his paperwork again.

'You have an impressive flying record, Trent.'

'Thank you, sir.'

'A pilot at the age of 16, crop-spraying in Winnipeg and Edmonton, six months delivering mail in Manitoba. You seem to have worked throughout the west of Canada.'

He put down his pen and held out his hand.

'Papers please, Trent. Birth certificate, school certificates, health records.'

Frank coughed. 'That's just it, sir. I seem to have mislaid them.'

Green's eyebrow raised and he sighed.

'I'm not going to ask you where you were born, son. I don't want to insult your intelligence.'

'No, sir.'

'In my experience, young men from Toronto are those most prone to losing their papers.' He smiled. 'Must be because it's so close to the United States, it makes them rather flash and wild. I find the accents fairly similar, as well. I gather that some people even mistake good Canadian boys like you for Americans.'

'Really, sir?'

'Really.'

Green gave him a bland look. 'So you're from Toronto.' It was not a question.

'Yes, sir.'

Green wrote on the paper.

'I guess you may have spent quite a bit of time in the United States?'

Frank caught his drift and nodded. 'Quite a lot, sir. It was almost like a second home.'

Green nodded, picked up a rubber stamp and pressed it to the piece of paper.

'Okay, Trent, here's proof of your Canadian citizenship. So you are now eligible to join the Royal Canadian Air Force.'

'Thank you, sir.' He took the document, scanned it nonchalantly, as if he were not that interested, and placed it in his pocket.

'Will some of our pilots go to Great Britain?' he asked.

'You're a member of the British Empire so that may be expected of you.'

'I have no problem with that, sir.'

'I guessed you wouldn't.'

Frank's heart beat fast with excitement.

'Now,' Green continued, 'bear in mind what I said about Toronto boys sounding a lot like Americans. The last thing you want is to be confused with a Yank. If the people in Washington think you're pretending to be Canadian in order to go fight in Britain they'll strip you of your American citizenship, put you in jail and throw away the key.'

'They can't strip me of citizenship, sir.'

Green looked bemused.

'Because I'm not American, sir. I'm Canadian.'

Green chuckled and passed him another set of papers. 'This concerns where you're going to next. The training school at Borden.'

Frank looked blank.

Green heaved a sigh. 'You should know it, son. It's close to Toronto.'

'Of course.'

Green shook his head ruefully before continuing. 'And then, if you're as good a pilot as you appear to be, you might be sent to England.'

He stood up and shook Frank's hand. 'Look me up when you're an Air Commodore, son.'

BITTER WORDS

February 1940

Claire Lamb took a deep breath and marched into Air Commodore Park's office. A silver-haired Flight Lieutenant gave her a cursory nod. She saluted and he gave a weary salute in return. He looked absolutely exhausted.

'Deputy Company Commander Lamb reporting, sir.'

The Flight Lieutenant gave her a cool stare. 'There's no such rank.'

She bit her lips. 'Sorry, sir. Section Officer Lamb. I can't get used to the new titles.'

'Only old pedants like me can,' he said. 'But everyone will get used to them, soon enough. Do you like the new WAAF rank titles, Section Officer?'

'Yes sir. To be honest I thought the old names were rather, well German. Commander, Commandant, Senior Controller.'

He raised an eyebrow. 'Never thought of it that way. Maybe that's why the top brass changed them. I assumed it was because the new titles sounded more like the male ranks. Squadron Officer for Squadron Leader, Wing Officer for Wing Commander. Easier for new recruits and the newspapers.'

He held out his hand. 'Call me Johnny if the big wigs aren't around.'

He pinched the tip of his nose wearily. 'Would you prefer to fly Spitfires or Hurricanes, Section Officer?'

Claire's mouth opened in surprise. 'I didn't think it would come to that, sir.'

He gave a chuckle. 'Just my little joke.'

The door opened and the Flight Lieutenant stood up.

'Relax, Longley,' Air Commodore Park said.

He strolled to his desk and looked at Claire. 'Ah, good to see you again, Section Officer. Welcome to Bentley Priory.'

She gave a nod. Although she had never been told so, her superior had hinted that Park himself had asked for her to work for him. She recalled the day he had observed her training Flo and Betty and said she had given them a harder time than the Luftwaffe would. She still wasn't sure whether it was a criticism or a compliment.

'I'll introduce you to Air Chief Marshal Dowding later today,' Park continued. 'He likes to welcome new staff himself.'

She was surprised to hear this. Air Chief Marshal Dowding had a reputation as a difficult, distant and irritable man; not at all the sort to bother himself with junior underlings like her.

Park sat behind his desk and immediately began to read through a pile of papers. 'Have the reports on the new RDF stations arrived yet?' he asked without looking up.

Longley handed her a folder and told her to take it to Park. He thanked her with a nod.

'Bring a chair here,' Longley told her. 'The best way to learn is by shadowing me.'

He spread out a map marked with twenty or so crosses around the coast and two dotted lines snaking over the Channel.

'RDF is short for Radio Direction and Finding,' he said. 'It's the system which tells you plotters where the enemy is.'

'I thought we got the information from the Observer Corp,' Claire said.

'That's correct, in part. But RDF is the extra powerful eyes we have.' He scratched his head. 'I think I heard someone refer to it as radar the other day.'

'It's a bit snappier than Radio Direction and Finding,' Claire said.

Johnny nodded and pointed out the crosses on the map. 'These are the stations, RDF, radar, whatever we want to call them. They give us warning of planes before they've even crossed the Channel. These lines mark the farthest point we can see.' He ran his fingers along the dotted lines, some of which reached as far as northern France.

He gave her a sharp look. 'Hush-hush. Very.'

His eyes widened suddenly and he leapt to his feet, saluting crisply. Claire immediately followed suit.

Although she had only seen photographs of him, Claire recognised that the visitor was Air Vice Marshal Leigh-Mallory. She thought that his responsibilities wore heavy upon him for he had a serious, almost grim demeanour, greying hair and clipped moustache framing tight-pressed lips. He was stocky with barrel chest and a strong, bull-like head.

'Morning, Air Commodore,' he said to Park. 'Is Stuffy in?'

Park got to his feet. 'Yes, sir,' he said. 'Sir Hugh is expecting you.'

Leigh-Mallory grunted and approached the inner door which led to Dowding's office. He knocked on it sharply with his knuckles.

There was a long silence. Leigh-Mallory shot a glance at Park, almost an accusing one, perhaps thinking he had misinformed him. But before he could say anything, a soft voice from the inner office told him to enter. He straightened his shoulders and walked in.

Park sat back down and gestured to the others to do likewise. Flight Lieutenant Longley continued to explain more to Claire about the role of radar but she noticed that his voice had lowered and he seemed to be keeping half an ear on something else.

She soon realised why. Five minutes after Leigh-Mallory had entered the Air Chief Marshal's office, the murmur of conversation grew suddenly louder. There followed a few minutes of quieter talk and then a loud cry from Leigh-Mallory followed by a barrage of complaint.

She looked at Longley who raised his eyebrow and gave a little grin. They then heard a sharp rapping on a desk and Dowding's voice suddenly loud in rebuke.

All this time, Air Commodore Park concentrated on his paperwork, seemingly oblivious to the row going on in the inner office. The only voice they heard now was that of Dowding. He sounded like a Headmaster chastising a naughty pupil.

The door flew open, Leigh-Mallory shut it firmly and stood in front of Park. He was red-faced and shaking, outraged and furious.

'The man is intolerable,' he snarled. 'I'll move heaven and earth to have him removed from Fighter Command. Just see if I don't.'

Park did not reply but got to his feet with a bland expression. 'Are you staying for lunch?' he asked, mildly.

'Certainly not.' And he strode out of the office.

Park turned to Claire and Longley. 'I'm sorry you heard that,' he said. 'Heat of the moment words, best forgotten.'

'Yes sir,' they chorused.

—

'Doesn't Air Vice Marshal Leigh-Mallory care for Air Chief Marshal Dowding?' Claire asked as she and Longley settled at a table for lunch. She was well aware that her question was a huge understatement.

Longley glanced around to make sure no one was in earshot.

'I don't think he likes anyone apart from himself. Did you notice how he completely ignored us?'

'Well, we are fairly junior.'

'Common courtesy to acknowledge fellow officers, no matter what their rank.'

She picked at her piece of fish, wondering what on earth could have caused the explosive argument in Dowding's office.

'My guess,' Longley continued, 'is that Leigh-Mallory was summoned from his Group because of problems there. He's well liked by his staff but not by his airfield commanders. He antagonises them, it seems. Maybe Dowding's got word of it.'

'Well you seem to have.'

Longley grinned. 'Of course I have; nothing much gets past me. But such tidbits doesn't always get to the ears of the top bosses.'

He pursed his lips, deep in thought.

'I bet I know,' he said at last. 'Leigh-Mallory never respected Gossage, the previous Head of 11 Group. Once he'd been moved on, Leigh-Mallory would have assumed that he'd be given the Group. But instead it was given to Acting Air Marshal Welsh who Leigh-Mallory believes is a glorified office boy. He must be seething at Dowding for denying him 11 Group.'

He put three large spoonfuls of sugar in his tea and stirred it gleefully.

'But why would Leigh-Mallory be so upset? He's already Head of a Group.'

'He is. But it's 12 Group, up in the Midlands. Leigh-Mallory knows that the crucial sector is in the south-east where the Luftwaffe will make their attack. All the fireworks will involve 11 Group. He believes he won't have much chance to shine now he's been denied it yet again.'

Claire's meal was getting cold but she didn't much mind. This gossip was far more interesting than what was on her plate.

'Mind you,' Longley continued, 'Dowding's on edge; as well as his job here, he's got personal worries. His only son is a fighter pilot. And Dowding knows the dangers he'll face better than most.'

'But surely he'll be kept out of harm's way.'

Longley scoffed. 'Do you think the old man would countenance that. Or the lad either, come to that. No, young Derek will be in the thick of it, I'm certain.'

Claire sipped her cup of tea.

'And what does Air Commodore Park think about all this intrigue?' she asked.

'He keeps his counsel, although he's very loyal to Dowding. The two of them have worked hand in glove to put the final pieces of the defence system together. Dowding has absolute faith and trust in Park.'

Claire almost hugged herself with delight. She was working for the man who had Dowding's ear. This could only mean a lot of excitement ahead, perhaps the opportunity for advancement in due course. Her brother would be thrilled.

She took a sip of her tea, not registering that it had gone cold.

'And what does Commodore Park think about Air Vice Marshal Leigh-Mallory?'

Longley inhaled sharply. He knew he shouldn't say more but Claire was paying him such close attention, and she was very pretty. He could not stop himself from wanting to sound well informed about everything.

'There isn't much love lost between them,' he said. 'I've seen the looks Park gives him, sort of doubtful. And I've heard that Leigh-Mallory is suspicious of Park's closeness to Dowding.'

'But Park's his deputy. They should be close.'

'True. But Leigh-Mallory thinks they're too close. Park's work on the Air Defence system gives him more clout than other Air

Commodores. Which also won't endear him to Leigh-Mallory. And he's not the only one with this view of Park.'

He swallowed the last of his tea.

Claire shook her head, thoughtfully. 'And I thought we were supposed to be fighting the Germans.'

Longley laughed. 'You'll find that the feuds at the top of the RAF are far more deadly and vicious. Mark my words.'

'As long as it won't affect how we fight against the Germans.'

At that moment someone approached, standing so close that the light from the window was dimmed. She was a young WAAF Aircraftwoman, a few years older than Claire and very attractive. Her hair was blond and curly, tucked into her cap but seeming to want to escape from it.

She stared at Claire with a sardonic glance.

'So, Johnny,' she said, without taking her eyes from Claire, 'I discover you with a dinner date.' She had a broad London accent.

Without another word she pulled up a chair.

'You want to watch this one, darling,' she told Claire. 'He's a real Casanova. Don't be fooled by his good manners.'

Claire was lost for words. Longley was her superior officer and a good twenty years older than she was. There was zero chance of any romantic relationship developing.

'I don't know what you mean —'

'That's what all the girls say, poor misguided fools.' She turned to Longley with one eyebrow raised.

'What are you doing here?' he asked, quietly.

She picked up a slice of bread, wiped up the last of the gravy from his plate and popped it in her mouth.

'I've been sent to take you and your boss to 11 Group HQ at 2.00. Besides, can't a girl meet up with her husband?'

'Not when she spreads scurrilous rumours about him.'

Longley gave a broad grin. 'Let me do the introductions. This is my new colleague, Section Officer Claire Lamb, who arrived here this morning. This is my wife, Jacqueline, who's a RAF driver. An Aircraftwoman, note, although she acts like she's an Air Marshal.'

'Only with you, honey.' Jacqueline gave him a peck on the cheek and held out her hand to Claire.

'Don't forget that Claire is an officer,' Longley said, 'as am I. We could have you on a charge.'

'You could try.' She gave him a pert smile and he seemed to dissolve with pleasure.

Claire's eyes went from husband to wife and barely suppressed a smile. He must be old enough to be her father. Yet they acted like youngsters: giggling, teasing and joking. Lucky things, she thought.

'So, do you live close to the base?' Jacqueline asked her.

Claire shook her head. 'I'm in digs in Hayes.'

'But that's miles away. I tell you what, we've got a spare room if you'd prefer to stay with us. We're in Edgware, not far from the Tube. We can be at Euston in half an hour easy, forty minutes to Leicester Square.'

She paused. 'You can pay us the same as your old digs. The extra cash would come in handy.'

Claire jumped at the chance. Her landlady was a curmudgeonly old woman, who frowned on any noise she made and even timed her soaks in the bath. The Longleys seemed an unusual couple and staying with them should be much more interesting.

'Okay,' she said. 'It's a deal. I must say I didn't fancy cycling ten miles or more in the black-out. I'll have to get my things tomorrow and bring them over.'

'Don't worry about that. Johnny will ask Commodore Park if I can take you to get your things this afternoon. He's very obliging over such matters. When I've dropped Park and his lordship here at 11 Group we can nip over and get your things.' She blew a kiss at Johnny.

Jacqueline proved an expert driver, speedy and assured. Claire had feared that her rather wild personality would make her impulsive and dangerous.

After they dropped the men at Uxbridge, Jacqueline and Claire sped off to Claire's digs. Her landlady heard her news in silence. Then she became even more difficult than usual, demanding a fortnight's rent in lieu of notice.

Claire insisted on only giving her one week's. When the landlady started to argue she reminded her that there was a war on.

The woman gave an angry look. 'I suppose your idea of war effort is to open your legs for any Brylcreem Boy you take a fancy to.'

Claire could find no words to answer but Jacqueline could. 'Jealous are you?' she snapped. 'You wizened old bat.'

'Get out or I'll call a constable,' the woman cried. She waved a fist at them as they carried Claire's belongings to the car.

'I'll leave her my bike,' Claire said. 'It's got a leaky tire anyway.'

She settled in the passenger seat and exhaled. 'I can't believe you said what you did,' she said. 'I wish I'd had the courage.'

'Plenty of practise, darling. You don't know my mother-in-law.'

'Is she a dragon?'

'Fire and brimstone. And she thinks that Johnny is the most wonderful thing in all creation. She spoilt him shocking and thinks I'm a gold-digger. Ha. She doesn't know about RAF wages.'

She put the car into gear and hurtled off.

They sped into the carpark at Uxbridge just as Park and Johnny appeared. Park was strangely silent on the journey back, engrossed in thought.

'Just drop me at the gate, Aircraftwoman,' he said. 'I need the fresh air. You two can get off home.'

Jacqueline and Johnny lived in a pleasant semi-detached house on the outskirts of Edgware. It had two bedrooms and a box room. Johnny carried the rest of Claire's belongings into the box room while she put her clothes in the wardrobe. It was a nice room with a double bed, a small wardrobe and a bedside table.

She stood at the window and looked out over a little garden. Most of it had been turned over to the growing of vegetables. There were signs of winter kale, early onions and carrots. Towards the rear of the garden, ridges of soil marched in ranks, presumably planted with potatoes. Dig for Victory, indeed.

But a tiny little patch had been left to lawn and a handful of daffodils poked their heads through the grass. They seemed to give a promise of an early spring.

This was the nicest place she had been in since joining the RAF, it reminded her of home. She hoped that the Longleys would let her stay for as long as she was at Bentley Priory.

They ate bread and jam for tea, with thin slices of fruit-cake for after.

'This cake is delicious,' Claire said to Jacqueline. 'Did you make it?'

'His lordship did,' she answered. 'He worked for a baker after he left school.'

She patted him on the arm. 'Come on then, darling, spill the beans. Why was Keith Park in such a stew on the way back.'

Johnny looked uncomfortable and gave a furtive glance at Claire.

'Oh, she won't tell on you,' Jacqueline said. 'Just as long as you don't say anything which will lose us the war.'

'It's Air Marshal Welsh,' he said. 'He's worried that we won't have enough Hurricanes and Spitfires in the summer if Goring unleashes the Luftwaffe. He wants Park and Dowding to try to persuade the Government to put all our resources into manufacturing fighters rather than bombers.'

'More bickering,' Claire said.

'Yes. And I'm afraid that neither Dowding nor Park are good at being diplomatic.' He exhaled wearily.

'Then let's just hope that Hitler will give up the fight,' Jacqueline said.

'I don't think that's likely,' Longley said. 'And I suspect that we'll need every Hurricane and Spitfire we can build.'

THE SQUADRON FORMS

March 1940

Frank Trent got out of the truck and looked around him. He had no idea where he was.

He shivered. Winters in Kansas were brutal but in March things began to look up. England, on the other hand, seemed to be enveloped in continual gloom. And here the air always felt damp so the cold seemed to invade his bones. His RAF clothes did little to combat this insidious chill.

'Get a move on,' a voice yelled from a hut across the field and he and the others hurried towards it.

A corporal with a clip-board was waiting for them, demanding their names. He exhibited none of the deference that Frank had been told the English showed to their superiors.

'The four officers are to use that barracks over there,' he said, pointing to a sturdy looking brick building in the distance. 'You three sergeants will sleep in that building, there.'

The building was actually little more than a hut, built close to the runway and rather ramshackle. Frank doubted it would do much to keep the cold out.

There were half a dozen men in the hut, lounging on camp beds, most of them doing their utmost to fill the air with cigarette smoke.

Frank noticed that of the beds which looked unoccupied, one was at the far end of the hut and distant from the door. It might be warmer there and he made a bee-line for it.

The man in the bed next to it scrutinised him as he threw his kit-bag onto the mattress. 'I hope you don't snore,' he said. 'Can't abide being kept awake by snoring.'

Frank's brow furrowed. The man had a deep, hard voice, and sounded as if he were sneering.

'I don't think I snore,' he said. 'Just kick me if I do.'

The man grinned, swung his legs to the floor. 'Don't fret yourself, I will. You're a Yank, aren't you? You sound like John Wayne.'

'Canadian.'

The man gave him a shrewd look. 'Of course.' He held out his hand. 'The name's Harry Smith.'

'Frank Trent.'

'Well there's a coincidence. I'm from Nottingham.'

Frank looked bewildered by the comment.

'Nottingham's on the Trent. The river Trent.'

Frank smiled. 'I've heard of Nottingham. Robin Hood, right?'

'And his Merry Men. And the lovely Maid Marian. You must have seen the film.'

'Olivia de Haviland,' Frank said, 'I like her.'

Harry nodded his agreement and then grinned. 'And Robin was played by Errol Flynn. An Australian pretending to be an American and acting the part of an English hero. There seem to be lots of people pretending they're from other countries, nowadays.'

'I wouldn't know,' Frank said stiffly.

'Of course not.' Harry gave him a huge wink.

Frank emptied his kit-bag and loaded the contents into the locker by his bed, aware that Harry was taking more than a passing interest in what it contained.

'You can tell a lot about a man from what he's got in his kit-bag,' he said, his voice now grown softer. 'Pictures of loved ones or none at all, sentimental items, good luck charms, letters from best girls, cigarettes.' He paused. 'Yours are American, I see. Lucky Strikes. I've heard about them.'

Frank handed him a packet. Harry took out one cigarette and handed back the pack.

'No, you keep it.'

Harry looked surprised. 'That's very generous of you.'

'I prefer Camels anyway.'

Harry opened a packet of Navy Cut and passed him a cigarette. 'Made in Nottingham, like me. I think you'll like 'em.'

Frank smiled to himself. He gave away a whole pack and got one cigarette in return. But then he guessed he knew the reason why. 'Are cigarettes rationed in England?'

Harry shook his head. 'Not for us in the Forces. Plenty of ciggies though pretty crap food. Here, are you hungry? We could go and get some dinner.'

Frank finished packing away his gear and followed Harry out of the hut. It had started to rain although Harry seemed not to notice.

'We sergeants have to Mess over there,' he said. 'Don't go into the officers' Mess unless you want a bollocking.' He noticed Frank's look of confusion. 'Getting shouted at, reprimanded.'

'The famous British class system,' Frank said.

'Infamous, more like. But we sergeants have one advantage over the officers. We can also use the NAAFI where the grub is better.'

'NAAFI?'

'Navy, Army and Air Force Institutes. They run cafes, shops even bars at sector stations. Come on, I'll show you.'

The NAAFI hut was on the other side of the airfield. Frank blinked as soon as he entered for the room seemed to consist of cigarette smoke more than oxygen.

They joined a queue at the serving area. Harry ordered fish and chips and Frank thought it sensible to follow suit. A big mug of tea was plonked on their trays without their having asked for them. Harry paid for both meals. They headed to a table where two men were already eating.

'Morning, Harry,' the older of the two men said, casting an inquisitive glance at Frank.

'Morning, Jack. This is a new pilot, Frank Trent. He's a Yank.'

'Canadian,' Frank corrected.

'Sorry, Frank, my mistake again.'

Jack grinned. The younger man, who looked slightly nervous, wolfed down the rest of his food and left.

'Doesn't he like Canadians?' Frank asked.

Jack grinned. 'He's young and daunted at the sight of pilots. Thinks they're too posh for him. He's never met Harry, of course. Citizen Smith, the RAF's own Karl Marx.' He laughed, amused at his joke as if he had never made it before.

Frank began to eat, pulling a face at the greasy batter on the fish. 'What gives with England?' he asked suddenly. 'I've heard about your class system but I thought it was only aristocrats and peasants and it had died out in the middle ages. Now I find it's still alive and kicking. And far more complex than I imagined.'

'You'll learn soon enough,' Harry said. 'The RAF will teach you everything you need to know about the class system. And more than you want to.'

'It's not as bad as the Army and Navy though,' Jack said to Frank.

'Don't be so certain,' Harry said.

Jack ignored him. 'Look at Harry and me,' he said to Frank. 'I'm an engineer, the sort who keeps your crates in the air. Wouldn't be able to fly if it weren't for us. So I'm the peasant but Harry's the knight in shining armour. Yet we both started up as apprentices in Halton.'

Frank frowned.

'Halton is where ordinary boys trained to be technicians,' Jack said. 'But then the powers that be decided they didn't have enough pilots and offered training to those who wanted it.' He glanced at Harry. 'Especially those who had trouble telling a screwdriver from a hammer. Golden boy here fitted both requirements and went to be a pilot.'

He reached across the table and undid the top button of Harry's tunic. 'I've told you that you have to dress the part.'

Harry laughed and offered both men a cigarette.

'Cor,' Jack said. 'Lucky Strikes Won the pools, Harry?'

'It's cause I get paid more than you,' Harry said.

'Either that or the pack was a gift from a stranger,' Frank said in a wry tone.

He lit all three cigarettes from the same match. The two Englishmen looked alarmed at seeing this.

'What's the problem?' Frank asked.

'Bad luck lighting three ciggies from one match,' Jack explained. 'We'll let you off this time, Yank, but don't do it again.'

Frank nodded, forgetting to correct him about using the word Yank.

'So why have you come to fight in the Mother Country's war?' Harry asked.

Frank shrugged. He had no ready answer to that and had pondered the same question all the way over the Atlantic. Maybe it was because his aunt had cousins here, maybe because he didn't like the idea of any country bullying another one, maybe to annoy his father by fighting for the British. More likely it was to get as far away from his father as possible.

He stubbed out his cigarette. It was all those things of course, but chiefly because of one even more important.

'I love to fly,' he said. 'I have to fly. I've been crop-spraying for years, did some work for the US Postal Service, even did some aerial acrobatic displays. But no flying I've ever done will test me like going up against a Messerschmitt Bf 109.'

Harry and Jack regarded him in silence.

'I understand this,' Harry said, finally. 'No heroics, no glamour, just a hunger for the air.'

Frank nodded.

Jack tapped Frank on the arm. 'By the way, you said you worked for the US Postal Service. I guess you meant to say Canadian.' He glanced around. 'Don't make such a stupid mistake again.'

'Definitely not,' Harry agreed. 'You run the risk of being kicked out penniless. And I hear that the USA might strip you of your citizenship. You'd have to take up smuggling. Or join the French air force. I'm not sure which would be worse.'

'I hear the French have a lot of planes and excellent pilots,' Frank said.

'Yeah, but they're led by idiots who prefer horses to aircraft. At least our bigwigs love the air. Most of them, at any rate. And the French planes are even worse than ours are.'

'The Hurricane's a good plane.'

'But there's not enough of them,' Jack said. 'They say the Spitfire is even better but I've never met anyone who's even seen one.'

'They're reserved for the posh boys at Tangmere, I expect,' Harry said. 'Or kept out of harm's way in 12 Group.'

Frank shook his head in disbelief. 'All this talk of class, posh guys and different Messes you can and can't go is crazy. I can't help thinking that you British prefer squabbling amongst yourselves than fighting the Germans.'

'You may be right, friend,' Harry said.

'At least for now,' agreed Jack. 'But when the fighting gets ugly, we'll show a more united front.'

'Let's hope so,' Harry said. 'Or we'll all be talking German by Christmas.'

A NEW COMMANDER

20th April 1940

Keith Park listened to Air Chief Marshal Dowding in silence. It was not unusual for him to share his thinking with his assistant but today he seemed unusually intent on doing so.

He opened a folder containing one sheet of paper and tapped it repeatedly.

'Not to put too fine a point on it, Park, I'm concerned about the readiness of Number 11 Group. Air Marshal Welsh is a very able officer, a deep thinker. He's a man with a grasp of strategy, the big picture. But both he and I know that he...'

Here Dowding paused for a moment, searching for the right words.

'Welsh and I both agree that he is not best suited to command of an operational group, especially one that will, inevitably, be at the forefront of battle. At the sharp end.'

He glanced out of the window before continuing. 'Welsh is not tactical enough to lead a Fighter Group. He sees too many variables, too many options. You and I know that a Head of Group needs to act speedily and without second thoughts.'

He closed the folder and stared at Park.

'So Welsh and I both agree that he is to be relieved of command and a new Officer in Charge appointed to 11 Group.'

Park was not overly surprised. Dowding had been worrying about Welsh's suitability since he had been appointed Head of the Group back in January.

'A good decision, sir.'

Park ran through the list of Air Vice Marshals, considering who might be the best man for the job. He felt certain that Dowding had already decided but he needed to be clear in his own mind in case he asked him for his opinion.

Air Vice Marshal Saul would be his first choice but he was already commander of 13 Group in the north and doing a good job there. His next thought was the South African, Quintin Brand, who he got on with very well. But Brand spent recent years on the technical side so the Air Staff would probably rule him out because of this. And, besides, he held the rank of Air Commodore and a number of people had greater seniority than him.

No sooner had he thought this than the image of Leigh-Mallory loomed in his mind. Park bit his bottom lip. Leigh-Mallory certainly had the seniority. He had been the youngest Air Vice Marshal in the RAF, had now spent over two years commanding 12 Group and was extremely ambitious.

Taking over 11 Group would be a sideways move rather than a promotion but Park had the feeling that Leigh-Mallory yearned to command it. Many of the hierarchy would support him in this. They considered Leigh-Mallory a safe pair of hands, the obvious choice to lead the sector which would experience the worst attacks and bear the brunt of any battle.

He took a deep breath, already formulating what he would say in response to Dowding's announcement.

'So, I've decided to put you in charge of 11 Group,' Dowding said.

Park blinked in astonishment.

'You're the best man for the job,' Dowding continued, 'no question about it. You've got a quick and decisive mind and I believe that you'll be able to deal with the pressure, which will be considerable. No one knows the Defence System as well as you do and no one has the knowledge to make as good a use of it.'

He took a deep breath. 'And besides, I trust you, Park. More than anybody I've ever worked with. I know you will do a good job. And by God, you shall have to.'

He pulled out an envelope and passed it to Park. It was confirmation of his posting.

'You'd better cut along straight away, no time for dallying. You can take any staff you want with you.'

Park nodded, rapidly coming to terms with what had happened.

'I'd like to take Johnny Longley, sir, we go back a long way. And Assistant Section Officer Lamb. She's a bright girl and works like a Trojan. And she would make an excellent lead plotter.'

'Just don't upset the apple cart, Park. You'll have to work with the staff already there. Be diplomatic.'

Dowding gave a sudden bark of laughter. 'That's ripe coming from me, I suppose. Never have time to be diplomatic.'

His face grew even more serious. 'The Germans will be bound to attack us in France, despite what Mr Chamberlain may hope. Our convoys will, therefore, be vulnerable to the Luftwaffe. In which case it may not be too long before food and other essentials won't be able to reach London.'

He said no more, he didn't need to. Such a scenario would be a disaster and might well make Chamberlain sue for peace.

'But there's more,' Dowding continued, his voice now so low Park could only just hear it. 'I have my doubts that we'll be able to hold the Germans if they attack our army. And if they reach the French coast they'll be only minutes from our shores. I've appointed you for the most vital task facing anyone in Fighter Command. You will have to keep our defences strong, keep sufficient of our planes and pilots functioning in order to continue the war. You must fight the Luftwaffe to a standstill, whatever the cost.'

He got up and shook Park's hand. 'Good luck, dear chap. Good luck.'

—

Jacqueline Longley screeched to a halt outside Hillingdon House. Claire almost fell into Park's lap.

Jacqueline had followed Park's orders to drive as fast as possible. He wanted to test how long it would take to get between Bentley Priory and RAF Uxbridge in an emergency.

'Thirty minutes, sir,' Jacqueline said. 'Door to door.'

Park gave a whistle as he climbed out of the car. 'I've known slower Fighter Pilots.'

He stood in silence for a little while, surveying his new command.

'It didn't take me long to get back here,' Claire said to Johnny Longley. 'I've only been away two months.' Her face clouded over. 'I suppose I'll have to eat humble pie and go back to my old digs with the gruesome dragon.'

'There's no need,' Johnny said. 'I've fixed it. Jacqueline and I are to have married quarters for the duration. And I got you a room in the WAAF Mess. A single room.'

Claire gave him a look of utter astonishment. 'How on earth did you swing that?'

He tapped his finger to his nose.

'Come on, you two,' Park said. 'Let's make our faces known.'

He strode off swiftly with Claire and Johnny hurrying in his wake.

The staff in the central office gave them a casual glance as they passed; they were used to seeing Park on previous visits. A few who knew Claire were more surprised to see her return. A number of her old colleagues waved and one asked if she'd join them for coffee at eleven.

'I'm not sure,' she said, wondering if any of them had an inkling about what was to happen.

Park disappeared into the Commander's office while Claire and Longley waited in the administrative office, rather uncomfortably, like spare parts.

Claire was surprised at the changes which had been made since she had left. Then there had been perhaps a dozen desks in the office, now she estimated there were at least twenty, all pushed so closely together she wondered how people could work with any degree of concentration.

'It's good to see you, Claire,' said Wing Commander Willoughby de Broke, the senior controller. 'What brings you here?'

She made a zipped motion across her mouth. 'Careless talk, you know,' she said with a smile.

'Of course. Absolutely.'

Claire gave Johnny a nervous look. But for once he showed no inclination to prove he was in the know about events.

A few minutes later Air Marshal Welsh stepped out of his office and rapped on a window for attention. The room fell silent. Keith Park stepped beside him.

'Ladies and gentlemen,' Welsh said. 'I am here to inform you that as of this morning, I am being posted as Head of Reserve Command. I am more than happy to announce that my replacement is Air Vice Marshal Keith Park. Many of you know him and will realise that, along with Sir Hugh Dowding, he has been the driving force behind the establishment of the RAF defence system. I can think of nobody better to lead this Group in the coming period. I trust that you will give him the whole-hearted welcome and support which you have shown me.'

And without further ado, he put on his cap and made for the exit. There was a hubbub in the room.

Park stepped forward and looked around, his glance putting an end to all conversation.

'I am more than pleased to have been given this opportunity to command 11 Group,' he said quietly. 'I know you people more than those of any other Group and you know me. I respect you. I hope that you will soon get used to me and my little ways.'

There was a slight ripple of laughter from some people. Most were not sure whether he had made a joke or not and remained silent.

'I don't need to tell you that there will be tough times ahead,' he continued. 'Adolf Hitler has been busy consolidating his grasp on Czechoslovakia and Poland. But it will not be long before his eyes are turned to the west. Our armed forces in France are second to none and the French army is the largest and best equipped in the world. I have no doubt that Hitler will get a bloody nose if and when he chooses to attack.

'But the sky knows no frontiers. Whatever the outcome on the ground we can be sure that Herr Hitler will unleash his Luftwaffe upon England. And 11 Group will be at the forefront of the battle. I am confident that we will prove his most lethal adversary.'

There was a burst of applause in the office.

Park gestured to Claire and Johnny. 'Come on,' he said, 'let's have a tour.'

The first place they went to was the most important part of the airfield. The Bunker, the underground operations room had only been completed in August, ten days before the start of the war. To Claire's mind the lobby still bore the faint odour of new paint.

Their papers were checked and they began to descend to the Bunker which was sixty feet below. The steps were very steep and had sturdy iron railings which, by some quirk of the designers, were cast with Art Deco patterns. It was the only thing in the Bunker which was not utilitarian.

The heart of operations was the plotting room.

On one wall was a colour coded clock linked to the one at Bentley Priory and above this the huge Tote Board with up to date information concerning every sector in the group and the squadrons attached to them.

Opposite this were the rooms where the most senior personnel could keep oversight of the operations, though some of the more elderly sometimes had to view the details with the aid of opera glasses. One of the plotters had once said it felt like being watched by angels. Another said by demons.

Below this was a raised dais where the controllers had a clear view of the map table below.

This was huge and showed the southern part of the country from the Wash in the north, south to the Channel and as far west as Cornwall and South Wales. It also showed all of the Channel and a part of the European coast from Cherbourg in the west to Rotterdam in the north-east. Seeing this gave Claire a queasy feeling, knowing just how close the Germans might be if they made a successful attack in France.

There was no activity this morning, however. Two Squadron Leaders sat chatting in the windowed rooms, the controllers lounged in their chairs on the dais and half a dozen plotters sat on either side of the map trying not to look bored. They all leapt to their feet and stood to attention. Claire recognised two of them immediately, her last charges, Flo and Betty.

Willoughby de Broke went over to the two controllers to tell them about Park's promotion.

'They're your two girls aren't they?' Park said to Claire, indicating Flo and Betty.

'Yes sir.'

'Well don't be stand-offish. Go and say hello.'

The girls could hardly contain their excitement at seeing her.

'What are you doing here?' Flo asked. 'I thought you'd gone on to better things.'

'I did. And now I've gone on to even better. I've been transferred back here.' She glanced at the plotting table. 'I don't know why, exactly. Maybe I'll be back here in the plotting room.'

'I hope you are,' Betty said. 'We don't like Squadron Leader Simpson.'

Claire followed her gaze to one of the controllers, a tall, slim man who wore his uniform well. He was lending only half an ear to de Broke; he kept an eye on Park who was scrutinising everything with the greatest care. But his greatest attention was on the three girls.

'He gives me the creeps,' Flo said.

'You mustn't say that about a superior officer,' Claire said sharply.

Flo looked as if she were about to argue but thought better of it. Then she straightened up, her face grown suddenly rigid.

'It's a pleasure to meet you,' came a voice from behind Claire's shoulder.

Claire turned and saw that Simpson was only inches from her. Involuntarily she took a couple of steps away. He moved forward, halving the space she had made between them

Squadron Leader Simpson looked like a Hollywood star. No, not a star, she thought but a - what was it called - a matinee idol. His face, while handsome, bore a curiously blank look, as if there was little of any consequence below the surface.

Simpson held out his hand and she took it. His fingers seemed to insinuate around hers. A shiver went through her but she was not sure if it was one of pleasure or alarm. It was meant to be a handshake but he did not move his hand in the requisite manner, merely held fast on to hers as if in an embrace.

She straightened her fingers, releasing her clasp and tried to slip them free but he held tight, all the time peering into her eyes.

Then he suddenly released his grip, and his gaze. 'Always a pleasure to meet new colleagues,' he said. He gave a complacent smile.

Claire felt disorientated, and a little unnerved by what had happened. But what had happened, exactly? A colleague had come over to welcome her, which was kind and to be expected.

But somehow that felt only the half of it. She thrust her confusion away and turned her attention to Flo and Betty.

'We've been given permanent roles as plotters,' Betty said. 'We got excellent results in our final tests.'

'Betty got higher marks than me,' Flo said, raising her eyebrows in exasperation.

Claire was not altogether surprised by this.

'Oh do say you'll come back to the plotting room,' Betty said.

Claire laughed. 'But surely you recall that I was a bit of a dragon?'

'A friendly dragon, though,' Flo said with a grin.

Claire gave a little cough. The conversation was getting a little too chummy, she had her position to think of.

'I really can't say where I'll be working,' she said, briskly. 'I've been helping Air Vice Marshal Park at Headquarters and maybe I'll be doing the same here.'

'Is he coming as well?' Betty asked.

'He's the new commander.'

'What about Air Marshal Welsh?'

'He's been promoted to Head of Reserve Command.'

'But that's the training division,' Flo said. 'How's that a promotion?'

Claire was rather shocked at her reaction and hastened to put an end to it. 'Because it is.'

'Yes, ma'am,' Flo mumbled. But Claire could see that she was still puzzling about it.

She's rather like me, Claire thought, always burrowing beneath the surface of thing. She smiled to herself, recalling the many times her superiors had told her it would get her into trouble. Maybe they'd been correct. But it had also, she believed, got her to where she was today. One of Air Vice Marshal's senior assistants.

And maybe someone who would have an important part to play if there was ever a battle to be fought.

THE END OF
THE BEGINNING

8th May 1940

Evelyn glared at her husband. 'If you're being sent into danger,' she said, 'then I want to be as well.'

'Don't be ridiculous, Evie. I don't want to be sent into danger. Nobody does.' Tony adjusted his tie in the mirror. 'Anyway, I doubt there'll be any danger. Hitler seems concerned solely with Poland. I doubt he will risk an attack against us and the French.'

'He made short work of the Poles.'

'The Poles are not the British. For goodness sake they've only been a nation for five minutes.'

'Tell that to the Poles. I had a Polish friend at school and she said that their first king lived a thousand years ago.'

Tony didn't answer. In the six months they'd been married he had learnt that she was far more knowledgeable than him about most things and could normally best him in an argument. He had an uncomfortable feeling that the long-simmering dispute about her doing war work would prove the same.

He took a deep breath. 'I told you that American citizens cannot do war work. Helping in some voluntary charity, maybe; but not serious war work. Our government won't allow it and yours most definitely won't.' He gave a wry smile. 'I'm pretty sure your Neutrality Acts forbid American citizens to fight on our behalf.'

'Then stop fighting me.' She took him in her arms. 'I want to do something to help. The sooner this war is over the better.'

She sensed his continuing reluctance, and pulled away from his arms. Her eyes narrowed dangerously and she squared up to him. 'And let's not forget that Winston Churchill is half American. If he can sit in the British Cabinet then surely a little American girl can also do her bit?'

He chose to ignore this and pretended to be having difficulty getting his tie to look right.

He kissed her on the lips. 'I'm off to take command of my new squadron. Don't let's fight. Please.'

She held him tight. 'You make it sound like you won't see me again.'

'I won't for a while. But France isn't far away and, as I said, all's quiet there.'

'Promise you'll keep out of danger.'

'I promise.'

He scooped up his kitbag and hurried out of the house. He didn't want her to see that his eyes were wet with tears.

She watched him get into his car and disappear. Her eyes were dry. There was no time for tears. She had work to do.

She picked up the telephone and asked the operator if she could make a call to Washington.

'County Durham?' the woman asked in surprise. 'Near Sunderland? I've never made a connection to so far away.'

'No,' Evelyn said, sharply. 'Washington DC.'

'I don't understand.'

Evelyn almost growled with anger.

'In the United States. It's the capital city.'

The operator was silent for a moment. 'I don't think I know how to connect you. Please hold and I'll ask my supervisor.'

They won't stand a chance in the war, she thought, angrily. They may as well give up now.

The telephone crackled and a new voice came on. 'You wish to telephone to Washington DC in America, ma'am?'

'I do. This is the number. It's to the White House. To Mr Harry Hopkins, President Roosevelt's aide.'

There was a short intake of breath.

'It will take a long while to connect you, I'm afraid.'

'I can wait.'

Thirty minutes later she heard Harry Hopkins' secretary voice. 'Putting you through. You'll have to be quick.'

Then she heard Hopkins' unmistakable, incisive voice. 'What can I do for you, Evie?'

——

Claire Lamb knocked on Air Vice Marshal Park's door but didn't wait for him to tell her to enter.

'I think perhaps you should see this, sir. It's a report about Parliament's debate concerning the Norway fiasco.'

Park gave her a stern look. 'Don't call it a fiasco, Lamb. Even if it is one.'

'Sorry, sir.'

He read the report carefully, his eyes widening as he did.

'Good God,' he said at last. 'Amery's a Conservative politician yet he said this to the Prime Minister.' He shook his head in astonishment.

'What do you think of this Lamb?' He read Amery's speech aloud.

'"You have sat here for too long for any good you have been doing. Depart, I say, and let us have done with you. In the name of God go!"'

He looked at Claire. 'Be honest, Lamb. What do you think?'

'I think that a lot of people would agree with Mr Amery, sir.'

Park nodded. 'True. But I doubt it will have much impact on the Government. Chamberlain's a tougher bird than he looks.'

'Perhaps so,' Claire said. 'But Mr Lloyd George has been even more scathing.' She went to hand Park a second sheet but he waved it away and asked her to read it aloud instead.

She took a breath and stood more upright, as if she were a schoolgirl ready to recite something to the class.

'"The prime minister must remember,' she began, 'that he has met this formidable foe of ours in peace and in war. He has always been worsted. He is not in a position to appeal on the ground of friendship. He has appealed for sacrifice. The nation is prepared for every sacrifice so long as it has leadership, so long as the Government show clearly what they are aiming at and so long as the nation is confident that those who are leading it are doing their best.

'I say solemnly that the prime minister should give an example of sacrifice, because there is nothing which can contribute more to victory in this war than that he should sacrifice the seals of office.'"

Park listened open-mouthed. 'Now that is damning,' he said.

He sat back and stared into space; her presence completely forgotten. She turned to leave but the door was flung open before she could reach it.

Air Chief Marshal Dowding entered, pushed past her without a glance, and lowered himself into the chair opposite Park.

'Have you heard?'

'About the debate?' Park nodded. 'Lamb has just told me.'

'It's the end of Chamberlain,' Dowding said. 'He can't continue, now.'

Park nodded, chewing his lip. 'Who do you think will become Prime Minister?' he asked.

'Whoever those blasted idiots choose. Halifax, probably, heaven help us.'

Claire was surprised at his vehemence.

He drummed on the desk, thoughtfully. 'I doubt if Halifax will be popular with the country though.'

Claire began to tiptoe towards the door but her movement caught Park's attention. 'You're old enough to vote aren't you, Lamb?'

'Two years ago, sir. So I've not had the chance to do so yet.'

'If there were an election,' he continued, 'who would you want as Prime Minister?'

She blushed furiously.

Park looked faintly amused at her reaction. 'Come on, Lamb. I won't bite.'

'Well sir,' she stuttered, 'I think that Mr Halifax is a bit posh, I think ordinary people would think the same as me. A bit out of touch.'

'He's not a mister,' Dowding said, 'he's Earl Halifax.'

'So he's possibly even more out of touch than people already believe,' Park said.

They fell silent. Claire wished the ground would swallow her up. She felt herself begin to shift from foot to foot and had to force herself to stand still.

'So if you think Earl Halifax isn't up to the job,' Dowding said slowly, fixing her with his gaze, 'who do you think would make the best Prime Minister?'

For a moment she thought he was having a little joke with her but then she realised that he was deadly serious.

'I don't know, sir,' she stuttered. 'Mr Lloyd George, perhaps. Or Sir Kingsley Wood.' She paused. 'But I rather fancy Mr Churchill for the job.'

The two men looked at each other.

'So do I,' Dowding said. 'Although I can't stomach the fellow.'

There was a long silence. 'You can go now,' Park told Claire. He made a zipping motion against his mouth.

'Of course, sir. Careless talk etcetera.'

She hurried out of Park's office and sank into a chair.

'What about Dowding rushing down here,' Johnny said, rubbing his hands together with excitement. 'He must have got word about the debate in the Commons.'

He gave Claire a questioning look. 'I wonder what he and Park think about it?'

'No idea,' she said and picked up a document, pretending to read it.

Johnny chuckled to himself. 'Well my money's on Churchill becoming Prime Minister. Care for a little wager?'

'I don't think it's the sort of thing we should bet on.' She was surprised at how prim she sounded. She was still flustered by what had just taken place in Park's office.

Johnny did not bother to respond. 'Mind you, it may be up to what Clem Attlee wants.'

'But he's Labour.' Claire was shocked that Johnny felt that Attlee's views might carry any great weight. 'And hasn't he already criticised the Government and said that we want different people at the helm?'

'Precisely. He was the first to say it. Before Amery and Lloyd George. Attlee's no fool, Claire.'

'My father thinks he's a Stalinist.'

'And I reckon he's more of a patriot than most of the Conservative party.'

She was surprised at his words but promised herself to think about it later. For now she shrugged. 'As long as we win this wretched war.'

'We might with Winston in charge. And with Dowding.'

She almost repeated the Air Chief Marshal's views about Churchill but stopped herself in time. She need not have bothered.

'Dowding doesn't care for Winston, though,' Johnny said.

Claire wouldn't gratify him by admitting how accurate he was about Dowding's opinion of Churchill. But she gave up all pretence of working.

'And Churchill doesn't much like Dowding,' he continued, delighted that she was proving a good audience. 'He thinks he's too cautious, and wants to fight a defensive war. Such a policy doesn't impress that vain old swashbuckler.'

'Vain old swashbuckler! I thought you want Churchill to be Prime Minister.'

'I do. We need swashbucklers right now.' He exhaled loudly. 'As long as they're not controlling our fighters. Cautious old Dowding is who we need, he'll conserve our fighters and strength.'

Claire groaned. 'You're impossible.'

Dowding came out of the office and Claire and Johnny shot to their feet. He walked past them but paused at the door and gave Claire a brief nod.

'You must have made an impression,' Johnny said after the door had closed behind him.

'Cut the chatter,' Park called, 'and get in here.'

He was standing at the window, glaring at the sky.

'Tomorrow morning, I want you to pack up this office and move us down to the underground Bunker. It will be a tight squeeze so only take what is absolutely necessary.'

He jammed on his cap and left.

Johnny crossed his arms. 'I think he senses something. He may not know what it is but I think he senses something.' They sat in silence for a few minutes.

Then Claire said: 'Let's move everything this evening. So we can start from the word go tomorrow.'

'You youngsters,' Johnny said. 'Never a moment's consideration for us old uns.'

Then he heaved out a heavy box and began to fill it with documents.

FRANCE

10th May 1940

Squadron Leader Nash surveyed the Hurricanes stretched out across the airfield. They were being kept in good shape because of the ground crew. But he worried about the pilots. They were getting sick of the lack of activity. They loved the training flights, sure enough. But for the last week these had been curtailed in number because the powers that be wanted to conserve fuel. The Allied campaign in Norway was draining large amounts of resources from other theatres.

Squadron Leader Maisfield came out of the administration block and gestured him over. He was standing next to a short, wiry man in French uniform.

'Bonjour, monsieur,' Nash said as he approached.

'Dzień dobry.' The man smiled at Nash's look of surprise. 'I am not French,' he explained.

'But I thought…' Nash gestured at the man's uniform.

'I am Polish,' the man said. 'But since I escaped from my homeland, I have been fighting with the French air force.'

'Good show.'

The man regarded him with some amusement.

'The thing is,' Maisfield said, 'that erm Mr Kacka…'

'Kaczmarczyk,' the man said.

84

'Yes indeed. Well the thing is Nash, that our friend here doesn't speak much French but his English is pretty damned good. He studied at the University of Birmingham before the war.'

'And I have not endeared myself to the French authorities,' Kaczmarczyk added. 'They make me fly old machines, little more than death traps and they won't listen to what I try to tell them about the Germans.'

'Our friend was in the thick of it last September,' Maisfield explained. 'Bloody good pilot, six kills to his name.' He tapped the side of his head. 'Sharp. Very. Wing Commander Wentworth thinks he'll be a marvellous addition to your squadron.'

Nash held out his hand. 'You're very welcome, Kackz —'

'Call me Tomasz. It's easier.'

Nash smiled with relief.

'I was a Major in my own air force, the same as you Squadron Leaders,' Tomasz said. 'But I am made a Pilot Officer by the French. If I join the RAF, that will change?'

Maisfield frowned 'Afraid not, old chap. Air Chief Marshal Dowding has said that all Polish officers must start at the rank of Pilot Officer. But you might get promoted.'

'Promoted to my actual rank?' The Pole's voice was a little mocking. 'Perhaps, when I have proved my loyalty to your king?'

'Something like that.'

'Or when you've knocked a few Jerries out of the sky,' Nash added quickly.

'I would welcome that,' Tomasz said. 'But your phony war means that nothing happens. Nothing happens while the Germans crush my country and people. It is not, I assure you, a phony war for us.'

Nash and Maisfield looked embarrassed. 'Come along, Tomasz,' Nash said. 'Let's meet the rest of the chaps.'

Harry Smith grunted as he turned the spanner and unlocked the nut. 'Bloody hell, that was tight.'

Jack White grinned. 'I must have loosened it for you. You'd never have got it free otherwise.'

Harry withdrew the bolt from the engine block and turned it in his hand. 'Completely bent. It's a wonder the whole engine didn't fly to pieces.'

'That's the beauty of Rolls-Royce,' Jack said. 'The Merlin's the finest engine in the world. Bar none. Even when a bolt bends it carries on working.'

'You would say that.'

'Of course. Rolls-Royce has the finest apprentice school in the world.' Jack tapped himself on the chest. 'And it turns out the finest engineers.'

'Maybe. But Raleigh Bikes have the best mechanics.'

'Except you're not a mechanic anymore, Harry. You're a pilot.' Jack shook his head. 'Not a particularly good one, if you ask me. You'd be more use to the RAF if you came back to ground crew.'

'But then I wouldn't get the girls so easily.'

Jack snorted. 'Pull the other one. I can't remember the last time I saw you with a girl.'

'Isabelle?'

'She's nothing to write home about. And I was told that French girls were supposed to be beautiful.'

'She's got a beautiful nature, Jack my lad. One of the finer things in life which you would not appreciate.'

'You there,' a voice called. 'You men.'

A man in pilot's uniform strode towards them. 'I've been watching you two. You've spent an age on this blasted plane.' He jerked a thumb behind him. 'Mine needs looking at and pretty sharpish, the engine damn near stalled on me. So get moving. Don't you realise there's a war on?'

He turned and headed back to the Officer's Mess.

'Who the hell was that?' Harry asked.

'Rupert Buckingham,' Jack said. 'He's just wangled a transfer to the squadron. It seems he wasn't very popular with his last Squadron Leader so he was happy to let him go.'

Harry whistled. 'I can see why.'

Jack's eyes narrowed and he took hold of Harry's arm. 'Why did you let him talk to you like that, Harry? Why didn't you tell him you're a pilot?'

Harry shrugged. 'Because it wouldn't make much difference to his sort. I'm only a sergeant and he'd look down at me almost as much as he does you. Besides, no one should talk to anybody like that. Doesn't matter if they're pilot or ground crew.'

Jack laughed. 'Thanks for the display of solidarity. So when are you off to Russia? Stalin would welcome you with open arms.'

Harry gave him a sardonic look and picked up a screwdriver. 'Come on, let's finish the engine.'

'So you don't want me running off to deal with his lordship's plane.'

'Mine first. And we'll take as long as we need.'

He watched Buckingham until he reached the Mess. He's a man to steer clear of, he thought.

It took only twenty minutes to fix the problem. At first Harry planned to work as slowly as possible but he knew that this would only cause problems for Jack. Besides, as Buckingham had so condescendingly reminded them, there was a war on. The sooner the planes were airworthy the better.

Not that there was any sign of fighting. It had been over a month since Prime Minister Chamberlain had announced that Hitler had missed the bus. Perhaps he was right, he thought. Maybe Hitler would content himself with conquering Poland and the war would fizzle out. He glanced up at the sky. At least the summer would be better in France than in England.

Jack packed up his tool-box and stared at Harry. 'I don't want you coming to help me with Buckingham's plane.'

Harry snorted. 'Don't worry about that, I've no intention of doing. I like keeping my hand in but only on my own kite.'

Harry began to make his way back to the administrative blocks. Buckingham was sitting outside the Officers' Mess reading a newspaper. He happened to turn a page as Harry approached and gave him an incredulous look.

'Where the hell are you going?' he demanded. 'I told you to fix my plane.'

'I don't work on other pilot's planes.' Harry just about managed to keep his tone civil.

'Other pilots?'

'I'm a pilot, just like you. A Flight Sergeant pilot but still a pilot.' He paused for a couple of heartbeats. 'Sir.' He managed to pack a world of contempt into the title.

'Best not to play at being Ground Crew then,' Buckingham said returning his attention to the paper. 'Helps avoid being confused with them.'

A man who likes the last word, Harry thought. Or is used to having it. He continued towards the Sergeant's Mess.

Harry was lounging in a basket-chair when he heard the sound of aircraft approaching. He shaded his eyes against the sun then cocked his head to listen more carefully. They didn't sound like Hurricanes. Perhaps they were Spitfires. He got to his feet, eager to see them land.

Twenty or so planes appeared from the east, moving fast. They'll never be able to land at this speed, Harry thought. And then he saw the bombs plummeting from the planes.

'Fucking hell it's the Jerries,' someone cried.

'Get them up, get them up,' Squadron Leader Nash cried.

Harry raced for his plane. He climbed into the cockpit. Then he cursed.

Surely none of the ground crew would brave the storm of bombs from the German planes. But he was wrong. Jack and a few colleagues were already at his plane, pulling the chocks away and clambering onto the wings to make essential last-minute checks.

'There's no time for that,' Harry cried. 'Get the hell out of here.'

He turned the ignition and pushed hard on the throttle. The power increased and he felt the Hurricane lift off. Out of the corner of his eye he could see a bomber heading straight for him, a stick of bombs already cascading from it.

He pushed even harder on the throttle and managed to climb above the bomber. He glanced down and caught a glimpse of the damage it was doing. The airfield was in chaos. Several Hurricanes were already burning, and large eruptions of flame showed where the fuel dumps had been bombed.

He prayed that Jack had made it to safety although he doubted he could have done.

But he shook such thoughts away. He had other things to worry about now.

He had been successful in the first priority which was to get his plane airborne. Now he searched for any bombers to destroy before they did any more damage.

Half a dozen bombers were bringing up the rear of the German attack and he raced towards them. Another Hurricane caught up with him and moved abreast. What speed is he doing, he wondered.

The two planes opened fire as they closed and the bombers skewed away, although not before one had been hit by a snarl of bullets. Harry chased after another of the bombers and it turned and dived, desperate to avoid him. He peppered its fuselage with bullets but it appeared to suffer little damage. Yet it was enough for the German and he hurtled back the way he had come.

Harry turned once more, seeking fresh prey.

He saw another Hurricane plunging into three of the remaining bombers, a burst of bullets and then the first of the planes exploded in flames, plummeting to earth a mile west of the airfield.

He glanced around. The rest of the bombers were now far to the north and heading to safety. There was nothing more to be done. He headed back to the airfield and prepared to land. This proved more difficult than he had imagined. The airstrips were littered with burning planes, both British and French. He found a likely spot, skimmed over a smoking Hurricane and touched down safely.

The first man who reached him was Jack.

'You made it?' Jack breathed.

'I was safer up there than you lot down here.'

Jack grinned. 'It will take more than a swarm of Jerries to do for me.'

Harry clapped his hand upon his friend's shoulder.

'Did you get any?' Jack asked.

'Possibly. Me and one other bloke hit a pack of Heinkels and fired at the same time. One of the buggers crashed. It might have been him who got the plane, might have been me. It's difficult to be certain.'

Jack ordered some of his crew to check over the plane and walked back to the barracks with Harry. Frank Trent was waiting for them just outside.

'Congratulations, Harry,' he said. 'You got the Heinkel.'

Harry laughed. 'Were you the bugger who caught me up?'

Frank gave a rueful smile. 'Of course it was me. Who else can fly so fast?'

'And you attacked alongside me?'

Frank nodded. 'But it was you who got the Kraut. Saw it with my own eyes.'

Harry looked dubious. 'Your eyesight must be a lot sharper than mine, Frank. I couldn't say whether it was me or you who got it.'

'It wouldn't do if the first kill of the war was by an American,' Frank said.

'You mean a Canadian?'

Frank grinned. 'Just testing that you were paying attention.'

Squadron Leader Nash approached. 'Well done, gentlemen. Which one of you got the hit.'

'Harry, sir,' Frank said. 'I'm faster than him but not as hot a shot.'

'I'll log it,' Nash said.

'I saw someone else get a hit,' Harry said.

Nash reddened. 'That would be me, I'm afraid. Pity really. I didn't want to get the first strike. It would have been better if one of you chaps had scored first.'

Harry grinned. This was typical of the man. He'll make a good leader, he thought.

Nash gave a low whistle. 'Well it looks like the phony war is over. This must be the real thing at last.'

Frank surveyed the airfield. There were half a dozen damaged planes and a fuel dump was ablaze. 'And I'd say the Krauts have had a better day of it.'

'Well let's make sure we're never caught napping again,' Nash said. 'Come on lads, let's get a cup of tea.'

Rupert Buckingham approached and held out his hand to Nash. 'I hear congratulations are in order, sir. You bagged one.'

Nash gave a nod. 'And so did Harry, here.'

Buckingham turned towards him with a look of surprise. 'Congratulations, sergeant.' His words were warm but his eyes were cold and glittering.

'I've got a good aim,' Harry said. 'All those years of shooting at policeman's helmets with my catapult.'

Buckingham frowned, uncertain whether to take him at his word or not.

'Tea, gentlemen,' Nash said. 'And then we'll all discuss how we can try to avoid another show like today.'

That night, at 9.00, they heard that Winston Churchill had been appointed the new Prime Minister.

THE LETTER

16th May 1940

'An American woman?' Squadron Leader Simpson said. 'You want me to take an American woman on to my staff?'

Park nodded.

'But official secrets, sir. Issues of security. She could be a spy for all we know.'

'Mrs Foster, the tea-lady, could be a spy for all we know.'

'But Mrs Foster's English.'

Park gave Simpson a cool look. 'And I'm a New Zealander. Does that make me suspect?'

'Of course not, sir.'

Claire stifled a giggle. Simpson shot her an angry glance.

'And the commanders of two of Britain's Fighter Groups are a South African and an Irishman,' Park continued. 'So, let's have no more nonsense about spies.

'In any case, we've no choice in the matter. Apparently, the lady's father is a friend of Harry Hopkins, President Roosevelt's most trusted aide. The American ambassador spoke to Mr Churchill who immediately agreed to her working here. So, whatever your misgivings, the American lady stays.'

Simpson nodded although he could not keep his face from displaying his reluctance.

Park went back to his office.

'Do you find something amusing?' Simpson demanded of Claire.

'No sir. It was just a cough.' She touched her throat. 'A little tickle.'

He gave a cold smile. 'Perhaps you should be careful what you put in your mouth, Lamb.'

'I don't smoke, sir.'

He stared at her. Both knew what he was insinuating. He marched out of the room.

A few minutes later a knock came on the door and a woman walked in. 'I was told to come here,' she said. 'To see Marshal Park.'

'Air Vice Marshal,' Johnny Longley said. He gave her a shrewd look. 'Is he expecting you?'

The woman shrugged.

'You sound American,' Claire said.

Evelyn pretended surprise. 'Even after living here for six months?' She held out her hand. 'I'm Evelyn Nash. Your friendly cousin from over the pond.'

Claire smiled, warming to her immediately. 'Are you the American lady who's to work in the Group?'

'You've heard? I didn't know I was that famous.'

'I think it's more that Harry Hopkins is,' Johnny said with a grin. 'Air Commodore Park is in his office.'

'Air Vice Marshal Park,' Claire said.

Johnny clicked his fingers. 'I still can't get used to his promotion,' he said.

Evelyn's eyes took in the office. 'What do you two do?' she asked.

'I'm Flight Lieutenant Longley —' Johnny began.

'So you fly?'

'Never in my life.' He pointed to his eyes. 'Colour blind, I'm afraid. I'm purely a paper pusher.' He gave a meaningful pause. 'And Air Vice Marshal Park's right-hand man.'

'And I presume you're Park's Girl Friday,' Evelyn said to Claire.

'That's one way of putting it.' The American's sardonic tone was beginning to grate and Claire's initial warm feelings towards her were rapidly cooling.

Evelyn sighed. 'So, what am I going to do?'

Johnny scanned a piece of paper. 'It says here that you're going to work in the plotting room.'

Evelyn's eyebrow rose.

'The plotting room is where we plot the progress of German air-raids,' Claire explained. 'But you won't be doing that, apparently. You'll be working in liaison, taking messages between the Observer Corps and the fighter controllers.'

She shot a glance at Johnny, warning him not to say more. The British deployment of radar was not something the Americans should hear about.

'How will I take these messages from the Observer Corps?' Evelyn asked. 'In a car? On a bicycle?'

'On foot,' Johnny said. 'The Observer Corps are positioned across the whole coast so you won't be travelling between them and us. You'll be taking messages between the controllers here. And as I said, on foot.'

Evelyn just about managed to hide her disappointment. This was not the glamorous, important work she had imagined.

'So who will be my boss?' she asked. 'One of you?'

'Squadron Leader Simpson,' Johnny said. 'He's in charge of all the plotters and liaison work.'

'And I guess he's never flown either.'

'On the contrary. He's a very good pilot. Air Chief Marshal Dowding insists on all controllers having flying experience.'

'Come on,' Claire said. 'I'll take you down to the Bunker.'

Claire spent the next hour helping Evelyn settle in. The American was quick to pick things up, partly because she was not afraid to ask questions. Nor was she shy about giving her opinion about things once she grasped them. Most of the time she was complimentary although even this felt condescending. Occasionally she was disparaging and suggested that things could be done differently. At first Claire bridled at this but then she realised that Evelyn thought she was being helpful and unaware that she came across as arrogant and sharp. And many of the improvements were things which Claire herself had argued for.

She'll have to get used to British ways, Claire decided. And perhaps we'll do well to get used to American ones.

⋙⋘

Claire was just about to pack up for the day when Air Commodore Park called her into his office. 'Can you type, Lamb?' he asked.

'Good. In that case I have an extremely important job for you. And a top secret one. The Air Chief Marshal's assistant has had an accident and he need someone to prepare a most important document.'

'Of course, sir.'

'Then we're to go across to Headquarters, immediately.'

Park was detained by one of the senior controllers and told her to go to Dowding's office without him.

She approached it with trepidation. She had not done much typing over the last few years and feared that she would be rusty and prone to mistakes. And Air Chief Marshal Dowding was notorious for being difficult to work for. She stood outside his door with her hands raised. She had knocked repeatedly on it but no answer had come from within. She opened it a little and peered in.

Her eyes widened is surprise.

It was not at all like the only other time she had been here, the day Sir Hugh had welcomed her to Headquarters. Then, the office had been neat and tidy, everything orderly, everything in its place.

Now, the desk was littered with discarded pieces of paper, scrawled upon with urgent script, most of the sheets tossed aside, a large number screwed up as if in rage or disgust.

The writer himself was bent over yet another piece of paper, pen in hand, writing intently, oblivious to the world, sighing and muttering to himself. She wanted to slip away but instead she took a deep breath, closed the door and walked towards him.

'Good evening, sir,' she said.

Dowding did not appear to have noticed her.

She took a seat at the small desk opposite him and considered the blizzard of papers. She was about to offer to pick them up when Dowding rummaged through the pile closest to him, retrieved a piece of paper, scrutinised it carefully and began copying something from it on to the page he was working on. She sank back in the chair, wondering what to do.

'Get me the note I showed to Churchill yesterday,' he snapped.

'I don't know where it is…' she said.

Dowding looked up in surprise. 'Who on earth are you? Where's Corporal Custance? I sent him out for supper an hour ago.'

'He had an accident, sir. A lorry blew a tyre and crashed into him. He's broken his arm very badly. Air Vice Marshal Park sent me to take his place. Just for this evening, I think.'

Dowding bent to his work once again and then looked up. 'The note I showed Churchill,' he repeated. 'It's in the folder marked secret.'

She searched through the folder, nervously.

'Custance will be okay?' she heard Dowding murmur.

'Yes, he will, sir. But the doctor says he won't be able to work for a month.'

'The note?' he repeated.

'I think I've got it,' she said. 'The one with the graph?'

She glanced at it as she took it over to him. It contained a red line, showing the number of Hurricanes available to Fighter Command. She blinked in surprise. The line appeared to be in free-fall.

Dowding put down his pen and took the document from her. 'Everything you hear and see here is absolutely top secret. You understand this?'

'Of course, sir. Careless talk and all that.'

'Good.' He glanced at the clock on the wall. 'If Park can spare you, I have a letter for you to type. Top secret.'

The door opened and Park entered.

'Problems, sir?'

'Yes,' Dowding said. 'Churchill has promised the French ten Hurricane Squadrons.'

Park looked horrified. He shook his head, stunned by the news, and sat on the edge of the desk. 'He can't mean it,' he said at last. 'It's impossible. We can't —'

'I've written this,' Dowding said, passing him the paper.

Park read it in silence. He gave a whistle of surprise.

'Tough words, sir,' he said.

'To match the times.'

Park read it once again and passed it back to Dowding. 'If Churchill takes umbrage this could destroy your career.'

'If he doesn't take notice he'll destroy Fighter Command. And that will be the end of Great Britain.'

Claire swallowed hard and hoped that the Air Chief Marshal was exaggerating.

Dowding glanced out of the window. It was growing dark. 'Churchill is a romantic and given to wild and extravagant gestures.

But he's also a pragmatist and I doubt he wants to go down in history as the last Prime Minister of Britain.'

He got up and took the paper over to Claire. 'Type this up, please, Flight Officer.'

Claire put a piece of paper into the typewriter. There were ten paragraphs in the letter and she began to type, more slowly than she normally did. She didn't want to make any mistakes.

After a minute she looked up. 'Sir, in paragraph two you say: "I hope and believe that our Armies may yet be victorious in France and Bedford but we have to face the possibility that they may be defeated."'

She gave a little cough. 'Do you really mean Bedford, sir?'

'Of course I don't. It reads Belgium.'

Park snorted with laughter. 'Your writing's getting worse, sir. Perhaps you should dictate it. Don't want Winston getting the wrong end of the stick.'

Dowding retrieved the piece of paper. 'I can read it well enough. What's wrong with the girl?'

'Dictate it to her. Please.'

Dowding gave him a cool look but cleared his throat and began.

'Paragraph 3,' Dowding continued. 'In this case I presume that there is no-one who will deny that England should fight on, even though the remainder of the Continent of Europe is dominated by the Germans.

'Paragraph 4. For this purpose it is necessary to retain some minimum fighter strength in this country and I must request that the Air Council will inform me what they consider this minimum strength to be, in order that I may make my dispositions accordingly.

'5. I would remind the Air Council that the last estimate which they made as to the force necessary to defend this country was 52 Squadrons, and my strength has now been reduced to the equivalent of 36 Squadrons.'

Claire gasped. So few squadrons? She did a quick calculation. That meant there were only five hundred planes to protect the whole country. Surely there was some mistake, or perhaps it was just a tactic on the Air Chief Marshal's part, a tactic to gain him more resources.

She glanced at Dowding. No, it couldn't be that. He wouldn't try to delude the Prime Minister. Things were not just bleak; they were unimaginably black.

'6. Once a decision has been reached,' Dowding continued, 'as to the limit on which the Air Council and the Cabinet are prepared to stake the existence of the country, it should be made clear to the Allied Commanders on the Continent that not a single aeroplane from Fighter Command beyond the limit will be sent across the Channel, no matter how desperate the situation may become.'

Stake the existence of the country, Claire thought in horror. She was so shocked she typed the next three paragraphs mechanically, aware only that Dowding emphasised that the German success meant they would now be able to attack directly from Northern France and that the Hurricane Squadrons remaining were seriously under strength.

The Air Chief Marshal paused and glanced at Park. 'Do you think that bit's too strong, Park?'

Park shook his head. 'It's strong. But if you believe it, then it's your duty to say it.'

Dowding nodded. 'We both know it to be true.'

He cleared his throat and began to dictate again.

'I must therefore request that as a matter of paramount urgency the Air Ministry will consider and decide what level of strength is to be left to the Fighter Command for the defences of this country, and will assure me that when this level has been reached, not one fighter will be sent across the Channel however urgent and insistent the appeals for help may be.'

Claire gulped. This was almost an ultimatum. She doubted that Dowding would keep his job after this.

'10. I believe that, if an adequate fighter force is kept in this country, if the fleet remains in being, and if Home Forces are suitably organised to resist invasion, we should be able to carry on the war single handed for some time, if not indefinitely. But, if the Home Defence Force is drained away in desperate attempts to remedy the situation in France, defeat in France will involve the final, complete and irremediable defeat of this country.'

Claire breathed a sigh of relief that he had finished. Her eyes had filled with tears on hearing that Britain might be on the brink of complete defeat and she had trouble typing the last few words.

Dowding held out his hand and she passed him the typescript. He and Park read it silently together.

'If this works it may save the country,' Park said.

'I pray to God it does.'

DUNKIRK

26th May - 4th June 1940

Jacqueline Longley raced into the base and screeched to a halt outside Bentley Priory. She loved to drive fast and now she had an excuse for it.

Air Vice Marshal Park exhaled loudly. 'Thank you for getting me here so promptly, Longley. No harm done. None of my bones are broken.'

'You ordered me to drive fast,' Jacqueline said.

'But not as fast as a Spitfire.' He gave her an amused look. 'How does your husband handle you.'

'With care, sir.'

'I bet he does. Wait here until we've finished.'

Claire followed him into the Priory. 'I want you to take notes, Lamb,' he said. 'Sir Hugh sounded anxious on the phone. Not like him at all.'

'Is there some flap on, sir?'

'It would appear so.'

Air Chief Marshal Dowding was pacing up and down in his office. His desk was strewn with maps and documents.

'Something big is about to happen,' Dowding said. 'We could lose the war in the next few days.'

'Shall I leave, sir?' Claire asked. 'If it's very hush-hush?' She thought she might faint.

'The Air Vice Marshal brought you for a reason,' Dowding said,' so you must stay. In any case, what we're about to discuss will be common knowledge soon enough.'

'Broadcast by that scoundrel Lord Haw-Haw?' Park said. He frowned. 'What's his real name? James Joyce?'

'William Joyce,' Dowding said with an almost absent air. 'James Joyce is an author.'

Claire looked surprised that the Air Chief Marshal had heard of the infamous author of dirty books.

'Good writer, Joyce,' he added. 'Racy but very clever.'

Park gave a polite cough. 'Something big, sir?'

'Yes. Forgive me. I had no sleep last night.'

Dowding jabbed a finger at a map of northern France. 'As you know, the British Expeditionary Force is bottled up here at Dunkirk. A quarter of a million men with all their equipment. Together with a hundred thousand French troops. Viscount Gort has insisted that they be evacuated to England.'

'That many men?' Park said. 'Surely that can't that be done?'

'Vice Admiral Ramsay has formulated a plan, Operation Dynamo. The hope is that we'll be able to evacuate as many as forty or fifty thousand men.'

'And the rest?'

Dowding shook his head.

Park took a deep breath. 'So what do we do, Fighter Command?'

'We support the Royal Navy as they undertake the evacuation. And we do our utmost to protect our soldiers on the ground.'

Park's brow furrowed. 'We have what, five hundred planes this side of the channel.'

'And a hundred in France.'

'So how many squadrons do we deploy?' He paused. 'Given the number you persuaded Churchill to leave here in England?'

'We will have to forget about that for the moment. This is today's crisis and we must do our utmost to deal with it. We shall have to send most of our squadrons into battle. And we will put our trust in God.'

'And our pilots,' Park said.

Dowding nodded.

———

They got back to RAF Uxbridge an hour later.

'There'll be no rest for us tonight,' Park said. 'Not while our troops are in such peril.'

He gave a few brief orders. As was typical with him, their brevity disguised their thoroughness and rigour. He had spent the journey back working out exactly what 11 Group should do and how they should do it.

It was now up to Johnny, Claire and the rest of his senior staff to formulate a plan to put his ideas into action. It was ready by six the following morning.

'The key thing,' Park told Dowding on the telephone, 'is that although we send the majority of our squadrons over to France we only fly them from airfields over here. If we deploy any planes from French airfields we risk them being captured by German ground forces.'

Dowding agreed and immediately telephoned the Air Ministry to inform them of the decision.

Claire managed to snatch a few hours sleep, returning to duty just after ten. She was surprised that she felt no fatigue. My blood must be up, she thought. She felt astonishingly alert, almost scintillating with energy.

The rest of the team swung into action. The only exception was Squadron Leader Simpson.

'It's utmost folly,' he said. 'The army is trapped and can't escape.'

'I could turn on the wireless and hear Lord Haw-Haw say the same,' Johnny Longley said. There was a gale of laughter at his words. Anxious, exhausted laughter but laughter nonetheless.

'Mark my words,' Simpson said. 'The army's doomed. And if we go to their rescue then the RAF will be doomed alongside them.'

Claire did not bother to hide her anger. 'Defeatist talk will lose us this war. Not how we fight it.'

He gave her a smug sneer. She made an instant decision, turned on her heel and marched into Park's office.

'Sir,' she began, 'I wonder if I could be sent to one of the sector stations. To work as a plotter. It's where I've got most experience.'

He looked astonished. 'Certainly not.'

'Why not, sir?'

'Because I need you here, with me. You've got a sharp brain, Lamb, and a good tactical mind. I shall have to deploy every squadron over Dunkirk and my controllers will be focused completely on organising the sorties. I need a sounding board I can trust when I make my decisions.'

She gulped. 'Very good, sir.' She made for the door but paused on the threshold. 'I hope I can live up to your expectations, sir.'

'Just as much as I do, Lamb.' It was the first time she had seen him look worried.

For the next nine days she only left Park's side to snatch a few hours sleep. The rest of the time they sat in the Bunker, watching the plotters at work as the controllers sent squadron after squadron across the channel.

Some squadrons were so badly mauled they had to be pulled back for a few day's rest. The rest were sent in every day, sometimes three or four times.

She had to harden her heart against the losses she knew were taking place.

Frank Trent flew as low as he dared over the beaches running north east from Calais towards Dunkirk. He gasped in surprise. The shore was filled with thousands of men, tens of thousands, with hundreds of vehicles and tanks abandoned to the rear. Long columns of men were snaking out into the sea.

He looked where they were heading and gasped. The sea was full of ships. Two dozen grey warships of the Royal Navy were stationed a mile from the shore, as close as they could get without foundering. Other large boats lay a little closer, coal barges, pleasure steamers, ferries. A makeshift armada collected from every port and estuary of southern England to make the hopeless dash to try to rescue a desperate, beleaguered army.

Between the larger vessels and the shore, a vast array of little boats - pleasure craft, lifeboats, fishing smacks and cockle boats - ferried soldiers from the hell of the beaches to the sanctuary of the ships.

From the skies above the beaches, a thousand planes of the Luftwaffe were hurling bombs and bullets on to the boats and soldiers below.

'Come on lads,' Nash called over the radio. His voice was a peculiar mixture of excitement, aggression and fear. Frank felt those same emotions churning inside him.

The squadron threw themselves at the German bombers. This is how it ends, Frank thought, this is how I die. A suicidal mission, with no hope of victory or survival.

Suddenly, he was in the middle of the German bombers. He fired his guns at the nearest one, his bullets smashing through the cockpit windscreen and mortally wounding the pilot. The plane swayed, stalled and plunged into the sea, narrowly missing one of the columns of men wading out into the water.

He glimpsed a Messerschmitt 110 heading towards him, threw his plane into a swerve which confounded his attacker, got behind him and raked his fuselage with fire. The rear gunner returned fire for a few seconds and then fell silent. Frank used the opportunity to get closer and pour more bullets into the cockpit of the plane. None of them proved fatal, for the pilot was able to make his escape.

He gazed around, searching for more prey. Two dive-bombers were wreaking havoc on the boats struggling slowly from the beach. He aimed at a third one, causing it to pull out of its dive and head out to sea. A Navy destroyer fired its anti-aircraft gun and brought it down. But then half a dozen other bombers attacked the destroyer in one screaming blast. The ship was lost to Frank's view for a moment and then he glimpsed smoke pouring from it and the crew leaping into the sea.

He chased the bombers and spent the last of his bullets on a Heinkel 111 without success. He turned back towards the battle although he knew that he would be able to play no further part in it.

'Watch your fuel, chaps,' came Nash's voice.

Frank glanced at his gauge, there was enough to get him back over the channel but not to undertake long, unarmed dogfights. He turned and headed back towards England.

He landed and saw the ground crew hurrying towards him. Even from a distance, he could see that some looked baffled. As he climbed out of the plane and watched the rest of the squadron touch down, he saw why. Of the twelve planes that set out an hour before only eight had made it back.

He joined the others as they gathered silently and stared at the empty sky. Nash, Harry Smith, Buckingham, Tomasz and the two new boys whose names Frank could not recall, were the only other survivors.

'We can't have too many shows like this,' Buckingham said.

Nash sighed. 'Then we'll just have to be more careful next time.'

The squadron returned to action early the following morning. Their new standing orders were to remain out to sea in order to protect the ships waiting to receive the troops. It meant that the beaches would be at the mercy of the Luftwaffe.

Although the RAF had lost many fighters and bombers, the Luftwaffe had fared equally badly and their commanders had decided to concentrate their attacks at dawn and dusk. For the next few days there ensued a merciless battle in twilight and shadows. Two more of the squadron's new boys were lost although one was picked up by a fishing boat and taken to a Navy destroyer.

Hour after hour, day after day, the RAF flew ceaseless missions to help the evacuation. Nash's squadron fought on every day.

Finally, nine days after the start of Operation Dynamo, all the men that could be taken off of the beaches had been and the deadly battle ended.

<hr>

Air Vice Marshal Park stared at the figures.

Bomber Command had launched 650 raids against the German artillery shelling the beaches. Coastal Command had operated against the German E-boats and submarines disrupting the evacuation.

But his eyes focused on the statistics concerning Fighter Command. It had flown 2,730 sorties, more than 300 each day of the evacuation. It was immensely gratifying and a credit to his people that they had achieved so much.

But a hundred fighter planes had been lost, together with their pilots. It was a catastrophe for Fighter Command.

The door opened to reveal Air Chief Marshal Dowding.

Park got to his feet.

'Sit down, Park,' Dowding said. 'Sit.'

He stared at Park in silence.

'You did well, Park,' he said at last. 'Your people did well. Because of what we did, and the magnificent work of the Navy and those brave volunteer sailors, we've brought back 338,000 men, of which 225,000 were British.

'Almost a thousand ships and boats were involved. A quarter of them were lost. Six destroyers were sunk and a further nineteen damaged. But it's not these losses which is the greatest worry.'

He unfolded a piece of paper and studied it for a moment.

'I have the final figures for our actions over the French coast. We lost one hundred and fifty aircraft. There are only 360 Hurricanes and Spitfires remaining to Fighter Command. Eighteen squadrons in all.'

Park groaned. 'Only a third of the minimum necessary to protect the country.'

'Precisely. If Hitler invades now, we cannot hold him back. The Navy is reeling from its losses, the army is stricken and without armaments. And we are but a shadow of our former strength.'

Park frowned and then called out, 'Lamb. Bring me those figures you showed me yesterday. The ones on factory output and pilot training.'

Claire hurried in with a couple of papers.

Park glanced at them and handed them over to Dowding. He read them swiftly and looked up in surprise. 'Where did you get these, girl?'

'I asked for them from the Air Ministry.'

Dowding frowned. 'I wish they were as forthcoming with me.'

'I think that Lamb may be a little more charming to them,' Park said.

Dowding grunted and studied the figures more intently. 'Well these give me hope,' he said, finally. 'The aircraft factories must be working every minute of the day and night. And the number of pilots in training is better than I thought.'

He glanced at Lamb. 'Well done, Flight Officer.'

'I'm a Section Officer, sir,' she said.

'Not anymore. Air Vice Marshal Park has recommended you for promotion to Flight Officer and I'm more than happy to agree it.'

She saluted and left the office. How bizarre, she thought. All those men have died, and I get promoted. She felt like weeping.

Harry, Frank and Tomasz threw themselves into the chairs in the NAAFI.

'Cup of tea, lads?' called one of the women behind the counter.

Harry frowned. 'Actually, no.' He tapped Frank on the shoulder. 'Come on you two, I think we deserve a pint. Not the Good Intent but somewhere quieter.'

They hurried to the bike pool and were soon cycling down the lane towards a nearby village.

The Badger was an ancient looking inn standing beside a duck pond. A group of people were lounging outside, enjoying the summer sun. Then one of them saw the three airmen.

'You bastards,' he cried. 'You cowardly, stinking bastards.'

The three pilots glanced behind them to see who the man was shouting at. There was no one there.

'It's you bastards I'm talking to,' the man continued. He was in his thirties, stocky and with angry eyes. 'My brother was on the beach at Dunkirk and you lot were nowhere to be seen. Skulking here, drinking whisky and having your hair done all fine and dandy.'

'We were there,' Harry said. 'And we protected our troops from the Luftwaffe.'

'As your brother will tell you,' Frank added.

'He told me the opposite. Told me there was no sight nor sound of you. And the poor lad lost one of his legs.'

'I'm sorry —' Harry began.

Suddenly a woman stepped forward and spat in his face. He was utterly shocked. He stared at her in silence, incapable of even wiping the spit from his cheek.

'You stinking little coward,' she said. 'If I had my way, I'd string you up.'

'You are wrong to say this,' Tomasz said. 'Harry is a courageous man.'

'And who are you? A bloody German?' The woman spat at him as well. She shook her hand in his face. 'Let's start with the Jerry. String him up.'

'How dare you call me that,' Tomasz cried.

The stocky man leapt towards them, fists flailing. Half a dozen other men followed him to the fray, three grabbing the airmen around the chest while the others landed punches on them.

Suddenly, it was all too much for Frank. He bellowed with fury and head butted the man aiming a punch at him. Then he twisted, as swiftly as he could manoeuvre a Hurricane, and hurled the man holding him to the ground. Harry managed to wriggle free and jabbed one of his attackers in the eye. Tomasz had already slipped free of his assailant and was throwing his fists around as if he were attacking Nazis.

A loud cry came from the pub. Two men, the landlord and an off-duty policeman charged out and bellowed to them to stop. The villagers looked disinclined to do so but then the policeman waded into the melee and clobbered a few of them around the head. He was a big man, six foot and sixteen stone, and they cowered away from him.

The place fell quiet apart from the excited yapping of nearby dogs.

'You disgust me,' the landlord said in a quiet voice. 'You attack these boys who have been risking their lives to protect us all.'

'But not the boys on the beach,' yelled the stocky man. 'Not my brother.'

The policeman stepped close to him. 'Your brother's an idiot, David Pierce, and you're an even bigger one. So shut your mouth before I shut it for you.'

'You can't threaten him,' said the woman.

'It was no threat; it was a promise.'

'You're banned, the lot of you,' the landlord told the villagers. 'You airmen come into the pub. I'll stand you drinks and something to eat. Forget about this lot. They're not worth bothering with.'

The mob sidled off with the policeman standing guard over the entrance until they had disappeared.

He followed them into the pub and put five shillings on the counter. 'Here's my contribution,' he said. 'And I think I'll join you.'

'Thanks very much,' Harry said. 'And thanks for weighing in on our behalf.'

'Don't take it amiss, lad. Some of them, David Pierce and his woman, are real scum. The rest are just too stupid to think for themselves. Any chance for them to have a little bust-up gives them something to do.'

'Why aren't they in the army?' Tomasz said. 'They're so full of aggression.'

'Not fit enough, probably,' the policeman said.

'Or malingers,' added the landlord. 'Petty thieves, poachers, spivs. This war is happy hunting ground for them.'

'Some of our friends have died to protect the likes of them,' Frank said.

'Aye lad. But also to protect decent folk. And there's far more decent folk than rotten ones, let me tell you.' He gave Frank a pint. 'Are you Australian?'

'American.'

'I didn't know you lot were in the war.'

'Not many of us are. But give us time and we will be.'

'I bloody hope so,' said the landlord. 'It looks like the Germans will be hard to beat.'

ALONE

22nd June 1940

'Get everyone into the filter room, Lamb,' Air Vice Marshal Park said. 'Don't let anybody go home. I have an announcement.' Her stomach crawled at his words. She had never seen him look so subdued.

She assembled everyone. Flo, Betty and Evelyn came and stood beside her. Johnny had positioned himself next to Willoughby de Broke. Despite their differences in background the two men got on very well. The war created strange bedfellows, Claire thought.

At eight o clock precisely, Park came out of his office. He had a single sheet of paper in his hand. Normally, everyone was relaxed in his presence but everyone immediately stood to attention. For a moment he didn't appear to notice. Then he waved them to stand at ease.

He glanced at the piece of paper and took a deep breath.

'This letter has come from the Prime Minister,' he said. 'It states that at six-thirty this evening the French and Germans signed an armistice. The new French Prime Minister, Phillipe Pétain, has ordered all French forces to lay down their arms.' He sighed. 'Pétain was a hero in the last war. I doubt that history will treat him kindly.'

There was a stunned silence.

'So we are alone,' Park said quietly. 'But Mr Churchill has said that we will continue the fight. That we will not surrender.' His hand briefly touched his forehead. Then he took a deep breath and said. 'I know that everyone here will continue to do their duty. Dark times lie ahead but if we are resolute and united, we will get through this trial.'

Everyone was silent for a moment, staring at their friends. Most had known that France was in a dreadful situation. But few had expected the Government to surrender. The battle had lasted a mere six weeks.

'What can stop the Germans now?' Simpson said, quietly.

Park overheard him.

'We can. The Royal Air Force. And we shall.'

He put the piece of paper on the table and his eyes swept the room. 'The German army is formidable. Adolf Hitler has announced that if we don't surrender, he will invade Britain. That he will defeat and conquer us. But before he can do that, he must be certain that his troops can cross the English Channel in safety. He can only do that if he is the master of the skies.

'His crony, Goring, has promised him that this will be an easy matter. The Luftwaffe is the largest air force in the world and, up to now, it has destroyed every enemy it has fought.'

He rapped once upon the table.

'But not anymore. Now, the Royal Air Force stands guard over these islands. Our bombers will destroy his invasion barges and his tanks. And we, Fighter Command, will fight the Luftwaffe wherever and whenever they appear. We will fight them and we will defeat them.

'And by doing so, we will prevent a German invasion.'

‐‐‐‐

'Do you think that Britain will fight on?' Evelyn asked the next morning. 'The Germans seem unstoppable.'

'So have a lot of our enemies in the past,' Claire said. 'We defeated the Spanish Armada, we defeated Napoleon Bonaparte, we defeated Kaiser Bill.'

'But Britain wasn't fighting alone then. You are now.'

'We've got the Empire. Canada, Australia, South Africa, New Zealand. Even India has declared war.'

'You mean the British Viceroy declared war on India's behalf. I doubt many of the people are keen to fight for their oppressors.'

'We're not their oppressors. We built them hospitals and railways.'

Evelyn gave a scornful look.

Claire put her cap on the desk and ran her fingers through her hair. Despite her brave words she felt sick to the stomach. She had been having nightmares about being chased by bears. Why bears she didn't know but they were frightening. Every night she dreaded going to sleep.

'You haven't really answered my question,' Evelyn said.

'What does it matter what I think,' Claire snapped. She picked up her cap and began to brush the material although there was no sign of dirt on it, not a trace.

Can we carry on the fight, she wondered. The Germans had defeated every army they fought, conquered every country. And now they were on the coast of France, only twenty miles away. Worse still, we have virtually no army left.

'That's why we need you Americans to come in to the war,' she said. She tried but failed to keep the desperation from her voice. 'Do you think America will?'

Evelyn shook her head. 'It's impossible, I'm afraid. Mr Hopkins, my father's friend, believes that Mr Roosevelt is sympathetic but his hands are tied. Too many folk in the US are isolationist. They want no part in England's wars.'

'But if Hitler wins, he'll turn his sights on America.'

'America's a very long way away. The Luftwaffe won't reach it and the Germans don't have much of a navy.'

'They will if they get their hands on ours.'

Evelyn picked up a pencil and turned it in her fingers.

'I suspect that Mr Roosevelt is worried about all these things,' she said quietly. 'And I guess that he'll do everything he can to help you, short of declaring war. If Mr Hopkins has anything to do with it, at least. My father says he'd declare war tomorrow if it were his decision.'

'A pity it's not.'

'Yep.'

'What can your President do?' Claire asked.

Evelyn shrugged. 'It's difficult. I'm sure he'd like to send you ships and airplanes. But he's worried about what might happen if we do.'

'In what way? We're hardly going to use your weapons against you.'

Evelyn took Claire's hands. 'He's worried that all our weapons will fall into German hands if you're conquered. And then, they may be used against us. By the Nazis.'

'Which is what I just said about our Navy. Surely the American people can see that if we're defeated, the Germans will have the largest army in the world and the most powerful Navy and Air Force.'

Claire tried to keep the exasperation from her voice. It was not Evelyn's fault that America had not joined in. And she was here, doing her bit, even though she was an American citizen.

And she was not the only one.

Claire knew for a fact that there were dozens of young Americans in the RAF. They were risking their lives and, if the American Government found out, they would probably lose their liberty and their citizenship. Everyone who knew turned a blind eye to it, pretending that they were Canadians. She wondered if President Roosevelt knew, but she thought it best not to ask Evelyn.

She stared out of the window at the number of personnel hurrying to and fro: administrators, cooks, cleaners, mechanics, instructors, pilots. Johnny said there were 20,000 people at Uxbridge, double what there were last year. She wondered what on earth they all did.

'Do you want a cup of tea?' she asked.

Evelyn took her hand and nodded.

'Me too, please,' came a voice behind them.

'Isn't it about time you made a cup, Johnny,' Claire said.

'I'd be happy to. But you wouldn't be happy to drink it.'

'Pathetic,' Evelyn said.

'Okay. You asked for it.'

He went into the little kitchen and clattered about for a little. He returned a few minutes later with three steaming mugs.

'So, what news?' Evelyn asked. She had learnt already that Johnny knew almost everything that was going on.

'The last of our forces in France are still being evacuated from the Western ports. Our boys are doing wonders to protect the retreat. There were almost two hundred thousand British troops still out there. I'm guessing that most of them will get home.'

'But what about the rest of the war?' Evelyn asked. 'Claire thinks the British will fight on.'

Johnny looked shocked at the question. 'Of course we will. We're not the sort to give up.'

He stared at his tea. 'In any case, what choice do we have?'

'You could do what France did. Ask for an armistice.'

'I think the French people will come to regret they did.'

He sighed. 'I don't blame the French authorities, not one bit. They didn't have the English Channel; their armies were wide open to the Germans. And they didn't have our Navy and RAF.'

He drained his cup of tea. 'Let's remember what Winston Churchill said. We'll fight the bastards everywhere, on the beaches, in the hills and the streets. We'll never surrender.'

Evelyn reached out and squeezed his hand. 'I'm glad. It might prove the saving of civilisation.'

SPITFIRE

8tth July 1940

Squadron Leader Maisfield walked out of the administration block and watched as the Spitfires landed. Eighteen of them, fresh from the factory. The Spitfire was already famous as the fastest aeroplane in the RAF. Perhaps the fastest in the world. Some wag had said that if the Hurricane was a trusty English carthorse then the Spitfire was an Arabian, beautiful as a goddess, swift as the wind.

Maisfield wrinkled his nose at that. He liked the Hurricane. It was a fine machine and had proved its worth in France and over Dunkirk. It was sturdy, well-armed, easy to maintain and repair and, after all, not much slower than the Spitfire. Equally important, it cost half the price of a Spitfire and could be manufactured in far less time.

And, perhaps best of all, it was easier to fly. This was becoming of vital importance as most of the pilots being posted to squadrons had far too few hours of flying practice. Fighter Command had no choice but to put these novices into the air sooner than they were ready. And in that case, the Hurricane was a safer choice than the Spitfire.

Maisfield scratched his ear thoughtfully as the Spitfires came to a halt. It would be good to see what all the fuss was about, fascinating to find out if the praise heaped on them was really justified.

Without giving it more thought he strolled up to the nearest plane.

The aircraftman beside it saluted him.

'Has she got much fuel?' Maisfield asked.

'Half a tank, sir. They've only just arrived from the factory at Southampton.'

Maisfield walked around the plane, examining it carefully, running his hands along the sleek metal fuselage. It was certainly a fine-looking machine.

He returned to the aircraftman. 'I'm going to take her for a spin.'

The man looked doubtful, almost as if he were about to argue but then nodded.

'There's fuel for about two hundred miles, sir.' He paused. 'There's no ammo.'

'I'm going to test the thing, not fight in it.'

'Very good, sir. I'll get you a harness.'

It had been a while since Maisfield had flown and the aircraftman had to help him put on the harness. Getting into the cockpit was more difficult than he had imagined, it was much narrower than any he had been in before.

He studied the controls. Nothing difficult here, he thought.

'Don't forget there's no ammunition,' the aircraftman said.

'I've told you, I won't be needing any. Chocks away.'

He turned on the engine and felt the powerful throb of the Merlin engine. He pushed on the accelerator and was soon racing along the runway. The plane lurched and swung, almost teetering on its narrow wheel-base. He was a skilled pilot but even he found it difficult to keep it going in a straight line. But then the nose lifted and he soared into the air.

Now the plane showed a very difficult character; it felt as light as a feather. He soon found that it was very responsive to his touch, a shade too much pressure and it would bank alarmingly. No wonder novices found it so damned difficult. He had more hours under his belt than he cared to remember but the Spitfire was taxing his skills. His tongue crept out of his mouth as he climbed, his concentration fixed on the controls. Soon, however, he felt as if he and the machine were almost as one, working in harmony. Just like a champion racehorse and jockey, he thought.

He speedily reached twenty thousand feet and slackened his rate of climb to conserve fuel. He knew it had a ceiling of forty thousand feet but he decided to stop at thirty. Once he had reached it he levelled out and increased speed. The engines growled a little more deeply and the plane surged forward.

He must have been flying for ten minutes when he saw it. A dark cloud far to the south. But it was moving fast, far faster than any cloud of the natural world.

He blinked. By God, it was the Luftwaffe. Dozens upon dozens of bombers with a loosely deployed pack of fighters as escort.

As he watched he saw a lone squadron of Hurricanes hurtling in from the west. It appeared that they were going to leap into the mass of bombers. It seemed suicidal.

Without thought or hesitation he increased speed and raced towards the enemy.

It was only when he got within a thousand yards that he recalled the aircraftman's words. The plane had no ammunition. He was unarmed and going into combat with the mightiest airforce in the world.

He was going so fast there was no time for him to alter course. There was only one choice open to him.

He moved the stick a fraction and aimed straight for the heart of the bombers. Instinctively he pressed on the trigger but, of course, there was no response. Now, his only hope lay in speed and manoeuvrability.

His eyes widened as he closed on the foremost rank of planes. Their pilots panicked. This was the first Spitfire they had ever encountered and they assumed that there must be more nearby.

The tight formation disintegrated as the bombers broke ranks, desperate to evade him. He found himself laughing aloud, part with joy, part with relief.

'Come on you bastard,' he cried and raced after one of the fleeing bombers.

The German pilot was incredibly skilled. He banked, climbed, swerved and dived in an astonishing display of acrobatics. But Maisfield hung grimly on his tail, inexorably closing the distance between them.

When he was three hundred feet behind the bomber his fingers pressed the trigger again. Damn it, damn it, damn it. No bloody ammo.

For a moment he wondered about crashing into the plane or sweeping beside it and clipping its wing. But then he thought about the cost of the Spitfire. What was it, £10,000? More than his salary for the next ten years.

Suddenly a hail of bullets thudded into the plane. Two Messerschmitt Bf 110's were on either side, their gunners aiming at him. He increased power and climbed at a rate which truly astonished him. It did the trick. In moments he had left the Messerschmitts far behind and was well above the battle.

He banked a little, studied the bombers which were now disappearing in every direction. He could do nothing more without ammunition and decided to head home.

The landing was more difficult than he anticipated. His face reddened as he hopped and slewed before coming to a hurried, undignified halt. The aircraftman ran over to help him out. His mouth opened wide at the sight of the bullets in the plane.

'I thought you were only going for a test-run, sir.'

'I was. I ended up in a fight. But I got lucky.'

'You're right there, sir. Very lucky.'

ATTACK

7th August 1940

Harry Smith and Frank Trent stared at the chess board. They had been playing since shortly after breakfast and neither had seized any advantage. Each suspected that the other was a slightly better player although they both realised that they were not actually very good at the game. But it passed the time and took their minds off any forthcoming danger.

Frank glanced out of the window. Low cloud filled the sky. 'And this is an English summer?' he asked in disbelief.

'Don't complain,' Harry said. 'While it's like this Jerry won't be flying.' He glanced at the clock. 'Come, on let's have an early lunch before the hordes arrive.'

Lunch was a choice of sausages with watery mash or a pie with a rather grey crust. Harry chose the sausages. Frank frowned as he examined the pie. 'Is this a steak pie,' he asked the kitchen assistant.

The man gave a derisive laugh. 'It's Woolton Pie, mate. Vegetables and gravy with a nice pastry crust.' He had been told to sound enthusiastic about it but the doubt in his voice spoke loud and clear. 'The WAAF girls like it but erm…' his words trailed off into silence.

'I'll try it,' Frank said.

The man looked surprised. 'Suit yourself.'

Frank took a seat next to Harry and began to eat. The pie was better than it looked and judging by the look on Harry's face, a little more appetising than the sausages.

'Sausages not good?' he asked.

Harry grimaced. 'They're made entirely of pig ears and nostrils.' But he ate it, nonetheless. Food was little more than fuel nowadays.

They returned to the station and resumed the game of chess. 'We'll play until two,' Harry said. 'Then I'm going for a kip.'

He'd no sooner said it when a bell rang across the station and the dispatch clerk raced into the room. 'Scramble,' he yelled.

Harry's throat seized at the sound. He leapt from his seat, grabbed his pilot harness and ran towards the line of Spitfires. It felt like he was in a childhood nightmare, being chased by some terrible demon where your feet are like lead and difficult to move. And you know, with dreadful certainty, that the demon is closing in on you.

He forced himself onward, ignoring all demons, his harness bouncing unheeded against his leg as he ran. Suddenly his legs seemed to move faster, like some crazy character in a silent film.

He reached the plane. Jack was already at the wing and stepped aside so he could clamber up to the cockpit.

Harry dropped into the seat and Jack clipped him into the harness, tapping him on the shoulder to show he had finished.

Breathe, Harry thought, breathe and calm yourself. He took a gulp of air and suddenly quietened. He pushed his helmet on and checked the radio was working.

'Everything's fine,' Jack said.

'Maybe for you,' Harry said, forcing a smile on his face.

He pressed the ignition and the engine growled into life. Like a tiger, he thought, like a flaming, angry tiger. He glanced across at Frank and gave a thumbs up just before Jack pulled the canopy over him.

The radio crackled and Tony Nash's precise tones filled his ears. 'Squadron Leader here. The Jerries are after a large convoy near Folkestone. We're going to teach them to mind their own business.'

Nash's Spitfire moved forward, picking up speed. The rest of the squadron followed, moving into line like soldiers on parade.

Harry pushed the stick and the plane gathered speed. A little bounce, a drop back, then another bounce, a second drop. And then the nose lifted and the plane was airborne.

The rate of climb was more impressive than that of a Hurricane and the pilots, still unused to this, were a little dispersed as they gained height.

'Close up, gentlemen,' Nash ordered.

The planes swung closer into the prescribed Vic formations. Nash flew at the front of A flight with Brooks leading Green Section to his rear. Buckingham, as the senior Flight Leader, led B flight a little to the right and rear of A.

They crossed the Thames and hurtled over the Kent countryside, following the line of the Downs south east towards the Channel. The Spitfires were extremely responsive and the slightest touch risked them sliding out of formation.

'Don't hold the controls so tight,' came Nash's voice. 'Treat the Spitfire like a lady, gently and with respect.'

Harry relaxed his grip and found that the plane flew more smoothly.

He was leading the three planes of Red section at the back of the squadron. Nash had asked him to fly this position, telling him to keep an eye on the new boy, just down from training. He agreed, of course, but he doubted he would fulfil the role as well as Nash expected. He berated himself for thinking so but could not shake off the sense of misgiving.

He glanced at the plane just ahead. He doubted Buckingham would entertain such uncertainties. Probably his only concern was that he wasn't the Squadron Leader. He acted as if he thought he should have been.

Harry glanced behind where Frank was flying Red Two. Because of the pattern of the Squadron he had one of the best views around. It also left him a little more exposed to attack. But Frank had the swiftest reactions of any pilot in the squadron and would, doubtless, easily outmanoeuvre any of the enemy.

Harry frowned, realising that he had no idea about the capabilities of the new pilot. Some of the novices flew their first mission with skill and success. Most made a real hash of it. A few never made it back.

He turned on his radio. 'Red Three,' he said.

There was no reply.

He shook his head wearily. 'Red Three, Red Three,' he repeated. He cursed under his breath. 'Hey, new boy. Answer for God's sake.'

A shaky voice came in his ear. 'Red Three here. I forgot that was me.'

'I thought you'd nodded off,' Harry said. 'Keep close to me and don't do anything stupid.' He paused. 'And remind me of your name?'

'Bob Wright.'

Harry chuckled. 'You couldn't have a better name. Just bob and weave and you'll come out all right.'

There was a silence and then he heard Bob gave a little laugh. 'That's funny. I didn't think there would be time for funny.'

'There won't be, shortly,' Harry said. 'The Channel is just ahead. And remember that up here you're not Bob Wright but Red Three.' He glanced at his clock. It was 13.50. They had flown sixty miles in under fifteen minutes.

As they came out over the Channel, he glimpsed the convoy far below, toy boats in a child's bath.

'Bloody hell,' Frank called over the radio.

Harry instantly saw why. Seventy German planes were below them, twenty bombers and fifty fighter escorts. It was the largest formation he had ever seen.

One squadron of Hurricanes was hurtling to attack them, head on. Twelve planes against seventy. A solitary David against a horde of Goliaths.

'They must be mad,' Harry muttered, forgetting that Frank and Bob would hear him.

'Come on, gentlemen,' Nash said, 'duty calls.' His voice was startlingly calm. 'We'll hit the Messerschmitts on the flank.'

He led the squadron to the east in a long graceful arc.

They sped east for a minute, five miles distance, enough to disappear from the enemy's sight. Then Nash led them into a turn, aiming at the heart of the German fighter escort.

Harry glimpsed three more Hurricane squadrons speeding from the west. Thank God for Keith Park, he thought, it's a more even match now.

The squadron loosened their tight formation and went into attack.

Up ahead, a Hurricane spewed fire at a Dornier but got too close and clipped its wing. The Hurricane's wing fell off and it spun out of control. Both planes plunged towards the sea. Harry forced his gaze away, sweeping the sky for signs of danger.

'Keep with me, Bob,' Harry said as they hurtled towards the Messerschmitts. The German pilots were surprised by this sudden attack from their flank but quickly responded, peeling away to get out of danger. Harry raced after the nearest plane, firing his machine guns as the Messerschmitt turned. His bullets raked the fuselage but did little damage. He glanced to his left and saw that Bob had obeyed his commands. He was sticking to him like glue.

'Keep your eyes peeled, Bob,' he yelled. 'Those bastards can turn on a sixpence and they'll be attacking us in a moment.'

The sky was filled with vapour trails as the planes dived and turned, engaging in furious combat. Harry kept after his prey, hanging on to his tail like a limpet. A Dornier slewed in front of him with a Hurricane following close behind, pouring bullets into the rear.

Suddenly he saw a stream of bullets spew from Wright's plane towards the Hurricane.

'Stop firing for fuck's sake,' he yelled. 'That's one of our Hurricanes.'

'Whoops,' Wright muttered.

'Whoops! Forget whoops and just concentrate.'

In this split second he had lost the plane he had been chasing. But as he scanned the air to his left he saw that two Messerschmitts were homing in on Nash's plane.

'Behind you, Leader,' he called as he accelerated after them. He was pleased to see that Wright turned to keep up with him.

'Red Three, Red Three,' he called over the radio. There was no reply. 'Bob bloody Wright.'

'Yes, sir,' came Wright's voice. 'Red Wright here. I mean —'

'That's Squadron Leader Nash at the front,' Harry said. 'I'd prefer it if you aimed at the Jerries and not at him.'

The Germans were unaware of them as they approached, closing to four hundred feet.

Harry fired his machine guns, saw the German pilot look round in horror and peel away. The other plane was slower to react and he closed on this. Just before he pressed his trigger he saw flames erupt on the fuselage. It flew straight for a couple of seconds and then keeled over, spinning towards the cliffs. Wright's plane soared above it.

'Well done, Bob Wright,' he yelled. 'First day and first kill.'

Nash's voice came over the radio. 'Well done, Red Three. But don't relax. Not for a moment.'

Harry turned in pursuit of a lone Messerschmitt below him. 'Keep with me, Bob,' he called. 'No heroics, mind.' He knew that the exhilaration Wright must be feeling at his first kill was a terrible enemy to him, could put him in real danger.

'Don't worry, sir. I think I'm too shaky to be brave.'

Harry smiled. Thank goodness for small mercies.

He plunged after the German plane but the pilot proved the more skilful, ducking and turning like a ballerina. Suddenly he was gone. 'Shit,' Harry said, searching the sky for sight of him. 'He got away.'

But then, out of the corner of his eye, he saw a Messerschmitt scorching through a bank of clouds towards Wright.

'Dive, Bob,' Harry cried, turning his own plane towards the German. He managed a few shots but the Messerschmitt veered off and disappeared from view.

'Keep your eyes peeled,' he ordered but even as he said it he realised the plane had returned and was swooping down on him.

'Jesus Christ,' he said, throwing his plane into evasive manoeuvres, 'doesn't he ever give up?'

'I'll get him, Harry,' came Frank's unmistakable drawl.

A line of bullets smashed into the rear of the Messerschmitt. It plunged towards the cliffs but, at the last moment, pulled up, turned and headed back towards France.

For a moment, Harry wondered whether to give chase. But no. He could inflict no more damage now and besides, the German was one hell of a brave pilot.

He turned back into the melee. The Hurricanes had worried at the bomber pack like hounds and the formation was splitting apart, the survivors releasing their bomb load in panic, already making the turn back towards France and safety.

The German fighters turned with their bombers, taking up a high position to try to guard them. Harry estimated there were still more than forty of them.

He felt sick. There were only twelve Spitfires and he feared that Nash would order them to the attack once again. They would stand no chance if he did.

'Well done, lads,' he called. 'We're to return to base but keep with the Hurricanes as they head towards London.'

Harry gave a whistle of relief and turned towards the north.

RAF MANSTON

14th August 1940

'I want you to go over to Manston,' Air Vice Marshal Park told Claire. 'It's taken a real battering and I'm hearing rumours that morale has been shaken. Badly shaken.' He drummed his fingers on the desk and gazed out of the window.

'I want you to check this out and report back. If it's as bad as I fear, we haven't got much time to solve it. So if you have any bright ideas while you're there then use them. Carte Blanche.'

Claire decided to drive herself. She had been given lessons by Jacqueline and felt confident enough to negotiate the almost empty London streets. It would take most of the morning to get there, which would be like a holiday from the constant pressure of Headquarters.

She drove through a golden morning mist which soon cleared to reveal clear blue skies and glorious sunshine. In former years she would have revelled in this. Now, such good weather foreboded danger. She glanced up at the sky. Thankfully it was empty of planes.

But that had changed by the time she reached the airfield. A flight of Spitfires soared low over the field, and glided in to land. She realised how incredibly difficult a task this was, for the airfield was littered with bomb damage. Buildings had been demolished, planes broken and destroyed, and there were craters everywhere, some big enough to swallow a plane. It barely looked like a functioning airfield.

She parked the car and watched the planes taxi to a halt, realising that she had never actually seen Spitfires in such close proximity. All these months they had been just names over the headphones, dispositions on a map board, a catch-all container containing victories, casualties and deaths.

Now she saw the reality, the glistening metal of the Spitfires, the bright blue, white and red colours of the roundels, the loud hum of the engines. And the young men clambering out of their cockpits, weary and still jittery after some dog-fight in the heavens.

The pilots headed towards a scatter of deck-chairs nearby, some of them casting appreciative glances at her. A few were more than just appreciative, and one man gave her a wolf-whistle which made her blush. No morale problems with these men, she thought.

But then her eye was caught by one of the planes. The pilot had not climbed down from it and a sergeant from the ground crew was squatting on the top, hammering at the canopy.

Intrigued, she went over for a closer look.

'Got a problem?' she asked the sergeant.

Jack White spared her a glance. 'Blooming canopy is jammed fast. We had trouble closing it earlier but our hero here insisted on taking off, regardless.'

He took a hammer and whacked it hard against the cowling.

Claire shuddered. Johnny had told her that a Spitfire cost more than she would earn in twenty years. And now, this man was hammering at it with considerable violence.

It did the trick, however, and the pilot was finally able to slide back the canopy. He hoisted himself out, grinned and slapped the mechanic on the arm. 'Thanks, mate.'

'I told you not to go up with the canopy jammed. You bloody fool.'

Claire was shocked to hear a member of ground crew talk to an officer like this.

'What if you'd been hit and caught fire?' the man continued.

'I didn't, Jack, so there's nothing to worry about. Besides, I know you'd get me out safe and sound.'

'If you landed, maybe.' He gave the pilot an almost angry look and both jumped off the plane.

'Hello,' the pilot said, blinking at Claire. 'I don't think I've seen you around before.' He held out a hand. 'Harry Smith.'

Claire raised an eyebrow. He obviously thought he was God's gift to women, although she failed to see why. With his pale, almost white skin, mass of freckles and light red hair, she thought him hardly the most attractive of men.

'Isn't it customary for pilot officers to salute their superiors?' she said.

'Whoops,' Jack said, swiftly saluting before leaning back to watch what would happen.

Harry gave a salute. 'Sorry ma'am.' He squinted at her arm band. 'So you're a —?'

'Flight Officer.' She could see him trying to remember the equivalent male rank but had no intention of enlightening him.

'Same as a Flight Lieutenant,' explained Jack. 'Above your rank, Harry.'

Harry gave a rueful grin. 'Does this mean I'm on a charge, Flight Officer?' He appeared not the slightest bit concerned.

'I've got more important things to do, Smith,' she said, coldly. 'As have you.'

He gave a lazy, rather sloppy salute. Then he strolled off to the deck chairs in front of the dispatch block.

'Are all pilots so full of themselves?' she asked Jack.

'Pretty much. Harry's not as bad as some.'

'Then heaven help us.'

She headed to the administration building.

The officers were startled to see her, even more when she explained that she was here to find out about morale.

Squadron Leader Nash gave her a sheepish look.

'The ground crew have been worst hit,' he said. 'They lost almost half their number in the raid two days ago. Now they're - how shall I put it - they're reluctant to face such risks again.'

'What on earth do you mean?' Claire demanded.

'They've gone on strike.'

'It's worse than that,' said another man. 'They've as good as deserted.'

'Keep your hair on, Buckingham,' Nash said.

Buckingham snorted with contempt. 'They've barricaded themselves in the underground shelters. Like rats refusing to come out.'

Claire turned to the Squadron Leader. 'Have you ordered them to?'

'Ordered them, pleaded with them, promised to listen to their grievances. The raid just knocked the stuffing out of them.'

Claire shook her head in astonishment. 'But what if we need to get the planes up?'

'The pilots from 600 squadron are helping out. We'd be sunk without them. Come and look.'

She followed Nash out of the building. Half a dozen pilots were working on the planes, checking ammunition and refuelling them.

'Are all the ground-crew refusing to work?'

'Not all.' Nash pointed out some men who were working on the planes. A few appeared to be telling the pilots from 600 squadron what to do.

She gave a sigh. Park had said that she should try to solve the problem but she didn't have the foggiest idea how to go about it. If the ground crew had been scared out of their wits, too terrified to do their duty, how on earth could she persuade them?

She had been at the airfield less than an hour when the sirens sounded. For a moment she didn't know what to do. Everyone was flying out of the room, heading for a shelter. She thrust her helmet on her head and fumbled for the strap. By the time she got outside there was no sign of anyone.

Where's the shelter? She searched hurriedly for a sign of it. The siren continued to wail, sounding more and more strident.

Where's the shelter? Her eyes located one at last and she raced towards it and pushed at the door. It was locked fast.

'Piss off,' yelled a voice from within.

She stumbled away and then suddenly she saw it, a mass of bombers on the edge of sight but moving fast towards the airfield.

Two squadrons were already streaming along the runway, the Hurricanes to the fore, the Spitfires close behind. Funny how graceful they looked, she thought. Like ballerinas gliding on to a stage.

Then she saw that there was one Spitfire still stationary on the ground. Harry Smith and his sergeant were on the top of the plane, both trying to manhandle the canopy shut. She began to run towards them, thinking she might help.

'Get to a shelter, miss,' Jack bellowed at her.

'Flight Officer,' she yelled back.

'I don't fucking care what rank you are - get to a shelter.'

The bombers were close to the airfield now, the British fighters plunging into them from below, an almost suicidal move.

Why the hell weren't they warned in time, Claire wondered.

'I'm going up,' Harry yelled, 'canopy or not.'

Jack stared at him in astonishment and then leaned into the cockpit and gave a powerful blow of his hammer.

'What do you think you're doing?' Harry cried.

'Saving your fucking life. You can't fly with a broken rudder so get out of the plane.'

He jumped off the wing and pelted towards a shelter, yelling to Harry to follow.

Harry raced after him. But then he saw Claire.

He ran back to her and grabbed her hand. 'Come on you idiot,' he cried.

They started to run, following Jack who was now already several hundred yards distant.

But they had not gone far when Harry slid on a wet bit of grass and fell. Exhaustion slowed him down as he struggled to his knees.

Claire stopped to help him up.

'Leave me, get to a shelter.'

'You cost too much to train for me to leave you to die.' She dragged him to his feet.

The bombs were falling on the runway now. One scored a direct hit on the damaged Spitfire, causing a blast of fire so fierce they were engulfed by its heat.

'No time to reach the shelter,' Harry gasped. 'A slit trench.'

He gestured to a line of sandbags and they raced towards it, throwing themselves into the trench. They were the only ones there. A slit trench might protect them from flying debris but a direct hit would be the death of them.

'Where's your helmet?' Claire demanded.

'Haven't got one.'

They heard a sudden whistle and looked skyward. A bomb was plunging towards them. They both ducked, even as they knew such a move was ridiculous.

The bomb hit a wooden building nearby, sending the framework flying high. The roof landed on top of the trench.

'That will really protect us,' Harry said, his voice thick with sarcasm.

The bombs continued to rain down, each explosion making them duck and cover their ears. Soil and gravel cascaded onto the roof, blotting out almost all remaining light.

'I'm going to die,' Harry said. 'Here on the bloody ground and not fighting in the air.' He gave a bitter laugh.

'I'm still a virgin,' Claire said.

He looked at her in amazement.

She grabbed him and kissed him violently.

'I don't want to die a ruddy virgin,' she said. She hoisted up her skirt and yanked down her knickers.

Harry shook his head in disbelief and then unbuttoned himself. He had just managed to pull his trousers to his knees when she pulled him onto her.

His lips found hers. She was panting hard. Her breath smelled sweet, he thought, like newly baked biscuits.

Then he entered her. She gasped, violently, partly from pleasure, mostly from shock.

The world seemed to fade from their consciousness as they moved, everything concentrated into the feelings of heat within them, the astonishment at their closeness and passion.

They cried out at the same time, shuddering with relief at the release. Harry ceased his thrusting, held her gently by the shoulders. She breathed into his face and sighed.

He slid off her and sat back on his haunches, watching her with disbelief.

She propped herself on to her elbows. 'Isn't this when we should share a cigarette?' she said. 'Like in the films?'

'I don't smoke,' he said.

'Me neither. My father said that smoking killed my uncles.'

Harry laughed, wildly. 'Bombs, bullets, a possible bloody invasion and you're worried about smoking.'

He kissed her on the lips. For a brief moment he thought he was in love with her.

She gave him a long, lovely smile. 'Thank you,' she murmured.

Then she began to pull up her knickers.

He risked a squint out of the trench. 'The bombers have gone,' he said. 'Let's try and get out.'

There was already the sound of men calling to them and a moment later a heavy piece of timber was dragged off the trench.

'You two alright down there,' a man called.

'Perfectly fine,' Claire answered. 'Safe, sound and shipshape.'

Harry held her hand to help her out of the trench. They stared at each other.

'Perhaps we can walk out together,' he said.

She smiled at his rather old-fashioned phrase. 'How very charming of you.'

She paused, her head to his side. 'Yes. Maybe. Although I'm stationed at Uxbridge.'

'I can fly there in minutes.'

'I doubt if that will be seen as a good use of a plane, Mr...?'

'Smith. Harry.'

'Not good use of a plane. Harry.'

He realised he was still holding her hand.

'I don't know your —'

'Claire Lamb,' she said.

He gave a wry grin. 'Flight Officer Lamb.'

'Yes. And don't you forget it.' She smiled. 'I won't tolerate insubordination.'

She let go of his hand and gazed around. The airfield had been a shambles when she had arrived. Now it was like a scene out of hell. The administration block she had just run from was in ruins, several hangers had been torn apart and there were bodies every-where. Screams of agony filled the air and the stench of burning flesh hit her.

One man, a ground crew corporal, careered about like a mad thing. His left arm had been severed and he clasped it to him as he ran. He didn't make a sound. And then he toppled over and was still.

Women were racing towards the injured: nurses, WAAFs, cooks, cleaners.

Claire did not have a plan, nor was she aware that she was making a conscious decision. But she marched over to the barricaded shelter and hammered on the door.

'Men are dying out here,' she yelled. 'Your colleagues, your friends. And if we don't get our planes back into the air it will happen again and again. The women here are doing all the work, all the filthy, bloody work. So get your rotten arses out here.'

There was silence. And then she heard the sound of timber being moved away. The door opened and a face peered out.

'Okay,' the man said. 'Okay. We know our duty.'

And the men who had barricaded themselves in safety for two days marched out to clear up the carnage.

Claire remained at the airfield for the rest of the afternoon. Everyone at the airfield gave their all. Pilots, ground crew, office staff all worked together and were soon joined by a crowd of civilians from the nearby town of Ramsgate. By mid-afternoon all the fires had been extinguished, the wrecked planes pushed to one side and the larger holes in the runways filled in with earth. It was still a shambles but it was just about operational.

Claire scanned the airfield. She wondered what she would report to Park. When she'd arrived, just five short hours before, the morale of many people had been dreadful, rock-bottom. For some it had developed into what some would term cowardice, desertion, perhaps even mutiny. But now everyone was working in unison.

The best thing, she concluded, was to tell the truth, not to try to hide the seriousness of the revolt but also to praise the way people had pulled together. The top brass might not like to hear the truth but, if the right lessons were to be learnt from what had happened, it was vital that they did so.

At 16.00 hours the remaining squadrons were scrambled. The exhausted pilots forced their legs to the planes, the ground crew fumbled to help them in. Harry Smith gave her a thumbs-up as his plane picked up speed along the runway. They had not exchanged as much as a word or glance since their time in the slit-trench.

As she climbed into the car to make her way back to London she wondered if she would ever see him again.

NEVER SO MOVED

15th August 1940

Claire arrived back at Uxbridge just after midnight. She was shaking with exhaustion from the long drive and from what she had witnessed at Manston. Throughout the journey the recollection of making love would stab into her mind, only for her to push it aside. She could not afford to think about this, not while she was driving.

She dragged herself into her room and just about managed to get ready for bed. She stood naked for a few minutes, her nightdress in hand. She could not believe what she had done. How foolish, how careless, how reckless. She rubbed her fingers along her tummy. What if I've fallen pregnant, she wondered.

She fell into a deep and untroubled sleep but woke just as dawn was breaking. The memory of what she had done immediately flooded over her.

She felt so ashamed. That was the sort of thing that only the most common girls got up to. Girls who were considered little better than prostitutes.

She hugged her blanket to her chest. What if she had fallen pregnant? What would she tell her parents? She imagined how they would take the news. The disbelief and hurt of her mother, the shamed look on her father's face.

Tears filled her eyes. How could she have been so stupid? And with a boy she didn't even know, one who she had only exchanged a couple of words with. And those not even friendly ones.

She sat up in bed and began to weep. Is this what his sort always did, she wondered. Had he considered her fair game, a lovely girl ripe for the plucking.

But then she blushed even more violently. 'I was the one who started it,' she gasped. 'I was the one who led him on.'

She bent her knees, grabbed them in her arms and rocked herself backwards and forwards. How could she have acted so madly?

She slipped out of bed and made for the washrooms. She wanted a bath and bugger the government stipulation that there should be no more than five inches of water. She felt guilty as she settled into the deepest bath she had enjoyed for a year. Perhaps, she thought, what she did yesterday would make her feel wicked for the rest of her life.

As she soaked, the thought of being pregnant consumed her. As well as having to tell her parents, she would have to leave the service. The only consolation was that she would not have to explain why. Unlike the other women's units in the Army and Navy, the WAAF allowed any woman to resign without needing to give a reason.

But she didn't want to leave. She loved what she was doing here and knew that she made a difference, however small.

And, she thought miserably, the idea of bringing up a child if Britain was conquered by the Nazis was just too horrifying to consider. Oh, why had she been such an idiot?

Suddenly, she had an idea and leapt out of the bath, towelling herself down as quickly as possible. She ran to the married quarters and hammered on the Longley's door. No one answered. A cleaning lady paused in mopping the corridor.

'Who you after love? Jacqueline left early to go off to London.' She leaned closer and lowered her voice. 'She told me it was something hush-hush.'

'It doesn't matter. Thank you.'

She went to the Bunker, her feet dragging with reluctance. But then she straightened her shoulders. She had a plan and she would see it through.

Thankfully the office was quiet.

She tapped Evelyn on the shoulder. 'Can I talk about something personal, really private? Something you won't breathe a word about?'

Evelyn looked astonished. Claire had never gone out of her way to be particularly friendly. She had been punctilious in her dealings with her but nothing more. If it weren't for the fact that she was British, Evelyn might have considered her downright frosty.

'Of course,' she said.

'Thank you.'

Claire seemed so grateful, Evelyn could not imagine what she needed to talk about.

They walked down a corridor and Claire ducked into a door. Evelyn followed and looked around in surprise. They were in the cleaners' room. Buckets, brooms and dusters were to be their only witnesses.

Claire blurted out the words all in a rush. 'I want to know when I might get pregnant.'

Evelyn nodded, surprised but sympathetic. 'I don't blame you. I guess you've had too much of all this terrible business. Becoming pregnant is a ticket to get out.'

Claire looked shocked. 'That's not it. Quite the opposit. I don't want to get pregnant. I'm doing something important here, I don't want to jeopardise it.'

She saw realisation creep across Evelyn's face. 'Oh, I get it.' She squeezed Claire's hand. 'You've had a little adventure and are worried about the consequences.'

Claire nodded. She dared not speak for fear of bursting into tears.

'When did you have your last period?'

Claire frowned. 'About a week ago.'

'About? You need to be a little more exact.'

Claire did a quick calculation. 'It ended on Sunday. Just before church parade.'

'And when did you have sex?'

Claire blushed so much she thought she would burn up. 'Yesterday.' Tears filled her eyes.

Evelyn patted her on the arm. 'These things aren't fool proof but that's about the best day to have sex if you don't want the stork to visit.'

Claire grabbed her hand. 'Really?'

'I'm not an expert, honey, but that's pretty much the case.' She frowned. 'If you don't mind me asking, why didn't you use a condom?'

Claire started to laugh, a tiny bit hysterically. 'There were no chemist shops nearby. I was in a shelter in the middle of an air-raid.'

Evelyn gave a whistle. 'So much for the stiff British upper lip.' She suddenly realised what she had said and just about stifled a giggle.

'Sorry, Claire. If it's any comfort I've heard that a brush with death sometimes makes people crave sex. Must be something to do with the survival of the species.'

'Do you think so?'

'I guess Darwin and Freud might say the same.'

Claire flung her arms around her. 'Thank you so much, Evelyn.'

'You can call me Evie,' she said.

Claire looked at her in surprise and then smiled.

'We'd best go,' Claire said. 'I'm late already.'

Evelyn refrained from commenting on what she had just said. She hoped she wouldn't be saying it in a month.

'Just remember to use a rubber next time,' she said.

Claire looked perplexed and then walked briskly back to the office.

'When did you get back from Manston?' Johnny asked as she sat down at her desk.

'At midnight.'

'No wonder you look so tired.'

He picked up a piece of paper and cursed. 'You'd think I'd have learnt to spell Messerschmitt correctly after all this time.' He picked up an eraser and rubbed furiously at his pencil-work.

'These rubbers are getting worse and worse,' he muttered, brushing away the black marks on its tip before flinging it irritably on the desk.

Claire picked it up. 'This is called a rubber isn't it?' she asked.

Johnny looked bemused. 'Of course it is. What do they call it in Norfolk?'

'The same.' She stared at the rubber. How on earth would using a rubber help prevent her getting pregnant?

'Jacqueline left early this morning,' Johnny said. 'Something very hush-hush.' He could not keep the pride from his voice.

'That's good,' Claire said, without interest.

Her mind kept returning to what had happened in the slit trench. Eventually a little smile played on her lips. The pilot had asked if they could walk out together. That, at least, was rather sweet. She picked up a paper and began to read through it.

'Get in here, Lamb,' Park called from his office.

She brushed her fingers down her uniform, checked herself in her compact mirror and went in.

She was surprised to see that Air Chief Marshal Dowding was also there. He gave her a swift nod and Park told her to take a seat.

'What did you find?' Park asked. 'At Manston?'

Claire took a deep breath. 'Well, sir, it was as we suspected. When I got there some of the ground crew had gone on strike.'

'As we suspected?' Dowding cried. 'We didn't think it was that bad. A strike. In the RAF. In wartime?'

Claire felt her heart begin to hammer. She'd been foolish in her choice of word.

'Carry on, Lamb,' Park said.

'In point of fact,' she continued, 'some of the men, not all, had barricaded themselves into a shelter and refused to come out. They'd been there a couple of days.'

Park and Dowding exchanged glances. The full extent of the problem had obviously been kept from them.

'And are they still there?' Dowding demanded.

'No sir. There was a very bad raid and they came out to help clear it up. They worked like dogs, sir.'

'They are like dogs,' Park said. 'But without the courage of dogs.' He took a deep breath. 'They'll have to be punished.'

Dowding pursed his lips. 'Maybe. Maybe not.'

Claire looked at him in surprise.

'Terrible experiences can unnerve some men,' Dowding said, his voice so low they could only just hear it. 'Just think about the last war with all that shell shock.

'Maybe that's what happened to those men. They couldn't take it any more - just temporarily.'

He took a deep breath. 'The last thing we want is some investigation, Keith. It will take a colossal amount of time and we've got precious little of that. As long as the chaps are back doing their duty I think we should quietly forget about it.'

Park looked dubious.

'What do you think, Flight Officer?' Dowding asked. 'You were there.'

Claire's lips trembled.

'Go on girl,' Park said. 'Answer the Air Chief Marshal.'

'I think Sir Hugh is right,' she said. 'After all, I'm sure that Goring wouldn't be so understanding.'

She blushed furiously, horrified at what she had said.

Park looked down at the desk. Dowding held her gaze.

And then he slapped his thigh and burst out laughing. 'Thank you, Flight Officer,' he said, wiping a tear from his eye. 'That's the drollest thing I've heard for months. And the kindest.'

'There's just one thing,' Park said. 'Why did the men go back to work after refusing to do so for days.'

'A sense of duty,' Claire said.

'Thank goodness,' he said. 'Right you are, Lamb, thank you very much. Now, back to work.'

Claire spent the next hour writing up the report of her visit to Manston. She took unusual pains over it, knowing that it might be vital evidence if there were any more examples of insurrection there or any other airfield.

This intense concentration was exactly what she needed. She almost forgot about what had happened between her and Harry Smith.

The telephone rang to say that a huge number of enemy craft had been sighted crossing the channel. She raced into Park's office to tell him.

The message from Fighter Command had led to a flurry of action at the plotting table.

Park was already barking orders to his senior controllers.

Three squadrons were scrambled and engaged the enemy. They were not enough. A formation of dive bombers damaged Hawkinge and Lympne airfields, putting them out of action.

Then came a concerted attack on radar stations at Rye, Dover and Foreness. Suddenly all direct communication from them ceased.

A few minutes later a telephone rang. 'The bastards have taken out the radar stations,' one of the controllers said. 'Buildings, power lines and towers all hopelessly damaged.'

Park looked horrified for a moment but mastered himself. 'We still have the Observer Corps. We're not blind.'

They watched with relief as the bombers turned back for home, still being harried by the British squadrons. But one lone swarm of BF110s managed to elude them on the way back and machine-gunned Manston airfield.

Claire's heart leaped into her throat. Would Harry be all right, she wondered. And what would this latest attack do to the fragile morale of the personnel there?

The last of the Germans disappeared over the Channel and the room went quiet. A few moments later the orderly hum returned as people went back to their regular tasks.

'Let's hope that's the last for the day,' Park said. 'Come on, Lamb let's get back.'

Johnny had already written up a report on the day's actions. He looked glum as he handed it to Park.

'Pretty ominous,' Park muttered as he read it. 'We've lost Hawkinge and Lympne completely. They'll be out of action for days.'

Claire licked her lips which had suddenly gone dry and cold. 'And Manston?'

'Thankfully it was only an attack by fighters. Machine guns and cannons but no bombs. Sixteen killed.

'A Squadron Leader Nash reported that morale there is much improved.' He glanced at her. 'You did well yesterday, it seems.'

'Me, sir?'

'Don't look so innocent. Nash told me the part you played.'

She blushed and looked down.

'Take an hour's break,' he said. 'You deserve it.'

———

Claire managed to catch a quick lunch with Betty and Flo but hurried back immediately to her desk. Being away in Manston meant she had a lot of work to catch up on.

She had only just sat down when Air Vice Marshal Park called for her to come to his office.

He was still on the telephone when she walked in. He looked troubled. Eventually he put the phone down and groaned.

'Are you all right, sir?' Claire asked anxiously. The last thing the country needed was for him to fall ill.

'What a day for the PM to decide to come for a visit,' he said.

Claire's face brightened. 'That's a relief. I thought you were feeling unwell.'

'I will be if Churchill wastes my time asking fool questions.'

He looked around. 'Tidy things up a bit, will you, Lamb. We want to look absolutely professional. I'm going for a wander round.'

She spent the next twenty minutes straightening up his desk. She wondered if he was normally a more organised man. Now, his desk was strewn with documents and memos, some of which should have been dealt with days before. There were two unfinished cups of tea and even a half-eaten sandwich. She realised that it was not only her own work which had suffered in her absence.

She had only just finished when the door opened and Air Vice Marshal Park gestured to the man beside him to enter.

Claire shot into the most rigid attention she had ever managed.

'Do take a seat, Prime Minister,' Park said, indicating a chair.

Churchill grunted, ignored where Park was pointing, marched around the desk and sat in his chair.

'You're a man of neat habits, Park,' he said, scrutinising the desk. 'I thought you'd have too much to do for you to worry about a tidy desk.'

Park's mouth opened, closed and opened again. 'I have a very good assistant, sir,' he said finally.

Churchill looked at Claire. 'And a very pretty one, if you don't mind me saying.'

She blushed with embarrassment but his eyes continued to gaze at her, regardless.

'Is it true that commanders choose the prettiest girls to run their ops rooms?' he asked. 'Someone told me it's called the beauty chorus.'

'I really wouldn't know, sir,' she said, in as neutral tone as possible

Churchill chuckled to himself and began to read the topmost of Park's papers.

Another man entered the room. Claire recognised him from the newsreels - Lord Beaverbrook, the Minister of Aircraft Production.

Johnny had nicknamed him pot stealer because he had appealed to the country to donate pots, pans and iron railings for the manufacture of new aeroplanes. Johnny was not the only one who knew that little of the metal was useful for that purpose, although everybody else kept quiet about it.

'Come in Max,' Churchill said to him.

Claire hurried to get Beaverbrook a chair.

Churchill pulled out a cigar and turned to Park. 'Now then, tell me how things stand.'

'You can leave us, Lamb,' Park said.

She could not get out quickly enough.

'It's the Prime Minister,' she whispered to Johnny.

He clicked his fingers, as if she has solved something which had been troubling him. 'I thought I recognised him from somewhere.'

'Very funny.'

She sat down with a sigh. She felt drained. The events of the day before, the long drive back, and now, seeing the Prime Minister, had all finally got the better of her.

She worked in a desultory fashion, keeping half an ear open to the murmur of conversation in Park's office.

A little while after, Evelyn appeared, unusually flustered. 'I think the Air Vice Marshal should come down. There's another big raid.' She hurried back to her post before they could answer.

Claire and Johnny stared at each other. 'Do you think we should?' Johnny asked. 'With Churchill talking with him?' For once his high-spirits had deserted him.

'We have to.' She knocked on Park's door and waited for the answer. It did not come. She knocked again a little louder and pressed her ear to the door. Still no answer.

She gave one last, very loud knock and opened the door.

The men inside looked surprised.

'Sorry to disturb you, sir, but there's a big raid.'

Park looked at Churchill who gave a fierce nod. 'Get to your duty,' he growled.

Park raced out of the room. Claire hesitated to follow him for a moment, wondering what to do about the Prime Minister.

'You girl,' he said. 'Take me to where I can see what's going on.'

'Right away, sir.'

She led him down the corridor, not moving at her usual brisk pace because of the Prime Minister's age.

'I thought it was an emergency,' he said.

'It is, sir.'

She increased her pace, even though she worried that he would not be able to keep up. But, despite his age and stoutness, he matched her stride for stride.

They arrived at the ops room at the same time as Air Chief Marshal Dowding and a General she had never seen before.

'You almost beat me, Ismay,' Churchill said, punching the General on the arm. 'Afternoon, Sir Hugh,' he said.

'Prime Minister,' Dowding said, gesturing Churchill to enter.

Claire slipped in behind them and made her way to Park. She glanced at the map below and gasped. A vast number of enemy aircraft were heading towards the English coast.

'With those radar stations down we're flying pretty blind,' Park told Dowding.

'The Observer Corps have increased the numbers of men on duty,' Dowding replied. 'Let's hope they can tell us what's happening.'

'I've sent up four squadrons to patrol,' Willoughby de Broke said. 'Extra eyes.'

'Good idea,' Park said. 'Scramble two more to be on the safe side.'

'Do you normally have squadrons on patrol like this?' Churchill asked. 'It seems to me it will waste fuel and fatigue the men.'

'We don't do it normally, Prime Minister,' Park said. 'But we lost some radar stations this morning. This is to try to make up for it.'

Not the type of foolish question the Air Vice Marshal had feared, Claire thought. Maybe he should worry that the PM would ask even more such acute ones.

'A message from Observer Corps,' one of the controllers said. 'Ninety Dorniers and a 130 strong fighter escort have crossed the coast between Dover and Folkestone.'

'Where are they headed?' Dowding murmured to himself. His eyes swept over the map.

'Tell the squadrons to attack,' Park ordered de Broke. 'And get 64 Squadron up from Kenley.'

'Seven squadrons?' Churchill said. 'You're pitting eighty planes against three hundred? Is that wise, Park?'

'He knows what he's doing, Prime Minister,' Dowding said.

Churchill was about to answer but General Ismay laid a hand on his shoulder to silence him. Churchill looked annoyed but grunted and returned his gaze to the map below.

'How do I know what's going on?' Churchill demanded.

Park touched Claire on the arm and gestured to her to stand next to Churchill. 'Tell him what's happening. Keep him out of my hair.'

She looked stricken but hastened to obey.

'Our fighters will head straight at the bombers, Prime Minister,' she said. 'That should scare them and force them to scatter.'

'And then what?'

'Then our boys will attack them.'

'Hunt them down?"

'Yes, sir.'

Churchill slapped his thigh with gusto.

Claire glanced at Park who gave her an encouraging smile.

'What about the German fighters?' Churchill asked. '130 of them. What will they do?'

'They'll attack our fighters. So our pilots will have to keep an eye out for them as well as targeting the Dorniers.'

Churchill looked astounded. 'Will they be able to do both?'

'Of course they will, sir.'

The German bombers now split into two distinct groups. One went north towards the Isle of Sheppey.

'They're headed for Eastchurch Airfield,' Park said. 'Alert coastal command that one of their fields is in their sights.'

'The other swarm appears to be heading for Rochester,' de Broke said.

'One of my factories is based there,' Beaverbrook cried. 'They're building the new Short Stirling bombers.'

'Three squadrons to protect it, Park?' Dowding suggested.

Park nodded.

De Broke gave the order. At the table below there was a flurry of activity from the plotters.

'Why are they pushing those tokens around?' Churchill demanded.

'To show the position of enemy groups and our squadrons, sir.'

'And that big board up there?'

That shows the status of all the squadrons in 11 Group. Twenty-three in total.'

Churchill exhaled. 'Plenty of them, then. So why doesn't Park use more of them?'

'He needs to conserve his forces, sir. The Jerries may launch another attack, and this raid could divert anywhere.'

She paused. 'As you said earlier, sir, we don't want to exhaust our boys or run out of fuel.'

Churchill's eyes locked on to her. 'Pretty and impudent.'

Claire looked horrified. 'Impudent —?'

'It's a compliment, girl. I like a bit of cheek.' He gave a chuckle and got out a match to light his cigar.

'I'm sorry, Prime Minister,' Claire said, wishing that some kind soul would come and knock her senseless. 'You're not allowed to smoke. The fumes would impair our vision.'

He looked outraged and about to argue.

'Do as the girl says, Winston,' General Ismay said.

Churchill grumbled and stared at Claire. 'What's your name, girl.'

'Flight Officer Lamb, sir.'

'Lamb! More like a lion.' He laughed aloud at his joke. Ismay joined in with a forced air. Claire wanted to die.

The battle unfolded beneath their eyes.

The two bomber groups, although continually harassed by the RAF squadrons, wreaked havoc on their target airfields. The aircraft factories were particularly hard hit.

'That will delay production of the Sterling,' Beaverbrook said. He remained silent for a long while, deep in thought. Then he appeared to brighten up. 'Might be good news for you though, Sir Hugh. If we can't build bombers, I'll switch production to more fighters.'

'Thank you, minister,' Dowding said. 'That seems a sensible response.'

At five o'clock the German attack switched to the west. Park breathed a sigh of relief but quickly hid it.

The status boards of 11 Group's squadrons changed to show that all squadrons had landed, although not all to their home airfields.

Cups of tea were brought into the operations room. 'Now what?' Churchill asked Claire. 'Is that the end of the day's fighting?'

'Not for 10 Group by the sound of it,' she said. 'They're fending off a large attack to the west. It seems rather dicey.'

At six o'clock there came more news of the fighting to the west. 'Middle Wallop airfield has been bombed,' one of the liaison officers called. 'One of the Spitfire squadrons just made it up. And Worthy Down and Andover have been hit but not too badly.'

'This is looking like the whole south of England,' Churchill said in dismay.

'Not entirely a bad thing, Winston,' Ismay said. 'Spreads the pain around instead of the Jerries constantly hitting our radar stations and Park's airfields.'

'He's correct, sir,' Dowding said. 'My biggest fear is that 11 Group will suffer too seriously.'

'So this is respite for them?'

Dowding nodded. 'It could be said so, sir.'

But the respite did not last long. Thirty minutes later, a swarm of Germans headed towards Kenley. But they must have made a navigational error for they bombed Croydon Aerodrome instead.

'It's not one of our proper airfields,' Claire explained to the Prime Minister. 'We've had to use it as an extra one after our other fields have been damaged.'

'Damn near London,' Churchill said angrily.

'Yes, sir.'

The tote boards were constantly flickering to show squadrons taking off, engaging in action, landing, refuelling and taking off for battle once again.

Finally, however, the Germans appeared to have had enough and began the flight back across the channel.

'Thank you for your assistance, little Lamb,' Churchill said, shaking her by the hand. 'She's a good girl, Sir Hugh. Brains as well as beauty.'

Dowding looked a little pained although Park could not prevent a smile.

'Come on girl,' Churchill said, 'walk me to my car. I may have more questions.'

But he made his way in complete silence.

As they approached the car, Ismay started to ask him a question but Churchill bellowed, 'Don't talk to me.' He pulled out a cigar. 'Never before have I been so moved.'

Claire saw that there were tears in his eyes. He brushed them away and looked up at the sky.

'I tell you, Ismay,' he said, quietly, 'never before in any conflict has so much been owed to so few.'

Then he climbed into the car and was gone.

TO RAF KENLEY

16th August 1940

'Could you give us a little tour on the way down?' Flo asked. 'My friend doesn't know London.'

'I'd be in the glass-house if I get caught,' the driver said. 'But seeing as it's you Flo, okay.'

Betty and Flo peered out of the window as the car sped through London. It was a bright and sunny morning with dark, almost black shadows thrown across the streets by the buildings.

Betty had never seen central London by car and she pressed her nose against the window in her excitement. 'What's that white arch all on its own?' she asked.

'Marble Arch,' Flo said. 'And that's Hyde Park to the right.'

Betty smiled to herself as she looked at the park. She had read a lot about romantic encounters there between wealthy lords and ladies of Regency times. Now rows of vegetables grew alongside the expanse of grass and they saw huge anti-aircraft guns pointing to the sky.

They drove on for a few minutes, turned right and hurried past a long, drab brick wall to their right. 'I expect the King and Queen are in there,' Flo said. 'And the young princesses.'

'Is Buckingham Palace over the wall?' Betty gasped.

'Yes. My dad says they hide it away because they've got lots to hide.'

Betty looked shocked at her words which pleased Flo greatly. The car swept around a large circle, with a dozen armed soldiers standing guard. Flo tapped Betty on the arm and pointed at the huge white building beyond the gates.

She just managed to catch a glimpse of Buckingham Palace and then it was gone. 'Ooh you rotter,' Betty said. 'That's not hiding it.'

How brave of the King and Queen to keep their daughters in London, she thought, when they could have sent them away somewhere safe in the country or to Canada or Australia. She doubted that Flo would be as impressed.

They turned left along a straight road with trees on either side. And then the trees were gone and they passed the huge and imposing bulk of Westminster Abbey to their right. Flo remembered going there once with her father who said he wanted to pay his respects to the body of Charles Dickens.

Her thoughts were interrupted by Betty grabbing her arm. 'Big Ben,' she cried in delight, pointing ahead. 'And that must be the Houses of Parliament. Oh Flo, do you think Mr Churchill is in there?'

'No, he'll be in Downing Street.' She looked at her watch. 'It's ten o clock. He's probably sozzled by now.'

Betty tutted disapproval at her words. She was incorrigible.

They crossed the Thames by Westminster Bridge and sped up even more now as they headed south.

Flo grew a little thoughtful. 'Do you know, I've never seen London look so quiet. It gives me the creeps a little.'

'It looks busy to me.'

Flo tapped her on the knee and whispered, 'Silly little country girl.'

She named each of the areas as they passed: Battersea, Clapham Common, Tooting Bec. None of them looked as lovely as their names.

After a further twenty minutes or so they entered a less congested area with fewer houses and more trees.

'Croydon,' Flo said. 'I'm going to live here when I'm married. Nice for the kids. Less soot and smoke. It's just like the countryside.'

Betty felt sorry for Flo if she thought that this was nice and healthy. It was nothing like the real countryside in Somerset where she had been brought up. She was used to brooks and meadows, sheep grazing in the fields, butterflies and bumble bees, and birds nesting in the trees. No, this was nothing at all like the countryside.

'Here you are, darlings,' the driver said after another half hour. 'RAF Kenley. But I'm not allowed to tell you the name in case Hitler's listening.' He chuckled at what he considered his wit.

There was a large perimeter fence surrounding the airfield, with concrete pill boxes at regular intervals along its length. Bored looking soldiers walked back and forth beside each pill box, marching if there was an officer nearby, strolling if not.

The driver halted at the main gate while their papers were examined. One of the men looked in at the girls at the back and gave a broad wink.

'Never seen ladies before?' Flo said, sharply.

'Not as lovely as you,' he answered. 'Are you Rita Hayworth by any chance?'

'Of course. And you must be Lon Chaney.'

'Very funny,' the man growled angrily, waving them through.

'That put him in his place,' she said with a smile.

The fighter planes were lined up in the distance, twenty Spitfires and twenty Hurricanes. Betty was surprised that such a huge place should contain so few planes and that so many people, officers, men and civilians, were considered necessary to maintain them.

It's a little like films, she thought. There were very few stars in each film but absolute hordes of people worked behind the scenes to make their appearances possible. Kenley was like a Hollywood Studio; huge and impressive but with only a handful of stars. The

Spitfires were like Errol Flynn or Clark Gable, she thought; sophisticated and smooth yet dangerous. The Hurricanes, were quieter and more steady, like Spencer Tracy or Leslie Howard.

They pulled up at the administrative hut.

'Watch out for Wing Commander Prickman,' the driver said. 'He's said to be a pleasant bloke but he can be as hard as nails if he has to be. One step out of line and he'll come down on you like a ton of bricks.'

'I doubt we'll see anyone as exalted,' Flo said.

'Don't be so sure. Kenley might look a big place but it's like a family. And Prickman is the daddy.'

Sugar daddy? Flo wondered. She nearly asked if the Wing Commander was married but thought better of it.

They were speedily processed in the main office and then told to report to Wing Officer Barlow. They knocked on the door, briefly looking over one another to make sure that they looked presentable after their long car ride.

'Come,' called a loud voice from within.

Wing Officer Barlow was in her late forties, small and a little stout with a long face and deep thoughtful eyes. She reminded Betty of the pony she used to give apples to on her way to school.

'So, you're the girls from Air Vice Marshal Park's outfit,' Barlow said. 'You're late.'

She told them to stand at ease while she read their files, all the while muttering under her breath.

'You both come with glowing references from Flight Officer Lamb,' she said at last, putting down the paper and gazing at them. 'In my experience that can mean one of two things. Either you're good and deserve your promotion. Or you're dreadful and your commanding officer is trying to get rid of you. Which are you?'

Flo and Betty glanced at each other, wondering which would be the most politic to answer.

'I don't think that Flight Officer Lamb wanted to get rid of us,' Betty said.

'Although I sometimes gave her a bit of cheek,' admitted Flo.

Barlow grunted and tapped on the paper. 'That's what it says here. At least you're honest. I like that in my girls.'

She gave Betty am inquisitive glance. 'You were in the Girl Guides, I see.'

'Yes, ma'am. I loved it.'

'Glad to hear it.'

She glanced at Flo. 'I don't suppose you were.'

'No ma'am. I was in a skittles team down the pub.'

The Wing Officer gave her a stony look. 'The first example of your cheek, I take it.'

'But it's true,' Flo said. She bit her lip. 'Sorry ma'am.'

'Don't be.' The Wing Officer laughed. 'We need an occasional bit of high spirits in these times. And with a thousand men on the airfield a girl needs to have a quick wit and tongue.' Then she leaned forward. 'But, Corporal Summers, just remember that I won't always take so kindly to your witticisms.'

'I don't know what they are, ma'am but I'll be sure not to give you any.'

'Ask Jones what a witticism is. She'll know. She didn't waste her younger days playing skittles.'

She stood up. 'Right, I'll take you to the plotting room. Bring your kit as we'll go by way of the dormitory.'

As corporals they were given a little anteroom off the main dormitory. There was no window and the walls were bare concrete. It contained two narrow, mean-looking beds, one small cupboard and a sink. But it felt like paradise compared to the large dormitories they had slept in before. They put their kit bags on the beds and hurried after the Wing Officer. She might be stout but she moved like a locomotive, fast and determined. Anyone she approached hastily got out of her way.

They went out into the sunshine and headed for a newly painted hut with hundreds of sandbags piled against it.

'Not as fancy as the plotting room at Uxbridge,' Barlow said with a smile. 'But it serves its purpose. They've finally found the money to start building a brick-built one but in the meantime, this has to serve. Come on, I'll show you where you'll be working.'

The plotting room was almost identical to the one they were used to at Group Headquarters although on a smaller scale. There was a sector clock exactly like at Uxbridge. But where Headquarters' imposing tote board displayed all the sector airfields in 11 Group, Kenley boasted only a small blackboard with details of the three squadrons based here. The map table was smaller than they were used to and consisted of only Kenley sector and those adjacent to it.

There were two controllers, and they sat, not in a mezzanine above the map table like at Uxbridge, but on a small raised dais to one side. One, a middle aged squadron leader, stared glumly at the empty table. The second was a younger man, who prowled the room like a watchful lion.

'Attention all,' Wing Officer Barlow called. Everyone stood to attention.

'These are Corporals Jones and Summers who are to work with you,' Barlow said. 'They come direct from Group Headquarters so you'd better be on your toes.'

Betty's heart sank at her words. She didn't want to be singled out in this manner. It might make the others decide to be difficult in order to test her. Flo, on the other hand, looked pleased as punch, preening herself visibly.

They were introduced to everyone in the room. The older Squadron Leader was very affable, taking a great interest in Flo especially.

Wing Officer Barlow gave him a shrewd look. 'How's Mrs Jerrold?' she asked him, pointedly. 'And the children?'

Jerrold blushed, gave a mumbled reply and hurried back to his chair.

Barlow shared a wry look with Betty and Flo.

The other man, Squadron Leader Norman, looked highly amused and resumed his prowling.

The atmosphere seemed very relaxed, almost informal. Some of the Wing Commanders that Betty had come across struggled to remember their subordinates' names. Wing Officer Barlow, on the other hand seemed to act almost like everyone's aunt.

'Right,' she said more briskly. 'Now I'll show you our systems.'

Most were similar to those they had been used to, although inevitably, there was less need to communicate with external units. Betty began to feel almost at home.

'Do you want a cup of char?' asked one of the young plotters.

But before they could accept the offer, the clamour of telephones interrupted them. Flo and Betty picked up unused headsets.

'A sixty-bomber swarm is coming in from Abbeville,' came the voice from the radar station, 'with forty fighters as escort.'

Flo was swiftest off the mark and hurriedly relayed the information to everyone. The WAAF privates, who had also heard the message, began to place the wooden plaques onto the board.

'A message from Headquarters,' Betty said. 'One squadron to scramble and head to Dover.'

'Scramble 154 Squadron,' said Squadron Leader Norman, '264 on standby.'

Jerrold glanced at some notes. 'Squadron 222 should be arriving shortly. I'll get them to refuel immediately, just in case we need them.'

The relaxed atmosphere of earlier had completely disappeared. The room was full of brisk seriousness.

Wing Officer Barlow took a seat beside a Wing Commander. She was the same seniority as him but, of course, could not take a controller's role. The RAF believed that only men who had been pilots had the knowledge and understanding to direct the battle.

Suddenly the room began to rock. A sound like the growling of a pride of giant lions filled the room and then ebbed.

'Squadron away,' Jerrold said.

Barlow turned to Flo and Betty and nodded her head. 'You're quick off the mark, ladies. Well done. I'm glad you've joined us.'

MISSING, BELIEVED DEAD

17th August 1940

Frank Trent groaned as the call to scramble sounded in the mess. He staggered up and hurried to the bathroom. His biggest fear was emptying his bowels in the cockpit.

Within minutes he was pulling his flying clothes on over his pyjamas. He gave a rueful smile. His aunt would have approved, it could be bitterly cold at thirty thousand feet.

'What bad bloody luck,' Harry said as they trotted down the corridor. 'Nash told me were going north for a week's respite. I'd hoped to see my family.'

'Little John and Friar Tuck?'

'Very funny.' A few days before, he would have found the joke amusing. Now he was too exhausted to respond.

They hurried towards their planes, passing by the Hurricane squadron just as Tomasz was climbing into his plane. 'You two are not as fast as your Spitfires,' he called.

'You're only jealous,' Harry said. 'They won't let you foreigners get your hands on a Spit.'

Tomasz glanced at Frank. 'So, is America still a British colony?' he said. 'Is Frank British after all?'

'No,' Frank laughed. 'But I can speak English.'

'Not as well as I can,' Tomasz said. 'And neither can Harry.'

The ground crew gave Tomasz the thumbs up and he closed his canopy.

The Hurricanes got airborne first, heading south to intercept the bombers. The Spitfires chased after them and then began to climb, racing to get higher than the German fighters.

'I wish Tommy was still with us,' Harry said over the radio.

'Me too,' Frank replied. 'He always had your back. Eyes everywhere.'

'Cut the chit-chat,' Nash said, 'and keep your ruddy eyes everywhere.'

They flew in silence for the next five minutes.

'Bandits a mile to starboard,' Harry said.

'Our visitors await,' Nash said. 'Follow me, gentlemen.'

He turned towards the Messerschmitts, the rest of the squadron peeling after him.

Frank rubbed his eyes and flipped up his goggles. He felt bone tired, could not recall a time he had ever felt as bad. He had lost count of how many sorties they had flown. Lost count weeks ago, in fact. Harry was right. They needed a rest, deserved a rest. A week of lounging around, drinking beer and sleeping late. Even the terrible British food would seem like paradise if it could be eaten without the threat of interruption.

What is up north, he wondered just as he closed with the enemy.

It was a bitter slog of a battle. The Messerschmitt pilots fought hard but Frank sensed that they were slower to respond than normal, had less verve and confidence. Perhaps they're as exhausted as we are, he thought. He banished the hope from his mind and fired a long burst into a plane but missed it by yards.

Suddenly, out of the corner of his eye, he saw Nash's plane had been hit. It began to spiral downward, plummeting horrifically fast. There was no sign of fire, thankfully. But then he realised that there was no sign of Nash either. He gulped. Perhaps he'd been killed.

He searched the skies for any planes but there were none nearby so he returned his gaze to Nash's plane. A thin white parachute line issued from the cockpit, a figure dangling beneath it. Then the canopy opened and Nash began the long descent to earth.

At that moment, a Messerschmitt sped towards the parachute and opened fire.

Frank threw his plane into a dive. He could not leave Nash prey to such an attack. He was on the German's tail in seconds, opening fire with stunning accuracy. Bullets riddled the cockpit and the nose of the plane abruptly pointed to the earth and fell. He guessed the pilot was dead.

He scanned the sky below for a sign of Nash. He caught a glimpse and then had to bank to avoid another attack. The last sight he had of Nash was of his body swaying helplessly beneath his chute.

Three planes did not return to base.

'Mick Radcliffe bought it,' one of the new pilots told Armstrong, the intelligence officer. 'There were flames everywhere. They got his fuel tank.'

Armstrong grunted and put the details in his log. 'Get yourself a cup of cocoa,' he said quietly. 'And a bite of breakfast.'

He glanced at Frank and Harry. 'Squadron Leader Nash?'

'His plane went down,' Frank said. 'He got out, his chute opened, but then the Krauts opened fire on him.' His voice was bitter.

'Bastards,' Armstrong said. 'Do you think they got him?'

Frank shrugged. 'I couldn't see for certain. But he didn't look to be moving. So yes, I think they did.'

'Missing presumed dead,' Armstrong muttered, writing this in the logbook. He looked up suddenly. 'Not sure you should tell the others just yet. I'll inform the Wing Commander.'

'Thank you, sir,' Harry said.

They stepped outside and drew breath. They walked towards the canteen in silence, too weary and upset at Nash's death to even speak.

———

Squadron Leader Maisfield dismissed the intelligence officer, picked up his cap and knocked on Wing Commander Wentworth's door.

'Sorry to disturb you, Miles,' he said. 'Thought you'd want to hear. Tony Nash bought it.'

Wentworth stared at him in silence and placed his pen on the blotter.

'We were at the Staff College together,' he said. 'I've known him for over ten years.' He exhaled loudly. 'I shall have to tell his wife.'

'It's not confirmed yet,' Maisfield said.

Wentworth looked a little hopeful.

'Apparently he bailed out and his chute opened,' Maisfield continued. 'But a Jerry opened fire and it appears that he was hit. No sign of life.'

Wentworth rubbed his eyes wearily. 'We'll have to appoint an acting Squadron Leader.'

Maisfield nodded. 'I'll do it straight away. Leave no time for uncertainty.'

'Who are the Flight Lieutenants?'

'Rupert Buckingham and Mick radcliffe. But one of the new boys thinks Radcliffe was killed. Apparently, his fuel tank caught fire.'

'A new boy saw it?'

'Not just him. One of the other chaps. More experienced, more reliable.'

'So that leaves Buckingham.'

Maisfield paused. 'Yes.'

Wentworth looked at him with surprise. 'Your usual certainty seems to have deserted you.'

Maisfield gestured to the seat opposite Wentworth. 'May I?'

Wentworth nodded.

'I'm not one hundred percent convinced about Buckingham's suitability. He's said to be reckless.'

'Can pilots be too reckless?'

'You know they can, Miles. It's bad enough with the new boys. We don't want a Squadron Leader to act the same way.'

Wentworth offered him a cigarette and lit one himself. 'Is that all?'

'Not entirely. I also hear that he's not well liked by the men. He reeks of ambition, which is probably why he's so gung-ho. And he can't seem to relate to the other chaps, nor hide his contempt for them.'

'A posh bloke?'

'Eton, Harrow or Winchester, I guess. Not like the rest of the squadron.'

Wentworth sucked in a lungful of smoke, held it and then exhaled.

'Well there's the rub, Stephen. Some of the top politicians are pretty peed off that most of our pilotss don't actually come from the better schools. Do we want be seen to be discriminating against one who's next in line for promotion?'

Maisfield frowned. 'You know as well as me that such things don't count a jot. Whoever's right for the job is the only consideration.'

'And you don't think Buckingham is?'

Maisfield spread his hands in a gesture of uncertainty.

'Well we've got to have an acting Squadron Leader.'

Maisfield sighed. 'We could get someone from another squadron but that won't do much for morale.'

'And we don't know for certain that Nash actually bought it.'

'No sir.' His expression suggested he believed otherwise.

'Then it seems we have little choice,' Wentworth said. 'Buckingham it is. But I'll make damned sure he knows he's only Acting Squadron Leader. Absolutely knows.'

'I'll send for him,' Maisfield said.

Buckingham left Wentworth's office twenty minutes later. His face was glowing and bore the unmistakable trace of triumph.

'Come in here, Stephen,' Wentworth called.

Maisfield shut the door behind him.

Wentworth was standing at the window, watching Buckingham strutting towards the mess.

'I didn't warm to him, Stephen,' he said. 'There's something - well just something about him.'

He lit a cigarette and then remembered to offer Maisfield one. 'But just as we're having to accept half-trained novices going straight into combat, I'm afraid we have to promote men who don't quite cut it.'

Maisfield grunted. 'I'll tell the men.'

Wentworth stopped him as he got to the door. 'I don't suppose there's any sign of Nash?'

'Sorry Miles. Not a dickey bird.'

━━━

Evelyn Nash marched up to Dowding's office and demanded to see him. His assistant refused at first but she complained so loudly that in the end he went and spoke to him. To his astonishment Dowding agreed to see her.

'My husband was killed by Germans as he parachuted to the ground,' Evelyn said as she strode into his office. She refused his invitation to take a seat. 'Murdered in cold blood.'

Dowding gave a little cough. 'Not murdered, Mrs Nash. It was an act of war.'

'But he was defenceless.'

'True. But our pilots who bail out usually survive and return to battle. It is, therefore, consistent with the Warsaw Convention, that they be classed as combatants. And as such, the Luftwaffe are perfectly within their rights to shoot them. War, Mrs Nash. Not murder.'

For a moment she was speechless.

'Yet you have said, Sir Hugh, or to be exact, you have ordered that RAF pilots are forbidden to shoot any Germans who've bailed out.'

'Quite right.' Dowding cleared his throat. 'You see the Germans stand no chance of returning to their units, no chance of continuing to fight. They are, technically prisoners of war.'

'Even when they're five thousand goddamn feet in the air.'

'Even then.'

She climbed to her feet. 'People have nicknamed you Stuffy,' she said. 'But that's not the right name. Heartless, cruel, unfeeling. That's what you are, Air Chief Marshal.'

He did not reply, although a pained look came over his face.

She strode towards the door and then turned. 'Your boy, your only son, is a fighter pilot. How would you feel if he was shot while hanging from a parachute?'

'Exactly as you do, Mrs Nash. Angry, bitter, inconsolable. And I would most certainly feel anger at the man at the top who told me that this is acceptable according to the rules of war.'

'You'd feel angry at yourself?' She shook her head. 'You're a strange man, Sir Hugh.'

She slammed the door behind her.

Dowding sighed. Then he returned to his work. He would have to find more planes and pilots.

He glanced at the clock. The production of planes was quickening all the time. But somehow he had to find more men and get them combat-ready more quickly. He picked up the telephone and asked for his Senior Air Staff Officer to come to see him.

Two minutes later, Air Vice Marshal Evill hurried into the office. 'Problem, sir?' he asked.

Dowding sighed. 'How can we get more men into active duty?'

Evill sat down wearily. 'We're squeezing the training programme as much as we can. The boys who are being sent into combat are green as grass.' He paused. 'Of course, there's always the foreign pilots.'

'I thought we were using all the commonwealth squadrons.'

'I mean the Poles and the Czechs.'

Dowding pursed his lips. 'I'm still worried about their poor English. It could be a disaster.'

'Then put their own men in as officers. They can happily chat in their own lingo. As long as they kill Jerry.'

Dowding seemed intrigued by Evill's suggestion. 'It's a possibility. But the Air Ministry is adamant that they remain Pilot Officer rank.'

'And I suppose that the only way that can change is if they see combat. But we're not allowing them to take part in combat. It leaves them in a cleft stick.'

Dowding did not respond. 'Which of them has the best English?' he said finally.

'The Czechs.'

'And the Poles?'

Evill shook his head. 'Not quite there yet, I'm afraid. They prefer to spend their time in Hurricanes and chatting in Polish about the best way to destroy Messerschmitts.'

'They'll have their chance. But only when they're ready.'

Dowding got to his feet and picked up his cap. 'In the meanwhile, make the Czech squadrons operational.'

'Very good, sir. Where will they be posted?'

A flicker of a smile crossed Dowding's face. 'Number 12 Group. We'll see what Leigh-Mallory makes of them.'

THE HARDEST DAY

18th August 1940

At 12.45, Claire hurried to Air Vice Marshal Park's office. 'I think you'd better come to the Ops Room, sir. There are 250 planes over the south coast. 100 bombers and the rest fighters.'

Park leapt from his seat and raced out of his office.

The map was crammed with plots. 'Good God,' Park whispered. He turned to his senior controller. 'Is this accurate?'

Wing Commander de Broke did not take his eyes from the map. 'Absolutely, sir. Radar and Observer Corps both say the same.'

'Anyone patrolling?'

'501 Squadron but they're returning to base.'

'Keep them up. And scramble another four.'

All eyes were on the plots as they crept onward towards London.

At 13.00 hours de Broke shook his head. 'The squadrons have made no contact over Kent.'

'They're too far to the north,' Park said.

'I'll order them south.'

Suddenly there was a flurry of activity below.

Claire picked up a receiver. 'There's contact now, sir. 501 squadron were attacked by Messerschmitts near Maidstone. Five Hurricanes have been destroyed.'

Park and de Broke looked at each other in shock. 'A surprise attack?'

'From above,' Claire said.

'Shall we put up more squadrons?' de Broke asked Park.

'Not until we know where they're headed.'

'It looks like London to me.'

Park shook his head. 'Intelligence is adamant that Hitler has forbidden any attacks on London. No, they're going for our airfields.'

He pushed his cap high on his forehead. 'Put up two squadrons from Kenley. And another two squadrons from Biggin Hill. And get on to 12 Group. Tell them we're facing a big attack and most of our squadrons will be on the hunt. Ask them to send planes to protect my airfields.'

One of the controllers made the call. Everyone's eyes were on the area north of Dover.

'They must be aiming for Rochester,' de Broke said.

Park nodded but he looked uncertain.

Suddenly, out of the corner of her eye, Claire saw a new plot on the map. A solitary marker. She picked up a pair of opera glasses to see the plot better.

She spoke to the plotter, demanding why the German planes hadn't been spotted earlier.

'They came in too low for our radar to pick up, ma'am.'

Claire had a sudden, sick feeling in her stomach.

'Nine Dorniers at Beachy Head,' she called. 'Heading west towards Lewes. I don't like the look of this.'

Park glanced at her in surprise but instantly returned his focus to the far larger threat to the east. Where could the 250 planes be headed?

Claire, however, continued to monitor the progress of the Dorniers. Her eyes widened with alarm. She realised where they were heading.

Betty listened to the report from the Observer Corps and moved the plot of the Dorniers over Brighton. She expected they would follow the coast west towards Portsmouth. Her brow wrinkled. The observers were now telling her that the bandits were moving north. She nudged the plot a little.

Suddenly, Flo stepped closer. 'The railway goes from London to Brighton. I bet the bastards are going to follow that.'

She watched for a few seconds as Betty moved the plot ever further north. Then she ran over to the duty officer, Squadron Leader Norman.

'I think the Dorniers are headed this way. Directly to us.'

He leapt to his feet. 'Any orders from Group?'

'Not since the order to scramble two squadrons.'

'And where are they now?'

'Doing a sweep,' Betty said. 'At twenty thousand feet.'

'And the Dorniers are how high?'

'Three thousand feet.'

Norman turned white. 'Give the air raid warning.'

Flo glanced at the clock. The hand seemed to have slowed almost to a halt.

'Any orders from Group?' Norman repeated.

'Still none,' Flo said.

'Bloody hell.' He bit his lips and reached for the phone. There was no reply. 'Christ, the Station Commander's phone is engaged.'

He bit his lip and then jabbed on the phone again. 'Croydon, this is Kenley. I need you to send a squadron here to protect my airfield. All our planes are up.'

Flo watched as he listened to the reply. He looked aghast.

'I can't wait for Group to give you an order,' he yelled. 'I need you to send a squadron immediately. This instant. Now.'

He listened in silence for a few moments longer and then gave a huge sigh.

'They're sending one squadron. Thank the lord. And their controller has told them to fly at 100 feet.'

He gestured to Flo. 'Take a look outside, Flo. Tell me what you see.'

Flo hurried out of the ops room. Sirens were blaring and men were winching up the anti-aircraft guns. Others, at the gun emplacements, hoisted their machine guns as high as they could go, knowing their only hope was to aim at the bombers as they passed overhead. Scores of men and women were hurrying towards the shelters.

Flo scanned the sky, south, east and north. She cried out with joy as she saw Croydon's Hurricanes racing over the airfield, so low they only just made it over the trees and power lines.

Then she heard the thrum of the Dorniers. There were nine and they seemed to be aiming straight for her. They moved apart, possibly having sighted the Hurricanes, and came in lower still. The Hurricanes swerved behind them and gave chase, guns blazing.

The bombers were over the airfield. Suddenly the air was filled with bombs, two hundred of them; they fell with deadly accuracy. The hospital, hangers, mess rooms and fuel dump were hit and a huge pall of smoke shot skyward. One of the Dorniers crashed as did one of the Hurricanes.

The anti-aircraft guns thundered but to no avail. The Dorniers were passing the airfield now. Without orders, Kenley's 615 Squadron had returned to protect their home airfield and they now joined the planes from Croydon in chasing after the enemy.

Too late, Flo thought. The airfield was ruined, utterly devastated in just over a minute.

She dashed back into the ops room. It was dark. All the power had been cut. No telephones sounded, nobody called out. The plotters were clutching their helmets and gasmasks, too shocked to even move.

Then Squadron Leader Norman bellowed: 'Don't just stand there - take cover! There's nothing you can do now!'

They ran towards the door, swallowing their fear so they could make an orderly exit.

Flo grabbed hold of Betty and they staggered out, almost retching at the smoke engulfing the airfield. There were dead and injured everywhere. One WAAF was desperately trying to staunch the blood gushing from her thigh. Betty ran to her, pulled a bandage from her gas-mask case and wound it round her leg in an impromptu tourniquet.

The only sounds were the crackle and spit of the flames, and the noise of collapsing buildings - timbers wrenching, muted explosions, breaking glass.

Flo saw Squadron Leader Norman at the door to the ops room. 'What shall we do now, sir?' she asked.

'Get to a shelter.'

She turned to do so but then paused. 'You did well, sir.'

He pointed out the ruined airfield. 'If this is doing well than I dread to think what doing badly means.'

'You got the squadron from Croydon here in time.'

He shrugged and then gave a grin. 'I'll probably end up with a court martial for ordering the scramble without authority.'

'My officer, my former officer, said that it's a station controller's prerogative to do that.'

'Well that's fine and dandy, then. Except for these poor buggers who have copped it.'

She touched him on the arm. 'Don't blame yourself, Anthony.'

'Get to a shelter,' he said. 'You never know when the Jerries will return.'

※

Frank Trent almost fell out of the basket-chair. Harry was shaking him violently.

'Wake up, Frank. Didn't you hear the order to scramble?'

'Obviously not.' Frank grabbed his flying kit and raced after Harry.

He wondered how long he'd been asleep. One minute he'd been thinking about his cousin Paul's new Buick, the next he had Harry yelling in his ear.

He strapped himself in and gave the thumbs up to the ground crew to remove the chocks. He picked up speed and took off.

'We're being vectored to cover Biggin Hill,' Buckingham said over the wireless. He sounded excited although maybe a trifle anxious. No wonder really, Frank thought, it's his first sortie as Squadron Leader. Everyone would be watching to see how he performed.

He turned and followed Buckingham to the west. There was little cloud cover which meant nowhere to hide, for them or the Germans.

He searched the sky to catch a glimpse of Harry. He spotted him after a moment, with young Wright close behind like a duckling keeping close to its mother. He took a deep breath, relishing these moments of quiet before all hell broke lose. Maybe the last moments he'd ever know.

'Holy shit,' he exclaimed as they got close to Biggin Hill. German planes circled above the airfield, a swarm of flies over rotting meat.

'Tally ho, boys,' Buckingham said. 'Let's show them our mettle.'

They dived towards the fighter escort which was bunched up more closely than usual. An inexperienced commander, Frank thought with relief.

He touched his ear-phones, for a moment expecting to hear Nash's calm voice alerting them to threats from behind and possible targets in front. But Nash was dead and now there was no sound. He realised that Buckingham was just as much a rookie leader as the German.

'On your tail, Red One,' Harry yelled in his ear.

Frank looked in his mirror and saw a Messerschmitt diving towards him. He flipped his plane and just evaded its guns. A quick glance saw that Harry and Wright were hot on the German's tail. Harry opened fire and the Messerschmitt spiralled out of control.

He returned his gaze to the front, seeking out a target of his own. A Messerschmitt 110 veered into sight, guns blazing. Easy prey, he thought, locking on to it.

But the pilot was good and handled the slower plane with astonishing skill, ducking and diving to get away. Frank wondered whether it was worth chasing him with so many 109s to tackle. But he was committed now and continued to chase.

He got it into his sights at last and gave it a three second burst. The plane wobbled slightly, managed to straighten and then turned back to the south. He must have caused too much damage for the pilot to continue the fight. He watched it for a second as the pilot nursed the plane towards the coast. Frank hoped he would make it back.

Most of the fighters were out of sight now, so he headed for the nearest group of Heinkels which, so far, had been unmolested. They saw him coming and split apart like sparks from a powerful firework. He took a moment to locate the best prey and hurtled after two planes which remained close together. As he closed, they saw him at last and began to separate.

He slowed a second, allowing the planes to turn to left and right. He let fly at the plane which had moved more speedily then nudged his plane a little and blazed away at the slower. The first plane got away but he managed to hit the cockpit of the second one and the plane plummeted to earth. As always, Frank prayed that it would not hit any buildings.

'I'll log that one for you, Frank,' Buckingham said in his earphones.

Frank could hardly recognise his voice. It was thick, low and breathy, as if he were about to make love to a woman.

'Thanks, Squadron Leader,' he replied. He guessed that Buckingham would relish being called this in combat.

A moment later a dozen Messerschmitt 109s hurtled out of the sun.

'Bandits, bandits,' Wright called, swooping away from them. It was the last thing he said. A storm of bullets raked his fuselage and his plane exploded.

A pang of sorrow swept over Frank but he had no time to indulge it. Two fighters were on his tail and he spent the next few minutes trying to escape. Minutes that seemed like hours.

Suddenly he felt his plane lurch. He'd been hit.

Frantically his eyes swept the cockpit for any sign of flames. There were none, thank the lord.

He checked the fuel gauge. It was steady. But his plane was careering strangely, almost as if it were drunk. He looked to his left. A piece of the wing had been shot away.

His mind raced. He would not be able to fight any longer.

The air around him was a nightmare. The 109s were taking a grim harvest of the squadron. Two more planes were hit as well as Wright's, although he could not see who. Thankfully, both men bailed out.

The sensible thing would be for him to also bail out. But something made him decide against this. What was it, he wondered. Not the cost of the plane because he didn't give a hoot for that. Not the desire to prove to the British that a Yank was as good a pilot as any of them.

No, he realised, it was because he felt that landing the plane would be a challenge, it would test his skills and knowledge of flying like nothing else. Madness, of course, but he could do nothing to prevent himself from attempting it.

He glanced down at Biggin Hill. There was no hope of getting down there in this maelstrom. The nearest airfield was Croydon but that was already being targeted by Germans. He did a quick calculation. Hornchurch was only twenty-five miles north, and if he took a slightly easterly track he would avoid the suburbs of southern London.

'Returning to Hornchurch, Harry,' he said. He felt a little guilty that he hadn't told Buckingham first. But he had no time for that as his plane was getting ever more sluggish.

His inclination was to get the hell out of there as fast as possible but he made a very slow and gradual turn, anxious not to stress the wing too much. It took all his nerves to do it. Then, suddenly he was clear of the battle.

Normally he'd be able to get to Hornchurch in five minutes. But he dared not push as fast as that. He nudged the speed down. The plane wobbled even more dramatically and heart in mouth, he struggled to regain control. He levelled out, fighting to keep level. He suddenly remembered when he had taken place in an arm-wrestling contest. He had come second to last in that. He cursed and fought with the control stick.

The flight seemed to last for hours although he knew it was only ten minutes at most. He aimed at the runway furthest from any buildings and gradually lowered the plane. It was only when he had almost touched down that he realised he was holding his breath. He inhaled just as the plane landed, lurching round as it did so.

He whooped with joy and turned the plane towards the hangers. It would be out of action for a while but he had made sure it would fight another day. And so would he, thank God.

It was not the same for the rest of the squadron. They were sent to Hornchurch at the end of their action and he watched them come in. He sighed. Twelve pilots went out but only seven followed him back. He'd seen Wright and two others hit but one of the others must have been as well.

'Dennis Taylor,' Harry told him as they went in to the administrative building to give their reports. 'Killed on his second day of action.'

'And Bob Wright,' Frank said glumly.

'He didn't have a chance. He was as good as ambushed.'

They paused a moment as they passed Buckingham. He looked shell-shocked.

'It wasn't your fault, old boy,' one of the older hands said to console him.

Buckingham held his hand up to silence him.

Harry watched him thoughtfully. For the first time he did not feel his usual loathing. Poor sod, he thought. Then he clapped Frank on the shoulder. 'Come on, let's go down to the Good Intent and get legless.'

It was the end of an exhausting day. Kenley had been battered to its knees but was being rapidly repaired. Biggin Hill had escaped lightly in comparison. Now, with the evening coming on, the worst of it was over.

At Headquarters, Claire slumped into a seat. 'I can't believe they have so many planes.'

Johnny Longley shook his head in disbelief. 'Perhaps we've been fooling ourselves. Maybe they have bigger reserves than we know. And, of course, they've been able to capture all those French planes.' He swore under his breath. 'Perhaps they even got hold of some of our planes. Heaven help us if they fly our own Spits against us.'

'Stop your chattering and get over here,' Park snapped.

'Are you okay, sir?' Claire asked. She had never seen him look like this. There was fatigue, of course, and worry. But the overriding emotion he was displaying was of a barely concealed anger.

'Did any planes from 12 Group get here in time to protect my airfields?' he demanded.

Longley stood to attention. 'I'm afraid not, sir. Not in time. Some of their squadrons arrived when the bombers were on their way back.'

'What the hell is Leigh-Mallory playing at?' Park cried. 'He'll lose us the battle at this rate. No, it's worse than that. He'll lose us the ruddy war.' He thumped his fist on the table.

He took a deep breath and finally mastered his rage. 'I want a conference tomorrow. All my senior controllers. And invite Sir Hugh Dowding to come. And Air Vice Marshal Leigh-Mallory. If he's not too busy.'

He pulled on his white flying suit. 'Now I'm going to visit my airfields to see the damage for myself.'

They watched him leave in silence. Then Claire heaved a great sigh. 'I wouldn't want to be Leigh-Mallory tomorrow.'

Johnny shrugged. 'I don't suppose he'll worry. He's got seniority over Park and has the ear of some of the top brass. The very highest brass.'

'But Sir Hugh supports Park, surely?'

'True. But who is there to support Sir Hugh?'

―――

Wentworth looked at the statistics for the day. The Luftwaffe had flown 800 sorties in daylight hours and 170 at night. They had lost seventy planes with more than ninety fatalities. Forty pilots had survived the battle and been taken captive. Wentworth wondered how much of the vast Luftwaffe fleet had been put out of action. Not enough, he guessed.

He turned to the report concerning the RAF. They had flown as many sorties as the Germans but had suffered fewer casualties. More than thirty planes had been destroyed in the air and eight fighters on the ground. Ten pilots had lost their lives and another nineteen were wounded, half of them extremely seriously. The toll was not as bad as the Germans had suffered but, nevertheless, it had been terrible, truly terrible.

Wentworth shook his head at the scale of the losses. It was the worst day of the battle so far. He wondered how much longer Fighter Command could continue, how much more the pilots could take. They had all the bravado and commitment of young men but they were being felled at an alarming rate. Just like their fathers in the Great War he thought bitterly. But the RAF's numbers were too few to fight much longer.

He felt sick at the thought and tried to banish it from his mind.

Squadron Leader Maisfield approached and gave him a weary salute.

'Have you seen the figures?' Wentworth asked.

'Yes, sir. Nash's squadron were the worst hit.' He paused. 'I mean Buckingham's squadron.'

'Do you think Buckingham's to blame?'

Maisfield considered this a moment. 'I don't think so, sir.'

'But he has a reputation for being reckless.'

'True. But his was not the only squadron bounced by the Hun. There were just too many of the buggers. Perhaps Park was at fault for sending the squadrons up piecemeal.'

Wentworth gave him a look of surprise. 'I didn't put you down as a Big Wing advocate.'

'I'm not. But things are looking bloody desperate. Perhaps we need to rethink our strategy.'

Wentworth lit a cigarette. He had almost finished his second packet of the day and it was not yet noon.

'What about replacements for the squadron?' he asked.

'Only green boys, I'm afraid. Barely out of training.'

Wentworth shook his head. 'I can't have that for a front-line squadron.'

'Is there any choice?'

Wentworth stared at the line of Spitfires and Hurricanes and then it came to him. 'We need to stiffen Buckingham's squadron with more experienced men. What about that Polish chap, Tommy what's his name? He's friends with several of the squadron, isn't he? He flew with them for a while in France.'

'Tomasz Kaczmarczyk?'

'That's the chap. We could move him into Buckingham's squadron.'

'He's only flown Hurricanes.'

'Over here, maybe. But I don't doubt he flew other planes in Poland and when he was in the French Airforce. Sound him out, Stephen. See if he fancies a transfer. If he does, I'll square it with the Head of the Station.'

THE RETURN

20th August 1940

The damage to Kenley had been extensive, including to the accommodation. Along with the other girls, Flo and Betty had spent the nights since the attack in tents. After three days, they were told they were going to be moved elsewhere.

They had no idea why or where they were going. They had been given half an hour's notice to get their kit together and say their goodbyes.

'I don't know why we're moving so soon,' Flo said.

'I don't mind,' Betty said. 'This place is frightful.'

A lorry pulled up in front of them and a driver hopped out and gave them a smile.

'Oh no,' Flo said, 'they're surely not expecting us to go in that thing?'

'Well you're the loveliest cargo I've ever carried,' the driver said. He pulled down the tailgate at the back of the lorry and helped them climb in.

There were two bench seats on either side with four men on each.

'Watch your language lads,' a corporal said. 'There's ladies present.'

The men budged up to allow the girls to sit on one of the benches. The men opposite cast surreptitious glances at them. Flo tutted loudly.

'Any idea where we're going?' Betty asked.

'Berlin, I reckon,' said a man who obviously considered himself a comedian.

'We don't know, miss,' said the corporal. 'They never tell the likes of us.'

'My name's Flo,' she said quietly, not wanting her name to be broadcast to all the men. 'And my friend's called Betty.'

One of the men took a sheet of paper and pencil out of his pocket. 'We've got a sweep-stake on where we're going, ladies,' he said. 'Care for a little wager? The favourites are Filton and Pembury but that's only because the lads want an easier time of it.'

'I don't bet,' Flo said. 'It's a mug's game.'

The men fell silent. They sensed that she was not a woman to tussle with.

'What about you, darling?' the man asked Betty.

She shook her head.

The journey took almost two hours and they were glad when the lorry finally drew to a halt. They waited for a few minutes for the paperwork to be checked and then drove on for another five minutes or so before coming to a halt. 'Everyone out,' the driver yelled, pulling back the tarpaulin.

The corporal jumped out first and helped Flo and Betty to the ground.

He glanced around. 'Hornchurch,' he said. 'That's bad luck. We'll be in the thick of it here.'

The airfield was lined with beds of flowers and shrubs which were in marked contrast to the armoured vehicles parked on every side. Every building on the airfield was camouflaged, as if ready for an assault on the enemy.

Flo and Betty were surprised to see that the runways were grass and not concrete. In fact, the whole airfield was a sea of green. If it wasn't for the rank after rank of huts and hangers, the armoured vehicles, the piles of sandbags placed at strategic points and the hordes of men in uniform it really would look a little like the countryside.

The men were marched away to the hangers while the two girls waited in the office. A few minutes later a rather stern looking Warrant Officer appeared and took them to the plotting room.

'You come with good recommendations from your superior officer,' she conceded.

'Thank you,' Flo said. 'But we've only just gone to Kenley. Why did they send us here so soon?'

The Warrant Officer shrugged. 'The powers that be must have their reasons.' She said it in a tone that intimated it was not for the likes of them to question such matters.

They walked across the airfield towards their quarters. They were surprised to see a pub on the edge of the airfield. 'I could fancy a drink,' Flo said. 'After all that journey.'

Betty sighed, wondering what her parents would think of her so much as considering going to a pub. But she guessed that Flo would have her visit there sooner or later.

Despite the losses of the day before, the Good Intent was busy as ever. Several of the drinkers had struggled here with various injuries, twisted ankles, bullet wounds or minor burns.

'Hello Tommy,' Harry said, as the Pole entered the bar. He held his empty glass. 'As you're going to the bar, I'll have a pint of mild.'

'Why do you persist in drinking this, Harry?' Tomasz said. 'I've been told that it's just the dregs of other beers.'

'That's a load of bull. You should try it. We drink it all the time in Nottingham.'

Frank made a face to warn him not to.

'I'll have what Frank is drinking,' Tomasz said.

They took their drinks outside to catch the early evening sunshine.

'I have news,' Tomasz said.

'Hitler's surrendered?' Harry joked. 'Well, thank the lord for that.'

'Almost as good. I'm joining your squadron.'

Harry clinked glasses with him. 'Excellent.' His face became thoughtful. 'What's the reason for it?'

Tomasz took a swig of beer before answering. 'Wing Commander Wentworth said you took heavier losses than other squadrons. He didn't want all of the replacements to be new boys.'

'At last a bit of sense from the big brass,' Harry said. 'Wonders never cease.'

'Have you had much time on Spitfires?' Frank asked.

'Not a minute.' Tomasz chuckled. 'How hard can it be to fly them?'

Frank laughed. 'Bloody hard for lots of guys. But I'm sure you'll soon fly them like an old hand.'

'Please, Frank.' Tomasz said, pulling a serious face, 'like a maestro.'

He laughed and swallowed the rest of the beer. 'Now I think you should buy me a drink to welcome me.'

'I'll buy one for you,' Harry said, 'but not for him.' His eyes went to the man making his way towards them.

'Hello, sir,' Frank said.

'Cut out the sir,' Buckingham replied. His usual bonhomie had evaporated. Now he appeared morose and uncertain.

'Hello, Rupert, then.'

'I prefer Buckingham.' He tapped his pocket. 'Do you chaps want a drink?'

Harry swallowed half his glass in one huge gulp. 'Wouldn't say no. Mine's a mild.'

'Bitter for me,' Frank said. He coughed a little in embarrassment and glanced at Tomasz.

Tomasz held out his hand. 'I'm Major Tomasz Kaczmarczyk. I have just been appointed to your squadron.'

'So I hear.' Buckingham frowned. 'Major?'

'The equivalent rank here is Squadron Leader,' Harry said. He feigned a look of surprise. 'Why, that's the same as you, Buckingham.'

Buckingham did not respond to him but glanced at the insignia on Tomasz's shoulder. 'But you're only a Flying Officer.'

Tomasz shrugged. 'Unfortunately, your Sir Dowding does not think much of us Poles. We all had to start as Pilot Officers.'

'That didn't last long for you, though,' Harry said. 'You were promoted pretty damn quick.'

'Yes indeed.'

'He's a bit of an ace, Buckingham,' Harry explained. 'A natural leader.'

Frank gave him a warning look.

'Well you're more than welcome to my squadron,' Buckingham said. 'I'll get you a drink. Oh, any by the way, it's not Sir Dowding, it's Sir Hugh.' He gave a supercilious smile.

'Cut him some slack,' Frank said to Harry as soon as Buckingham was out of earshot.

Harry gave him a skeptical look.

'You do not like your new Squadron Leader, Harry?' Tomasz asked.

'Acting Squadron Leader. No, I don't like him one little bit, and the feeling is mutual. I'd rather have you as Squadron Leader, Tommy, even though you pull all the girls.'

Tomasz laughed. 'That will never happen. The men at the top of the RAF think little of we Poles. One said that he thought we were untrained, inexperienced and lacking in morale. Yet we fought like demons against the Nazis.'

'Your guys will have your chance,' Frank said. 'I guess the language issue is one of the factors.'

'The solution is simple,' Tomasz said. 'Make men like me squadron leaders. Men who can speak both Polish and English.'

'That's too good an idea for the top brass,' Harry said. 'And they think that only private school boys have any ideas worth considering.'

Buckingham came back with a tray full of drinks.

Harry looked askance. 'I asked for mild.'

Buckingham pretended a contrite look. 'Sorry, Smith. Couldn't quite understand your accent. Got you bitter instead.'

They drank their beer in silence.

'Yesterday was a bad day,' Tomasz said.

Buckingham rankled, assuming he intended his words as criticism. 'For lots of squadrons,' he said. 'Not just mine.'

'I meant for the whole of the RAF. Fortunately, it was even worse for the Nazis.'

Buckingham grunted, embarrassed that he had jumped to his own defence so hastily.

'Do you think we need to change tactics, Buckingham?' Frank said. 'One of the Canadians at 242 Squadron said that his Squadron Leader is pushing the idea hard.'

'Douglas Bader,' Buckingham said. 'He's very full of himself, I'm afraid. Shoots his mouth off a lot.'

Harry heaved a sigh. 'Why on earth do they make arrogant men like that Squadron Leaders?'

Buckingham's eyes glittered but he decided not to rise to the bait. He swilled his beer in his mouth as if he wanted to rid himself of an unpleasant taste. He glanced around, desperate to see if there was anyone else from his squadron to go and speak to. But as he did so he caught sight of a familiar figure strolling towards them.

'Bloody hell,' he said, words echoed by Harry and by Frank.

'Thought you'd seen the last of me, did you?' Tony Nash gave them a broad smile.

'We thought you were —' Harry said.

'Dead is the word, Harry.' Nash clapped him on the arm. 'Never thought I'd find you lost for words.'

Harry pumped his hand. 'Well I'm bloody glad to see you're alive.' The others echoed his words.

Nash turned to Buckingham. 'I'm sorry but I'm going to have to take my squadron back, Buckingham. Wentworth and Maisfield say you did a splendid job.'

'Thank you, sir. We took a lot of hits, I'm afraid.'

'It won't be the last. I'm grateful for you stepping up to the plate.' He held out his hand to Tomasz. 'I'm glad you've re-joined us, Tommy. I didn't want you to leave after Dunkirk.'

'There were several Poles in the squadron they moved me to and they needed a nursemaid. I'm glad to be back with you, Tony. And looking forward to flying Spitfires.'

'I gather you've had no experience of them. Put that right, first thing tomorrow. I'm not having you in combat until you've done a good couple of hours.'

Tomasz looked amused but gave a nod of acquiescence.

'So what happened to you, sir?' Harry asked.

Nash ran his fingers through his hair. 'I took a dive but managed to bail out. Just about evaded some German bullets and landed in a tree. I cut myself loose from the chute, scrambled along a branch and fell onto my head.'

He gave a little self-deprecating laugh. 'Survived combat, survived the drop and fell out of a bloody tree. I got concussion and apparently was gabbling like some bloody foreigner.' Here he gave Tomasz an embarrassed glance.

'The locals thought I was a Jerry,' he continued, 'and carted me off to a local hospital under the guard of some frightful women. I swear she claimed she was an Amazon warrior.'

Harry chuckled. 'You must have been delirious.'

'Didn't they think to check your papers?' Buckingham asked.

'Seems not. And I found out later that I was spoiling for a fight. It appears I thought I'd come down in Germany. No one could get near me until I'd quietened down next morning.'

'Does your wife know, sir?' Harry asked.

'I telephoned her from the hospital. She came and collected me.'

'She must have been relieved.'

'Absolutely. It was rather nice. We stayed in a hotel in Whitstable. Fabulous oysters.'

'Well we're relieved as well,' Frank said. 'Glad to have you back, sir.'

'Thanks boys. Now, I'm told there will be no ops for us for the next few days so how about another drink?'

Four glasses were thrust towards him.

At that moment two young women entered. The pub immediately went quiet.

'Oh my gawd,' Flo said. 'I thought we'd come to a pub but it turns out its a monastery. Looks like they've never seen a girl before.'

Most of the men laughed with good humour. It wasn't so much the fact that women never came in here, for some did. It was that few of them ventured in alone and certainly not two such young and pretty ones.

Tony Nash strolled over. 'Good evening, ladies. Would you care for a drink? I was just about to buy a round.'

'You're quick off the mark, Squadron Leader,' Flo said. 'I'll have a gin.'

'A lemonade for me, please,' Betty said. She looked alarmed at the fact that the man had pounced on them so soon.

'Don't think I'm forward,' Nash said when he saw her look. 'I'm a happily married man. It's just that I had a fairly narrow escape a few days ago and I'm celebrating rather.'

'I hope your wife was pleased to hear you're okay,' Flo said.

'She was delighted.' He held out his hand. 'My name's Tony Nash,'

'We worked with a Mrs Nash,' Betty said. 'What a coincidence.'

'An American lady,' Flo said. She gave him an ironic glance. 'Do you happen to know her?'

'Possibly. My wife's called Evelyn. And she works for Keith Park at Group Headquarters.'

'Oh, gawd,' Flo said. 'That's our friend.'

Nash beamed with delight. 'Any friend of Evie's is a friend of mine. I hope you don't mind if I take you under my wing.'

'Wing?' Flo said. 'I thought you was only a Squadron Leader.'

Nash didn't get the joke for a moment but then laughed. 'Come and see some of my chaps.'

They followed him over to the four men of his squadron.

Frank's eyes grew wide the moment Flo approached. It was as if the whole of the rest of the room had faded into insignificance. The rest of the men said their hellos but he stood rapt and unmoving.

'Cat got your tongue?' Flo said. Then she gazed into his eyes and her heart surged.

He reached out and took her hand. She wanted to smile, to say something else to keep the advantage. But, for the first time in her life, words failed her.

'These ladies worked with my wife at HQ,' Nash said.

Harry blushed. 'Do you happen to know...' He shook his head and fell silent.

'Know who?' Betty asked.

'Flight Officer Lamb,' he mumbled.

'Know her? She was our commanding officer. She trained us. She's wonderful.'

She nudged Flo in the side. 'This chap knows Claire.'

Flo did not even notice.

'How do you know her?' Betty asked.

Harry went scarlet. 'We met. Just briefly.' He tipped his glass to his mouth before he realised it was empty.

Nash pursed his lips thoughtfully and turned to see how Frank had reacted to his friend's odd reaction.

But Frank had not moved. He was still holding Flo's hand and gazing into her eyes.

DOWNFALL

27th August 1940

The few days respite that Nash had mentioned was over all too soon. Within a week, Harry was leading half the squadron on an observation flight when he glimpsed bombers ahead. He calculated that it was a big swarm, fifty bombers with half a dozen Messerschmitt 110s as escorts. Then he saw a solitary squadron of Hurricanes drive head-on into the pack. Twelve planes against fifty. Courage or desperation, he wondered. Or merely doing what was expected of them.

Instinctively he began to calculate the odds. Five to one.

The bombers appeared to be escorted by fewer fighters than normal. But this may have been deceptive. There might be others nearby, waiting to attack the British fighters.

Harry searched the sky for any sign of the enemy. Suddenly, screaming out of the sun, came twenty Messerschmitt 109s.

He opened the throttle and sent the Spitfire into a dizzying climb, ordering the other pilots to do the same. They obeyed instantly, each choosing a different trajectory to try to confuse the enemy.

The Luftwaffe pilots had expected the Spitfires to veer to right or left and were surprised at Harry's manoeuvre, that his planes were heading straight for them from below. They had no idea how to respond for it seemed an almost suicidal move. It gave Harry the time he needed and he sped into the centre of the pack.

A German came into his sights and he volleyed a quick burst at it. But he fired too soon and none of the bullets made contact. He slewed to the left, evading the fighter's answering fire. His eyes moved fast, searching for planes which might prove a danger to him or his pilots.

'Watch out Red Two,' he called. 'Bandit on your tail, Blue Three. Get the bugger, Frank, get the bugger.'

He levelled out, looking for a target. Two seconds later, a German appeared from the sun, guns blazing. He felt the shudder of some of his shots hit home.

Harry flipped away, climbed, turned and was instantly on the Messerschmitt's tail. He pressed his trigger and poured a long blast into the plane. It turned to avoid him and he managed to get a final few shots, just below the cockpit.

He saw the plume of smoke rise from the engine and then the tell-tale flickers of flame on the fuselage. Get out, you idiot, get out.

It was almost as if the German had heard him. The cockpit cover was flung back, the plane rolled and the pilot dropped out. His eyes followed the man's descent for two seconds, saw that he was heading for a good landing close to a nearby village.

And then he felt a judder. He moved the stick but the plane barely responded. He pushed even harder and he felt the plane do a slow turn, almost reluctantly. Sweat leapt onto his brow. His rudder had been damaged. He was a sitting duck.

'Take over, Frank,' he yelled. 'My plane's been hit.'

Part of him hoped that some of his men would follow his descent, provide protection. But he did not expect that, did not wish it. Their job was to continue to fight, with or without him.

He gritted his teeth and pulled at the stick again, hoping to regain more control. It was hopeless. The plane was a goner and there was every likelihood that he would be as well.

He searched the skies as he flew, fearful to see a Messerschmitt on his tail. But he had fallen so fast he had now gone beyond their reach.

He reached up for his canopy, and then cursed. He could not roll the plane for an easy exit; he would be forced to try to climb out. But the fields below appeared to be hurtling towards him. Even if he managed to get out there was no longer enough time for his chute to deploy.

There was only one thing left to do, try to land the plane.

He wiped the sweat from his eyes and peered ahead to try to find a place to aim for. This part of Kent was full of hop gardens and, thankfully, only sparse woodland.

Just below was the little village he had seen earlier, with the German pilot's parachute drifting to earth close to it. He thought he could make out the shapes of people running for shelters. Why haven't they got there already, he thought. Christ, almighty, if he ploughed into them he'd be a murderer.

Desperately he pulled on his stick and the plane responded a little. At the same time, he saw a tongue of flame flicker along the fuselage. His stomach lurched. If the fuel tank blew, he would have only seconds to get out. And how could he do so now that he was so close to the ground.

He grunted as he pulled still harder and the plane lifted a little more, clearing the roofs of the houses by only a dozen feet. He heard his own voice moaning, like a child in pain and he aimed at a patch of land which looked fairly level.

He had no time to deploy the under-carriage and gritted his teeth as the plane slewed along the ground. The sound of metal being wrenched apart filled his ears. The plane skidded to a halt.

He took a deep breath and reached for the canopy. He yelped in alarm. It was stuck.

He rose from his seat and pulled the canopy with frenzied strength. But it refused to budge.

The flames on the fuselage were growing fiercer. The plane would blow any minute. He hammered on the canopy in desperation, hoping he would be able to shift it or shatter it, anything to escape the maelstrom about to engulf him.

It was hopeless. He was trapped.

He heard a loud thump, then another and another. A man was on top of the canopy, hammering furiously at it but to no avail.

Then he pulled out a pistol, fired at the bolt and pulled the canopy back, reached in and grasped Harry under the armpits. He dragged him out onto the wing and then both men rolled across it and onto the ground.

'Renn du Idiot,' he cried. 'Das Flugzeug wird explodieren.'

The man grabbed Harry and dragged him twenty yards from the plane. Parachute lines still hung from his belt.

There was a sudden roar and the Spitfire burst into flames. The heat was so intense they had to shield their faces.

'Kommen Sie,' the German yelled. 'Come on.'

Harry went to move but a sudden pain seared his leg and he almost stumbled. The German bent his head and lifted Harry's arm over his neck. 'Kommen Sie. I help you,' he said.

They stumbled a couple of hundred yards from the plane and then, without a word, halted and sat on the ground.

'Exhausting work, almost dying,' the German said. Now that they were out of danger he spoke in very good English.

'You're Luftwaffe,' Harry said.

The man nodded his head. 'Ja. The Luftwaffe pilot you shot from the sky. But I also shot you. I think.' Then he grinned and held out his hand. 'Oberleutnant Diederichson.'

The same rank as me, Harry thought, and younger than I am. Maybe they're being killed off as fast as we are.

Harry shook his hand. 'Flying Officer Smith.' A sudden pain shot through his leg but he ignored it. 'You're a prisoner of war now. I suppose I'll have to take you into custody.'

Diederichson shook his head. 'No. I think those men will.'

Two elderly men were struggling across the field towards them.

'Home Guard,' one of them yelled. 'We're armed.'

'I doubt it,' said Diederichson. 'But I am.'

He pulled out his Luger and brandished it at the men. He was not sure what to do next. There was a wood five hundred metres distant and he could run for that, possibly even get to the other side and try to make it across country. But how far would he get, in his uniform?

'We are armed,' one of the men said, his voice betraying his nerves.

Diederichson laughed at the man's attempt at deception. 'I've shown my gun,' he said, 'now it's your turn.'

The two men gave each other an uncertain look. One waved a stick at him. 'There's two of us.'

'And there's one of me,' came a steely voice. 'And I've got a knife.'

Harry glanced up in surprise.

A woman had crept up from nowhere and was pressing a large butcher's knife into the German pilot's neck, just by his jugular. She was middle aged and slight of build but looked determined enough to fight to the death.

'Be careful, Enid,' cried one of the Home Guard anxiously.

'Commander Bowles to you,' the woman said.

She pressed the knife harder into Diederichson's flesh, drawing blood. 'I'm not afraid to use this,' she said.

'I can tell this,' Diederichson said. He handed her his gun.

'I'm Group Commander Bowles of the Amazon Defence Corps,' the woman said. 'I shall take you into custody.'

She waved his Luger at him. 'And no funny business. I've been trained in the use of weaponry.'

'I'll tell the vicar what you're doing, Enid,' one of the Home Guard men complained. 'And your husband as well. Christopher won't like it.'

'He'll be proud of me. Although I doubt he'll ever hear of it from the middle of the Atlantic.'

She waved her gun again. 'Come on, prisoner, stand up.'

Diederichson got to his feet. Harry did likewise but immediately buckled over in pain.

'You're bleeding,' Commander Bowles said.

'A bit of shrapnel, I think.' He glanced at the two Home Guards. 'Could you lend a hand, please.'

They set off across the fields but it soon became clear that the old men did not have the stamina to help Harry.

'Let me,' Diederichson said, bending his head once more for Harry to put his arm around it. 'If that's alright with the Amazon?'

Group Commander Bowles nodded and they made their way to the village.

'My name is Jurgen,' the young pilot told Harry. He sipped the mug of tea which the Home Guard had provided.

'Mine's Harry.'

'Like your king. At Agincourt.'

'I doubt I could ride a bloody horse though.'

Both pilots were in the school hall, guarded by members of the Home Guard. Their captain was a veteran of the Great War and actually had a gun but Harry doubted he would use it. A good job really because he appeared unconvinced when Harry said that he was in the RAF. To Kentish ears, Harry's Nottingham accent sounded suspiciously German.

Even when Harry pointed out his uniform and showed him his identity papers the captain remained doubtful. 'You could have taken them from one of our boys,' he muttered.

The captain still looked doubtful when one of his men brought the airmen their tea. He watched them intently, a ferocious and suspicious look on his face.

'A fearsome lot,' Diederichson said, jerking a thumb in the old man's direction. 'I'm sure they will throw our invasion back into the sea.'

Harry laughed. It was a good natured joke. And the man had saved his life.

'I wouldn't underestimate them,' Harry said. 'Members of the Home Guard will do everything in their power to defend their country.'

'Which is as it should be. I do not doubt that German grandfathers would do the same.'

Harry frowned. Here was an opportunity to find the answer to a question which had been increasingly troubling him. 'Would they, though? Would old men fight for the Nazi party? For Hitler?'

Diederichson tapped the insignia on his uniform. 'I do, Harry.'

There was a long silence. 'But do you believe in what you're fighting for?'

'I fight for my country and my people.'

'And for Hitler?'

Diederichson did not answer for a moment and then he gave a little shrug. 'I have no feelings about the Führer. Neither good nor bad.'

'But you fight for him?'

'You fight for Winston Churchill. Do you like him?'

Harry stared at the young German for a long while. 'Not particularly. Perhaps we're the same, you and I. We're both fighting for our people and that's all.'

'I think that the English and the Germans are very similar, my friend. I got to like you when I spent a few months here.'

'You did? What brought you here?'

'I was in the Boy Scouts. Pretty high up. I was sent over to your headquarters to see how you English did things. That was before it was disbanded by the Nazis.' He gave a wry smile. 'We were replaced by the Hitler Youth.'

Harry thought it best not to ask if he had joined that.

He sipped his tea, moving his leg a little to try to ease the pain. He wondered if the Home Guard had any biscuits.

'That Amazon woman was someone to be reckoned with,' Diederichson said, after a while. 'I think she would actually have killed me.' His voice was full of admiration.

Harry chuckled, put down his mug, and got out his cigarettes.

A door was thrown open and Enid Bowles marched towards them; a harassed elderly man struggling to keep up with her.

The Home Guard Captain looked annoyed at her arrival, put out and flustered. 'I'm in charge here,' he said.

'I'm taking over,' she replied.

'But Mrs Bowles —'

'No arguing. I'm a Group Commander. I far outrank you.'

'But you're not official.'

'Not as yet. But the Amazon Defence Corps will be recognised fairly soon. Our leader, Venetia Foster is confident of it. So I'm taking charge.'

The Captain glanced at the knife and the German Luger thrust into her belt. 'Have it your own way,' he muttered.

She approached the two pilots and indicated the elderly man. 'This is Dr MacQuirter,' she told Harry. 'He'll check your leg.'

The doctor bent to the task, cleaned and bandaged Harry's wound and told him he would be okay to travel.

'Okay, Flying Officer,' Group Commander Bowles said. 'I've a car waiting to take you to RAF Manston. They'll fix you up, I don't doubt. The Jerry will go to London for interrogation.'

'I think that standing orders say he should go to the nearest airfield,' Harry said mildly. 'In which case he should come with me.'

Mrs Bowles looked at him coldly. He was right, unfortunately. 'If you say so,' she snapped at last.

The Home Guard soldiers approached Harry to help him but he waved them away, looking at Diederichson to continue with the task.

Enid Bowles scowled, showing her disapproval.

But then she touched Harry on the arm. 'Oh, and by the way, thank you. You would have slaughtered half the village if you'd landed in the middle of it.'

It took thirty minutes for the ancient, dilapidated car to reach Manston. The men at the gate looked astonished at the occupants but, seeing Harry, let them through.

As soon as it stopped, Enid Bowles leapt out, pulled out the Luger and indicated that the airmen should come with her.

Then she marched straight to the administration block.

The station commander was bemused at the sight of the three people who entered his office. He had never seen a captured Luftwaffe pilot before and searched his mind for what he should do with him. But it was the willowy woman in front of him who was his biggest concern. He stared anxiously at her pistol.

'Do you have a licence for that thing?' he asked.

'Of course not. It's contraband of war. I'm confiscating it for the Amazon Defence Corps.'

'But are you chaps even official?'

'Chaps,' she cried. 'Are you blind, Wing Commander? Chaps?'

'I mean ladies —'

'Women, Wing Commander. We are the women of the Amazon Defence Corps. And we shall play just as big a part in the defence of these islands as do the Home Guard.'

He sighed wearily and brushed his fingers through his hair. 'I don't doubt it. If they're anything like as fierce as you are, erm…' He peered at her armband.

'Group Commander,' she said. 'Bowles.'

'Ah, the same rank as me.' He gave a sudden smile, got to his feet and shook her hand. 'Well done, Group Commander. Capturing the Jerry, I mean.'

'This young man shot him down,' she said indicating Harry.

'And well done you too, Flying Officer.'

He turned his gaze to Diederichson. 'And I should say well done to you as well. You're doing your bit, just like our chaps. But the war's over for you, I'm glad to say.'

'He saved my life,' Harry said.

The Wing Commander turned to him in surprise.

'My Spitfire was about to blow up. He risked his life to come and get me out.'

'Good show,' the Wing Commander said. 'Good show all round.'

He heaved a sigh. 'Soon,' he said, 'one day, we'll all be friends again.'

'I think they're friends already,' Enid Bowles said. 'And yes, a cup of tea would be splendid, I think. If it's on offer.'

'Good idea,' said the Wing Commander.

He shook her hand vigorously, then Harry's. He gave a moment's pause and then reached out and shook Diederichson' hand. 'Do you take sugar, Oberleutnant?'

SECTOR CONTROLLERS' MEETING

27th August 1940

Air Vice Marshal Park stared at the sky. The rain was pouring from a dark grey cloud more normal in November than August. There was no hint of the sun.

'And the weather report says this will last all day?'

'Yes, sir,' Claire answered.

'Right. Get all the sector controllers over here for a meeting. And ask Sir Hugh if he can make it.'

A few minutes before eleven Claire and Johnny checked the meeting room for a third time. The door opened and the sector controllers came in, led by Willoughby de Broke. This was the first time they had been called to such a meeting since June and there was a palpable air of anticipation.

Claire directed them to their seats and then withdrew to a chair beside Johnny at the back of the room. Their job was to run any errands Park might have, retrieve any documents not to hand and generally help ensure that the meeting went smoothly.

A few minutes later Park and Dowding entered the room. Dowding gestured Park to take the chairman's seat and sat beside him.

'Thank you for coming, gentlemen,' Park said. 'It seems unlikely that Jerry will attack in such foul weather but if he does, I know your deputies will manage things more than adequately in your absence.'

He was not a man for addressing meetings and he took a sip of water to give himself time to prepare his next words.

But before he spoke, the door opened to reveal the Deputy Chief of the Air Staff, Air Vice Marshal Sholto Douglas.

'Hope you don't mind me attending, Park,' he said. His tone suggested he did not actually care what Park thought.

'Of course not,' Park said. He sounded as though he minded a great deal. 'I'm sorry but I didn't think to invite anyone from Air Staff.'

'Don't worry. We got wind of it.' He stared at Willoughby de Broke. 'May I?' He placed his document case on the table in front of de Broke.

De Broke looked a little disgruntled but gave up his chair. Sholto Douglas slid into it.

Claire leapt up, carried her chair to the bottom of the table and helped de Broke move his things there.

'Get yourself another chair, Lamb,' Park said. She got a chair from the outside office and took it to the back.

As she sat down, she noticed Sholto Douglas stare at her. He had a morose look, with sharp nose, thin, unmoving lips and deep set, wary eyes. She hoped that she had not angered him by helping de Broke so promptly.

Dowding looked pointedly at his wristwatch.

'I've called this meeting,' Park said, 'to discuss strategy and tactics in general. In particular, I want to discuss whether we are doing enough to protect 11 Group's airfields from attack.'

Sholto Douglas raised his eyebrows and made a note. The very move seemed to aggravate Park. His face reddened.

'I would think that attacks are inevitable,' Sholto Douglas said, after he had finished writing. 'As Prime Minister Baldwin once said, "the bomber will always get through."'

'I think Fighter Command is proving this not to be the case,' Dowding said, brusquely.

'Apparently not,' Sholto Douglas replied. 'Park has just said he's not able to protect his airfields.'

'The point of the matter is,' Park said, 'that my airfields are being attacked when my planes are airborne, fighting the enemy. And this, despite the fact that I request assistance from my fellow Group Commanders.'

'Which, of course, is always provided,' Sholto Douglas said. 'Where possible.'

'It's always given by 10 Group,' Park said. 'Air Vice Marshal Brand reacts in a speedy, almost instant manner. I have never had to ask twice.'

Sholto Douglas smiled but did not reply.

A heavy silence filled the room.

Finally, Park spoke into it. 'I cannot, however, say the same about 12 Group.'

Sholto Douglas wrote once again in his notebook. He paused for a moment but did not look up. 'Perhaps, Park, you would not need to ask for help so much if you deployed more squadrons. If you acted with greater aggression. Took the fight out to the enemy over the Channel instead of allowing them to arrive at your airfields.'

Claire bit her lip, noticing that Park did not take this suggestion at all well.

'I do not send more squadrons up,' he said, 'because I need to husband my resources. If I don't there will be no squadrons left to defend this island.'

'I don't think we need to be so alarmist, Park,' Sholto Douglas said.

He turned towards the controllers. 'How do you chaps feel? I take it you're confident that we will win the battle.'

'We will if we pull together,' said one of the younger men. 'Every member of the service. Every Group.'

Sholto Douglas stared at him with cold contempt. 'I have been assured that Air Vice Marshal Leigh-Mallory responds with alacrity to all requests for assistance.'

'Leigh-Mallory offers assistance,' Park said. 'But I'm afraid it is not always on time or at the right place.'

He hastened on before Sholto Douglas could interrupt.

'Yesterday, for example, I asked 12 Group to intercept a Dornier formation before they reached my airfields north east of London. By the time Leigh-Mallory's squadrons finally arrived the Dorniers had got through as far as Debden, bombed the airfield and headed home.'

He glanced at Debden's controller who nodded in affirmation.

'I have been informed,' Sholto Douglas said, 'that the request for assistance came too late. So it was little wonder that the squadrons from 12 Group were unable to find the raiders in time.'

Claire and Johnny exchanged glances. They had heard Park request help from 12 Group in ample time.

'The German bombers had to fly twice the distance than fighters from 12 Group,' Park continued, 'and are much slower. Yet Leigh-Mallory could not give Debden the protection it needed. Damn it man, it's only a dozen miles from 12 Group's Duxford airfield.'

'I gather that one squadron did get through.'

'Yes. One solitary squadron.'

Air Chief Marshal Dowding leaned forward. 'I think the point is that our Station Commanders need to feel confident that their airfields will be protected when their own planes are going up to intercept.'

The controllers all murmured in agreement.

'Leigh-Mallory is fully cognisant of this,' Sholto Douglas said.

'In one instance,' Park continued, as if he had not heard the last remark, 'there was no patrol over North Weald until long after the bombing was over. And as far as Debden and Hornchurch are concerned I have still failed to get confirmation that Leigh-Mallory's squadrons had even been seen.'

'It's easy to put the blame on other commanders, Park —'

'I don't have the time nor resources to check if 12 Group have actually been ordered to patrol my airfields,' Park snapped.

Sholto Douglas did not respond although his face turned black with anger.

'If Leigh-Mallory weren't so wedded to his notion of the Big Wing he'd be able to protect my airfields,' Park continued. 'It takes time to form squadrons into a wing and by the time they've arrived at the scene of combat it's too late.'

'Leigh-Mallory points out that the Big Wing shoots down more planes than single squadrons,' Sholto Douglas said. 'Better to bag them when they're scurrying home than when they're headed our way and are fresh and alert. Even if it means they've dropped their bombs.'

'But they're dropping their bombs on my bloody airfields,' Park cried. 'And I, for one, have not seen any hard evidence that the Big Wing gets more kills than individual squadrons.'

'Air Vice Marshal Leigh-Mallory says they do.'

Park glared at him.

'And I say there's no evidence.'

'Noted,' Sholto Douglas said, writing in his book.

The meeting broke up at twelve thirty. The station controllers almost sprinted for their planes, so anxious were they to get away from such a venomous atmosphere.

Claire and Johnny cleared up the room. The air felt almost electric.

'I've never seen Park so angry,' Claire said, after checking that no one else was in earshot.

'Me neither. But can you blame him?'

'Do you think that Leigh-Mallory really said that that he didn't mind if the Germans bombed our airfields?'

'I wouldn't put it past him. But I wouldn't believe all that Sholto Douglas said either. I suspect he might be manoeuvring to get Dowding's job.'

Claire raised her eyes. 'I can't believe they quarrel so much between themselves.'

'You have to realise that a lot of them were comrades in the Great War. Friendships and rivalries last long and run deep. Hardly any of them have seen combat in the last twenty years but that doesn't stop them from believing that they know all about air warfare. Nowadays, they're just as much desk-job men as I am. But they still think they're air aces.'

Claire looked at the table where de Broke had been sitting. It was littered with scraps of paper he had torn from his note-book. Yet he was normally the most unflappable of men.

'I thought that Air Chief Marshal Dowding agreed with Park's tactics,' Claire continued. 'Why didn't he support him more in the meeting?'

'Stuffy can't be bothered with politics. He just wants to win the war and assumes the Heads of Groups will work together. And he has no time for Sholto Douglas. I'm not sure he has much for Leigh-Mallory either.'

They continued clearing up in silence. They had just about finished when Park came into the room and handed Johnny a document. 'I got so damned heated in the meeting that I forgot to tell the controllers that our squadrons are not to be drawn into combat with

German fighters unless they prove to be a threat. We're losing as many planes as the Germans in these dog fights and we just can't bloody afford it.'

He gave Claire a little wave of apology. 'Sorry about the language.'

'Don't worry, sir. I've heard worse from our pilots.'

'Yes, but they're fighting for their lives. I'm not and haven't got that excuse.'

Claire smiled. 'Perhaps you should get some lunch, sir.' She glanced out of the window. 'This rain looks set for the day so we might have a quiet patch.'

'Let's hope you're right.' He strode off.

Poor man, she thought. He's got the weight of the battle on his shoulders and yet some of his colleagues don't give him support. She hoped he would be able to put this meeting behind him. The country needed him terribly.

CATASTROPHIC LOSSES

30th and 31st August 1940

Claire passed the details of the previous day's fighting to Evelyn. 'Only three deaths,' she said. 'A pretty quiet day.'

'President Roosevelt will be pleased when he hears it,' Evelyn said.

Not like Joe Kennedy, she thought. The American Ambassador was convinced that Britain would be defeated and often sounded as though he hoped it would be. But that was information she would not share with anyone here.

At 09.00 hours the plotters were beginning to fidget. They had been on duty for two hours, there had been no raids and they were getting bored. Claire leaned over and looked at the huge map below her, wondering how long this quiet patch would hold.

Suddenly the plotters leapt to their feet and rushed to the table.

'They've started, sir,' she called to Park.

A number of sorties swept over the south coast but the Observer Corps said that they were fighters and not bombers.

'They're trying to tempt us up to fight them,' Park said. 'Well we're not going to be tempted. They might be able to afford to lose planes and pilots but I can't.'

He gave the order that no squadrons were to be scrambled to attack fighters.

The pattern was repeated for the next hour. Numerous sorties of German fighters crossed the channel and criss-crossed the airspace until their fuel got low and they had to return to France.

Most of the people in the Bunker were relieved about this. Park, however, was getting increasingly anxious. 'I don't like the look of this,' he muttered to himself.

At 10.30 a mass formation of two hundred bombers was spotted heading across the channel. They crossed the Kent coast at Dover and immediately split up.

Claire glanced at the clock as the minutes drifted by. The bombers were like a swarm of locusts over southern England. It was almost impossible to determine where they were heading.

She turned her gaze back to the map. Suddenly, she discerned the beginnings of a pattern.

She called out. 'It looks to me like each raid is targeting a different airfield, sir.'

Park snatched up some opera glasses and scanned the map. 'Get the squadrons up,' he yelled.

He cursed himself. He had been too busy thinking about the earlier German feints, too determined to avoid fighter to fighter combat. Now his every airfield was in jeopardy.

'How many should we scramble, sir?' the duty controller asked.

Park studied the map, made a quick calculation. 'Fifteen squadrons. I want every airfield covered.'

The controllers all exchanged anxious glances.

———

Harry and Frank were eating a late breakfast when the order came to scramble. 'Bloody hell,' Harry said, stuffing a slice of toast into his mouth. 'If the bastards don't kill me, I'll die of starvation.'

They were airborne within two minutes.

'Don't forget the high-ups forbid us to tackle the Jerry fighters,' Nash said over the headphones. 'We're only to target the bombers.'

His mind raced. The order had been given too late for his planes to climb above the bombers. That meant they would have to try the tactic they had been discussing for the last two weeks. The head on attack. He knew that Air Chief Marshal Dowding opposed this idea because he felt it was too dangerous. It was especially so for the novice pilots, many of whom were killed in attempting it. But Park appeared sanguine about it, knowing it could prove the most effective tactic of all.

Nash made his mind up.

'Harry, take your flight and climb above the bombers. Attack when you've got good sight of them.'

The planes peeled off immediately and began to climb.

'Frank, Rupert and Tomasz stay with me,' Nash continued, 'the rest of the squadron in staggered formation behind. We're going to attack head on.'

Frank laughed aloud. This was the sort of fighting he liked.

A head on attack meant that the Spitfires and Hurricanes would not be vulnerable to the gunners at the rear of the bomber. And any German fighters would be reluctant to attack for fear of hitting their own bombers. Best of all, the cockpit was the most vulnerable part of the bomber. It was the optimum place to make a kill.

The only problem was that a head on attack required nerves of steel.

He chose a target and raced towards it. The closing speed of the two aircraft was a combined six hundred miles an hour, almost three hundred yards a second.

His target was a Heinkel and at four hundred yards he gave a short burst of gunfire. At the same time, he pulled back on his stick and soared above the bomber, avoiding a collision by yards.

The three men by his side did the same although the man following Nash left it too late and crashed into the German. Both planes erupted in flames and plunged to earth.

The bombers were now peeling away at speed. There was no chancethat they would be able to regroup so the danger to any airfield was now minimised. Nevertheless, he gave chase to one of the bombers.

'Watch out, Frank,' Tomasz yelled. 'Messerschmitt on your tail.'

Frank instinctively dived and the bullets missed by inches. He looked up and saw Tomasz launch himself on the Messerschmitt. It was over in seconds. The German plummeted to the earth and Tomasz leapt on another German.

Getting his revenge for Poland, Frank thought before targeting another bomber.

Minutes later, it was all over. British and German planes were now too dispersed for any further action.

'Well done, gentlemen,' Nash called. 'Let's get back for a rest.'

The squadron streaked back to Hornchuch. But they had little time for a rest.

—————

At 11.30 a second wave of bombers filled the skies above Kent. Park took no chances now and immediately ordered sixteen squadrons to scramble with the other six waiting on standby.

The fighting was intense and vicious but the fighters just about managed to keep the Germans from bombing the airfields.

'It looks like Goring's sending over the whole bloody Luftwaffe,' Johnny said.

'But we're holding our own,' Claire said.

At 12.00 noon radar picked up another wave of bombers heading towards Kent.

'Get every squadron up,' Park yelled. 'Pull them away from the airfields and send them to attack these fresh waves.'

'That's every squadron,' Claire said to Johnny. 'We've got nothing in reserve.'

'Ask 12 Group for assistance,' Park said. 'Tell them every plane we have is now in the air.'

The duty controller yelled the request down the phone.

At 12.15 Biggin Hill was hit.

'What's happened to 12 Group?' Park asked. 'They were supposed to send support.'

'They sent two squadrons,' the controller said. 'But they appear to have missed the Jerries coming from the south.'

'Then pull back two of our squadrons to cover Biggin Hill and Kenley. One more attack and they'll be out of action.'

It was a desperate time but by 13.00 many of the Germans began to pull back.

Park flung his cap onto a table.

'Well done everybody,' he said. 'And pass on that message to all the stations.'

He took a deep breath. 'Now, someone pass me a phone.'

His eyes were like pin pricks as he put the speaker to his mouth. 'Get me Air Vice Marshal Leigh-Mallory.'

Claire watched him as he waited. His hand constantly clenched and unclenched.

'Leigh-Mallory?' he said after a short while. 'Keith Park here.'

He was determined to be calm and professional. 'Where were your fighters? They were supposed to protect my airfields.

He listened to the reply for a moment. 'They couldn't find the enemy?' he said in astonishment.

Then he exploded in rage. 'They weren't supposed to go looking for the enemy. They were supposed to be above my airfields, waiting for the enemy to come to them.'

He listened to the reply with stony face. 'Good day to you, as well,' he said. He slammed the phone down and swore.

Evelyn thrust a sandwich into his hand. 'Here you are, Park. Chew on this instead of Leigh-Mallory's ear.'

He looked at her in astonishment. 'Nobody here calls me, Park.'

'I'm a Yank. Get over it. Or should I call you Keith?'

He took a bite of the sandwich. He cursed himself. It was stupid of him to shout at Leigh-Mallory in front of his junior staff, unforgivable.

'Claire,' he called. 'The next time I phone Leigh-Mallory, remind me to make the call in my office, would you?'

'If I know you're going to, I will.'

'Good.'

He frowned. 'Did I just call you Claire?'

'Yes, sir.'

'Good God, it must be catching. Damned Yanks. My apologies.'

'None necessary, sir.'

———

The next few hours were quieter with only the occasional sorties from the Germans.

'They've had their fingers burnt,' Johnny said to Claire and Evelyn. 'They won't be back in any force again today.'

At four o'clock they proved him wrong.

A huge number of bombers streamed across Kent and along the Thames Estuary. For a moment Park looked stricken but then he shook his head. 'Get every squadron up,' he ordered his controllers.

'They've been at it all day, sir,' Wing Commander de Broke said. He could not hide the anxiety from his voice.

'I know,' Park said, 'but they have to go.'

He paced up and down a few steps. 'Get me 12 Group.'

He held out his hand for the telephone, weighed it in his hand for a moment and then passed it to Claire. 'Ask them to send as many squadrons as they can,' he said. 'And this time tell them that I need them to engage in combat with the enemy and not just guard my airfields.'

Air Chief Marshal Dowding walked into the room and peered at the map.

'This is worse than I feared,' he murmured to Park.

'I know, sir. I've got every squadron in action and have just asked 12 Group for assistance.'

They fell silent.

'I've found you another squadron, by the way,' Dowding said. 'I'm certain it will help.'

Park looked baffled.

'I've ordered 303 Polish squadron operational and transferred it from 12 Group to you.'

'Thank you, sir.' Park frowned. 'But is their English good enough to take part in combat?'

'It seems it is.' Dowding gave a ghost of a smile. 'Six of them were engaged in a training exercise over St Albans when they saw some German bombers. One of the Poles attacked immediately, without waiting for orders, and destroyed two German planes. When he got back to base he was reprimanded for indiscipline, of course. And congratulated at the same time.'

Park grinned. 'That's the spirit we need.' He thought that transferring the squadron to 11 Group would also annoy Leigh-Mallory.

Claire put down the telephone. '12 Group are sending half a dozen squadrons,' she said.

'Good to see you and 12 Group working well together,' Dowding said.

Park gave him a bleak smile.

'We've got the final reports,' Johnny told Park. 'Thirty-nine planes destroyed, including eight Spitfires from Hornchurch. We got forty-one Jerries though.'

'Not enough,' Park said. 'We need a kill ratio of at least two to one if we're to beat them.' He drummed his fingers on the table.

'The radar stations at Pevensey, Beachy Head and Foreness have been badly damaged,' Johnny continued, 'but they're going to work on them overnight and hope they'll be okay by tomorrow.'

He took a deep breath. 'Two hundred civilians died in the raids, sir.'

Park closed his eyes for a moment. 'Anything else?'

'Yes, sir. Biggin Hill suffered extensive damage including forty personnel killed and thirty seriously injured. It's virtually out of action.'

Park placed his hand over his mouth and groaned. Losing his sector stations was what he he feared most. He would have to do something and fast.

'Transfer control of their sector to Hornchurch,' he said. 'Bouchier should be able to handle both for a day or two.'

'Are you certain, sir?'

'Hopeful rather than certain. But what else can we do?'

'I'm afraid I must go,' Dowding said. 'The Prime Minister wants me to report progress.'

He went to leave and paused. 'Well done everybody. I'm proud of you all.'

———

Claire and Evelyn went to have tea together. It was ten at night and they had been working since early morning, a double shift. The canteen was crowded with the afternoon shift eating supper and the evening shift getting their breakfast.

'I'm whacked,' Evelyn said. 'And you look shattered.'

'I'll be all right.'

Evelyn gave her a searching look. 'Are you worried about that boy? The one you…the one you made friends with in the shelter?'

'Yes I am. It's ridiculous because I don't even know him.'

'It's not ridiculous. It's all quite natural.'

'What about you? Isn't your husband a squadron leader?'

'Yep. And knowing Tony, he'll be in the thick of it.'

Claire frowned. 'I think I met a squadron leader called Tony when I went to Manston. Perhaps that was him.'

'He's a skinny guy with a thin moustache.'

'That could be half the pilots in the RAF.' She stirred her tea. 'Does he look a little like Robert Donat? Or even Clark Gable?'

Evelyn laughed. 'I'm flattered you think so. But you're not the first to say that. Yep, I guess that was him.'

'More like Clark Gable,' Claire said. Gable was more dashing than Donat and a fib was sometimes justified.

'His squadron's getting leave in a few days,' Evelyn said. 'They're going to be sent north. I've managed to get two days off to be with him.'

Claire nodded but she was only half listening. 'Does your husband fly Spitfires or Hurricanes?'

'Spitfires.'

'In that case he might be my friend's squadron leader.'

'I'll ask when I telephone him later. What's your guy's name.'

'Harry Smith. I think he's a Pilot Officer.'

She was getting ready for bed when there came a knock on the door. It was Evelyn.

'I've just spoken to Tony. Yep, your guy is in his squadron. Except he's not a Pilot Officer anymore but a Flying Officer.'

Claire nodded. She knew too well that casualties meant people were getting promoted astonishingly quickly.

'Thanks very much for finding out,' she said.

'No problem. And Tony says Harry's absolutely fine and looking forward to his leave.' She gave an arch smile. 'Maybe you could meet up with him. Although I'd suggest a hotel this time and not a hole in the ground.'

Claire laughed. 'Goodnight, Evie. Thanks for finding out.'

―――

Park arrived at the Bunker at five thirty the next morning. He had sent up squadrons too late the day before and did not intend to make the same mistake today.

The day was already warming up and the light haze over the Thames estuary was clearing. The rest of southern England was clear and fine, the sort of conditions which the Luftwaffe would be quick to take advantage of.

A figure approached and held a cup of tea out to him.

'Thought you might like a cuppa, sir.'

'Goodness, Lamb. You're up early.'

'Couldn't sleep, sir. I feel perfectly alert though.'

'Good. I suspect we'll need all our wits about us today.'

The truth of it was that she hadn't slept for worrying about Harry. She'd tried to tell herself to stop it. After all he was only one airman out of hundreds engaged in combat every day. And they had only had the one fling, and that totally unplanned. To be honest, she wondered if her terror would have made her have sex with anybody. That Harry was the one only because he happened to be in the trench with her.

He did not appear to share these thoughts, however. He had written a charming letter to her, saying that he would be happy to take her out to a restaurant when he had his next leave. She had read the letter three times during the night.

Now, this morning, she could not afford to think about him. Her entire focus would be needed on the task in hand.

She turned towards Park as he sipped his tea. 'Did you have breakfast, sir?' she asked.

He shook his head.

'You should do, if you don't mind me saying. Wasn't it Napoleon who said that an army marches on its stomach? It must be the same for the air force. I'm going for mine now, if you care to join me.'

Park smiled, finished his tea and followed her to the canteen. Not even Johnny Longley had invited him to eat and he doubted he would have accepted even if he had.

The canteen was almost empty but as soon as they went to the counter Claire realised that she was starving and asked for scrambled eggs and bacon instead of her usual toast. It looked fairly unappetising but she was too hungry to care.

'Fried bread or toast to go with it?' the server asked.

'Both please. I'm famished.'

The woman smiled and put a slice of toast and another of fried bread on her plate. Then she winked and gave her a second rasher of bacon.

'I'll have the same, please,' Park said.

'Of course, sir. We've got some sausage if you'd like.'

'Yes please. As long as I get the same amount of bacon as the lady.'

'More, sir.' She heaped the food on his plate. 'England's relying on you. Can't have you fainting from hunger.'

They took their plates to an empty table. 'I'm not sure I'll be good for anything after all this,' Park said, eyeing the food. But he wolfed it down, nonetheless.

They returned to the Bunker at 6.15 and caught up on the reports of the night raids which had been alarmingly intense. The night shift left at seven and the day shift arrived. Although most of them looked exhausted they were at their posts within minutes.

At 7.55 radar picked up two German groups, one over the Thames Estuary and the other headed towards Dover.

'They don't give up, do they?' one of the controllers said.

'And nor will we,' Park said. 'Scramble two squadrons to intercept.'

Claire leaned over and watched the girls moving the plots across the map.

'They're coming in fast, sir,' she said. 'Looks like fighters to me.'

Park looked at the senior controller but he said he had no definite information as yet. Five minutes later he called to Park. 'The squadrons are in visual distance and report they're Messerschmitt 109s, flying at 25,000 feet.'

Park bit his lips. 'They're superior to Spits at that height. Are you sure there are no bombers?'

The controller picked up his opera glasses and studied the map below. 'Positive, sir.'

'Then call the squadrons back. I'm not allowing fighter to fighter combat.'

The controller gave the order. Park paced up and down waiting for more news.

'253 Squadron have returned to base,' the controller said after a few minutes.

Park spun round. 'What about the other one?'

'1st Canadian Squadron, sir. They don't appear to have received the message, sir.'

'Damn. Keep trying them, man. They must return to base immediately and not, repeat not, engage in combat.'

They heard nothing for perhaps thirty seconds. Then there came a flurry of movement below, the sound of telephones and one WAAF plotter talking into her headset.

Two minutes later, she glanced up. She looked anxious and spoke to her supervisor who immediately contacted one of the controllers. His face looked grim as he heard the news.

'The Messerschmitts pounced on the Canadians, sir,' he said. 'Three of their planes destroyed.'

'Christ in heaven,' Park said.

He turned to Claire. 'Find out why they didn't receive the order. And send out another memo, word it as tough as you want, absolutely forbidding any more fighter to fighter combat.'

He looked more exasperated than she had ever seen him.

She returned to the Bunker fifteen minutes later and showed him the memo she had written.

'That's fiercer than I would have put it,' Park said appreciatively. 'Get it out to all airfields. And make sure that the Station Commanders see it and acknowledge that they have.'

At 8.25 the telephone from 12 Group rang.

A sergeant listened to the message and gestured to Park. 'I think you should take this, sir.'

Park grabbed a phone.

'Okay, everyone,' he said. 'Forty Dorniers are headed towards Duxford. 12 Group seem to have been taken by surprise and Duxford's controller has asked us for assistance.'

He glanced at the tote board. 'Divert 111 squadron there.'

Five minutes later, the controller gave the thumbs up. '111 has spotted the bombers. They've got in front of them and are going to meet them head on.' He gave a derisive laugh. 'Lucky for Duxford that we're not scratching together a Big Wing.'

Park did not respond apart from to smile. A feather in 11 Group's hat, he thought.

A few minutes later they heard that the bombers had been dispersed over Duxford but another swarm had sneaked in and dropped a hundred bombs on nearby Debden airfield.

'That's one of ours,' Squadron Leader Simpson said.

'I'm aware of that,' Park shot back, icily.

Claire bit her lip. Simpson would not be the only one to criticise Park for assisting 12 Group and leaving his own airfields defenceless.

More raids arrived just after 12.00. Biggin Hill was attacked and many buildings destroyed. The temporary power and telephone cables which had been put in overnight were badly damaged.

'Biggin Hill's down,' one of the controllers called.

'Switch control of the sector to Hornchurch again,' Park said. 'Let's hope they remain unscathed.'

***

'Not again,' Harry cried, throwing his knife and fork onto his uneaten meal. 'Goring must have a spy watching when I'm about to eat.'

He sprinted to his plane. The process was now so automatic he was able to put his harness on as he ran and spring into the cockpit with one leap.

As he did so he saw a fleet of bombers coming in low over the trees. He thrust his control stick forward and sped down the runway, taking off in a storm of falling bombs. None hit him and he soared above the bombers. Others were not so lucky. Three Spitfires were destroyed on the ground, two of them while they were on the brink of getting airborne.

He banked savagely and hurtled after the bombers. He got a Dornier in his sight but not before the rear gunner had seen him. A hale of bullets erupted from the German but none of them hit.

Harry's aim proved better. His bullets tore the gunner's canopy to pieces and killed him outright. He stopped firing for a moment, edged closer and then gave the bomber two seconds of concentrated fire. Flames erupted from the fuel tank. The pilot managed to get his canopy open but he was too close to the ground and he hit it in a huge fireball.

The nine remaining Spitfires continued to play havoc with the bombers but only for a few minutes before Nash ordered them to return to base.

'There might be more of the buggers waiting in the wings,' he said. 'We should refuel and rearm.'

Landing at the airfield took every bit of the pilots' skill. The low-level bombs had done incredible damage, with massive craters everywhere.

Everyone on the airfield was heaping earth into the holes, including Hornchurch's controller, Wing Commander Bouchier.

Who's minding the shop, Harry wondered when he saw this. But then again, there was not much of a shop left to mind.

He climbed out of the cockpit and grabbed a shovel while the ground crew refuelled the plane.

Fortunately, there were no further attacks and within three hours the runways had been returned to a reasonable state. Bouchier hurried back to his operations room and his voice soon echoed over the airfield congratulating everyone on a splendid job.

'I reckon he has a hankering to work at the BBC,' Jack said to Harry.

'Maybe he should become a British version of Lord Haw-Haw,' Harry said. 'He can tell the Jerries they're going to lose the war.'

His laughter stopped in his mouth. 'Oh bloody hell. Here they come again.'

Another swarm of bombers was heading towards them.

Every plane managed to get airborne unscathed this time and the bombers were dispersed. They managed a few hits on the airfield but nowhere near as many as earlier.

Harry met up with Frank and Tomasz on the runway and they made their way back to the canteen. Harry's untouched plate was still on the table. Without a word he took a seat and began to eat.

Park stood down his controllers for a quick break. It was getting dark now and the only activity was a huge bombing raid on Liverpool.

'That's Leigh-Mallory's concern,' Johnny said to Claire, with a sigh. He picked up a piece of paper and went over to Park.

'I've got the interim situation report, sir,' he said.

'Just the summary please, Longley.'

'Forty-one Spits and Hurricanes have been destroyed or lost at sea.'

Park's lips tightened.

'Twenty-two pilots bailed out,' Johnny continued, 'and half of them were badly burned and won't see action any time soon.' He took a deep breath. 'And nine pilots killed or posted missing.'

'The Germans?' Park asked.

Johnny glanced at the paper. 'Sixty planes destroyed, sir.'

'It's good,' Park said, 'but not good enough. Sixty of them but forty of ours.'

'But the Jerries are either dead or prisoners,' Claire said. 'They won't be able to fight against us anymore. Whereas our boys can get back in action.'

Park sighed. 'Good point, Lamb. But I wonder how much more our pilots can take.'

'As much as necessary,' Longley said. He knew that he was not the person to say it, never having flown, but he felt it his duty to buck up his commander.

'I believe you're right, Johnny. Thank God.'

And without another word he made his way, exhausted to his quarters.

SLEEP WITH ME

1st September 1940

Frank Trent paced up and down nervously. He couldn't believe that he was walking out with a girl as pretty as Flo. No, pretty was not the right word. Lovely, gorgeous, beautiful. He frowned. These words weren't quite right either. They made her seem like some glamorous woman in a Hollywood film that he'd watch at the cinema. Flo was more down to earth than that, more real and well… just more.

Pretty was the best fit after all, he decided. Pretty and lively and fun.

He saw her walk towards him and his heart leapt.

'Here she comes, you lucky dog,' Harry Smith said with a wink.

Frank blushed. Flo was his first girlfriend although he would never admit this to anyone. To her maybe but not to his mates. And he didn't even know how to tell her. What if she thought he was pathetic, not much of a man? Would she ditch him for someone else? Someone more exciting and devil may care like Rupert Buckingham perhaps?

'Hello, handsome,' she said, pecking him on the cheek.

'Handsome,' chorused his friends with great amusement.

She turned to them with a bright smile. 'You're just jealous, boys. Jealous of my Frank. As if any of you stand any chance compared to him.' She put her hand on her hip in a provocative manner.

'You take care, Frank,' Harry said. 'She might be more dangerous than a Messerschmitt.'

'And you're about as exciting as a Great War biplane,' she said, blowing him a mocking kiss.

'A Sopwith Camel,' one of the men cried.

'Camel,' a sergeant said. 'That's just the right name for Smithy.'

'Harry Camel,' Jack White said.

Harry groaned. He knew, just knew, that he would be lumbered with this name for the rest of the war.

Flo hooked her arm in Frank's. 'Come on then, handsome,' she said, 'take me away from all this.'

They walked into Hornchurch and headed towards the cinema. He'd wanted to see Laurel and Hardy in A Chump at Oxford but Flo had set her heart on Rebecca.

'You'll like it,' she said. 'It's a dark mystery, about brooding and passionate love.'

'Okay,' he said, instantly converted to the idea. Brooding and passionate love was exactly what he was beginning to feel for Flo.

She was engrossed in the film and managed to meet his rather clumsy advances with experienced skill, just enough to satisfy him while she kept her eyes on the film. When the second feature came on she allowed him a great deal more success.

As she did so she sensed something different in him. And in herself, for that matter. She liked him. She realised that she liked him a lot, far more than most of the boys she went out with. It was partly his rather gentlemanly behaviour with her, partly the rather gauche way he acted.

But mostly, she thought, it was because he seemed incredibly besotted by her.

She'd had her share of moon-struck boys before. More than her fair share if she were honest. But Frank felt different. He was smitten, definitely smitten.

Maybe, she thought, he even loves me. She was not at all sure how she felt about the idea. Love was a very big step and not one to take lightly. Especially in war. She dismissed the idea from her mind, concluding that she was almost certainly wrong, that Frank was merely experiencing an excess of excitement.

'I love you,' he whispered.

'Oh, my,' she said.

'I do,' he continued. 'I realised it a few days ago. I can't stop thinking about you. I go to sleep thinking about you, I wake up thinking about you. Even when I'm flying.'

'Well don't do that, you silly thing. I want you to concentrate when you're in the air, not go day-dreaming about me.'

He fell silent.

She squeezed his hand. 'I've got a soft spot for you too, Frank.'

He gave a huge sigh. 'I'm so glad. I wasn't sure whether to tell you or not. But I just couldn't help myself.'

She put her lips to his and her tongue crept into his mouth, tickling his tongue. He almost bit hers in surprise.

'I've never kissed a girl like that before,' he said. She chuckled and kissed him once again.

The film ended and the lights came on. People on either side stood up and began to push past them, anxious to leave before the National Anthem started and kept them standing there.

Flo grabbed his hand and bolted for the door, just making it out before the music started.

They walked back to base slowly, hand in hand. They stopped for a while and stared at the late evening sky. There were no street lights because of the blackout so the stars were already growing bright.

'They're beautiful aren't they,' he said.

'As beautiful as me?' she teased.

'Not quite.'

She giggled.

He suddenly pointed out a bright star low down in the sky.

'Do you see that star, Flo? My mom died when I was four years old. A few years later, my dad lost his temper with me, a terrible rage. I was distraught and told him I missed her and wanted her back. Why did she leave me, I asked.

He slapped my face and threw me against the wall.

My auntie Mildred, his second wife, wiped my tears and took me out into the garden.

'Your mommy didn't leave you, Frankie,' she said. She pointed out that star. 'There's your mommy,' he said. 'She's in heaven but she comes out every night to watch over you. She never forgets you and never will.'

Flo felt her eyes fill with tears.

'I didn't know you'd lost your mother,' she said. 'You poor thing.'

He shrugged. 'I haven't told anyone before. You're the first.'

'Well this is a night for finding out about you,' she said.

She kissed him tenderly and then with more feeling.

'You're a good kisser,' she said when they finally broke their embrace.

'Thank you.'

He paused and bit his lip. Then he made his decision.

'I've not had many girl-friends before, Flo. In fact, you're the first.'

'I know.'

He looked at her in surprise.

'You know? But how?'

She gave him a quick kiss. 'I could tell. Don't ask me how.'

She gave him a rather strange look. 'Actually I'm rather flattered.'

His heart hammered. 'So you don't think I'm a bit of a drip? Not really a man?'

She pulled him close and squeezed him tight. 'How could I think that, silly. When you go up in your Spitfire day after day and face the enemy. You're not just a man, you're a very brave one.'

He laughed loudly, a great gust of mingled joy and relief.

She closed her eyes and rested her head upon his shoulder.

After a little while she whispered. 'I've got some leave soon. If you could wangle it, we could go into town for the evening. Maybe see my mum and dad.'

His mouth opened but no words came.

The thought of seeing her parents was terrifying. Yet, at the same time, he was happy for it meant that she thought he was her special boy.

'Go and see your parents? You and me?'

'Yes. My Uncle Ted's got a pub with a few rooms. I'll ask him to put you up for the night. That way we can have a real good evening of it.'

'Oh yes please,' he said. 'Oh very yes please.'

FAREWELL TO NASH

3rd September 1940

'Well done, chaps,' Tony Nash said. 'I make it one definite and a probable.'

'I'm not sure about the probable,' Frank said. 'I think the Hurricane may have got it.'

'You're too bloody honest, Trent,' Buckingham said.

'That's us Canadians for you.'

Harry laughed aloud at his words. Frank was certainly not honest in claiming he was Canadian.

'Back to base, gentlemen,' Nash said. 'I'll see you in the Good Intent at nineteen hundred hours. The first round is on me.'

The squadron made a lazy circle and headed back towards Hornchurch. The skies were clear of planes and it was a wonderful evening.

Suddenly Harry cried out. 'Tony, on your tail.'

The Messerschmitt had come from nowhere. Its young pilot had got separated in the melee and got lost. He had finally found his bearing and was on his way home when he saw the squadron streaming back towards their base.

Still smarting from his failure in the battle, he chanced one last attack on the solitary Spitfire bringing up the rear of the squadron.

It was a lucky shot. His bullets tore into the cockpit.

The squadron watched Nash's plane plunge in horror. They kept their eyes on it, praying that a chute would appear. But it did not and the plane smashed into the earth.

Harry turned, vengeance flooding through his veins, and gave chase to the Messerschmitt.

But he was too late. The plane was too far distant for him to catch.

The squadron flew back to the base in silence. When they were a few minutes away, Buckingham flipped on his radio and reported their loss.

The men climbed from their planes and stood on the tarmac in silence, not able to look at each other. They thought they had lost Nash a fortnight before yet he had proved them wrong.

There would be no return this time.

Two figures walked towards them, Wentworth and the sector controller, Wing Commander Bouchier.

'You're sure of this?' Bouchier asked.

They nodded. 'Five of us saw his plane go down,' Buckingham said.

'He didn't bail out?'

'No, sir.'

The silence hung heavy upon them.

'He's got a wife, sir,' Frank said, at last.

'I know her,' Wentworth murmured. 'I'll telephone her.'

'Doesn't she work at Group HQ?' Bouchier asked.

Wentworth nodded.

'Then best take a plane over there and tell her in person.'

Wentworth hurried over towards the hangers.

Bouchier turned towards the others, thinking carefully about his words and tone.

'Bad business,' he said. 'Nash was a good man and a fine leader. He'll be missed by everyone at the base but by you most of all.'

He took a deep breath. 'He wouldn't want you to grieve for too long. He did his duty, unflinchingly. We will honour him best by doing the same.'

The men mumbled in agreement.

'He usually stood you a round in the pub didn't he?'

One of the younger men nodded.

Bouchier felt in his pocket and gave Harry a pound note. 'Have a drink to his memory, gentlemen. And have a good rest tonight.'

The squadron trudged down to the Good Intent in silence. They were so distressed, none of them noticed that Buckingham was not with them.

When they reached the pub, Frank put his hand on Harry's arm, delaying him until the rest of the men had gone in.

'I hope they make you Squadron Leader,' he said.

Harry looked astonished. 'Me? I've only just become a Flying Officer. There's no chance.'

'You're a bloody good pilot. And the men would follow you.'

Harry shook his head and laughed. 'We're not a republic, Frank. It doesn't matter what the men think.'

'So only the views of the top brass count?'

Harry shrugged. 'And what school a person went to.'

Frank shook his head in disbelief. 'If that's the case, then Buckingham should be a shoo-in. He might not be as good a pilot but he's one rank higher than you and I'm guessing he went to a better school.'

'An open and shut case. They won't even look at me.'

'Are you disappointed?'

Harry shook his head. 'Buckingham's welcome to it. He's wanted it all along. Pity he's such a bastard though.'

Frank stared at him for a moment, wondering if Buckingham being promoted might make him suddenly discover his own ambition.

Harry pushed open the door and they went in.

The landlord had been changing the barrel. He hurried into the bar and gave them a cheery welcome. Then he checked himself and scrutinised the men.

'Your Squadron Leader?' he asked, quietly.

Harry felt a huge lump in his stomach, heavy and cold as a stone. He kept trying to remember the first day he saw Nash, the first words they had exchanged. But he could not recall them at all.

Harry passed Bouchier's pound note over the bar. The landlord knew the men's orders by heart and silently began to get their drinks.

Harry took his pint of mild and led the way outside.

The sky was still bright and clear. Before the war he welcomed clear skies with delight. Now he knew that they heralded only danger and death.

He raised his glass in the air and sensed several of the other men doing the same.

'Tony was a good man,' he said. 'And a very good squadron leader.'

The others murmured in agreement and began to drink. None noticed that Buckingham was not with them.

Wentworth marched towards the administrative buildings at Uxbridge. He felt sick inside. He did not know Evelyn Nash very well, having met her only once or twice. But she had seemed very pleasant, full of spirit and rather feisty. She would need all these qualities and more in the days ahead. He opened the door to the operations room and looked around for her.

She was putting a document in an envelope when she happened to glance up and see him. Something in his look made her stop what she was doing.

Everything around her faded into a dim sepia morass. The only thing she could see was Wentworth as he approached; his determined step, his upright bearing and, in stark contrast, the look of sympathy on his face.

'It's Tony,' she said.

He took her hand. 'I'm afraid so, Evelyn.'

'Wounded? Burned?'

He shook his head. 'He didn't make it. I'm sorry.'

Tears blinded her vision. She thought she would fall and reached behind for the desk to steady herself.

'Is this definite?' She heard herself ask the question. It sounded like it was coming from miles away and not her own voice at all.

'I'm afraid so. Half his squadron confirmed it.'

'We should have stayed in the States,' she mumbled. Yet she knew that this would have been impossible for Tony to have even considered for a moment.

'If there's anything I can do…' Wentworth began.

She tried to answer but her tongue felt immense and unwilling to act for her anymore. She managed a brief nod.

Then she felt an arm around her.

'Sit down,' Claire murmured in her ear. 'Sit here for a while.'

She found herself being lowered into a chair.

'A cigarette,' she managed to mutter.

Wentworth produced one in a moment, put it in her lips and lit it.

'Thank you for coming, Wing Commander,' Claire said.

Wentworth nodded. He gestured to the exit.

'Yes, of course,' Claire said. 'They'll need you back at the airfield.'

Wentworth touched Evelyn briefly on the shoulder and made his way out.

Evelyn felt her heart begin to clench, unclench and clench again so tight it felt like an angry fist punching wildly.

And then she sobbed. A tiny, almost silent sob. The tears fell more swiftly then and she grabbed hold of Claire's hand. She felt as if she were drowning.

'Shall I take you back to your room?' Claire asked.

'No.' Her voice sounded panicky, terrified. 'I don't want to be alone.'

Claire glanced at Johnny. 'Fetch Jacqueline,' she mouthed. Evelyn would need her friends around her now.

Suddenly Evelyn looked up. 'I'm not going back, Claire. I'm not going back to the States. I'm going to stay here and work and toil until those bastards are defeated.'

Claire squeezed her hand tightly.

'It's what Tony would have wanted,' Evelyn whispered. And then she began to weep without cease.

A NEW
SQUADRON LEADER

3rd and 4th September 1940

Rupert Buckingham left Wing Commander Bouchier's office and headed across the airfield. His mind was in a turmoil. He had wanted to be a Squadron Leader for a long while now, wanted to be promoted even higher, in fact. He had always assumed that the process would be an ineluctable one of moving from squadron to squadron, taking the place of a man who had been promoted elsewhere. But he had never considered that he would get the job because his own Squadron Leader had been killed. It felt like he was filling the dead man's shoes.

He'd admired Tony Nash, he liked him. And he knew that he would be a hard act to follow. His superiors had valued him, his men had trusted him completely. Yes. A bloody hard act to follow.

Forty Spitfires were lined up on the runway and he paused to stare at them. The people of England thought they were like the steeds of knights of old; noble, fearless, loyal to their masters. Those who flew them were well aware that they were responsive, graceful, superb planes. Yet they also knew that they were agents of death; honed to perfection as killing machines. If not of the Germans then of any man lacking the skill to fly them.

He gave a grim smile. He knew that he was an extremely accomplished pilot, one of the best. Quick to sum up a situation, able at a glance to identify the most promising targets, swift to pursue them and fearless in the attack.

He was a far better pilot than Nash had ever been. In fact, Nash had told him so on numerous occasions.

At such times he had prickled a little, suspicious that Nash thought of him solely as a fighter, well suited to take part in any battle but not fit to lead it. Well, he would prove otherwise. He would show everyone that he had what it took to be both a deadly fighter and a first-class leader.

A flock of starlings surged across the sky. He watched them for a long while, marvelled at their astonishing acrobatic dance. The world seemed quiet and peaceful now, and the calm seemed to reach out and caress him. He knew it was an illusion but for the moment he savoured it.

He took a deep breath and continued on his way.

Most of the squadron were already in the Good Intent, subdued, nursing their beers. Their eyes followed him as he entered. He stopped in his stride for a moment, wondering how best to announce that he had been made Squadron Leader. What combination of humility and confidence would work best for him.

'I hear congratulations are in order,' Frank Trent said.

Buckingham's mouth opened wide. Trent had robbed him of the opportunity to make a good impression.

'You've heard?' His tone was a little aggrieved at being robbed of making the announcement himself.

'The news got here quicker than you did.'

Buckingham cursed himself for spending so long watching the starlings fly. The men looked at him, expectantly.

It took him a while to think of something to say. 'Tony Nash will be a hard act to follow.'

He expected a chorus of voices saying that he would do well, that he would be a splendid squadron leader. But the men merely nodded, gloomily.

'Nash was an excellent leader,' Tomasz said. He raised his glass. 'Salut, Nash and find peace. We will avenge you.'

The others repeated his words. Buckingham joined in the chorus of praise, at the same time realising that he alone did not have a drink with which to salute his lost leader. Then it came to him.

'I think Tony deserves to be remembered in splendid fashion,' he said. 'All the drinks are on me.'

A few cheered loudly, some clapped him on the back. Yet, even so, there were a few less friendly glances, as if they suspected he was trying to buy their favour.

He collected a beer from the bar. He would telephone his sister later, he thought. Tell her the news. She, at least, would be unstinting in her congratulations.

The scramble came at 7.00 the next morning. Buckingham led the run to the Spitfires. He tried to recall if Nash had called out as he ran, words of encouragement, words of good cheer.

He'd reached the plane before he remembered that Nash always made some disparaging quip about the Germans. Too late to do the same thing now.

He paused on the wing, turned round and raised both his thumbs in the air. Half of the men didn't see him. The rest returned his thumbs up. It was something.

'Good luck, sir,' the corporal said as he helped strap him in. 'You'll be fine.'

Buckingham almost choked at his words. At least someone showed confidence in him.

He waved for the chocks to be removed and accelerated along the runway. He pushed the plane hard and was the first into the air. He switched on his headphones and listened to the instructions from the controller.

He opened up his channels. 'Squadron Leader here. There are bandits over Folkestone, heading this way. Let's go and say hello.'

He led them in a steep climb, setting a southward course.

Five minutes later, Frank Trent called out. 'Bandits below, Squadron Leader.'

'They look to be headed towards Chatham,' Buckingham replied. 'Let's give them a surprise.'

He led the squadron in an easterly loop to bring them above the German flank. He meant to disperse them before they had a chance of dropping any bombs on the town.

Suddenly, Harry Smith called, 'Heinkels heading for RAF Gravesend.'

Buckingham was startled, so intent was he on the Dorniers heading for Chatham. He searched the sky desperately for sight of the Heinkels but a bank of cloud restricted his view.

'Maintain course for Chatham,' he ordered.

'The Heinkels are approaching Gravesend,' Harry called.

'I can't see them, Smith. Maintain present course.'

There was a moment's silence and then Harry spoke once more. 'I could take my flight to intercept them.'

'I've given the squadron my orders,' Buckingham snapped. 'Attack the bandits over Chatham.'

'RAF Gravesend here,' came a voice over the radio. 'A swarm of Heinkels are heading our way. Can you intercept?'

'Is it okay if I go now?' Smith said.

He turned off his radio before Buckingham could reply and dived towards the Heinkels, followed a moment later by the other two planes of his section.

Buckingham's hands clenched in rage but he mastered himself and got ready to lead the attack on the Messerschmitts over Chatham. He glanced around and saw that his squadron was the only one in the area.

'There's no Hurricanes here,' he called. 'We shall have to go for the bombers.'

'Frank and I can hold off the Messerschmitts,' Tomasz called.

'Right ho. Tally Ho the rest of us.'

He aimed his plane at the nearest bomber.

Five thousand feet below, Harry pushed his plane into an even faster dive. He caught the Heinkels completely unawares. His fire raked one of the bombers and caused it serious damage. A newcomer, Bert Fowler, finished if off and then destroyed a second bomber.

'That's your fifth, Bert,' Harry called. 'You're officially an ace.'

They were almost his last words. A Messerschmitt pounced upon him from nowhere. He wrenched his stick and got away.

His course took him into the main pack of bombers and he hurtled towards them. The German pilots saw there were only three Spitfires attacking but assumed there must be others nearby. They darted away in panic and raced for home, dropping their bombs in the Thames estuary.

'Well done, lads,' Harry said. 'Let's get back to the others.'

They reached the rest of the squadron as they were tearing into the bomber force. 'Bert, go and help Frank and Buckingham' he ordered. 'Carter with me and at the Dorniers.'

In two minutes, three of the bombers had been damaged and one destroyed. The rest continued gamely on to Chatham but in their panic they dropped their bombs wildly, completely missing the Naval dockyard.

'Back to base,' Buckingham said. His voice was hard and cold.

As soon as they landed he stormed over to Harry Smith.

'What the hell do you think you were doing?' he demanded. 'I told you to attack the raiders over Chatham.'

'Gravesend sounded desperate,' Harry replied. He was about to pretend that he had lost radio contact but decided it would be wiser not to.

'So you thought you could ignore my orders?'

Harry looked him in the eye but did not reply.

'I see,' Buckingham railed. 'Dumb bloody insolence. The working man's favourite weapon.'

The rest of the men shifted from foot to foot with embarrassment. They did not wish to be party to such a public dressing-down.

Harry Smith crossed his arms and waited for Buckingham to say more. But instead he marched off towards headquarters.

'You shouldn't have done that, Harry,' Frank said. 'You should have maintained formation with the rest of us.'

'Probably. But if Nash had still been here he wouldn't have reacted in that manner.'

'Are you sure? You disobeyed orders.'

Harry shrugged. 'Heat of the moment, mate.'

Frank shook his head, a slight look of dismay on his face.

———

'He bloody well disobeyed my orders,' Buckingham repeated.

Wing Commander Wentworth frowned. 'That's erm, that's not good. Not good at all.'

'Then what will you do about it, sir?' Buckingham's rage was so intense he could not stop pacing the room.

Wentworth pursed his lips. 'Well Gravesend did ask for assistance. And your squadron was the only one that could give it.'

'But my orders were clear. Attack the Dorniers over Chatham.'

Wentworth half lifted his hand, part in agreement, part to try to calm him.

'I followed the controller's orders,' Buckingham continued. 'I have every right to expect my men to follow mine.'

'You're right. You do.' Wentworth was acutely aware that Buckingham was in a dreadful position. It would be a disaster if he were seen as an easy touch, a new Squadron Leader who could be defied at will. His mind ran over what steps to take to deal with it.

'I want Smith in front of a court-martial,' Buckingham said.

Wentworth looked astonished. He rubbed his chin slowly, wondering how best to answer.

'You've every right to demand this —'

'I know I have, sir. And it will be best for the other men.'

Wentworth gave him a hard look. 'I hadn't quite finished, Squadron Leader.'

He kept silent for a moment, holding Buckingham's gaze. 'You've every right to demand a court-martial. That's absolutely the case. But I have to advise that it's perhaps not the wisest thing to do.'

'Whyever not?'

'Harry Smith is a popular chap. And it might seem a little hasty for his new Squadron Leader to want to press charges against him. A little lacking in perspective.'

'But he disobeyed orders.'

'Indeed he did. And that is not to be condoned.'

He was already thinking what other punishment would be more suitable.

'And reducing his rank would not be sensible,' he continued, keen to forestall any such suggestion from Buckingham. 'It would throw your whole command structure to smithereens.'

'What then?'

Wentworth took off his cap and scratched his head furiously. 'I'll talk to him.'

'Talk to him? And that's it?'

'Look, Buckingham, I know you're upset. But this is an issue we want to nip in the bud, not one we want to make worse. So I'll talk to him and I promise I shall come up with some suitable punishment.'

Buckingham gave a stiff salute and left the room, slamming the door behind him.

'Dismissed,' Wentworth said wearily to the door. He could well do without this.

He called his corporal in. 'Fetch Flight Lieutenant Smith. Straight away.'

The door opened almost immediately. 'He was just outside, sir,' the corporal said, before quickly dodging out of the room.

Harry saluted. Wentworth got to his feet and glared at him.

'What the hell do you think you were doing?' he demanded.

'I'm sorry, sir,' Harry replied. 'I have no excuse. I shouldn't have gone for the Heinkels.'

Wentworth scowled. It was always more difficult to harangue a man when he'd admitted he had done something wrong.

'No, you bloody well shouldn't. Not when your commanding officer ordered you otherwise.'

Harry did not reply, although he looked contrite.

'What was the excuse? Problems with your radio?'

Harry gave a ghost of a smile but swiftly hid it.

'You do realise what a devil of a position you've put me in?'

'I do. I'm sorry, sir.'

'I could demote you and it would be totally justified. But I guess it would not be much of a punishment for a man like you. You've never exactly hidden your disdain for rank and titles.'

'I'm sorry if that's the impression I give, sir.'

Wentworth did not reply. He stared at his desk, then pulled out a piece of paper and scribbled on it.

'This is a chit docking your pay for two weeks. You're lucky it's not two months.'

'That's probably as bad as being busted down to Flying Officer, sir.'

'You think you'd only lose the one rank? I'd be quite justified in demoting you to sergeant.'

Smith nodded although both knew that such a dire punishment was not in the power of a Wing Commander.

He pushed the chit over to Smith. 'Take that to the pay clerk.'

'I'd like to apologise to Squadron Leader Buckingham,' he said.

Wentworth's eyes narrowed. He was far from convinced that the apology would be genuine. It was more likely designed to get him out of any further hot water.

'See that you do.' He gave a weary salute and dismissed him.

Harry hurried over to the rest of the squadron and sought out Buckingham. He gave a crisp salute. 'I'd like to apologise, sir. It won't happen again.'

Buckingham stared at him in surprise, unsure if the apology was genuine or not. The rest of the men felt the same. And so, to his surprise, did Harry.

'Apology accepted,' Buckingham said.

There was a palpable sense of relief from the men.

Buckingham reached inside his tunic for a packet of cigarettes and held it out.

'Thank you, sir,' Harry said. 'Don't mind if I do.'

A TRYST

6th September 1940

'Now don't be nervous,' Flo said. Frank's hand was damp with sweat and clung like a limpet to hers.

'I'd rather attack half a dozen a Messerschmitts,' he answered.

She gave him a sweet smile and wondered if that might not actually be the truth.

She pushed open the door and dragged Frank inside.

'Hello Flo,' her mother said. 'Is this him?'

Frank coloured a beetroot hue.

'Good afternoon, Mrs Summers,' he said, aware that he was stuttering a little.

'Handsome isn't he?' her mother said in a playful tone. 'He's quite the proper Brylcreem Boy.'

'Don't be rotten, Maggie,' said a man coming in from the kitchen, wiping his hands on a towel. He was short and fat, with a happy, friendly look. He kissed Flo on the cheek and then held out his hand to Frank.

'George Summers. Pleased to meet you.'

His face showed surprise at how damp Frank's hand was and he wiped his own hand once again.

He looked embarrassed in case Frank had noticed. 'Been gardening,' he explained quickly. 'Have to wash my hands thoroughly or I cop it from the wife.'

He gave his daughter a quizzical look. She normally went for more confident boyfriends. Too confident for his taste in fact. This was one the complete opposite.

'Flo tells me that you're American.'

Frank nodded. It seemed futile to keep up the pretence of being a Canadian.

Flo's brother Raymond, a young boy of about ten, looked Frank up and down. 'Where's your horse then?' he demanded. 'I thought all you Yanks had horses.'

'Cheeky little sod,' Flo said, raising her hand as if about to wallop him.

He poked his tongue out and retreated to what he imagined to be a safe distance.

His father clipped him around the ear.

'Done any flying, Frank?' Mr Summers asked.

'I'm not supposed to say…'

'Official Secrets?'

Frank nodded.

Raymond was immediately all suspicion. 'Why don't you go out with a real pilot, Flo?' he asked. 'One who fights.'

'He is a real bloody pilot, if you must know,' she snapped. 'Goes up to fight the Jerries every day.' She stood a little higher. 'Killed five of them. That makes him an ace.'

Frank went even redder.

'Cor blimey,' Raymond said. 'Killed em dead?'

'Afraid so,' Frank said.

'Then well done, you,' Flo's mother said. 'You're a real hero. You can have Raymond's sausage as a thank you.'

Raymond looked outrage but a glare from his mother stopped him from arguing.

They went into the kitchen and squeezed around a small table. Frank's knees got caught in the cloth and he almost dragged the whole contents of the table to the floor.

'Steady on, son,' George said. 'I hope you're not planning on a dog-fight with my supper.'

The meal was sausage and mash. Frank was given two sausages although he noticed that Flo's mother sliced her own sausage and gave half to Raymond. Sidney, the younger brother, laughed at his short rations so their mother cut a portion from his sausage and put it on Raymond's plate.

'You're handling those sausages like Mr Park does with his squadrons, mum,' Flo said with a laugh. 'Splitting them up, moving them round. You could make an Air Marshal.'

'Marshals are in the Wild West, stupid,' Raymond said, poking out his tongue.

'That's what you think,' Flo said. 'Don't they teach you anything in school?'

'Don't go much,' he said. 'Morning's only for the dration.'

'Duration,' his father said. 'The word's duration. For the duration of the war.'

Raymond shrugged and wolfed down a forkful of mashed potato.

They finished the meal quickly. Frank sipped his cup of tea. It was thin and murky. He guessed that the tea leaves had been used several times.

'Had enough Frank?' Flo's mother said, hoping that he said yes as there was little else to give him.

'Absolutely.' To be honest he had lost much of his appetite since meeting Flo.

'Good. It will line your stomach.' She collected the plates to wash up.

'Flo says you're staying at the Nag's Head,' her father said.

'Yes. Your brother has been very kind. He's letting me stay for nothing.'

'So I hear. He usually charges a pretty penny for his rooms.' He glanced at his daughter. She returned his look with open gaze.

Frank relaxed after his first drink. It was not only Flo's uncle who was generous. Her father made it abundantly clear that Frank was not to pay for anything.

It was a good-humoured, boisterous evening. Flo's Uncle Ted could not look more different than her stout, round-faced father. He was tall and lean with a face like a horse. Yet, despite his reputation as a careful businessman, he made it clear that Frank could have anything he wanted on the house.

'Beer, whisky, brandy, cigarettes, anything you take a fancy to.' He thrust a large tumbler of whisky beside the glass of beer in front of him.

Frank went to pick it up but Flo put her hand on his to stop him. 'You don't want to get tipsy,' she said. 'Not tonight.'

Frank nodded. It would not do to make a fool of himself in front of her family.

'This is my Flo's favourite,' her father called as he sat at the piano and launched into a galloping, off-key rendition of Puttin' on the Ritz.

'I do like this,' Flo said.

'You should stay at the Ritz,' Frank said fervently.

She hit him on the arm. 'As long as you're paying.' She gave him an odd look. 'We could stay in the Honeymoon Suite.'

He looked startled and took a sip of his beer.

The evening wore to a close and the customers began to drift home. George played a final song, covered up the keyboards and approached his family.

'Time we were off home,' he said. He reached for Flo's arm, drew her to her feet and made for the door.

'Nice to meet you, Frank' he called. 'Ted will look after you.'

The pub suddenly seemed empty. Ted came over and gave Frank a grin. 'Your room's at the top of the stairs. Have a good night, son.'

Frank thanked him, grabbed his bag and made his way to the stairs.

Ted began to whistle tunelessly as he tidied up. First the empty glasses which he put in the sink for the cleaner to attend to in the morning. Then the ash-trays which he emptied into a large bin and carried outside to the yard. He took a huge brush and swept up the room, ceasing his whistling to concentrate on getting every bit of dirt up.

Finally, the job done, he got out his keys and went to the door. He was just about to lock it when he gave a tut. 'You'd forget your head,' he murmured, put the keys back in his pocket and went upstairs.

Ten minutes later the door opened and a figure stepped inside.

Flo did not need to put on the light even with the heavy black-out curtains for the pub was like a second home to her. She slipped across the bar, passed the piano and began to climb the stairs.

'Who's that?' Frank asked, sitting up in bed.

'Who do you think,' Flo answered. 'Winston Churchill?'

'What are you doing here?'

'What do you think, silly boy.' She took off her coat and slipped into bed.

'You've got no clothes on,' Frank said in amazement.

'And nor should you,' she said, undoing the buttons of his pyjamas.

The sound of someone rapping on the door woke them.

'Best get home, Flo,' Ted called. 'If your dad finds out you're here he'll have my guts for garters.'

She sat up, rubbing her eyes. Frank stared at her, eyes wide with disbelief and joy.

'Thank you,' he whispered.

'My pleasure,' she said, giving him a peck on the lips. 'And hopefully it won't be the last time.'

She put on her coat and made for the door. She paused for a moment and gave him a thoughtful look. 'And I've still got a hankering for the Honeymoon Suite at the Ritz.' She blew him a kiss and disappeared.

When Frank got downstairs, Ted was nowhere to be seen. A cleaning lady said he'd popped down to the warehouse to order more beer. She put a plate of bread, margarine and jam on a table for him. 'How many sugars in your tea?' she asked.

He ate his meal in silence, still marvelling at the events of the night before.

Like all young men of his age, he had continually talked about sex, thought about sex and constantly rehearsed in his mind what it would be like to have sex. But the reality was more incredible than even his most fervent dreams.

Flo had been wonderful. Apart from her sheer sexiness and fun she had coaxed him and encouraged him, made him get over his nerves.

And she had been - he struggled to decide exactly what she had been for a moment.

Yes, he decided at last. She had been generous with herself. Yes that was it. Generous with herself.

He felt like a god.

The door opened and she walked in.

He leapt to his feet, knocking his plate to the floor in the process.

'The cleaner will see to that,' Flo said. 'We need to get back to the airfield.'

She walked up to him, rather shyly and folded herself into his arms.

'Hello, darling,' she whispered.

He could not find the breath to answer.

'How was your evening?' Betty asked that afternoon.

Flo glanced around to make sure there was no one in earshot.

'It wasn't the evening that was the best part. It was the night.'

Betty's mouth opened wide in astonishment.

'You didn't?'

'I did.' She gave a self-satisfied smile. 'He was lovely. Lovelier than I thought he'd be, in fact.'

Betty blinked in amazement. A hundred questions raced through her head but she didn't think it was her place to ask them.

Finally, one question refused to be stifled.

'Was he your first?'

'Of course not,' Flo said. 'I worked in a betting shop for three years before joining the WAAF. I had lots of boyfriends, including the manager.'

Betty bit her lip. 'And erm…'

'Yeah, I was Frank's first. How sweet.' She touched Betty's arm. 'Don't tell him what I said, though, about my previous times. I told him it was the first time for me as well. Men like to hear that.'

'But won't he guess?'

'I doubt it. I reckon I pulled the wool over his eyes in that regard.'

'So when will you see him again? To walk out I mean.'

'We're going to the pictures tonight. He wants to see some cowboy film so I agreed. Can't stand the things but what can you do?'

Betty sighed. 'And will you get married?'

Flo looked astonished at her question. But before she could answer she realised that she was nodding. Tentatively, uncertain but most definitely nodding.

She put her finger to her mouth in something approaching consternation. Then she reached out and touched Betty's hand.

'Oh no, Betty. I've just realised that I love him.'

She burst out laughing, such a contagious laugh that Betty could not help but join in.

'I'm really happy for you, Flo.'

Flo stopped her laughter and wiped her eyes.

'Not half as happy as I am.'

'WE MUST PULL TOGETHER'

6th September 1940

'I have to go over to Bentley Priory,' Park told Claire. 'Air Chief Marshal Dowding has called a meeting with Air Vice Marshal Leigh-Mallory and myself. He said I was to bring you.'

'Why, sir?'

'I've no idea. Come along.'

Jacqueline Longley was waiting for them on the road outside the Bunker. She gave a crisp salute to Park and an altogether more casual one to Claire.

'Bentley Priory, sir?' she asked.

He nodded.

'Are the other Heads of Group coming, sir?' Claire asked.

'No. Brand and Saul are staying at post.'

He fell silent after this, pondering what the meeting was about.

Dowding was gazing out of the window when they entered his office. He normally wore a thoughtful, almost stern expression but now he looked troubled.

He gestured Park to take one of the two seats in front of his desk.

'And Lamb?' Park asked.

'Over there,' Dowding said, pointing to the little desk opposite. Why isn't Corporal Custance here, she wondered. But then she recalled hearing that his mother had died. First, he was hit by a car and then this. He seemed to have had a lot of bad luck recently.

There came a sharp rap on the door and Air Vice Marshal Leigh-Mallory walked in. This was the second time that Claire had seen him, the last time being February when he had been summoned by Dowding for a dressing-down and left his office spitting blood.

Park had only been an Air Commodore then. Now he was of equal rank to Leigh-Mallory and held an even more vital post. But the atmosphere between the two men was cool, verging on icy.

In all honesty, she felt a little sorry for Leigh-Mallory. Events had turned against him.

He had been promoted to the rank of Air Vice Marshal almost two years before the start of the war and made Head of 12 Group when it was believed that any German raids would come from Germany and fall mainly on his area. He had been one of the youngest Air Vice Marshals in the RAF and his future must have looked golden.

Park, on the other hand, had been promoted to command of 11 Group only this April, a mere four months earlier. The Germans had invaded France shortly after.

This meant the Germans were only twenty-five miles across the English Channel and they launched the majority of their raids on 11 Group, making it the most vital theatre of the war. Leigh-Mallory was said to be manoeuvring to replace Park. Dowding had vetoed it.

'Thank you for coming, gentlemen,' Dowding said. He gave Claire a sharp look. 'You're here to take notes, Lamb.'

'Sorry sir,' she said, fumbling for a pencil and pad.

'As you are aware, gentlemen,' Dowding continued, 'the situation is bleak. Fighter Command has been in action every day since the invasion of France in May. We were badly mauled at Dunkirk and since then, things have only grown worse.'

He fell silent and straightened a piece of paper. It had got unaccountably out of alignment with the angle of the desk.

'Our squadrons in the south are exhausted, utterly exhausted. We've had the luxury of sending them to the north for respite but we've had to curtail the length of time they are away.

'Not only this but —'

'We know all this, sir,' Leigh-Mallory said.

Dowding held up his hand to stop him.

'I'm well aware that you know it,' he said. 'Allow me the courtesy of sharing my thoughts.'

Leigh-Mallory reddened. 'Of course, sir.'

'Spitfires and Hurricanes are being lost at a far greater rate than they are being replaced.' Dowding continued. 'In just two weeks Fighter Command has lost 295 planes with 171 badly damaged. One hundred of our pilots have been killed and a hundred more wounded. I gather that some of your squadrons, Park, now have only sixteen pilots attached to them.'

'Yes sir. Ten fewer than the norm.'

Dowding took a deep breath.

'Gentlemen, we have squadrons that have been involved in combat from first light right through until dusk, they have operated like this for weeks on end. And this includes many of our experienced squadrons who we are reliant upon. These men are not immortal, they are human beings. Day after day of prolonged combat has made them exhausted.'

Leigh-Mallory shifted in his seat, believing that he was about to be given a reprimand. And in front of Park and some slip of a girl. It was intolerable.

'That is why,' Dowding continued, 'I have decided that these men must be replaced by men who are fresh. We cannot win if we have pilots who can barely stand up.'

Claire's heart was in her stomach. She knew that things were bad but now that Dowding was emphasising it, they suddenly seemed terribly so. Was he about to tell them that Fighter Command could no longer fight on? That they were finished and the country was now open to German invasion?

Dowding glanced at the two men. 'Because of the utter peril of the situation I have come up with the following.' He gestured to Claire to take down his words.

Both Park and Leigh-Mallory thought that he was about to pronounce on the argument about the use of Big Wings. They began to marshal the arguments for their own case.

But Dowding did not refer to this.

'I have decided', he said, 'to categorise all squadrons across the country, whatever Group they belong to. Category A will consist of all those squadrons in the front line of defence.'

Park and Leigh-Mallory glanced at each other briefly. Did this mean that their commands would be amalgamated? And that someone else would be placed in command?

'Category B,' Dowding continued, 'will be those squadrons that are not in the front line but prepared and ready to be transferred to a front-line airfield.

'Category C will be all those squadrons that have reached exhaustion or have not yet reached the level required for operations in the front line. Squadrons in training, some of the pilots of our allies and those who we would normally deem unfit because of wounds and injuries.'

'What does this mean, exactly, sir?' Park asked. 'For the existing Groups?'

'It means that you two must give thought to which of your squadrons you consider should be in category A, ready for action. And which you shall put in category B, on the back burner, so to speak. Remove the pressure from them and let them know it. If only for a few days.'

'You think this will give them sufficient respite?' Leigh-Mallory asked.

'I hope so.' He glanced away for a moment.

'You may want to consider moving your category A squadrons to more forward airfields' he said to Leigh-Mallory. 'And Park, designate twenty-five percent of your squadrons to category B and move them back out of the hottest spots.'

A long silence filled the room while the two commanders took in the implications of what they had just been told.

'There is more,' Dowding said quietly. 'This is of the greatest secret imaginable and not to be discussed beyond these walls.'

He glanced at Claire who put down her pencil and made to leave the room. But before she could get up, Dowding continued.

'The War Ministry has informed me that tonight they will issue Alert Number 3. Invasion probable within three days.'

Park and Leigh-Mallory exchanged glances. The RAF had failed after all. They had failed to stop the invasion.

Dowding put his hands on the table and stared at them.

'I for one do not believe that an invasion will take place.'

His voice took on a more strident, more urgent tone. 'Fighter Command is not finished. We are exhausted but not finished. And I am convinced that we can fight on.'

The Air Vice Marshals mumbled their agreement.

Dowding stood up and gestured them towards the door. Then he said quietly, 'We must pull together. We must win.' He waved his hand in dismissal.

Claire sat in silence all the way back to Uxbridge.

Invasion probable within three days, the War Ministry had said.

She shuddered at the thought of it.

Polish pilots had told of the cruelty of the German army, of people forced out of their homes, thrown into prison camps, shot on the streets.

It was rumoured that things were better in the other occupied countries. But perhaps the Germans only treated them more leniently because they had surrendered.

Britain's continuing intransigence enraged Hitler, however, and his most recent pronouncements promised only conquest, death and destruction.

She tried to remember what Mr Churchill had said in June about fighting on the beaches, on the landing fields, in the fields and streets. It had all been stirring stuff.

Then, suddenly, there came to her mind, the final part of his speech. Churchill had said that if the country were subjugated and starving, our Empire would carry on the fight. He made it clear he did not believe this would happen. But if this were the case, why did he say such a thing at all?

Subjugated and starving.

She imagined her parents and little brother, no longer safe even in the country. Defeated, despairing and afraid. The quiet streets she had known all her life echoing with the sound of German boots and tanks. The town hall with a huge swastika flag hanging from it. People being rounded up, thrown into camps, murdered.

She felt sick inside.

They reached Uxbridge and walked towards the Bunker. 'Don't forget, what you heard is absolutely top secret,' Park said.

She nodded.

He stopped and touched her on the elbow. 'Sir Hugh knows more about the defences of the country than anyone, even those in the Air

Ministry and the War Cabinet. If he thinks we can fight on then we should believe him.'

'I do, sir,' she said.

Even though she didn't.

NEVER GIVE UP

6th and 7th September 1940

Evelyn packed her case with the essentials. Change of frock, underwear, make-up, a light coat in case the night turned chill.

She picked up a nightdress and felt a terrible despair clutch her. Tony had especially liked that one; it was rather revealing. She held it in her hands for a moment longer but then put it back in the drawer. She pulled out another one which had no special meaning for either of them.

She stared at a photograph of Tony and laid this on top of her clothes.

Then she snapped the case shut and marched out to the bus stop.

Air Vice Marshal Park had given her a week's leave. Not that she needed his permission, of course. Or did she? A frown crossed her face. She was not certain whether she was bound by British regulations or not. But that didn't matter. She would not give up now; would not scurry back to America no matter how much she yearned to. No, she would carry on the fight for Tony's sake.

The bus came and she got on board and climbed the stairs to the top deck. She had felt hemmed-in ever since she had heard of Tony's death. Confined spaces made her feel constrained, almost claustrophobic. Being on the top would, at least, give a clearer view of things.

'Where to, love?' the conductress asked her cheerfully. She was very young, probably not yet twenty. But she was doing her bit, just like everyone.

'I don't really know,' Evelyn said. 'Central London?'

'I can take you as far as Marble Arch.'

'That will do fine.'

'Travelling alone, are you?' the girl asked as she punched the ticket.

The question stabbed Evelyn painfully.

'Yes. Why do you ask?'

'Because there's some wide boys in central London you need to watch out for. Black marketeers, spivs and even worse.' She glanced around. 'They prey on girls like us,' she continued. 'The pretty ones.'

Evelyn forced a smile. 'I don't feel very pretty.'

'Oh but you are.' She counted out the change into her hand. 'Just remember what I say. Keep your eyes peeled for any trouble. I'm afraid this war brings out the worst in some blokes. As soon as they see one of us on her own.'

Thank goodness I'm not on my own, Evelyn thought, I've got... But then she remembered. She was on her own, now. She shivered and turned away from the conductress.

She was not aware of the long drive towards town. The bus seemed trapped in an endless web of streets and shops, houses and gardens. Eventually the houses gave way to large apartment blocks, offices and department stores. She heard a pounding up the steps and the conductress appeared.

'We're at Marble Arch, love,' she said. 'We turn east now and go on to King's Cross and Holloway. So if you want the West End you should get off here.'

Evelyn thanked her and stumbled down the stairs.

The conductress came hurrying after her, carrying her case. 'Here love, you forgot this.' She stared at Evelyn a little anxiously. 'Are you all right?'

Evelyn brushed her fingers through her hair. 'Yes. Absolutely. Couldn't be better.' She took the case and stepped down from the bus.

The streets were emptier than when she had been here last. She stood on the corner, not sure of which way to go or even where she was going. But then she recalled that there were plenty of hotels in Bayswater and she made her way along it.

Ten minutes later she found a rather down-at-heel hotel on the Bayswater Road.

'A single or double?' the manageress asked.

'A double,' she answered automatically.

'Husband joining you later?' the woman asked. Her tone was rather suspicious.

'Actually no he's not. I'll take a single.'

'That will be three and six.' The woman gave her a disdainful look. 'There's no porter to help you with your luggage.'

'The war, I suppose.'

'That's right. The porter joined the Navy. Don't know why. He hated the water, I never saw him wash in all the years he worked here. Talking of which, the bathroom is at the top of the stairs. It's sixpence extra if you want to take a bath.'

Evelyn paid out the sixpence. 'I shall. Thank you.'

The room was on the top floor and it was tiny. In the past, when the hotel had been a family home, it had been the bedroom of the junior maids. Now, because of the room's size and location, it was reserved for travelling salesmen in the main. Or, perhaps, for women the manager considered disreputable.

She put her case on the bed which gave a loud, complaining squeak. She plonked herself beside it. 'Oh Tony, why have you left me?' she murmured.

At seven o clock she realised that she had not eaten all day. Although she did not feel hungry, she thought she had better try to eat something.

There was a Lyons Corner House a little further along the road and she went there. It was homely British food and off ration, so she decided to treat herself to some fish. It was river trout with a rather muddy taste to it. But she forced it down, nevertheless. The coffee she had after the meal was execrable and she felt a sudden longing for home. But no, she told herself, she would stick it out in England.

The bed was uncomfortable and she tossed and turned until the early hours of the morning. She woke at first light with a thumping headache and raw, bleary eyes. Her pillow was damp and she realised she must have been crying in the night.

How can I act like this? she thought angrily. What would Tony think if he saw me moping around?

She went down to the breakfast room where a surly older woman served her one slice of bacon and some concoction of eggs which looked and smelled disgusting.

'It's made from powdered eggs,' she explained, when she saw Evelyn pull a face. 'It's all we can get on account of the war.'

She decided then and there that she would not stay another night. She packed her bag and went to pay her bill. The manager gave her a withering look as if her suspicions about Evelyn being a woman of ill repute were confirmed. But she took her money swiftly enough.

It was a glorious day. She headed up Queensway and stumbled on Whiteleys. It was said to be the largest department store in the world and she could well believe it. There were countless halls, offering a huge range of goods, from food to clothes and household items. But she guessed that the war had made it only a shadow of its former self.

Many of its displays were half empty and the customers seemed lost in the vast space of the store. Nevertheless, she wandered its halls for hours, and had a cup of coffee in one of the cafes overlooking the central atrium. It was the best coffee she had tasted since arriving in England.

She went outside and walked along pleasant streets to the west of the store. Finally, she chanced upon a church with a dome. She smiled to herself. It was Greek Orthodox, and the sign outside proclaimed that it was Saint Sophia's Cathedral. Some of her ancestors had come from Athens. Perhaps she had chanced upon it for a reason.

The outside was rather plain, looking more like an educational institute than a church. But inside took her breath away. The interior was sumptuous, a kaleidoscope of gold and blue with astonishing art-work and gracious, ornate pews and lecterns. She stood beneath a large dome, decorated with benign old men, saints presumably. Looking up at it felt as if she were gazing into heaven.

A sense of peace descended upon her, calm more than peace, acceptance more than calm. She breathed a few words of prayer, not to God or Jesus or any saint, but to Tony.

Then she took a deep breath and left.

The streets nearby felt enclosed after the cathedral. She felt the need for open spaces so she made her way towards Kensington Gardens.

She had strolled here with Tony on crisp early evenings soon after they arrived in England. She had liked the ornamental gardens there and remembered that there was also a statue of Peter Pan nearby. She took a deep breath and strode off in that direction.

There were some gun emplacements on the edges of the Gardens but after she had passed them it took on its more usual look. The grassy fields looked tired and frazzled after such a hot summer, but trees in full leaf cast welcome shade and people sat beneath them snatching a hurried sandwich. She realised that it must be lunchtime although she did not feel the slightest bit hungry. There were fewer children here than when she had last been here, she realised. Many had been evacuated, of course.

The Gardens had never felt quieter or seemed more a haven of peace. Even the hum of traffic was subdued. She might almost have been out in the country. The war seemed a world away.

Two men were walking towards her and slowed as they approached. She suddenly remembered the words of the young bus conductress. She put on her determined, don't mess with me, New York face and picked up speed.

The men stopped as she approached.

'You seem in a hurry, darling,' one of them said. 'Care for a sit down and a chat?' He grinned like a hungry hound might if it chanced upon food.

'I'm meeting my husband,' she said.

She craned her neck and gave a cheery wave to a man a little way away. The two men turned to look at him although, fortunately, too late to see the puzzled look on his face.

She did not give them a second glance but headed towards the man.

'Do I know you?' the stranger asked mildly as she approached. He appeared to be in his late middle years, more her father's age than Tony's.

'No. Sorry, my mistake.'

He glanced towards the two men. 'Are those men bothering you, may I ask?'

She gave a brittle laugh. 'I didn't give them a chance.'

'Well, just to be sure they don't, I'd be honoured to accompany you for a little while. Where are you going?'

She gestured in front of her. 'The place with all the little fountains.'

'Ah, the Italian Gardens. Splendid.' He gave a little chuckle. 'I'm rather fond of them, myself.'

He spoke to her continually as they walked, in a companionable, almost familiar manner. It was almost as if he realised that she did not want to speak much herself.

'My name's Hartley,' he said. 'Leslie Hartley.'

She smiled but did not give him hers.

They reached the gardens and she was disappointed to see that the fountains and water cascade had been turned off.

'It's because of the war,' Hartley said, forlornly. 'There's been so many changes caused by that horrid man, Hitler. We were a different country then. Before this wretched war.'

Tears filled her eyes.

'I'm dreadfully sorry,' he said. 'You've lost somebody.'

She nodded. 'My husband. He was a fighter pilot.'

Hartley looked up at the sky, almost as if he might discover her husband there. 'Please accept my condolences,' he murmured.

She took a deep breath. 'Isn't there a statue near here? Of Peter Pan?'

'Yes, indeed,' Hartley said eagerly, glad of the change of topic.

They strolled down a path until they came upon the statue.

Evelyn stared at it in silence for a while.

'It's lovely,' she said, finally. 'Tony, my husband, said he wanted to be Peter Pan when he was a boy. He brought me here once.'

Hartley touched her hand fleetingly. 'It's a good place for kind and lovely memories.'

He pointed to the statue. 'I like that Peter's holding his pipe with his left hand while his right seems to be dancing in air, almost like he's conducting a secret orchestra.'

'Dancing in air,' she said, softly.

She stared at the statue in silence.

After a little while Hartley pointed to the west. 'J.M. Barrie lived a little way further along.'

Evelyn looked perplexed.

'J.M. Barrie, the author. The man who wrote Peter Pan. He lived in a lovely house overlooking the park. When he met the boys who inspired Peter Pan.'

'Does he still live there?'

'He died a few years ago, I'm afraid.'

'You sound as if you knew him.'

Hartley nodded. 'I did a little. I know his secretary better, Cynthia.'

'And how did you come to know such a famous author, Mr Hartley?'

He blushed slightly. 'I write a little myself. Short stories and a novella.' He gave a rueful smile. 'I was once dubbed one of the most promising writing talents in England. But that was a dozen years ago, I'm afraid.'

He gave her a thoughtful look. 'But I'm still writing,' he said finally. 'For the last fifteen years I've been working on a novel about my sister and myself as children.'

He gazed at Evelyn. 'It's important never to give up, my dear. Vital, in fact.'

Tears filled her eyes.

He took her hand and squeezed it. 'Would you care for a cup of tea?' he asked gently. 'There's a cafe in the park.'

'No thank you, I need to walk.'

He reached inside his jacket and gave her a little card. 'If you ever need a chat or a cup of tea, just give me a call.'

She was too touched by his kindness to say anything for she thought she might begin to cry.

She walked along the south bank of the Serpentine, almost to its end. She sat on a deck chair and watched the swans and ducks moving across the water. They were not concerned with the doings of humanity, she thought. Lucky them.

She remained there for almost half an hour when she had a sudden idea and rummaged in her handbag. She found her diary, looking for the address of Tony's parents. But she realised that she had forgotten to write it down.

Then she remembered that his father's church was in the East End. She racked her brain for its name but nothing came. Eventually she recalled that it was in Cable Street. Mr Nash had been very proud that the local people had halted the Black Shirts' march there.

She would go there and see him, tell him about Tony. She felt guilty that she had not thought of this before.

———

Claire saw the first indication of a raid just before noon. 'It looks like a small formation a mile or so from the coast,' she said to Park.

'Probably trying to draw our fighters out,' he replied.

'66 squadron are on patrol near there,' Willoughby de Broke said. 'Shall I send them to intercept?'

Park nodded. 'But just them. And remind them that our aim is to destroy bombers and not fighters.'

'You'd better go if you're to join Air Chief Marshal Dowding for lunch, sir,' Claire said.

Park nodded, put on his cap and made for the door. He paused on the threshold.

'Lamb, remind all controllers and squadron commanders that, wherever possible, they must attack with two squadrons, one Hurricane to target the bombers and one Spitfire for the fighters. They are to obey my orders exactly, and without any modification. We'll lose too many planes and pilots otherwise.'

'He's a bit grumpy,' Johnny said when he had disappeared.

'Show some respect, Longley,' de Broke said.

'Yes, sir.' He raised an eyebrow. 'I guess the Air Vice Marshal is under a lot of pressure.'

'You'll be under even more if you repeat such a thing,' de Broke said.

Park reached Bentley Priory just after 1.00. It was a lovely afternoon with only a few wisps of cloud in the sky. Some of the staff were on the lawns beside the main house, sipping tea and smoking cigarettes, taking advantage of the warm weather. They got to their feet when they saw him but he gestured to them to relax.

'A pleasant day, Park,' a familiar voice called.

To Park's surprise, Dowding was also outside enjoying the sun, standing by the entrance and gazing at the surroundings.

Park recalled that he had been a very athletic man, in his youth. Being chained to a desk all day must be quite unpalatable to him.

'A pleasant day and a very quiet one, sir. Only one small raid so far today.'

Dowding grunted. 'Good. It gives everyone the chance of a break.' He glanced along the drive. 'I'm expecting visitors.'

A ministry car drove up and a dapper figure with a lugubrious face stepped out. Sir Archibald Sinclair was Secretary of State for Air and a close personal friend of Churchill. It was vital that he be treated well.

Dowding held out his hand. 'Welcome, Sir Archibald. Luncheon is ready if you are.'

'Delightful.' He gave a smile which lit up his face. 'I usually grab something on the run as I'm sure you chaps do. Although, somehow this never seems to apply to Winston. He always finds time for a first-class meal.'

They took their seats in the dining room. 'Sholto Douglas had planned to join us,' Sinclair said, 'but I'm afraid he couldn't make it.'

'Ah,' said Dowding.

Park unfolded his napkin thoughtfully. He should try to find out if there was any special connection between Sinclair and Sholto Douglas. Perhaps sound out Johnny Longley. If anyone were to know such gossip, he would.

The luncheon was a very pleasant occasion. For a politician, Sinclair was remarkably well informed about operations and asked focused and sensible questions.

The one point he kept coming back to was what Fighter Command would do if there were an invasion in the next few days.

'A two-pronged strategy, Sir Archibald,' Dowding said. 'Assist Coastal and Bomber Commands if they need help attacking the invasion force. And, more importantly, we shall continue to knock the bombers and fighters out of the sky. Stop them from seizing control of the air.'

He paused. 'If we fail, I fear we will lose the war.'

Sinclair nodded, glumly. 'And your airfields? How are they standing up to the attacks?'

'They're carrying on, despite the damage,' Park said. 'We won't let the Luftwaffe beat us.'

'Glad to hear it.' Sinclair raised his glass. 'Your health, gentlemen. You and your staff are doing an excellent job.'

They concluded the visit with a tour of the operations room. As they left, Sinclair shook their hands.

'We're glad that your retirement was postponed, Sir Hugh,' he said. 'Not what you were expecting, I suppose?'

'True. I was looking forward to a quiet retirement, fishing and skiing. But we must all do our duty.'

'And now you sound like Nelson,' Sinclair said with a laugh, heading towards his car.

'Was I diplomatic enough, Keith?' Dowding asked as they watched his car disappear from view.

Park looked surprised, both at the question and even more at Dowding's use of his first name.

'Exceptionally so, sir.'

'You mean for me?' Dowding gave him a rare smile.

Then he frowned, recalling what Park had told him earlier. 'You said there had only been one small raid today. That's odd.'

'Let's enjoy it while we can, sir.'

Dowding rubbed his eyes wearily. 'Will you stop for a little longer, Park? Maybe have a little snifter at seven or so.'

'I'd be delighted, sir.'

'Let's just pop back to the operations room,' Dowding said.

They got there at 15.45. The duty controller was lounging casually in a seat above the operations room. He looked a little guilty when he noticed Dowding and Park and hurried over to join them.

'It's very quiet, sir,' he said.

'Hmm,' Dowding said. 'A bit worrying, don't you think?'

'Possibly, sir. But fingers crossed.'

Park glanced at the room below. The WAAFs were sitting around the empty plotting table, chatting quietly. Some were sipping cups of tea, a few even reading newspapers. Nevertheless, most of them still had their headsets around their necks with a couple of girls still wearing them over their ears.

Five minutes later, one of the plotters put her hand to her headphones. At the same time, she reached into a tray and picked up one of the markers indicating the number and height of approaching aircraft. She placed them on to a small plaque and used her long pole to push it across the map table, just north of the French coast.

The rest of the plotters were also on their feet and reaching for their poles.

'Perhaps I spoke too soon,' the duty controller said.

Within five minutes there were more plaques on the map, showing increasing numbers of aircraft approaching.

'Have you got a good man back at Uxbridge?' Dowding asked Park.

'Willoughby de Broke.'

'Excellent. Then you'd best stay here. You can keep in touch by telephone.'

Fifteen minutes later, the duty controller spoke. 'Maidstone Observer Corps have said they've spotted a hundred Germans.'

The plotters were intently shifting the plaques across the map.

The telephone rang again and the controller listened for a moment. 'Make that two hundred plus,' he said.

A few seconds later the phone rang again. The controller's face grew incredulous. 'You're certain? Three hundred plus and building?'

Down below the plotters were working at a furious pace.

Within minutes they could see that over a thousand enemy planes were crossing the coast.

Park picked up a phone and spoke with his headquarters. Within the next twenty minutes thirteen of his squadrons were airborne with a further five on their way from 10 and 12 Groups.

The German force had split up by this time and were heading in different directions.

'They seem to be going for all your airfields, sir,' the duty controller said to Park.

But soon after, they appeared to be changing targets.

One large group headed north-east as if intent on attacking the airfields of Essex and East Anglia. Another headed west towards London.

Shortly afterwards, an even bigger German armada arrived. The whole of southern England was under attack. The German planes were stacked one and a half miles in height and covered eight hundred square miles of sky.

The large formation split into smaller groups. One group flew north-west, banked over Guildford, then turned back towards west London.

'Good God,' Dowding said. 'It looks like they're heading for us. Tin hats everyone.'

The planes passed by, however, and headed east towards the docks.

'They're wrong-footing us,' Park cursed. 'Where the hell are Leigh-Mallory's squadrons?'

'They're forming a Big Wing, sir,' one of the controllers said. 'Douglas Bader and two squadrons are airborne but they've slowed down to wait for a third.'

'Christ in heaven,' Park said.

The British could not get through to the bombers because they were outnumbered ten to one by German fighters and could only snipe at their flanks. The major success came when a Polish Hurricane squadron worked with a Spitfire squadron, destroying a total of eleven bombers.

'Bader's Big Wing has been attacked,' a controller said, 'and they won't get to their vectored position over Maidstone.'

'Then tell them to go to the estuary,' Park said, 'and shoot down anything they can find.'

But it was all too late. The bombers launched a storm of bombs and incendiaries on the docks and oil storage tanks along the Thames. Those that missed their targets destroyed and damaged hundreds of houses and factories in the East End and beyond.

Canning Town, East Ham, West Ham, Poplar, Stratford, Wapping and Whitechapel were all ablaze. It was horrifying.

As the sun went down, Park and Dowding went outside and looked over London. A huge pall of smoke was rising from the fires and the sky glowed an ugly red.

'The bastards have switched to bombing London,' Park whispered. 'But at least they're no longer targeting my airfields.'

Evelyn left Whitechapel Underground station, pulled the slip of paper from her bag and peered at the address. She headed south along Canning Street Road and had almost reached Cable Street when there came the ominous wail of sirens. She automatically reached down for her tin hat and realised she had left hers at headquarters.

An Air Raid Protection Warden came racing along the street. 'Get under cover,' he yelled at her. 'Get to a shelter.'

'I don't know where they are.'

'Gawd help me,' he said. He hurried her to the end of the street and pointed to the right. 'There's a tube station down there. Off with you.'

The words died in his lips as a whistling came overhead. It was too late. He grabbed her by the hand and dragged her to an arch beneath the railway. 'It's the best we can do,' he said.

They pushed themselves to the back of the arch and ducked as the bombs crashed into the houses nearby. Huge amounts of masonry flew everywhere, hurtling into the air and along the streets Luckily, none reached them.

The warden swore under his breath each time an explosion sounded. 'My wife said that being an ARP Warden was a bit of a joke,' he said. 'It doesn't seem so funny now.'

'You saved my life,' she said. 'You should tell her that.' But even as she said it, she half wished he had not bothered.

A bomb landed on a warehouse nearby, crashing through three floors and setting fire to the materials within.

The warden looked horrified. 'There's tea in there,' he said furiously. 'The bloody Jerries are even gunning for my morning cuppa.' He raised his fist at the sky.

The bombing went on for over thirty minutes. At last the thunder of planes and bombs ceased. Now the air was full of bells, police, ambulances and fire engines.

'You wouldn't believe they had so many planes,' the warden muttered as he peered up at the sky. 'We were told the RAF pilots had destroyed most of the Jerry planes.'

'They're doing their best,' Evelyn said. Her voice was angry and bitter. 'Getting terrible injuries, being burnt alive. Losing their lives. They're doing their best.'

He looked at her in astonishment. 'You're right, miss. I'm sorry I suggested otherwise.'

The air raid siren wailed once again and she moved back to the rear of the arch.

'It's the all-clear,' the warden said. 'The bombers have gone.'

He pushed his helmet more firmly on his head. 'I must go and do my duty now, miss. I hope your husband is okay. Fighting the Luftwaffe, I mean.'

How did he know, she wondered.

'There's a church hall just down the road,' he continued. 'Saint Cuthbert's. Go along there and you can get a cup of tea.' He gazed at the burning warehouse. 'If there's any still left, that is.'

He touched her arm and raced off.

She stumbled out of the arch and looked around. The fires had turned the sky a fierce orange. The air tasted acrid and smoky and she almost gagged.

The buildings nearby were terribly damaged. The tea warehouse was engulfed by fire and already a fire crew was battling to put it out. The water gushing from their hoses appeared insignificant against the raging flames.

Many houses had lost their roofs and most of their front walls. Others were completely unscathed. A school had been virtually demolished. Desks, chairs, books and blackboards lay strewn across the playground. Thank God the raid had come in the evening, she thought.

The sound of the emergency vehicles was punctuated by the wails and cries of people nearby. Some were the sounds of terrible injuries. Many were cries of grief as people discovered that loved ones had been killed.

One voice in particular rang loud above the tumult. 'Elsie,' the man called. 'Elsie, where are you?' His cries continued for a very long time.

She picked her way through a mass of bricks and tiles and broken glass. An ambulance man was dealing with an elderly woman who lay on the rubble in front of her house, thrown out from the force of the blast.

'I got under my table, like the wardens told us,' she said, brightly. 'It was just as good as an Anderson shelter.' Her leg was broken but she was too shocked to notice the pain.

Scores of people were crowding into the church hall. They stumbled as they walked, almost as if they had been woken suddenly from the deepest sleep. They looked traumatised, unable to believe what they had just witnessed. Some of the youngest children were crying. A few of the older ones were already running around the hall, many of the boys with arms outstretched, pretending to be Spitfires. Occasionally, they were given a clip around the ear but it didn't seem to stop them.

A long table stood at the rear of the hall. Cheap cups and saucers had been set on it and people were queueing to collect a drink. Two women were wielding huge, heavy metal teapots, battling valiantly to fill the cups.

Evelyn pushed her way through the crowd. 'Do you want some help?' she asked.

'We could do with some help from you Yankees,' one man said bitterly, catching her accent.

'Yes, please,' said one of the women. 'You can bring a jug of milk and more cups. Ignore Bert Higgins, he's a pig.' She gave the man an angry look.

Evelyn collected a jug of milk from the kitchen and heaved it to the table. It was more an urn than a jug and it was all she could do not to spill some.

'Fill the cups, duck,' the woman said.

For the next fifteen minutes all she did was fill cups, collect cups, get more jugs of milk. The British capacity for tea seemed insatiable.

At last, every adult had been given a cup, they had found themselves a space to stand and were sipping quietly at their drinks. Like babies at the bottle, she thought. She found herself smiling, for the first time since she had heard the news of Tony's death.

'Evelyn,' came an astonished voice from the crowd.

'Mr Nash,' she said.

Her father-in-law made his way through the crowd, stepped behind the table and gave her a hug.

The two women beside her raised their eyebrows at this.

'You don't need to say anything,' he said, disengaging from her arms. 'We got a telegram from the authorities.'

'I should have contacted you earlier...'

'You're here now,' he said. 'And we're grateful for it.'

'Would you like a cup of tea, Reverend?' one of the women said, holding up a cup. 'And maybe your friend as well?'

'She's my daughter-in-law,' the vicar said, 'not my friend.'

'Oh.' The woman seemed disappointed.

'Well you are my friend, of course, Evelyn,' he continued, stumbling over his words in embarrassment. 'I meant that we were not just, you know —'

'I understand.' She smiled and her eyes went to the two women. 'And don't worry. A bit of scandal would have brightened their lives. They need it after all this.'

The vicar blushed furiously and sipped his tea, scalding his mouth as he did so.

'You must stay with us,' he said. 'Winifred will be pleased to see you.'

No she won't, Evelyn thought. But she gave him a smile and thanked him.

'I'm so sorry,' he said, touching her hand. 'For you, for Winifred and for Tony, of course.'

'He knew the risks,' she said. 'He was doing his job.' She wondered if her words sounded harder than she intended.

'His duty, yes.' He sipped at his tea. 'I shall miss him very much.'

He wiped a tear from his eye. 'This wretched war. Those wretched Nazis.'

Now she touched his hand to give him comfort.

'I'm sorry for you as well Mr Nash. For you and Mrs Nash.'

He looked pained. 'Don't call us that, please Evelyn. We're family, after all.'

'Then what shall I call you?'

He shrugged. 'Father, perhaps? Or Stanley.'

'Stanley,' she said.

He smiled. 'We'll wait here until people drift off and then try to get home. It's a bit of a walk, I'm afraid.'

'I'd welcome that.'

'In the meanwhile, shall we go into the vestry? Say a prayer for Tony?'

The vestry was tiny and crammed with items intended for physical comfort rather than spiritual. They picked their way past cans of food, blankets, boxes of toys and stacks of toilet paper.

He cleared a little space and got down on his knees. She knelt beside him and he began to pray.

She could not remember the words he said. His prayer was not a formula, not by any means. It was full of love and passion and pride. Full of regret and yet acceptance.

He fell silent, got to his feet, and gazed at her thoughtfully. He held his hand out to her.

'I'm sorry,' she said. 'But that didn't give me any comfort. I feel numb. Just numb.'

He smiled. 'That is God's gift. It's His way of protecting you from the worst pain. When you feel stronger, He will allow you to feel more. Let you feel more grief, more anger, more despair. And eventually you will gain understanding and peace.'

'That all seems a long way off.'

'It is a long road. But God will walk beside you, I guarantee it.' He sighed. 'And now let's go home.'

There was a crescent moon and this, together with the light from the fires in the East End, meant they did not need to use their flash-lights. They arrived at the apartment after an hour.

They found Winifred Nash in the lounge, staring at the red glow from the fires.

'Thank goodness you're safe,' she said. 'I heard about the raids on the wireless. And then I decided to open the curtains and watch.'

'I'm quite all right, Winifred.'

She dragged her gaze from the window and noticed Evelyn.

'How did you get here?' she demanded.

Evelyn felt herself redden a little. 'I went to Mr Nash's church —'

'Canon Nash,' she said.

Evelyn took a deep breath. 'I went to your husband's church to see him.'

'And?'

Evelyn looked nonplussed.

'To see how we were,' Stanley said. 'It was very considerate.'

'We got a telegram about Antony,' Mrs Nash said. 'When did you see him last?'

Evelyn shook her head, not at all certain. 'A few weeks ago, I think.'

Mrs Nash looked away.

Stanley gestured to Evelyn to sit down.

'I suppose you'll get a pension,' Mrs Nash said, with her head still turned away. 'As Antony's widow.'

Evelyn went to answer but shook her head, unable to speak.

'How about a glass of sherry?' Stanley said.

'To toast my son's death?' Mrs Nash said bitterly.

'No,' Evelyn said. There was anger in her voice. 'Your husband and I have just come from the middle of a bombing raid. It was terrible. We could both do with a drink.'

She glared at Mrs Nash. 'And if we are to toast Tony, and perhaps we should, then let it be for his life and his courage and his wonderful nature.'

Mrs Nash did not answer although Evelyn wondered if the light in her eyes were tears or a reflection from the fires.

'You must stay tonight, Evelyn,' Stanley said.

'That's very kind. I shall go back to work tomorrow.'

'Didn't they give you leave?' he asked.

'Yes. But after what I saw tonight, I want to get back on duty.'

Mrs Nash stared at her and said not a word.

⬛

Later that morning Air Vice Marshal Park landed his Hurricane at Uxbridge. He had flown all over London to see for himself what damage had been done. He returned to the Bunker with his face looking worn and dismayed.

'Is that a cup of tea?' he asked Claire.

'Yes, sir. I just made it for Johnny Longley.'

'He can wait.' He took the cup and swallowed a huge mouthful.

Claire gnawed on her lip, anxiously.

'Were you able to see much, sir?' she asked, when he had finished.

'The destruction was terrible, Lamb, truly dreadful. Factories, warehouses and homes destroyed. Streets flattened from Tower Bridge as far as Woolwich.

'It was burning all down the river. It was a horrid sight.' He closed his eyes.

He fell silent, thinking deeply.

'The only consolation,' he said at last, 'is that the Luftwaffe may have switched to attacking London because they believe our airfields have been knocked out. This will buy us some time to get things back in good order.'

'A pity for the Londoners, though, sir.'

Park nodded. 'They're in the front line now, I'm afraid.'

He stoked his chin thoughtfully. 'Can you ask Sir Hugh if he can arrange a meeting with Lord Beaverbrook? We need to speed up our plans to produce night fighters.'

'I didn't know we had any.'

'We haven't. Not yet. But if London's going to avoid destruction, we need to build them pretty damn quick.'

AFTER THE BLITZ

8th September 1940

News about the Blitz came over the wireless the following morning. It was Sunday and Flo and Betty had a rest day so were sitting down to enjoy a more leisurely breakfast.

Flo had just started to scrape the margarine on her toast, chattering away to the other girls about going to the cinema. 'Broadway Melody is on at the Odeon, I think I'll try to catch the matinee. I like Fred Astaire, he's not good looking but he's a lovely dancer —'

'Be quiet, Flo,' Betty said. 'Listen.'

There was something in her voice.

Flo stopped what she was doing and stared at the wireless. The news reader was calm and dispassionate as he gave the details of the raid, the numbers of bombers sent and shot down and the docks, factories and warehouses which had been targeted. Finally, he mentioned the names of the residential areas. West Ham, Silvertown, Canning Town, East Ham, Poplar, Stratford, Wapping and Whitechapel had all been extensively damaged.

'Oh God,' Flo cried, dropping her knife. Her hand went to her mouth and she stared at Betty.

Then she stumbled to her feet. 'I've got to go home,' she said.

Betty raced after her. 'You can't just walk out.'

'Just let them try and stop me.'

'Just hang on a minute.'

Betty ran to the officers' mess. Her immediate superior wasn't there, in fact she didn't recognise anyone. She turned to leave and almost collided with someone she did recognise, the officer in command of the airfield, Wing Commander Bouchier.

'Sorry sir,' she stammered.

'What's the hurry, Corporal?'

'My friend's family are in the East End and she wants to go there to see if they're all right. I came to ask permission of our Section Officer.'

'And has she given it?'

'I couldn't find her, sir.'

He pursed his lips and finally gave a nod. 'In that case, I suppose I shall have to give her permission.' He held her gaze for a moment. 'And I think you'd better go with her.'

She saluted and went to the door.

'What's your names?' he called.

'Corporal Jones. My friend is Flo Summers.'

'Then tell Miss Summers I hope that her family are safe. And she can take two days leave.'

Betty saluted once again and raced out to find Flo.

She found her at the gate arguing with the guard.

The man gave Betty a despairing look. 'Can you tell your friend that they'll have my guts for garters if I let her leave without a chit.'

'We've got better than a chit,' Betty said. 'Wing Commander Bouchier has given us permission to go.'

The guard's eyes narrowed. 'Pull the other one.'

'It's true. I just bumped into him and he said we can go.'

'Where's the chit?'

'He doesn't write chits, you idiot.'

The man heaved a huge sigh. 'It's so unbelievable it must be true. Go on, off with you before I change my mind.'

He opened the gate. 'I hope everyone's safe,' he called as they hurried off.

Flo led them along the street towards Hornchurch Underground Station. Even with its reduced Sunday service it should be quicker than by bus.

They were halfway to the station when a car pulled up and a driver wound down her window. 'Are you Summers and Jones?' she asked.

They nodded.

'Then hop in. Wing Commander Bouchier has told me to take you to London.'

The girls looked at each other in amazement and then climbed in.

Flo squeezed Betty's hand throughout the journey. Her mind was in a panic, maddened with thoughts which could not be stilled or contained.

What if they're terribly injured? What if they're dead? What if I never find them?

Memories of her mother making Sunday dinner returned to her time and time again. Her intense concentration, the continual complaints that she spent hours making dinner yet her refusal of help, nonetheless. The family gobbled it down in next to no time with no thanks, of course, but it was this which gave her the greatest pleasure. Woe betide anyone who left even a morsel on their plates.

What if she's too hurt to ever cook again? Who will look after Dad? Will I have to leave the WAAF to look after him? What if he's hurt? What if he's dead?

Her thoughts circled like a merry-go-round that was not merry at all.

She imagined herself at the morgue identifying her parents and her brothers, their faces cold, white and accusing. She saw herself at the funeral with Betty the only person who came to help her grieve. She saw herself pulling bricks from her demolished house and the calls of her grandmother for her to hurry up before she died.

They looked in horror as they drove through the streets. Flo began to weep, silently, continuously. This was worse than she had even imagined.

'It's up there,' she whispered to the driver.

They turned into Flo's street. It was almost completely destroyed. Every house had its windows blown out, some had no roof. Bricks and roof tiles had been strewn across the street by the force of the bomb blast. There were ambulances everywhere and ARP wardens and police swarming over the rubble searching for anyone buried there.

'My house,' Flo whispered.

She got out of the car and stared at her home. It was a shell. The whole of the front wall had disappeared, revealing every room of the house. The front room was full of dust and debris and little could be discerned there. Yet the bedrooms looked remarkably intact. They could see the beds and the wardrobes, a bedside chair, the pictures on the walls, the chamber pots below the beds. It was terrible to have displayed such a stark, clear view of what had once been a private world.

Flo saw a policeman, hurried over to him and grabbed his hand. 'What about the people who lived there?' she demanded.

'I don't know for sure, miss.' He groaned as he stretched his back. He had been searching for survivors for eight hours now. 'Most people are in the pub on the next street along.'

'The Nag's Head?'

He nodded.

Flo raced off with Betty trying to keep up. The driver followed more slowly, anxious to avoid the rubble in the road.

Her uncle's pub had no windows in it but was otherwise little damaged. Flo took a step towards it and then halted, too fearful to go further. It looked like she would never move again.

Betty took her hand. 'We'll go in now,' she said, gently.

The driver got out of her car and stood beside them. 'I'll wait here,' she said. 'As long as you need.'

Betty pushed open the door and led Flo inside. The room was crowded, as crowded as the year before when they had come for Flo's grandmother's birthday.

Flo pushed her way through the crowd, her eyes darting everywhere.

Betty gazed at the people milling around. They looked exhausted and bewildered. Some were in their ordinary clothes, quite a few in their nightwear. A number had blankets draped around their shoulders yet were shivering uncontrollably.

Many were clutching cups of tea, some chewing on thick slabs of bread. A few were drinking bottles of beer.

Suddenly a voice called out, 'Flo. Flo Summers.' A young woman hurried towards her, with a baby in her arms. She put her hand on Flo's shoulder.

'Do you know where my mum is?' Flo asked.

'She was hurt in the raid,' the woman answered. 'She's been taken to hospital. Don't know which one. She was helping your grandma get to the Anderson Shelter when the bomb dropped. Your grandma is fine.'

'My dad?'

'He's okay. He's gone to the hospital to keep an eye on your mum.'

'Thanks, Connie,' Flo said. 'Are you alright?'

'Not a scratch. Nor the baby.' She squeezed Flo's hand. 'Hope your mum gets better soon, Flo.'

'There's your uncle,' Betty said, nudging Flo.

Ted Summers made his way towards them. He looked filthy and exhausted.

'Hello sweetheart,' he said. 'Has Connie told you?'

Flo nodded. 'She said Mum's gone to the hospital. What happened?'

'The bomb blast took the roof off the house and a chunk of wood hit her in the neck. She's in a lot of pain but cursing Hitler like a trooper.'

Flo gasped. 'That's all right then. I'd be worried if she was quiet.'

'Do you want a drink, sweetheart? It's out of licencing hours but the police are turning a blind eye this morning.'

'On the house? For me and my pal?'

He grinned. 'Of course.'

'Then I'll have a port and lemon.'

He turned to Betty.

'I'll have the same please, Mr Summers.'

Ted led them to the bar and prepared their drinks. 'How did you get here?' he asked.

'One of the officers sent us in a car,' Flo said. 'The top man himself. Ooh. Could the driver have a drink as well?'

'Of course. Is he outside?'

'He's a she, uncle. All the men are flying planes.'

'I'll go and get her,' Betty said.

'We'll all go,' Ted said. 'Get a breath of fresh air.'

The air was anything but fresh. It was hot and heavy with dust from the rubble and smoke from the fires at the docks.

But the scene that confronted them was looking better by the minute. Ambulances had taken the most injured people to hospital and the rest were being tended by first aiders.

Two women had lit a fire under a tin bath and were cooking a huge batch of soup in it.

A policeman approached and gave a doubtful look. 'Get some buckets of water in case you need to put the fire out,' he said. 'And save me a mug.'

A few shops were opening their shutters. 'Sunday trading laws are suspended by order of the King,' one of the shopkeepers called.

'I bloody doubt that,' the policeman muttered as he turned and hurried out of sight.

'Do you want a drink?' Betty asked the driver.

'Not on a Sunday, thanks. My dad's a churchwarden.'

'Get yourself a cup of tea then,' Ted said.

He walked over to Flo and put his arm around her shoulder. She leaned in to him and began to weep.

A small boy came up and regarded her thoughtfully. 'What a sissy. I thought you was in the RAF.'

She reached out and smacked him round the head. 'Don't give me any cheek, Sidney Summers.'

'Oh,' he said, rubbing his head. 'I'll tell mum.'

She folded him in her arms. He glanced around, alarmed in case any of his friends saw him being hugged by his big sister. But they all had concerns of their own.

'We'll grab a bite and then we'll go to the hospital,' Ted said.

'I can take you all,' said the driver as she emerged from the pub with a cup of tea. 'Boy Bouchier's orders.'

'You shouldn't call him Boy,' Betty said in shock.

'Oh, I think he likes it.'

'Soup's ready,' yelled one of the women.

'Okay,' Ted said. 'You can have some of Ethel and Maggie's tin bath soup or one of my meat and onion pies.'

'Pie, please,' Betty said, eyeing the concoction in the bath with alarm.

'Good choice. Come on ladies.'

They grabbed a quick bite and started off to the hospital. Flo's brothers realised that she was going in a car and pleaded to go with her. Their mates clambered onto the running board until the driver said they'd end up in jail if they didn't get off.

The hospital was overflowing with people. Every bed and trolley were being used for the injured, with many more sitting on chairs or even the floor.

'Where can we find Maggie Summers?' Ted asked.

The harassed clerk ran her eyes down the list. 'Queen Mary Ward. Top floor.'

They found her sitting up in bed with a cardigan around her shoulders.

'Flo,' she called, waving her arms frantically. She gave her a stern look as she approached. 'What are you doing here. Shouldn't you be fighting those buggers who did for our house?'

'I'll fight them later, Mum.' She kissed her on the cheek and then gazed around. 'Where's Dad?'

'Gone for a pee. He couldn't hold it any longer.' Her mother gave a broad smile. 'He's been a brick, Flo. Carried me into the shelter out of harm's way. Patched up my neck which was bleeding fit to burst.'

'Will you be all right?'

'So the doctor says. They'll keep me in for an hour to make sure I'm all right and then I can go home.'

Flo sighed. 'There is no home, mum. All the front's been blown off.'

'You can all stay at the pub with me,' Ted said. 'We'll make room, Maggie, never fear. Your mum can come as well, as long as you make sure she doesn't try to drink all my profits.'

'What you doing here, Flo?' came a voice from the door.

'Wondering why you didn't take better care of Mum,' she answered. She got up and hugged her father, giving him a searching look. 'Are you okay?'

'I am. But my greenhouse is just a pile of glass. It was the Chrysan-themum show next week and every last flower's been destroyed. I was in with a good chance to win. Bloody Jerries.'

'He cares more about them ruddy flowers than about me,' her mother said.

'It's 'cause they don't give me any grief,' he said. 'You should learn from them.'

He turned to Flo with a grin. 'She's going to be okay, Flo.'

'Apart from the pain in my neck,' her mother called.

'You shouldn't call Dad that,' Flo said.

They burst out laughing at her joke, so much so that her mother yelped in pain.

'You get on back to work now, girl,' she said. 'Thanks for coming but we'll be all right.'

Flo nodded and made to leave. But her father detained her.

'Just you take care, Florrie,' he whispered. 'What with all these Jerry bombs attacking your airfield.'

'I've got the feeling they may have stopped aiming at us, Dad. It's you lot who will cop it from now on, I reckon. So make sure you get to a shelter in good time.'

'Tell your mother and grandma that,' he said ruefully. 'It's like herding kittens.'

LACK OF MORAL FIBRE

8th – 9th September 1940

Squadron Leader Buckingham gesticulated at the ground crew, desperate for them to speed up. His body was hot, broiling hot, but his head was cold and clammy. Fire and ice, he thought, passion and ruthlessness.

The chocks were pulled away and he began to accelerate, waiting for that exquisite moment when the Spitfire would lift a little, touch down briefly, lift once again and then suddenly soar into the heavens.

Within moments he was climbing furiously, glancing at his altimeter, watching as the needle showed that he was entering the killing field.

He glanced around him, making sure that his squadron were assembled. Automatically they moved into the Vic formation that had been drilled into them. A formation which he believed to be dangerous.

'Finger-four, gentlemen,' he said. 'Finger-four, please.'

'Wilco, skipper,' sounded the voices in his ear, relieved that he was telling them to move into the pattern which experienced pilots considered better than the regulation Vic.

Buckingham felt a thrill of pleasure at their enthusiasm.

Harry Smith was the first to make the manoeuvre which was especially gratifying. He might be a jumped-up little shit but there was no denying that he was a fine pilot. Presumably, that was why Wentworth had promoted him to Flight Lieutenant. A complete mistake, of course, but one he would have to learn to live with.

The squadron sped south towards the approaching Germans. There were fifty bombers with a close escort of about twenty Messerschmitt 109s. Buckingham glanced to his right and saw fighters approaching from the west. He assumed they would be Hurricanes and ordered his men to gain height to attack the German fighters.

For a moment they swept into cloud and were temporarily blinded. But he kept his course and ordered the squadron to follow him. They climbed for ten more seconds

'Don't forget the guns have been harmonised from 750 to 250 yards,' he said. 'Hold your nerve and hold your fire. We'll get more of the bastards this way.'

The men acknowledged his words, a few with excitement, the rest more doubtfully. It might be fine for the better shots in the squadron but flying so close to the German planes seemed hideously dangerous to the others.

He ordered the attack.

The Spitfires dived downward, hurtling out of the cloud a thousand feet above the Messerschmitts. Buckingham aimed for the centre of them, his teeth clenched tight, his finger hovering over the trigger.

He was a thousand yards from them, eight hundred. He cursed when he glimpsed a few of the men beginning to fire too early, despite what he had told them. But he held on, he would show them, he would lead them.

Those last five hundred yards seemed like miles, the seconds like hours. But then he jammed his thumb down. A Messerschmitt immediately burst into flame and he had to swerve like a demon to avoid it. Another German flew into his sights and he aimed a burst at it but missed. The plane banked sharply to flee. But the Spitfire's circle of turn was tighter than the 109s and he was soon on its tail, sending five seconds of fire into the fuselage and wing, five hundred bullets tearing at his foe.

The plane began to plummet, black smoke billowing from it. He glimpsed the canopy open and the pilot try to clamber out. He managed to deploy the chute but the plane was spiralling so quickly the lines got tangled on the wings. The last thing he saw was the pilot being slammed against the body of the plane before it smashed into the cliffs.

The bomber pack had now disintegrated and the Messerschmitts disappeared, their ammunition spent and unable to protect their bombers any longer.

He turned and led the rest of the squadron in pursuit of the bombers. Most were too far off now, but he caught a Heinkel and spewed the last of his ammunition against it although with no effect.

He looked around, saw there were no fighters nearby and ordered the squadron home.

His heart pounded with excitement, so hard and fast he thought it might drown out the noise of the engine.

He felt a raging fire within, a savage, harsh exultation. He had killed, killed again, killed twice. Two less enemies to launch mayhem on the country.

He started to laugh. It was a cold and reckless laugh which went on and on, throughout the flight back, even as he made the descent to the airfield.

He landed, still laughing and coasted to a halt. His face twisted with uncontrollable glee.

But then he shuddered. He felt as if the world were disintegrating around him. Suddenly, his joy fled. There was the taste of ash in his mouth and he thought he would vomit. He looked down and saw that his hands were shaking uncontrollably.

He began to howl, like a dog in the dark midnight. He smashed his hands upon his knees, again and again, heedless of the pain.

And now he wept. The tears came in great, heaving gasps, uncontrollable, unstoppable, as if a dam had burst and the waters were pouring out to engulf every last thing in its path. A deluge which threatened to sweep him away.

He felt rather than heard the canopy being pulled back, saw as if from a vast distance, the frightened looks upon the faces of the ground crew.

'Sir?' one said doubtfully.

He looked at the man and screamed.

Wing Commander Wentworth put down the sheet of paper and sighed. The report spoke of lack of moral fibre. In the last war it would have been called cowardice.

'Buckingham's shot to pieces, Maisfield.' He tapped his head. 'In here.'

'He's had five kills now, sir,' Maisfield said. 'It makes him an ace.'

'Doesn't matter. Lack of moral fibre. Even Dowding won't countenance it and he's soft at heart. You know as well as I do that LMF is like a plague. It can rip through the men in days. And Buckingham being a Squadron Leader makes it worse. He'll have to go.'

Maisfield pursed his lips. 'Who makes the decision, Miles? You or Boy Bouchier?'

Wentworth drummed his fingers upon the desk. 'I give a recommendation. Bouchier makes the final decision.'

Maisfield nodded. The room fell silent apart from the ticking of the clock. He vaguely recalled a film he had seen with the same unrelenting noise, perhaps a film about a murder, perhaps when the judge was about to pronounce the punishment.

'The squadron's already lost Nash. It won't help morale if it were to lose Buckingham too soon.'

Wentworth sniffed. 'But Buckingham's not popular.'

'True. But you know how contrary the men can be. The fact they dislike him will make them rally round him. They have the right to loathe him, we don't.'

Wentworth sighed. Maisfield was right, he thought, wearily.

'So what do you suggest?'

'Send the boy home. Four days of rest and recreation. Hopefully, that will do the trick.'

'And who will take over from him?'

'I recommend Harry Smith.'

Wentworth pulled at his moustache. 'But he started as a sergeant. And before that he was an apprentice at Halton.'

'He's a damned good pilot and the men like him. Respect him. I think he'll make a good Squadron Leader.'

Wentworth looked a little doubtful. 'It won't go down well with the powers that be.' He gave a little laugh. 'Not when they find out that he's has never ridden to hounds.'

'Nor have you or I, Miles.'

'We went to good schools though. What about Smith?'

'An elementary, I expect.' He leaned closer. 'But I'm confident he'll make a good Squadron Leader.'

Wentworth pondered a little longer, then shook his head.

'I don't want any ructions,' he said. 'I'll transfer Watson from 41 Squadron until we hear more about Buckingham. He'll do fine.'

Maisfield looked less than convinced.

━━━

'What are you doing here?' Buckingham's father demanded. He prodded him in the chest. 'Are you wounded? I can't see any wounds.'

'He's here for rest and recreation,' his mother said. 'Isn't that what they call it, Rupert?'

His father did not even look at her. His eyes bored into his son's.

'I've heard less mealy-mouthed names for it, boy,' he said. 'Lack of moral fibre. Although we had a more accurate name in the last war. Cowardice, boy. Cowardice in the face of the enemy.'

Buckingham began to shake. He feared he would start to weep.

'My two brothers, died at the Somme,' his father continued. 'Your uncles.' He held his hand to his forehead. 'The best of my generation died in that war.'

'And yet you survived, father.' Buckingham spoke the words coldly. It was the bravest thing he had ever done. 'You survived.'

His father stared at him as if he could not believe his ears. Then he slapped him hard across the mouth and stormed out of the room.

Buckingham did not move, not even to touch the sting upon his face, did not respond to the sensation of his lips beginning to swell.

His mother gave him a peculiar look, part anguish, part rebuke, and hurried after her husband.

Buckingham gave a derisive laugh and went out in search of his sister.

'Of course you must stay here, Rupie,' his sister said. 'Don't let the old bastard win.' She poured him a gin and tonic which he nursed but did not so much as touch.

She took a long swallow of hers. 'How long is your leave?'

'Five days.' He put down the glass. 'I'm not sure I can last that long, Vi. Not after what he said.'

Tears pricked his eyes now. He wiped them away, angrily. 'If he only knew. If he only knew what we go through. Every day, every bloody day. Two, three, sometimes four sorties a day. Fighting terrible odds. Outnumbered five to one, ten to one, sometimes more.'

She sat next to him and held his hand.

'It must be frightful.' She put her hand to her mouth.

'Goodness, Rupie, I didn't mean anything by that. Didn't mean to imply you were frightened. It's the situation I meant. Frightful, dreadful.'

Buckingham picked up his glass now and took a sip. It seemed to have no taste or kick.

'You spoke truer than you realised, Vi. It was frightful and I was frightened.'

She squeezed his hand fiercely. 'I'm sure you weren't. You're an ace, for goodness sake. You shot down five of the Hun.'

He stared into her face, clinging to it as if it were a life-jacket. 'I was more than frightened, Vi. I was terrified. Absolutely terrified. No words can capture it. Fear, terror, funk, lack of bloody moral fibre. Cowardice. Nothing can describe what I felt.'

He began to weep now, the long pent horror of combat spilling from him as if it were blood.

She knelt and held him, rocking him back and forth as if he were a baby.

'We'll go to Auntie Jessica,' she said. 'You won't have to stay here.'

He shook his head. 'That would be to let him win. I'm not going to do that, Vi. I've been doing it all my life. Not anymore.'

———

That afternoon, Buckingham went into the sitting room and his father folded up his newspaper with studied deliberation, got to his feet and stalked past him without a glance. From that day forward, he refused to be in the same room as him.

Violet shook her head in disgust.

'You'll have to take your meals in the sitting room,' their mother said. 'You can use the card table. I'll get Mrs Baxter to set it up for you.'

'Then I'm going to eat with him,' Violet said.

'Oh darling, you can't.'

'Just try and stop me.'

'But it will drive a wedge between you and your father.'

'He's done that himself. By being so beastly to Rupert.'

Her mother sighed but said nothing more. She had long ago lost any battles against her husband, long ago lost any will to fight.

The next few days were as bad as any of the family could remember.

Taking their meals alone together was the best part of the day for brother and sister. That and walking in the grounds.

On the third day they strolled towards the lake. It was fairly small but when they were children it had felt as big as a sea. There was a little jetty with a rowing boat. It was still tied up but no longer usable. The long years of neglect had made it decay, tarnished its paint work, eaten away at its timbers.

'I used to love this boat,' Rupert said.

'We'd pretend we were pirates,' she said, putting her arm in his. 'Sailing the seven seas to do battle on the Spanish Main.'

She glanced at him. 'Is it really awful?'

He did not answer for a moment. 'Why do you think I'm here, Vi? It's so bloody awful I couldn't take it any longer.'

He bit his lips. 'We have to aim at the Jerries, you see. Aim our Spitfires right at them. We're closing at something like six hundred miles an hour. At three or four hundred yards we've got only seconds before impact. So we blast away for a second and then bank or dive. And pray that the enemy won't perform the same manoeuvre and crash into us.'

He ran his fingers through his hair. 'It's madness. The only way we can fight properly is to virtually commit suicide. Russian roulette but without the safety margin.'

'Then you're not a coward, Rupert. Far from it. I can't imagine the courage it takes.'

'It would take more courage not to do it.'

She frowned and shook her head, not comprehending.

'The other chaps would think you were a yellow belly, Vi. They'd never trust you again, become more distant.'

Like Father, she thought, although she did not say it.

'It's not like here,' he said. 'Not like with Father. The other chaps don't hate someone who's scared because we all experience the same fear. But they're never quite the same with him again. They can no longer fully trust him, you see.'

But even as he said it he wondered if he had ever really experienced that trust. Suddenly, he felt a burning need for it.

They headed back towards the house.

'I wish you'd come for a canter,' Violet said. 'You'd feel much better for it.'

Violet loved to ride and so did Rupert. But when his father had raged at him for refusing to join the Horse Guards he had determined never to ride a horse again.

'You know I can't.'

She sighed. 'Sometimes I think you're every bit as stubborn as father is.'

'Do you really?' He looked horrified at her words, betrayed even.

She punched him on the arm. 'Not really. You're a much nicer person than he is.'

'Not a chip off the old block, then?'

She paused a moment before shaking her head vigorously. 'Of course you're not.'

But he died a little because of the pause.

'I'm going back tomorrow,' he said quietly.

'So soon?'

He nodded. She wanted to dissuade him but realised she shouldn't. 'I'll miss you,' she said.

⬛

Buckingham got back to Hornchurch early the next morning and requested an immediate meeting with Wing Commander Wentworth.

He had woken that morning feeling completely fine. More importantly, he felt desperate to go back to duty and prove his father utterly wrong. He smiled as he drove up to the airfield. His father's vile behaviour had been exactly what he needed to get him to return to duty.

He saluted crisply when he entered the office and then blinked in surprise. Wing Commander Bouchier was sitting in the corner of the room.

'Don't fret,' Wentworth said. 'It's not an interrogation.'

'But the Station Commander —'

'Wanted to see how you were doing,' Bouchier said. 'You've come back early from your leave.'

'I have, sir. I'm feeling much better.'

'I think the doctor will be the best judge of that,' Bouchier said.

'If you say so, sir.'

Wentworth leaned forward, a concerned look on his face. 'The fact of the matter is, Buckingham, that you had a bit of a turn.'

'I know, sir. I think it was because I had a fever.' He tapped his head. 'It affects some people on occasion. But my doctor at home gave me some aspirin and my temperature is fine now.'

Bouchier and Wentworth exchanged looks. Doubtful ones.

'Wait outside, Buckingham,' Bouchier ordered.

He saluted and stepped outside. The typist gave him a brief sympathetic look and returned to her work. He heard the low murmur of his superiors through the door. After five minutes, Wentworth appeared and gestured him back in.

'We want you to pop along to the doc,' he said. 'If you're given the all clear you can go on operations again.'

'But not as Squadron Leader,' Bouchier said. 'Not immediately. If your - fever as you call it, is settled then we'll review our decision.'

'Yes, sir. Very good idea, sir.'

'Dismissed.'

He left the office and cursed. He'd neglected to ask who the acting Squadron Leader was.

ORDEAL

11th September 1940

The morning started very quietly and Park prowled up and down. The previous day he had become convinced that the Luftwaffe command had changed their tactics. Before this week they had launched three or four widely spaced attacks each day, which had tried the nerves of controllers, pilots and ground crew and exhausted their stamina.

But the gaps between the attacks had given Fighter Command vital breathing space in which to ready themselves for the next combat. The Germans appeared to have recognised this. Now they began to deploy mass raids of three hundred planes, sometimes four hundred, in two waves about fifteen minutes apart.

Because of this, Park realised he would have to alter his strategy and had discussed it with Dowding by telephone earlier.

Dowding had decided to come to Uxbridge for the meeting and now sat quietly at the back of the room.

Park rapped on the table for attention and began to outline the change of strategy.

'As you know, the Luftwaffe are hitting us with huge numbers in very quick succession. From now on we need to combat this by resisting the temptations to send too many squadrons to intercept the first attack.

'The second German wave has always been much larger than the first and we need to hold back enough squadrons to tackle this.'

The controllers muttered in agreement. It felt a sensible response to the new situation.

'In what ratio?' a senior man asked.

'40 per cent to tackle the first wave. 60 per cent held back until the second wave arrives. We can review this on a daily basis.'

He paused. 'We're never going to get it completely right because we're having to second-guess our enemy. They've sent up a smaller wave first until today but it doesn't mean they will continue to do so. I certainly wouldn't. I'd keep the enemy guessing.'

'You haven't got the Germanic mind, sir,' de Broke said. 'They keep on going like a steam roller without changing their course. That's even more the case now with the Nazis in control. I'm guessing they don't give their commanders much free rein.'

'Good point,' Park said, although he wished he hadn't used the term steam roller.

Park took a deep breath before continuing. 'There's one other thing. Single squadrons are no longer adequate to deal with such large numbers.

'I want to reiterate that, wherever practicable, two squadrons are to be paired, ideally one of Hurricanes and one of Spitfires. They are to act together with the Hurricanes targeting the bombers and close escort fighters while the Spits gain greater height and pounce on any fighters lurking nearby. The squadrons that are brought to readiness most quickly should attack the first wave of planes.'

He paused. 'I'm not advocating a Big Wing, of course.'

Everyone chuckled at his joke.

'The remaining squadrons should be put on fifteen-minute readiness. They're to attack the second wave when it appears.'

'Will there be any reserve?' de Broke asked.

Here Dowding spoke up. 'The Air Vice Marshal and I have discussed this. We feel that one squadron in five should be held back as a reserve, in readiness to aid squadrons needing further assistance.'

'And,' Park added, 'to provide essential cover of airfields and industrial facilities.'

He glanced at his controllers.

'That seems an excellent plan,' de Broke said.

'Good.'

Park turned to Claire. 'Get this off to all Sector Commanders and controllers. And they are to inform their pilots, every last one of them, of the new tactics.'

Wing Commander Cecil Bouchier listened to the new orders from headquarters and smiled. The last few days had been the worst of the battle so far. Husbanding his squadrons in the way Park described made a lot of sense. It would mean the second wave of Germans would be in for a surprise and more likely to be dispersed.

He called a meeting of his Squadron Leaders, controllers and pilots and told them the news. There were murmurs of agreement and relief. This should give a boost to morale, he thought.

He went back to the operations room. Within an hour there came the call to scramble.

'Which squadrons are ready?' he asked.

'Two from here, a Hurricane Squadron at Hawkinge, and another at Rochford.'

'Send one from here and the one at Rochford. The others to be readied for take off in fifteen minutes.'

'Reserves, sir?'

He glanced at the sector map. 'One of the squadrons from here and a Hurricane squadron at Gravesend.'

He watched as one of his Spitfire squadrons hurtled down the runway. 'Is that Nash's old squadron?' he asked Wentworth.

'Yes.'

'Who's the Squadron Leader? Watson?'

Wentworth shook his head. 'Watson got badly shot up the first time he led the squadron. But Rupert Buckingham seemed absolutely fine on his return to combat. Went at the Jerries like a terrier after rats. The doctor gave him the all clear so I put him back as Squadron Leader.'

Bouchier sighed. It was some relief. He had lost over half his squadron leaders since the beginning of July and every other sector commander reported the same. They were having to make do with less experienced and, sometimes, less suitable men. The loss of so many pilots and planes was bad enough. Losing experienced leaders was even more worrying.

'Let's hope Buckingham remembers he has to lead as well as fight,' Bouchier said. 'The new boys we're getting are greener than ever and they need a hell of a lot of guidance.'

He checked his watch. 'Two minutes from the scramble order to airborne. That's good.'

It was better than good, considering how exhausted the men were.

His eyes wandered to the calendar on the wall. When would autumn come? The deteriorating weather would mean that the threat of invasion would be lifted for six months at least. Equally important, the cloud and storms would provide the respite they so desperately needed.

'Is everybody with me?' Buckingham asked.

Harry and Frank confirmed that they and their flights were right behind him.

'Excellent. Tomasz I want you to ride shotgun.'

'What is shotgun?' the Pole asked. 'Please speak in the King's English.'

'It means riding to one side of the rest of the squadron and keeping watch for the enemy.'

'Why shotgun? Why riding?'

'It's from the Wild West,' Frank explained. 'An armed guard would ride beside a stagecoach and keep his eyes peeled for bandits and hostiles.'

'Shotguns, stagecoaches, peeled eyes,' Tomasz said. 'And to think my compatriots were the ones forced to go to school to learn English.' He gave a derisive scoff and banked off to the right.

They headed over the Thames Estuary, climbing all the time. They levelled off at thirty thousand feet and headed towards the south Kent coast.

They had just passed over Canterbury when Tomasz alerted them to an oncoming mass of bombers with close fighter escort.

Buckingham banked and saw the huge formation of bombers five thousand feet below them.

'Bombers,' he said to his squadron. 'The Hurricanes are going for them, I'm afraid. We've been ordered to keep out of the fray unless we see fighters attacking our Hurricanes.'

He itched to get down amongst the bombers. They seemed like chickens ripe for plucking.

He watched as a Hurricane squadron smashed into them and cast his gaze around for any sign of fighters.

'Messerschmitts to your left,' Tomasz said.

Buckingham saw them, a swarm of twenty Messerschmitt 109s to his left and a little below. He launched himself directly at the foremost fighters, the rest of the squadron following him.

Suddenly, he felt a strange lightness and, at the same time, an incredibly heightened awareness. He felt as if he and his Spitfire were one, joined together.

Not just that, it felt as if the whole world, the sky, the clouds, the earth far below, was now as much a part of him as his hands, his feet, his heart.

'Tally ho,' he cried as he closed on the Germans. The Messerschmitts peeled away.

The two fighter formations swept apart as if in some complex dance, seeking the most advantageous positions.

Tomasz scored a hit and the Messerschmitt exploded. Frank hammered his guns at another, causing enough damage for it to pull out of further conflict.

Another German managed to put two of the Spitfires out of contention but both men managed to bail out. Then it turned and chased after a third victim.

'A Messerschmitt on your tail, Hopkins,' Buckingham called, at the same time rattling his guns at a German.

Hopkins cried out, whether in alarm or terror was impossible to say. He dived, swerved and dived again but to no avail. He was aznovice, the Luftwaffe pilot chasing him a seasoned hunter.

Buckingham realised that Hopkins was a dead man. He had only seconds to live.

He did not think about it but turned and swooped after the Messerschmitt. He opened fire and the German banked savagely to avoid being hit.

'Now get away, Hopkins,' Buckingham yelled.

'Thank you, sir. Oh shit, sir, look out.'

Buckingham saw the Messerschmitt turn and head back towards him, an incredible, almost impossible manoeuvre. He saw the bullets streaming from his guns.

His cockpit glass shattered and then he heard a whoomp like the last bit of water draining from a plug.

His trousers suddenly became wet and for a moment he thought that fear had opened his bladder. But then he saw the fuel from the tank flooding over him.

Another whoomp and the engine exploded. The fuel burst into flame, a searing sheet of agony. His clothes caught fire and the cockpit became an inferno.

He tried to fight down the panic.

But then he saw Canterbury below him, with scores of people racing for shelter. A thought flashed through his head. *If I crash, I'll kill them.*

He banked savagely and swerved away from the town. He could hear himself screaming.

'Roll the plane, Buckingham,' yelled Harry. 'Roll your bloody plane.'

He obeyed instantly, turning the plane upside down while simultaneously struggling to undo the canopy. His hands were burning and slow to respond but he managed it at last and the canopy dropped to earth.

He took in a lungful of air, unbuckled his harness and fell from the plane. His first instinct was to pull the ripcord but his fingers would not respond. He plummeted to earth, screaming with pain and terror.

But the speed of his fall was fortunate, for the plane exploded within moments. If the chute had deployed, he'd have been burnt to shreds.

He finally managed to pull the ripcord and the chute opened.

He did not feel the impact of his landing for his body was a searing mass of agony. He struggled to sit up. His trousers had burnt away and the skin of his thighs was flapping like tissue paper. His flying jacket was smouldering but not alight.

But it was his gloves which were worse; they were like flaming torches. The leather burned away and he saw to his horror that the skin on his hands had been consumed, leaving only a mass of bloodied flesh.

His eyes closed and he sobbed.

Two women came running towards him, shouting in alarm. One carried a basin of water. She flung it over him to extinguish the flames.

'There, there darling,' she said. 'You're safe now. You'll be alright.' But the look of horror in her eyes said otherwise.

A NEW LEADER

14th September 1940

'Come in Harry,' Wing Commander Bouchier said. 'Take a seat.' Harry's eyes narrowed. What on earth could Bouchier want with him? His mind ran over the last few days to see if he'd done something to justify an official reprimand or even a warning. He'd cursed and complained enough, admittedly, but never to the extent of questioning tactics or strategy. Not since the attack on Gravesend.

'I guess you know why you're here.'

Harry frowned. 'I haven't a clue, sir.'

Bouchier's eyes closed wearily for a second. 'I'm not sure if that's the best start but never mind.'

He took a deep breath. 'I'm making you Squadron Leader, Harry. Effective immediately.'

Harry blinked in astonishment.

'But surely there are better blokes. Tomasz for one.'

'Tomasz is a Pole. The high-ups wouldn't stand for it.'

'Frank?'

'For all his papers say he's Canadian, he's a Yank. He's fighting illegally.' He peered at Harry. 'I must say I'm disappointed that you're not more enthusiastic.'

Harry exhaled. 'It's just that I'm shocked. I never expected it.'

'You're one of the two Flight Lieutenants.' He opened a packet of cigarettes and offered one to Harry.

Like a king knighting a squire, Harry thought.

'I don't, however, want to give the impression that you're only being made Squadron Leader because you're British.'

'Well —'

'If that were the case I could have drafted in any of two dozen chaps from other squadrons.'

He lit Harry's cigarette and then his own.

'I'm making you Squadron Leader because you're the best man for the job.'

Harry tried but failed to keep the doubt from his face.

Bouchier chose to ignore it.

'You're a good pilot, Harry, brave but not reckless and a good tactician. But even more important, you've got what it takes to lead the men. They like you, they see you as a man of integrity.' He paused. 'I don't need to tell you that the more vital thing is that they respect you. And that they trust you and want to follow you.'

A queasy feeling slithered through Harry's stomach. He'd never given the concept of leadership such consideration. Bouchier clearly had.

A poisoned chalice, Harry thought. He thrust the thought aside.

'I'm honoured to have been chosen, sir,' he said. 'I'll do the best I can.'

'I know you will. Make sure that my trust in you is fully justified.'

Harry got up and saluted. Bouchier came round the desk and shook his hand.

The squadron pilots were lounging around in the afternoon sunshine. There had been no sorties that day and they were hoping that there would be none now.

As Harry approached, Frank and Tomasz got to their feet. They had a hopeful look in their eyes.

'Well, lads,' Harry said. 'I'm your new Squadron Leader.'

The men leapt to their feet and cheered.

Oh shit, Harry thought. I hope I can live up to it.

A moment later the dispatcher yelled, 'Scramble.'

They began to run.

'You're like Olympic runners,' Harry yelled. 'Goring's too fat to join our squadron.'

'He eats too much sauerkraut,' Frank called.

'Sauerkraut would make him fart and go faster,' Harry replied. 'Too much sausage inside him, I reckon.'

They clambered on board their planes, laughing for the first time in weeks.

'Who's the new boss?' Jack said as he helped him strap up.

'I am. Wish me luck.'

'Bloody hell. Wonders never cease.' His face cracked in a wide smile and he gave the thumbs up.

Harry's squadron was airborne in record time and the other Spitfire squadron not far behind.

'Congratulations, Harry,' the controller said, warmly. 'Now, just remember that it's my job to tell you what to do. So keep your mouth buttoned until I've finished.'

'Okay, Wheatcroft. I'm all ears.'

'Bandits approaching along the estuary,' the controller said. 'Between fifty and a hundred. You're to rendezvous with Hurricanes from Northolt, Squadron 1 Royal Canadian Air Force. Your mate Frank should like that.'

'He's no more Canadian than you or me,' Harry said.

'I didn't hear that Squadron Leader,' Wheatcroft laughed.

Harry grinned. Squadron Leader! What would his folks say when he told them?

They had a few minutes to wait until the Hurricanes arrived so Harry ordered the squadron to climb to thirty-five thousand feet, some five thousand feet higher than they normally reached.

'Wanting a grandstand view?' Frank asked.

'Just an inkling that the 109s will be pretty high,' Harry said.

His intuition proved correct. Seventy bombers were heading west along the estuary with thirty Messerschmitt 109s above them and to their flanks. His squadron were now far above them.

'That's a lot of 109s,' Tomasz said. 'I think they're trying to draw up more of our fighters.'

'Squadron 1, RAFC here,' came an unmistakable Canadian drawl. 'I'm told we're to act in concert.'

'That's right,' Harry said.

'Then, may I ask, where are you?'

'Way above you and way above the Messerschmitts.'

'That's fantastic, fellers. We're attacking now.'

Harry banked a little and watched as the Canadians flew at the bombers. The Messerschmitts immediately dived to attack them.

'That's all of the Krauts in action,' Frank said after a moment.

Harry caught a glimpse of a second Hurricane squadron attacking the German flank with the other Hornchurch Spitfires racing to their side.

'And all our boys in action,' Frank said. He sounded edgy, keen to get started.

'I know,' Harry said. 'I'll tell us when to attack.'

He counted to five in his head then cried, 'Dive boys, dive.'

He hurtled earthward with the rest of the squadron racing alongside him.

They took the Messerschmitts completely by surprise, blasting them with cannon and machine guns. Three were hit and plummeted towards the estuary. A couple more were damaged and swerved away, fleeing to France and safety.

For the next thirty minutes the British and German fighters engaged in furious dogfights while the Hurricanes tackled the bombers. By 16.00 hours it was all over.

Harry led the squadron back to base. The Ground Crew applauded him when he got out of the cockpit.

'So the guttersnipe made good,' Jack said, clapping him on the back. His eyes were shining with pride and pleasure.

'More luck than judgement.'

Jack grabbed him by the arm. 'Don't ever say that, Harry. You can bet a pretty penny that the rich boys would never say the same. There are plenty of people who'll be unhappy that a lad like you has got so far. Don't let them think that you have luck but no talent.'

Harry looked at him in astonishment. 'You want me to lie?'

'No. But I don't want you to spurn all credit or belittle yourself.'

Harry looked a little dubious but mumbled his thanks. 'I'll stand you a pint tonight,' he said.

'And I'll drink it, no fear.'

Harry started to walk towards the mess but suddenly felt dizzy. He reached for the tail of the plane to steady himself.

'I wish I had a camera,' Frank said. 'You look like the noble hero patting his steed.'

'Actually, I feel fucking wobbly.'

'It's the strain of command,' Tomasz said. 'I felt this the first time I led men into battle. It's much worse than the actual fighting. It will pass.'

'It better do.'

Tomasz reached for Harry's hand. 'You did well today, Harry, you held your nerve and waited to attack until the most favourable moment. I don't think I could have done that.' He glanced at Frank. 'And our American friend certainly wouldn't.'

'Praise from a real hero,' Harry muttered as he watched Tomasz march towards the mess.

'I guess we're all heroes,' Frank said. 'Although I sometimes feel like a charlatan.'

Harry punched him on the shoulder.

Harry was surprised to see Wing Commander Bouchier waiting for him as he approached the administration building to make his report. It was unheard of for the Station Commander to greet a Squadron Leader like this.

His stomach did a somersault, thinking Bouchier would reprimand him for delaying the attack. Perhaps he might even be accused of cowardice.

Instead Bouchier gave him a broad grin. 'I wanted to congratulate you on leading your first sortie, Harry. I'm told you got into an excellent position and held firm before launching your attack. That takes nerve and fine judgement.' He shook Harry's hand.

'It was nothing, sir,' Harry said. 'Beginner's luck.' He cursed himself for forgetting Jack's advice so soon.

'Beginner's luck, nonsense,' Bouchier said. 'It showed real leadership skills.' He held Harry's eye. 'And that's not something that's taught on the playing fields of Eton.'

'I didn't go to Eton, sir.'

Bouchier raised his eyebrows. 'Well what a surprise, lad. And I thought you were a toff.' He gave a broad grin. 'I'll let you into a secret. My father worked in hotels and I didn't go to private school but to a Grammar School. I worked as a clerk and then a travelling salesman.'

Harry gave a grin. For the first time since joining the RAF he felt he belonged.

'Come back to my office,' Bouchier said, 'and we'll have a beer.'

Harry made his report and then knocked on the Commander's door. Bouchier was sitting with his feet on the desk and his arms behind his head. Two bottles of beer were open on the desk in front of him.

Bouchier swung his legs down and gave Harry a bottle, chinking his against it. 'Cheers, young man and here's to many more successful sorties.'

'Thank you, sir.' He took a sip and glanced around the office. Earlier, when Bouchier had promoted him, he'd been too shocked to notice anything about it. Now he was surprised to see a fez hanging on the wall and a hookah pipe beneath it.

Bouchier caught his glance. 'Mementos of my time in Egypt,' he said. He patted a small statue of an elephant on his desk. 'And this was given to me when I left India. It's supposed to bring good luck.'

'You were the first commander of the air-force there weren't you, sir?'

Bouchier nodded. 'I was. I loved India. Wonderful country, wonderful people.'

Harry bit his lip. He had wanted to ask this question ever since being posted to Hornchurch. 'All the flowers that grow around the airfields, sir. Did you plant them?'

Bouchier chuckled. 'Not personally, no. But I thought the place needed brightening up. Do you like them? I know lots of my colleagues thinks it's foolish.'

'I like it a lot, sir. Gives the men a touch of home. Makes them remember what they're fighting for.'

The telephone rang. Bouchier listened to it for a moment and put his hand over the mouthpiece. 'Do you know anyone at Group Headquarters?'

'I've seen Air Vice Marshal Park but that's all.'

'What about a Squadron Officer Lamb?'

Harry shook his head and then blushed.

Bouchier handed him the phone. 'The young lady wants to talk to you.' He took his beer and left the office.

'Harry,' the voice said over the line. 'It's Claire Lamb here.'

'Yes.'

'I hear that you've been made Squadron Leader.'

'Yes. How on earth did you know.'

'My boss is Keith Park, silly.' She gave a giggle. 'I know everything.'

His heart surged.

'And I hear you've been in action and did very well.'

'Yes.' It was only half an hour ago. He could hardly believe that she'd heard about it so soon.

There was a silence.

'So you've become the strong, silent type have you?' Claire asked. 'Is yes all you can say.'

'No.'

'Ah. Yes and no. Well there's progress.'

Harry grinned.

'Anyway I just wanted to telephone to congratulate you. And to tell you to take care.'

'Claire,' he cried, alarmed that she would hang up.

'What is it?'

'Here's some more words,' he stammered. 'Would you like to go out one evening?'

He bit his lips, thinking she'd refuse, and desperately tried to come up with something to make his request appear a little lighter, a bit more casual.

'Now I'm a Squadron Leader I'm flush with cash, you see. I could treat you to dinner in the West End.'

There was a heart-beat of silence. 'I'd love that, Harry. Very much. When?'

Harry licked his lips which were suddenly very dry. 'How about next weekend? I'm due two days leave then.'

'I'll see if I can fix some leave,' she said. 'I'll get a message to you on Tuesday at the latest.'

'Wonderful.' He grinned like the Cheshire Cat.

'Bye then. And congratulations again.'

He put the telephone in its cradle, swigged his beer and headed out of the office. Bouchier was perched on a corporal's desk, swinging the bottle back and forwards.

'By the look on your face you have an admirer already,' he said. 'You'd better get off. Your chaps will be expecting you at the Good Intent.'

'I'm standing the squadron and ground crew a drink.'

'Excellent idea. Just make sure you keep enough money to entertain your lady friend.'

Harry smiled and made for the door, only just remembering to turn and salute.

Bouchier touched his head, not really a salute, more a casual goodbye.

As he hurried towards the pub, Harry realised he had never felt happier.

NO RESERVES

15th September 1940

Claire glanced at the sky as she walked towards the Bunker. The ground was wet from heavy overnight rain and the sky was overcast. She was delighted for it meant that there would probably be few raids today.

She hurried down the steps to the plotting room and picked up the weather forecast. She pulled a face. It looked like the clouds would clear away in the late morning and no rain was expected.

She looked up as Park entered. He looked very troubled.

Her heart began to hammer. What had he heard? Was the invasion going to come today? Had it started?

'Are you all right, sir?' she asked nervously. She dreaded to hear his answer.

'No, I'm not. He straightened his cap and scratched his forehead. 'It's my wife's birthday and I forgot all about it. No gift, no card, and no birthday wishes.'

Claire felt profound relief but she made her expression stern. 'That's awful of you, sir.' Her tone was a mixture of sorrow and admonishment.

Then she grinned. 'You'll have to do something nice for her later.'

Park smiled. 'She said that a good bag of German planes would be an excellent present.'

Claire nodded. Park's wife was an East Ender and she must be anguished and vengeful at the destruction being wrought there.

'The weathermen predict a mixed day,' she said, giving him the weather forecast. 'Patchy cloud this morning but clearing this afternoon.'

'So, a quiet morning in store. Good. The men could do with a rest.'

He glanced at her suddenly. 'Have you got a boyfriend, Lamb?' He shook his hands vigorously in embarrassment. 'None of my business. Forget what I said.'

'That's all right, sir. I have met one chap.'

Park glanced away. He hoped he was not a pilot.

'He flies Spitfires from Hornchurch. Actually, he was made Squadron Leader yesterday.'

'Then give him my congratulations.' Park forced a smile but he sounded far from congratulatory. The chances were that the boy would be dead or injured within a week. New squadron leaders were especially vulnerable. They had too much to do and they often failed to look out for themselves.

He shook the thought from his head. If he ever allowed himself to worry about individuals, he would find it impossible to take the decisions that he needed to. He recognised the danger of losing sight of the big picture.

He studied the weather forecast carefully. Intelligence reports suggested that the Luftwaffe were going to launch a huge attack in support of the planned invasion. He had no idea when it would come but he thought it would be soon. But not today, by the look of the morning's weather.

At nine o'clock Evelyn hurried into the operations room. 'Guess what, sir?' she said. 'The Prime Minister and his wife have decided to pay a visit.'

Park pulled a wry face. 'Thank goodness it looks like a quiet day.

'Bring him down, Evelyn,' he said. 'And tell him that your father's friend is delighted at how we're doing against the Germans. That he tells President Roosevelt this all the time.'

'Of course. Why only last night Mr Hopkins sent his warmest wishes.'

Claire gave a doubtful look. 'Did he really? Did you even speak to him?'

'Of course I didn't. But if I had I'm pretty sure that's what he'd have said.'

'Then tell that to Mr Churchill,' Park said. 'He'll be delighted.'

'You and Evelyn look after him,' he said to Claire. 'If things heat up, try to keep him out of my hair.'

A few minutes later they heard the heavy tread of the Prime Minister and a low growling voice of complaint. He entered the room with his wife, Clementine.

'How deep is this blasted hole?' he demanded.

'Sixty feet, sir,' Park said. 'It's designed to withstand a direct hit.'

'You mean designed to exhaust me.' He stuck a cigar in his mouth and went to light it.

'Sorry, Prime Minister,' Claire said. 'But no one's allowed to smoke. The air conditioning can't cope with it.'

'Damned impertinence,' he said. He peered at her and wagged his finger. 'Didn't you tell me the same thing last time I came here?'

'I did, sir. And the ventilation system still can't cope with cigar smoke.'

Churchill grunted and stuck the unlit cigar further into his mouth.

'I just happened to be passing,' he said, 'so I thought I'd call in to see what's happening. I don't want to disturb you, Park. If necessary I can go and work in my car.'

'Not at all, sir. Things are fairly quiet so far.'

The telephone rang.

325

'Radar has reported enemy aircraft approaching Dover,' Johnny Longley said. 'And more gathering over Dieppe.'

Park tossed the weather report aside. It appeared that they were not going to get as quiet a morning as they had hoped.

'It looks like you will see some activity, Prime Minister,' he said. He turned to de Broke, the senior controller. 'Tell the station heads at Biggin Hill, Hornchurch and Kenley to put a couple of squadrons each on Standby.'

He looked down at the map table below. 'I think this may be what we've been waiting for,' he told his controllers. 'I've got a feeling something big is about to happen.'

'Show me what's happening, Park,' Churchill demanded.

Park looked perturbed, needing to concentrate on the forthcoming battle.

'You can see exactly what's happening from the map down there, sir,' Claire said.

She gestured to the Prime Minister to come over to the window. 'You can see the progress of the battle here.'

Churchill's face lit up and he hurried over.

Park gave her a thankful look.

She adroitly positioned herself between Park and the Prime Minister as they stared at the map below.

'What are the Nazis doing, Park?' Churchill asked.

'They're staying out over the Channel,' Park said. 'They're putting up feelers, trying to entice my squadrons into the air.' He frowned. 'Not their usual tactics.' His eyes narrowed thoughtfully.

'And the girls down there? With their long poles?'

'The markers show that there are forty German planes near Dover,' Claire said.

'Come here, Clemmie,' Churchill told his wife. 'This is fascinating.'

Another of the WAAFs leaned over the table and placed a new marker on the board.

'And that's the formation that was forming over Dieppe,' Claire said. 'Now they're heading across the Channel. It looks like another forty planes.'

'Tell the squadrons on Standby to go to Readiness,' Park said to his controllers. 'And put another half dozen on Standby.'

'What does all that mean?' Churchill asked.

Park's eyes slid to Claire.

'Standby means the pilots are strapped into their cockpits ready for immediate take off,' she said. 'Readiness means they can take off within five minutes.'

'Why aren't they all on Standby?'

'To conserve fuel. And being on Standby is quite intense for the pilots.'

Churchill looked annoyed at this sign of less than martial valour. 'Battle is meant to be intense.'

'But it's probably best for the pilots to keep calm before the battle,' his wife said.

His mouth worked but he did not argue with her. Clementine raised her eyebrows and smiled at Claire.

'The Germans are turning back, sir,' one of the controllers said.

'Then tell our boys to return to base.'

'Is this normal?' Churchill asked.

'A good question, sir. No, it's not.' Park rested his chin in his hand and stared anxiously at the map.

Evelyn handed cups of tea to Churchill and Clementine.

'You sound American,' Churchill said. 'My mother was American.'

'Lucky her,' Evelyn said.

Churchill laughed. 'And what, may I ask is an American doing in the WAAF?'

'My husband - my late husband - was a squadron leader. I wanted to help him by doing my bit.'

'Late husband?'

'He was killed a couple of weeks ago.'

Churchill's eyes filled with tears of sympathy. 'I'm so sorry, my dear.'

'Thank you.'

He made his way towards Park who quickly said, 'Corporal Nash's father is a friend of Harry Hopkins. Mr Roosevelt's friend.'

Churchill glanced at her. 'Is he indeed?' They could almost hear his mind working.

He took Evelyn's hand in his. 'I would be most grateful if you could inform Mr Hopkins that we are holding our own but we would welcome any help and matériel from our friends across the Atlantic.'

'I certainly shall, Mr Churchill. Why only last night, Mr Hopkins told me that he was very impressed at how the British are fighting.'

'Did he indeed? Well I trust he wasn't surprised.' He gave a deep chuckle.

At 10.30 the telephone rang and the plotters in the map room below swung into action.

'This looks like a bigger raid, sir,' Claire told Churchill. 'A hundred and more.'

He plucked up an opera glass and studied the map below. 'And you can tell that from the labels on the wooden blocks?'

'Yes, sir.'

'Then it looks like trouble's brewing.' Another marker had been placed behind the first, indicating a second force of 150 planes.

'You're correct, Prime Minister,' Park said. 'This looks like a big one.' He stared at the map table for a minute then said to de Broke. 'Tell the sector station controllers to put all planes on Standby.'

He gazed at the plots as they inched slowly towards the English coast.

Churchill moved beside him. 'There appear to be many aircraft coming in.'

'They should arrive over the coast near Hastings a little after 11.45 hours. We're ready for them, sir. There'll be someone there to meet them.'

'With more success than Harold had against William the Conqueror, I trust.'

Park did not reply, did not take his eyes from the map.

Suddenly he called, 'Scramble all squadrons on Standby.'

'Thank God for that,' Harry said when he heard the order to scramble. He had been sitting in the cockpit on Standby for five minutes but it had seemed like a day. He pushed the accelerator and his plane thundered along the runway.

'Lots of bandits over Hastings, lads,' he said. 'Looks like the Jerries have ended their holiday.'

'I wish we could have ours,' Frank said. 'Coney Island would suit me.'

They turned to the south and began to climb. They reached the coast a minute before the German formations did.

'Bloody hell,' Frank said.

The German armada stretched for almost two miles. They were arranged in swarms of three to seven planes, stretching between fifteen and twenty-five thousand feet, giving the appearance of a vast herringbone. Messerschmitt 110's were flying in close support of the bombers with the 109's wheeling above them.

'There's more planes than we thought,' Harry said to his controller. 'We're going in now.'

He got a 109 in his sight and closed on it. He recalled playing chicken in the high street when he was a child. One of his friends had misjudged the speed of a tram and been killed. He shook the thought away and opened fire, pulling away just in time. The German had continued to hold his course. He was either inexperienced, had stronger nerves or was better at playing chicken.

He had no time to see if the plane was damaged for two more Germans were racing towards him. He swerved to avoid a hail of bullets but one of the planes immediately swooped on the newest member of his squadron. '109 on your tail, Jarvis,' he yelled. The novice just managed to get out of trouble as Tomasz pounced and smashed the attacker to shreds.

'Keep your eyes peeled for Jerries attacking you,' Harry told Jarvis. 'Your job is to put the wind up them and stay out of trouble.'

'They're putting the wind up me,' Jarvis answered. He sounded terrified.

'Good. It will keep you on your toes.'

The combat was intense and deadly. The pilots on both sides were exhausted and this made them angry and bitter, unwilling to give even the slightest quarter. The sky was full of smoke as plane after plane spiralled to the earth.

Hell's bells, Harry thought. I might be the shortest serving squadron leader of all time.

Park pressed his head against the window. His fighters had slowed the Germans but not dispersed them. The numbers were just too huge. He glanced at the tote board.

'Get the Standby squadrons airborne,' he said. He felt a growing horror in his chest but his voice was low and deadly calm.

'Every squadron?' de Broke asked. His normally impassive face showed his alarm.

Park nodded.

'All squadrons airborne,' de Broke said a few minutes later.

Park nodded and turned his attention from the board to the map.

There was a long silence and then Churchill turned to Park. 'How many reserves have we?' he asked.

Park answered, 'There are none.'

Churchill looked horrified but he quickly masked it and returned his gaze to the map. His wife slipped her hand into his.

'If they defeat our fighters today,' he murmured, 'Hitler will launch his invasion.'

Claire gazed at Park. He looked in command and in complete control, his mouth set firm and his eyes taking in the details of the battle. But then she happened to glance down. His left leg was shaking like it had the palsy.

Churchill saw where she was looking and followed her eyes. He stared at Park for a while. Then he quietly placed a hand upon his shoulder.

―――

The Hornchurch controller came over Harry's radio. 'Park's ordered the whole of 11 Group airborne,' he said. 'Someone should be with you in five minutes.'

It was the longest five minutes any of them had experienced. But then Frank whooped with delight. 'Here comes the cavalry.'

Harry glanced round and saw three squadrons close on the enemy. It was a welcome sight but it brought fresh dangers.

Although he had told Jarvis to keep his eyes peeled it was all but impossible. The sky was full of planes, British and German, more numerous than a swarm of midges. Enemy fire was no longer the only danger. He saw several planes collide and a handful more have near-misses.

'Try to get height,' he ordered. 'Attack from there.'

They swung into a swift climb for almost a minute, two thousand feet above the battle. Then the squadron swept down upon the German fighters, taking them by surprise.

'Like a knife through butter,' Frank yelled in delight.

The dogged resistance of the British was having an effect on the German planes. The attacks by the Hurricanes had forced them to continually manoeuvre out of trouble which slowed them considerably. At the same time the Spitfires somehow managed to keep the German fighters from giving close protection. The German formations slowly but surely began to unravel.

Dozens of the German fighters were forced to pull back, damaged, out of ammunition or running low on fuel. Some of the Spitfires pursued them to the coast and beyond.

Harry was ordered to break off and attack the bombers. He led the squadron in a swift turn and pounced. It was like swatting flies, he thought.

Many of the bombers peeled away, desperate to evade the British fighters. A large number dropped their bombs on open countryside in order to lighten their load and give them a better chance of escape.

Most, however, continued towards London, suffering dreadful casualties as they did so. Only a third of the 109s were still with them and as they reached London one of 12 Group's Big Wings appeared from the north, four fresh squadrons. They crashed into them, sending the already ragged formation into tatters.

Harry asked his men how much fuel and ammunition they had.

'That's enough for one more attack,' he said. And they again swept into battle.

The Germans fought desperately but this last attack proved the breaking point. They disengaged and headed home at maximum speed.

'Well done, lads,' Harry said. 'Say your names.'

Nine men answered. He stifled a groan. Three planes down. He prayed that their pilots had got out alive and unwounded.

They reached Hornchurch at 12.30. Harry sat in the cockpit for five minutes, too weary to climb out.

When he reached the operations room he was told that two of three pilots had survived. But Jarvis, the new boy, had been killed. It was his first combat.

'It's not your fault, Harry,' the intelligence officer told him. 'New boys are always the most vulnerable.'

Harry stared at him, stricken. It might not have been his fault but he felt a dreadful sense of guilt.

Frank Trent approached and put his hand on his shoulder. 'Well done, Harry. Let's get some lunch.'

Harry shook his head. 'I can't eat,' he said.

Frank put his hand on his shoulder and gently steered him towards the canteen.

'Sit down,' he said. 'I'll get us some bully beef sandwiches.'

Harry started to argue but knew it was pointless. And then suddenly he felt a ravenous hunger.

'Let's eat them outside,' Harry said when Frank returned. 'I need the air.'

They walked across to the dispersal hut and collapsed into a couple of basket-chairs.

'I'm knackered, Frank,' Harry said.

Frank laughed. 'Oh what you northern lads do to the language of Milton and Shakespeare.'

Harry grunted. 'I lost three planes,' he said at last. 'And young Jarvis.'

'Don't beat yourself up about it, Harry. Jarvis told me he'd only had six hours flying Spits. It's not enough. I don't know what they're thinking sending us boys like that.'

'No choice I suppose. We're losing too many men and they have to replace them somehow.'

'Well, Pete and Andy made it okay. I saw them bail out.'

Harry frowned. 'Then where the hell are they?'

'Taking a slow coach back here, I suppose.'

Frank finished his sandwich and leaned back with his hands behind his head. They sat in silence for ten minutes, their presence more reassuring than any words they might have found. The clouds disappeared and the sun began to shine on them.

'I like September best of all the months,' Harry said at last. 'I burn in the summer, you see. Too pale. But September is lovely. Still warm but with a hint of cold in the morning. And the light always looks golden. It makes the fields look like they belong in fairy tales.'

Frank opened his eyes and stared at him. 'Where's all this come from? You sound like a poet.' He punched him gently on the arm. 'You must be in love with that girl from headquarters.'

Harry shook his head. 'Love's too dangerous, Frank. We all know that.'

Frank chuckled. 'It's not as dangerous as a Messerschmitt up your backside.'

'It is, you know. Far more dangerous.'

Then he closed his eyes and thought of Claire. And a slow smile crept over his face.

He woke an hour later. Pete and Andy were approaching with big grins on their faces. Andy was limping quite badly.

'So you decided to join us at last,' Harry said. 'What happened to you?'

'I came down in Woolwich,' Pete said. 'Near a pub, fortunately. The landlord stood me a drink and a sandwich while I waited for a ferry to cross the Thames.'

'I landed in Poplar,' Andy said. 'Twisted my foot when I landed.'

'Isn't Poplar where Flo's from?' Harry asked Frank.

He coloured slightly. 'Yeah.' He closed his eyes to prevent further questioning.

─────

'Thank goodness he's gone,' Park said to Claire as they returned from escorting Churchill to his car. 'I suppose I should be grateful he didn't get in the way as much as I feared.'

'He was very interested, sir. It will probably do us some good. Perhaps he'll provide us with more planes.'

'That would be wonderful. But what I really need is more pilots.' He frowned. 'I wonder if the training schools could trim their training schedules a little more?' Then he shook his head. 'No, the trainees aren't getting enough flight experience as it is.'

'Air Chief Marshal Dowding is on the phone, sir,' Evelyn said as they returned to the operations room.

Park spoke with him for ten minutes, giving a breakdown of the morning's activity and of the Prime Minister's visit.

'Is 11 Group holding up?' Dowding asked, eventually.

'Barely, sir.'

'And are you getting the support you need from the other Groups?'

Park took a deep breath. 'Absolutely from Brand —'

'And 12 Group?'

'They came through, sir. Not as quickly as I'd have liked but they came through.'

'Just make sure you give them enough warning. As much as humanly possible.' Dowding paused. 'Thank all your people from me. And keep up the good work.'

Park got off the phone to see Evelyn beckoning to him. He joined her at the window. The map below was filling up with the plots of enemy aircraft.

'Bugger,' he said. 'They've given us no respite.' He called to de Broke. 'Get the sector commanders on the blower. Tell them to scramble the squadrons in the same order as this morning.'

Claire glanced at the tote board. Harry's squadron had left the ground and was heading towards battle yet again. Her heart began to hammer.

'It looks to me like another large force,' Evelyn said.

Park peered at the plots and quickly calculated the numbers. 'Two hundred bombers and four hundred fighters.'

He stared at the board in silence. His fingers moved in the air as if they were doing a little dance.

De Broke was about to tell him that the British squadrons were in the air but noticed that Park seemed almost in a trance.

The controllers exchanged anxious glances. Claire took half a step towards him. Was the strain finally proving too much for him?

Still he stood there, immobile apart from his fingers moving in the air. Suddenly he straightened up. He had made up his mind. He would have to change tactics.

'Tell the most forward squadrons to ignore the bombers and concentrate on the fighter escorts.'

'Ignore the bombers completely, sir?'

'Yes. If we can engage the German fighters for long enough, they'll run out of fuel and ammunition and have to pull back. That will leave the bombers undefended and we can move on to them.'

'More of the bombers will get to London if we don't attack them,' de Broke said.

'True.' He bit his lips. 'When we scramble the second wave instruct them to patrol nearer London and wait for the bombers.'

He rubbed his hands together. 'The Jerries won't expect this.'

Harry sighted a formation of fifty Dorniers over Canterbury at 14.30 hours.

'You're supposed to go for the fighters, Harry,' Digby, the senior controller said.

'Roger.' He scanned the sky for any sign of fighters. 'I can't see any fighters in the vicinity.'

'Hang on while I check,' Digby said. A moment later he told him that Bouchier had given him the go-ahead to attack the bombers. 'But keep an eye out for fighters.'

'Let's get em,' he cried.

He led the squadron at the Dorniers and the formation split up immediately. Harry chased after one Dornier and got a hit. It wheeled away towards the Channel with a thick trail of black smoke billowing from it. He saw Frank rake a fourth plane and this too banked away to limp back home.

Two more Dorniers exploded nearby. None of their crew escaped.

But at that moment a dozen 109's hurtled down upon them from the clouds. Harry's men banked quickly to evade them, scattering over a large area.

'Regroup,' Harry yelled.

They did so in moments and turned back to battle. Out of the corner of his eye Harry saw the Dorniers carrying on towards London. He had to ignore them and focus on the Messerschmitts. His squadron were fighting for their lives now.

'Wear them down,' Harry ordered. 'Make them use up their fuel.'

It was a desperate business. The Messerschmitts and Spitfires slogged it out for several minutes. Harry tried to conserve his ammunition but soon there was precious little left. He cursed when he saw two of his planes badly damaged.

'Get out of it,' he yelled to the two pilots. 'Fly to the nearest airfield.'

The Messerschmitts began to disengage now, half hurrying to catch up with the Dorniers, the rest, presumably out of ammunition, making for France.

'Let's get after them,' Harry said.

'What's your fuel and ammo situation,' Digby demanded over his headphones.

Harry got a summary from his men and relayed it to the controller.

'Best come back to base then,' he said.

Harry breathed a sigh of relief and ordered the men back.

He knew that the planes would be refuelled and rearmed in minutes and they would be sent back into battle. But the wait on the ground and the journey there and back would give them perhaps an hour's respite. An hour they desperately needed.

The planes taxied to a halt and the pilots surged out. Most threw themselves into the chairs outside the dispatch hut but a few raced off to the toilets. Harry found Armstrong, the intelligence officer and gave his report.

'You look all in, Harry,' he said.

'I'm all right.' But he swayed as he said it and had to reach out for the wall.

Armstrong raised an eyebrow. 'Get yourself a cup of tea, lad.'

Harry ignored his suggestion and went over to his men. They were watching the ground crew working furiously on their planes.

He looked at his watch. It was 15.30 hours. There was plenty of light for more battles. Someone thrust a cup of tea in his hand and he sipped it. He revived almost immediately.

'One more show, lads,' he said. 'And then the pub.'

The loudspeaker in the operations room was turned on. Bouchier's voice rang out over the airfield, giving an account of the battle over London. He had started doing this a week or so before and he was obviously enjoying it.

'He sounds like a commentator on a football game,' Frank said with a grin. 'He'll be selling hot dogs and soda next.'

Harry slumped in a chair and listened as Bouchier continued his commentary.

'Is he supposed to do this?' one of the younger men asked.

'Almost certainly not. But I doubt he'll stop, even if he's ordered to.'

He took another sip of tea. Boy Bouchier was living up to his nickname with a vengeance. He was a one-off and he would do what he thought best for his people. They liked him for it although he doubted he'd get any thanks from the high-ups.

He finished his tea and leaned back in his seat. The sky was still clear but the clouds were beginning to come in from the west. He knew that murderous conflict was taking place over London but here over the airfield the sky was tranquil and at peace.

The ground crew signalled that the Spitfires were ready for combat again. Harry glanced at the dispatcher who gave a shrug of his shoulders. 'Nothing yet,' he said.

The minutes ticked by. Any second now, Harry thought.

'I'm going for a crap,' Frank announced.

'Make it quick,' Harry said. 'We may get the scramble soon.'

A gentle wind blew over the airfield, ruffling his hair. He glanced at his watch again. It was now past four. His mother would be getting tea ready, he thought. He wondered if she was able to get any fish paste for her sandwiches. She had them once a week, for her brain, she used to say. Where did the notion that fish was good for the brain come from, he wondered.

He realised that Bouchier had stopped giving his commentary on the battle. Here it comes, he thought. He looked around for Frank, willing him to hurry up and get back before they were ordered to scramble.

Then Bouchier spoke again. 'We can stand down, ladies and gentlemen. The Jerries are high-tailing it back to France where a heavy storm is imminent. There'll be no more raids tonight.'

Harry whistled with relief. Then he saw Bouchier and his senior staff fanning out across the airfield with cartons of beer in their arms.

Bouchier thrust a bottle into Harry's hand.

'What's this, sir? Your birthday?'

'That's next month and I'll try to get some cake. This is for a bloody hard day's work. Well done.'

He ambled off to hand out more bottles.

'He's definitely not supposed to do this,' Harry said to the new boy.

Beer had never tasted better.

TACTICS

16th September 1940

The following morning was dark and overcast, more like November than September. A cold wind blew in from the North Sea and throughout the morning there were sudden downpours.

'I like this,' Harry said to Tomasz as they sat in the canteen. 'I don't think even Goring is mad enough to send out his planes in these conditions.'

'But will it last?' Tomasz asked. 'I have learnt that the English weather is as fickle as you claim. Spring, autumn and winter in one day.'

'You forgot summer,' Harry said.

'Not just me. God forgot to give the English any summer.'

Frank sat beside them and opened a packet of cigarettes. The others reached out for one before he offered.

'Hey, get off fellers. This is my only pack.'

'We're helping you,' Tomasz said. 'Smoking is bad for your health.'

'And fighting in this war isn't?' He looked at Harry. 'I came to find you actually. There's a meeting for all officers of Squadron Leaders and above.' He slapped Harry on the leg. 'That includes you now, buddy.'

Harry grimaced, pocketed the cigarette and made his way to the meeting.

Harry took a seat at the back of the room, a position he had adopted from his earliest school days in order to avoid the attention of the teacher. There was a quiet hubbub of talk, some about the previous day's action, most about the weather and the chances it would set in for the day and give them some respite.

Wing Commander Bouchier and Air Vice Marshall Park entered the room. The men shuffled to their feet but Park hastily gestured to them to sit down before most had time to get to attention.

Harry stared at him as he took his seat. This was Claire's direct superior and the man who held their fate, and that of the nation, in his hands. He was younger than he had expected. And, perhaps stranger still, he gave no impression of worry or strain. He must have broad shoulders, Harry thought. Which was fortunate for everyone.

Bouchier introduced Park, then took a seat beside him, moving it at an angle so that he could watch his superior speak.

Park stood up and his eye roved around the room. 'First of all, gentlemen,' he said. 'I wish to commend you for your work yesterday. It was a damned hard-fought battle and the Germans had the worst of it.'

The men looked at each other, nodding and smiling.

'However,' Park continued, 'I do have some slight misgivings. Yesterday, 1,600 German aircraft came across the Channel. This morning's press claimed that 175 of them were destroyed.'

He held up a copy of the Daily Herald for them to see.

'I wish that had been the case. But, according to our intelligence, 56 enemy planes were shot down. That is good, let me say.'

He paused for a moment and scanned the room.

'But I'm afraid that it's not good enough. We have an advantage over the Germans as we're fighting over our own airspace, we don't have to keep such a close eye on dwindling fuel and ammo and we have the better planes.'

He took a deep breath. 'We sent up 300 planes yesterday. And only bagged 56. You can work out the ratio for yourselves.'

Bouchier looked uncomfortable. 'I'm thinking that's not the whole picture, sir,' he said. 'I guess that many of the German planes were damaged.'

'True. But they can be fixed and come back to attack us.'

The men looked crestfallen. They had expected to be praised and instead, they felt like they were being chastised.

'I don't think that's altogether fair, sir,' came a voice from the back. Park looked over, expectantly.

'We sent the Jerries packing, sir. We stopped them bombing their targets and we sent them home with a flea in their ear.'

'You did,' Park said, 'and I am proud of you for that.'

'Then what more do you want of us?'

Park sighed. 'I know that you are all giving everything you have. But I have to ask for even more. I have to ask you to be, not just brave and skillful fighters, because it's abundantly clear that you are. But I have to ask you to be better still. Every army has had its champions. Achilles, Lancelot, William Marshal, our own Albert Ball.'

'Don't forget the Red Baron,' someone said.

'Yes, even him.' Park smiled and paused. 'Well I'm asking every one of you to be champions. And I know that I do not ask in vain.'

The atmosphere in the room lifted, became charged and resolute. He placed his hands on his hips and held the men's eyes for a moment before continuing.

'And we are changing tactics slightly. And it affects this base and Biggin Hill more than others. For 11 Group as a whole, I want to continue the policy of having Hurricanes attack bombers and Spitfires attack the Bf109's.' He held up his hand to forestall any interruptions. 'Yes, I know that this is not always possible but we should aim to do so, nonetheless.'

He took a sip of water, using the time to gauge the attitude of the men.

'But from now on, I would like the Spitfire squadrons here and at Biggin to rendezvous in pairs, at height if possible but, if the weather's like today, below the cloud base. Then you are to increase altitude as quickly and as high as possible to gain advantage against the Messerschmitts. They won't be expecting to see two squadrons of Spits at their throats. It should give us the edge against them.'

He rubbed his chin for a few moments. When he spoke again his voice was quieter.

'I know what it's like to fight in combat. The fear, the exhilaration, the confusion. But I fought in the last war, in a Bristol F2 biplane, the Brisfit. Perhaps your fathers and grandfathers remember that old plane. Wing Commander Bouchier and I certainly do.'

Bouchier pretended to look shocked at his words and the men chuckled at it.

'Our top speed was 123 miles per hour. Can you believe this, gentlemen? 123 miles per hour? But the Germans were equally slow. One day I remember filling my pipe as I atarted a dog-fight.'

He paused. 'That was the day I got shot down.'

The laughter was louder now.

'So I know the sort of thing you're up against. Although I don't know, can't know, the sheer intensity of it. But I also know this. You are England's champions. And not just England's but New Zealand's too.'

Many of the men looked confused by this but Park ignored it. 'And champions of the rest of the Empire. And the whole world.'

'Except for Germany, of course,' Bouchier added. He got to his feet and clapped Park.

The rest of the men did the same.

Bouchier held up his hands for quiet. 'I'd like to thank Air Vice Marshal Park for sharing his thoughts on the battle. As it's twelve o'clock he's going to join us for a spot of lunch. And, I'm reliably informed by the Met Office that this wonderfully horrible weather will last all day. So it looks like we can put our feet up for the next twenty-four hours.'

The men cheered and hurried out of the room to eat.

———

'You got away with it, Keith,' Bouchier said as they headed towards the Mess. 'You told them that you expected them to do even better than they are already, which I have to say, I found rather surprising. But you also gave them a big pat on the back and made them feel like heroes. Astonishing carrot and stick. I remember you doing the same when you commanded 48 Squadron. You kept referring to the motto.'

'Forte et fidele.'

'Forte et fidele. By strength and faithfulness. That's what you're expecting now, aren't you? Strength and faithfulness.'

'Not just expecting, Cecil. Relying on.'

A waitress brought over their plates.

'This is welcome,' Park said. 'I usually only manage half a sandwich.'

He grinned at Bouchier. 'I hope you dine better than me, Boy. I hear that you think creature comforts are as important as bullets. Even Dowding has commented that you give the men beer out of your own pocket.'

'Don't say he's going to reimburse me?' he said with a grin.

'Definitely not. Although he did say that he approved.'

He gestured towards a nearby table. 'What's the name of that red-headed fellow? The one who told me that I wasn't being fair.'

Bouchier didn't even look up. 'Harry Smith. I made him squadron leader a couple of days ago.'

Park looked surprised. 'Well he certainly wasn't overawed by my presence.'

'Nothing overawes Harry. That's why I think he'll make a splendid leader.'

Park frowned. 'One of my staff, Claire Lamb, has a boyfriend here. She said he was a red-head.' He pursed his lips. 'A chap from Nottingham, I think she said.'

'That's Harry. Our very own Robin Hood.' He held Park's gaze. 'He's a good man, Keith.'

'I don't doubt it. I like a chap who's not afraid to speak out when he needs to.' He put down his knife and fork and beckoned Harry over.

'Oh shit,' Harry said to Frank. 'I'm about to be busted down to sergeant.'

He approached Park and gave a rather half-hearted salute.

'Take a seat, Harry,' Bouchier said. 'The Air Vice Marshal wants a word.'

'You're a cheeky bugger aren't you, Smith?' Park began.

'So I've been told, sir. All my life.' His eyes narrowed as if he were about to engage in a fist-fight.

'So was I at your age. And the Wing Commander here, even more. I like that in a man.'

He leaned forward. 'I wonder, did you understand what I was doing this morning?'

'Yes sir.'

Park gave him a questioning look.

'The eternal one two, sir,' Harry said. 'A quick slap on the head followed by a pat on the shoulder.' He shrugged. 'I learnt that one from my dad.'

'And fathers always know best.'

'In my family's case, yes.'

'Wing Commander Bouchier says you've made a splendid start as a Squadron Leader, Smith. I'm sure you'll continue in this vein.'

Harry wanted to say that he was finding it harder than he imagined but he would not give him the satisfaction of admitting it.

Park gave him a thoughtful look. 'Are you the young man who's walking out with my assistant, Squadron Officer Lamb?'

Harry swallowed nervously. 'Yes, sir. I'm sure she must be doing a good job.'

'I couldn't do without her. I shall tell her I've met you. That you're a cheeky young bugger but a good one.'

He picked up his knife and fork and Bouchier gestured Harry to leave.

'What was that all about?' Frank asked.

Harry gave a serious look. 'He just asked me to replace Leigh-Mallory as the Head of 12 Group. But I told him I wanted a rest from Nottingham so I'd stay here.'

Tomasz scoffed. 'You can't bear to be parted from us,' he said.

'Can't manage to stop spinning yarns,' Frank said. 'Seriously, what did he want you for?'

'Carrot and stick, my friend. He said he was impressed by me but that he'd marked my card.'

'Then you'd better be careful in the future,' Frank said.

Harry nodded. Although he wondered how much of a future this war would leave anyone.

NO SON OF MINE

20th September 1940

Harry and Frank followed the directions to the Burns Ward. There were thirty beds in the room, with men lounging on them, reading magazines and chatting. At the entrance to the ward a nurse asked who they were visiting and directed them to a ward further along the corridor. The sign above the door read Acute Cases.

This ward was made up of half a dozen cubicles with curtains drawn and four small rooms on either side of the door.

'We've come to see Squadron Leader Buckingham,' Harry said to the nurse on duty.

Her mouth made a little movement of disquiet. 'Are you family?'

'As good as,' Frank replied. 'We're from his squadron.'

'His parents are seeing him at the moment,' she said. 'It's their first visit. You'll have to wait, I'm afraid.'

'That's okay. Is there someplace we can grab a coffee?'

'The tea trolley's coming round in a minute. You can get a cup of tea then.'

She pointed out two chairs where they could wait and lowered her voice. 'He's very badly burnt.'

'We guessed that,' Harry said.

'Very badly.' She bit her lips. 'Are you quite sure you want to see him?'

'That's why we've come.'

She nodded. But she doubted the wisdom of them seeing him, wondered if it would terrify them, traumatise them, make them unwilling to climb into another plane and fly off to fight. Her mind worked, wondering if she should call the doctor or the sister. They were such handsome young boys.

At that moment the door opened and Buckingham's parents came out of the room. His mother began to weep, having held back the tears while she was in there.

The father's face was set rigid.

It must be terrible for them, Harry thought. To witness their son with such dreadful injuries.

'Poor Rupert,' his mother sobbed. 'We must get him home as soon as possible. Build him up, cherish him.'

'Have you lost your mind?' her husband said. 'That thing? Do you want to see him around the house? See that filthy, burned up face staring at us every moment of the day?'

He shook his head. 'I disown him. I'll pay for him to be taken care of somewhere but that's all. I don't ever want to see him again. He's no son of mine.'

Harry and Frank looked at each other in disbelief.

Buckingham's father took his wife's elbow and made for the door.

Harry opened his mouth to say something but had no chance. Frank took one step towards the man and punched him in the eye. He slumped to the ground.

'Get the police,' he managed to gasp. 'I'm a magistrate. Have him arrested.'

The nurse knelt to attend to him. 'But what on earth for?' she said. 'You slipped and banged your head. I clearly saw it.'

'The man punched me, God damn it.'

'No he didn't, sir. You're mistaken. Perhaps the fall has given you concussion.'

She jerked her head towards the room and Harry hustled Frank away.

'I don't regret it,' Frank whispered.

'And nor should you.'

They turned their gaze towards Buckingham. It was all they could do not to gasp. The whole of his upper body was burnt. The flesh was a mixture of black and red, shrivelled and torn. But it was his face which horrified them. Or what had been his face.

The skin was all but gone, seared and burnt into a gooey mass of purple and grey welts. He had eyes and a mouth but his nose was a disfigured lump and one ear had been entirely burnt away. Only his chin looked the same, untouched, a brave reminder of the man he once had been.

Harry felt the gorge rise in his throat. Not just at the sight of Buckingham's face, terrible though that was.

For he could see himself reflected there, imagine that he was the victim of just such an inferno, feel the torment of a body and life ravaged beyond recall. He began to shiver and shake, and felt that he might faint.

'Hello boys,' Buckingham whispered. 'Didn't think I'd see you so soon.' His voice was low and weak, as if he were speaking from the furthest reaches of a cave. 'I appreciate it.'

'Don't flatter yourself,' Frank managed to say. 'We really came to see the pretty nurses. You were just the excuse.'

Buckingham's eyes widened with amusement.

A heavy silence fell, each of them frantically thinking of what to say.

'Parents have just been,' Buckingham murmured.

'We saw them,' Harry said.

'Surprised at the old man. We never cared for each other. Good to see mother, though. I've told my sister not to come yet.'

'Your mother looked very nice. Younger than my mother. Very well turned out.' Harry cursed himself for the banality of his words. But what he wanted to say he could not, dare not utter.

'I guess you'll be here some time,' Frank said at last. 'Till they get you back on your feet.'

Buckingham raised a finger as if to agree. 'I expect I look a mess.'

They did not reply.

Buckingham stared at them, realisation in his eyes. 'That's the answer no one's been willing to give,' he said, his voice a mixture of bitterness and relief.

'They can do wonders now,' Harry said, quickly. 'Surgery, skin grafts…'

Buckingham sighed. 'Let's hope so.' He held up his right hand, tried to flex his fingers but failed. 'I think my flying days are over, boys. How will you cope without me?'

'We'll do our best, sir,' Harry said.

Buckingham stared at him and his face moved in the tiniest of smiles. 'Thank you, Harry.'

Harry looked confused. 'For what?'

'For calling me sir. It's the finest thing. The best thing I've heard since…'

Again a silence fell. The tick of the clock on the wall filled this silence, counting down the seconds, foretelling the coming minutes, the hours, the days, the years.

'Perhaps you'll get a medal,' Frank ventured. 'You were pretty bloody brave.'

'A medal? Well that will win the hearts of all the fair maidens.'

Buckingham's voice took on a bleak tone now. Any pretence was proving unsupportable.

'How long will you be here?' Harry asked.

Buckingham did not answer. How could he?

'Quite some while,' came a voice from the doorway. The doctor was a middle-aged man who looked as if he had not slept in months. 'But your friend will be okay, I promise you that.'

He held out his arm, indicating gently that they should leave. They leapt at the chance with relief.

'We'll be back to see you as soon as possible,' Frank said, turning to give Buckingham a wave.

'Win the battle first,' Buckingham said. 'And get some of the bastards for me.'

They went out into the corridor. They could see the young nurse looking at them anxiously.

'He will recover,' the doctor said. 'He'll look better than that, we hope. And eventually, he should be able to walk and lead a fairly normal life.'

'Normal?' Harry said.

'We'll do our best.'

He stifled a yawn and stumbled towards the door.

'Take care,' the nurse said to Harry and Frank. 'Take care.'

THE WORST NEWS

27th September 1940

'Bandits at three o clock,' Harry said.

This was their third sortie of the day and he knew that his men were as exhausted as he was. The sooner they got this one over and could head for home, the better.

'Up and at 'em, lads,' he said.

They approached line abreast. But just as they were about to close, a second swarm of Messerschmitt 109s dived out of the morning sun, guns blazing

Frank was the quickest to react. He gave a touch on his stick which sent his Spitfire soaring above the German planes.

He glanced right and left. Harry and Tomasz were by his side. Others of the squadron were not so quick. He banked a little and saw two planes being set upon by half a dozen Messerschmitts. One was a new boy but the other was Carter, as experienced a pilot as any in the squadron. He managed to shake off one of the planes but the other two pursued him relentlessly. The new boy managed to dive out of danger.

Frank turned and fell upon the Messerschmitts attacking Carter. He gave two of them a couple of three second bursts, enough to send them skidding away from their attack. The third plane was riddling the fuselage of Carter's plane.

Frank fired once more but this time nothing happened, His guns must have jammed. He had no other option than to aim his plane at the German in the hope he would break off his attack. For a moment he thought he wouldn't but, with seconds to spare, the Messerschmitt dived and Frank was able to correct his course.

'Thanks, Frank,' Carter said.

Frank climbed, searching for more targets.

'One on your tail, Frank,' Tomasz called.

Frank banked savagely and evaded the bullets. As he levelled out he saw a pair of Messerschmitts racing towards him. He dived rapidly but they followed. For the next few minutes the three planes performed a dizzying chase and flight, the German guns hammering, Frank's silent.

Finally, Frank managed to get above one of the Germans. He tried his guns again but there was still no response. It was hopeless, he had to get out of there.

'Guns are jammed,' he called to the others.

'Then break off,' Harry said.

'I'm gonna.'

He swept around in a long arc and headed for base. He pushed against the accelerator and there was a kick of speed. Then, abruptly the surge ended.

His eyes shot to his fuel gauge. It was plummeting. His fuel tank must have been hit. A moment later the engine cut out.

He calculated that he was forty miles south of Hornchurch but only thirty from Gravesend. If he was lucky he might make it to the nearer airfield. If there was a lot of turbulence, he would have to try to find somewhere to ditch it. He moved his fingers gently on the stick and brought the plane into a level glide.

He recalled the time when he had been hit by the flock of birds back in Smith County. It seemed a lifetime ago now, but he had managed to land without power then. I've gotten more flying hours under my belt, now, he thought and brought his attention back to the task.

He was five miles south of Rochester when a swarm of Messerschmitts saw him. They must have realised he had no power and was defenceless because they chose to ignore him.

'Good guys,' Frank muttered. 'I'd send you some Bourbon if I could.'

But then one pilot had second thoughts, unable to resist an easy kill and notch up his score. He made a lazy turn and hammered after Frank.

Frank swallowed hard. Part of him realised he was a dead man, but more of him determined to fight to the last. The German came close, blasting the Spitfire's fuselage with bullets. One cracked the cover of the cockpit but it was only a glancing shot and did not shatter it.

The Messerschmitt came in for a second attack. Frank had only one chance. He pushed the plane into a dive and dodged the German's bullets.

Then, to Frank's relief he turned and hurried after his comrades. He must have run out of ammunition or thought he'd already done for Frank.

Bastard, Frank thought. Hope you run into Harry and the boys.

The dive had brought him much lower to the earth, dangerously lower. He did a quick calculation; there was now no chance of him reaching Gravesend.

He scanned the ground below to find somewhere safe to ditch. He cursed; it was too heavily wooded.

He checked his altimeter. If he bailed out now, he had just about enough height for his chute to open. He might survive. He pulled at his canopy but it did not move. It was jammed.

He cursed. The German's final shots must have damaged the canopy more than he thought.

He concentrated on the landscape below. There was nothing else for it, he would have to make a landing on a road. He'd managed it with a crop sprayer but the Spitfire was two tons in weight and English roads were notoriously narrow and winding.

He glimpsed a likely candidate to his left and turned towards it. It was a typical country lane and he glued his eyes to its many twists and turns. But as he closed on it the lane took a sudden long curve. Hidden behind it was a small village.

He cursed and raised the nose a touch higher, managed to gain enough height to skim over the houses, avoided the squat tower of the little church by a few feet.

But then he saw a school ahead of him. The playground was full of children. They must have heard him hurtling towards them and stared up transfixed. Some began to wave.

'Run, kids, run,' he yelled although there was no chance they could hear him.

A couple of teachers raced into the playground, screaming at the children to flee. For a moment none obeyed but then they began to run like kittens, this way, that way, heedless in their panic.

Frank felt blood run into his mouth. He'd bitten through his lip.

It was no good, he was too close, he would crash into the kids in the playground.

He pushed hard on the control stick, pointing the nose towards the ground. The Spitfire fell like a stone, crashing a mere two hundred yards from the school.

The rest of his squadron soared over the village. Harry saw the fireball below and guessed that a plane had been downed.

The squadron landed at Hornchurch twenty minutes later.

Harry went to the Intelligence Officer to give his report.

'Has Frank landed?' he asked. 'Or did he have to use Gravesend?'

Armstrong looked at him, put down his pen, shook his head. 'We've had a report from the Kent police. It's bad news I'm afraid.' He reached out his hand and touched Harry's arm gently.

Flo had finished her shift and was eating her tea in the canteen. She looked up suddenly.

Harry Smith stood a few yards away; motionless, staring at her.

She put down her sandwich. A horrible chill seized her stomach. He stepped towards her.

'I'm very sorry, Flo,' he said. 'But Frank's plane was hit. He crash-landed. I'm afraid he didn't make it. He was very brave. He ditched the plane to avoid a school full of kids.'

She heard someone howling and only gradually came to realise it was her.

The other girls in the canteen flocked around her, nudging Harry out of the way, crooning soft words of comfort and care.

One of the girls hurried off to the ops room to take Betty's place and send her here.

Gradually, very gradually, Flo's wails began to quieten.

Harry Smith shifted from foot to foot. It was the first time he fully realised the grief caused by the death of his friends. He felt bad that he could not feel the same. Then he experienced a slow dawning of relief. If he were to feel anything like Flo did he would never function at all.

Betty rushed past him, and the girls parted to let her through.

She crouched and Flo threw her arms around her.

'Frank's been killed,' she cried.

Betty looked up and caught a glimpse of Harry. He nodded in confirmation.

Flo's tears welled up now, soaking Betty's neck and collar.

'Hush, darling,' Betty murmured, rocking Flo gently as if she were a little child who had woken from a nightmare.

She wanted to tell Flo it would be all right but she knew that was not the case. Not now. Probably not ever. She had been alarmed at the speed with which Flo had fallen in love with the young American. Alarmed at the intensity of her feelings. And now she was going to pay the price.

'I'll take you to our room,' Betty said, helping Flo to her feet.

They headed out of the canteen and towards the women's quarters.

But Flo stopped and shook her head. 'I don't want to be inside. I'd feel trapped. I want to see the countryside.'

They moved slowly past the ranks of Spitfires, past the hangers, past the gun emplacements. One of the soldiers on duty went to stop them but a look from Betty made him turn a blind eye.

They reached the eastern part of the perimeter fence and looked out. Close by were a glade of trees and beyond them, the rich farmlands of south Essex. The river Thames threaded its way close to them.

'I thought that after the war, Frank and me might live round here,' Flo said. 'Unless he took me to America, of course.'

Betty was shocked that she had made such plans already. She did not know how to respond.

'Southend's along there,' Flo continued. Her voice was cold, detached. 'I went there on holiday once. Lovely sand, lots of pubs and cafes and amusements. I don't suppose it's like it now, though. I promised Frank I'd show him the pier.'

She began to weep again. Betty squeezed her hand, murmuring nonsense with no meaning but much heart.

Eventually Flo stopped and reached into her pocket for a handkerchief. She wiped her eyes, turned to stare at Betty and her face was fierce.

'I loved him, Betty. It happened so quick. I didn't mean it to happen, I didn't want it to. And he loved me.'

Her eyes looked up to the sky. 'Maybe knowing that he loved me was what made me fall so quick and so deep.'

'He was a lovely boy,' Betty said.

'He was, wasn't he?' Flo sounded as if they had just discovered something new and astonishing.

'He was really lovely,' she continued, softly. 'Better than all the blokes I've been out with before, much better. We fitted, you see. We fitted together.'

Her hands clasped, fingers interlocking.

She held them up for Betty to see. 'Fitted together.'

'I'm glad we spent that night together,' she murmured. 'Glad for him most of all. Oh he wanted me Betty. He needed me. He was an orphan. From a little boy. He had no one. Not until I came along.'

She started to weep again.

Behind them the sun began to set and their shadows grew long across the woods and meadows.

CALM AND STORM

October 1940

As October wore on, the day-time raids grew more infrequent. On these occasions, the squadron was called up only once a day, sometimes not even that. The fights were just as desperate, the injuries just as terrible, the deaths just as frequent. Yet the gaps between raids allowed some slight relief.

The days turned chillier and every eye looked to the heavens hoping for heavy cloud and rain. Some days this was the case, and the pilots were able to hunker down and try to rest.

Harry found these quiet days almost as troubling as the days of deadly combat. His mind kept going back to the members of the squadron who had died since the start of the battle three months before. He could not remember them all for some had joined the squadron only a day or so before losing their lives. He thought in total it might be a dozen, perhaps more.

But it was the death of Frank Trent which most tormented him.

'You never realise how much you like someone until they're gone,' he told Tomasz one morning.

'Frank was a good man,' Tomasz said. 'And he died bravely, heroically.'

Harry nodded. 'Thirty children would have died if he hadn't ditched his plane.'

This was the one thing which made Frank's death seem less painful. At least for him, he thought. He doubted it did for Flo.

He had spoken to her every day. She was distant, detached, as if she were sleep-walking. Her friend Betty said that she would be okay, in time, but he wondered if that were true.

———

'Are you okay?' Betty asked Flo as they ate lunch in the canteen.

She was growing increasingly worried about her.

For the last few weeks, Flo had seemed constantly tired, which was not too surprising because she tossed and turned all night. Most of the time she was listless and miserable, but then her mood would change abruptly and she would become lively and excitable. This would normally be followed by a bout of tearfulness.

Wing Officer Lewis had already reprimanded her for not concentrating. She'd shown not a trace of sympathy for Flo's loss and told her to snap out of it and focus on the task. It led to another bout of weeping.

'Miserable cow,' Flo had said when she'd dried her tears. 'Frumpy old maid doesn't know what it's like to have been in love.'

She had forced herself to concentrate since then and just about managed it. The other girls covered for her on the days when things got too much for her.

'Are you okay?' Betty repeated. 'You've not touched your food.'

'I'm okay, Betty,' she said, pushing her plate away. 'But if I ever see a bloody Woolton Pie again, I'll scream.'

'You have to eat,' Betty said. 'You've got an important job to do and you need to keep up your strength.'

Flo sighed. 'I don't fancy it, Betty. I feel sick most of the day. The thought of eating makes it worse.'

'Perhaps you've got a bug.'

'Maybe. I've been sick several mornings in a row.' She bent over and groaned.

'What's the matter?' Betty asked anxiously.

'I've got stomach cramps. Well, more a tingling and a pulling.'

'Maybe it's your period.'

'It's not the same. Anyway, I'm late this month.'

She pushed herself up from the table. 'Come on, back to work or Fraulein Curtis will haul me over the coals again.'

It was a quiet day for raids. One of the girls had plotted a small formation of planes over Canterbury but that was all.

'I'll take over,' Flo said. 'Get yourself some dinner.'

She put on her headphones, picked up the plotting pole and leaned over the map. Suddenly it reared up to meet her.

'That's peculiar,' she thought as her head crashed onto the map.

She woke up in the sick bay with Betty sitting beside her.

'Oh God, what happened?'

'You fainted,' Betty said. 'All over the plotting table.'

She squeezed Flo's hand. 'How do you feel?'

'Drunk. And like I've been force-fed a dozen Woolton Pies.' She held her hand to her mouth as if about to vomit.

The orderly saw she was awake and called for a doctor.

Doctor Newmarch was an elderly man, called out of retirement a few months previously. He had a round face, curly eyebrows and a warm smile. He was growing a little white moustache, thinking it would suit his new role in the RAF.

'You fainted,' he said, with an air of authority.

'So I've been told,' Flo said in a distinctly unimpressed tone.

He took her hand and felt her pulse.

'Your friend says that you've been upset recently,' he said. 'That your boyfriend died.'

Tears filled her eyes.

'Maybe you should take some leave.' He spoke in a kindly, compassionate tone.

'Frank wouldn't want that.'

'Frank?'

'My feller. He'd want me to carry on.'

The doctor let go of her hand and lowered it to the sheet.

'Your pulse is a little high but nothing out of the ordinary.'

He placed a blood pressure cuff around her arm and pumped at a little bulb while watching a gauge.

'Ouch, that's tight. What are you doing?'

'Testing your blood pressure. He pulled the cuff off. 'A little high but nothing untoward.'

He peered into her eyes. 'Any other symptoms? Apart from the fainting.'

'I'm a bit down, I suppose.'

'That's not to be wondered at given the circumstances. Stick your tongue out please.' He placed a little stick on it and examined it carefully. 'Anything else?'

Flo gurgled and pointed at her tongue.

'Sorry. You can put it back in now.'

'I'm off me food, doctor. I get stomach cramps and headaches. And I feel sick a lot.'

'Nauseous?'

'Sick. In fact, I keep being sick.'

'When exactly?'

Flo shrugged. 'In the mornings, mostly. For the last three days.'

'For the last week, more like,' Betty said.

The doctor leaned back and looked at Flo. 'What about menstruation?'

Flo shook her head, not knowing what he meant.

'Your period?'

'Oh, why didn't you say so? That's a bit late.'

He sighed. 'Tell me, young lady, in confidence...' He gazed at Betty. 'Perhaps we could have some privacy.'

'There's nothing you can say to me that Betty can't hear,' Flo said. 'We're like sisters.'

'Very well.'

The doctor gave a little cough. 'Tell me...' he glanced at the name on her chart, tell me Flo, are you a virgin?'

Flo coloured. 'Not much.'

There was a silence. 'You either are or you're aren't.'

'Then I aren't.'

He nodded. 'And when did you last have relations? Sexual relations?'

'At the beginning of September. At the pub.'

'The location is hardly relevant. Did your boyfriend take precautions?'

Flo shook her head. 'It wasn't really planned.'

'And have you had a period since then?'

Again she shook her head.

He sighed and took her hand. 'Then I have to tell you that I think you may be pregnant.'

'Oh bugger,' she said.

Harry reached for a cigarette and tried to focus. His hands were shaking. He had first noticed this a few days before. The phrase lack of moral fibre kept haunting him.

'You look tired,' Tomasz said. 'A bit shaky. You should try to get more rest.'

'Then telephone Hitler and ask him to stop sending planes against us. Tell him Harry Smith is knackered. Ask him nicely.'

Tomasz snorted. He could not understand how the British treated Hitler as a figure of fun.

A corporal popped his head around the door. 'The boss wants to see you, Harry. Urgent.'

Harry picked up his cap and went outside. He glanced at the sky. It was dark and brooding with a bank of clouds threatening rain from the south. What could Bouchier want? Surely the squadron wouldn't be told to go up in this weather? And surely the Germans weren't stupid enough to mount a raid in such conditions.

The rain began to fall and he hurried to the station commander's office.

'Come in Harry,' Bouchier said. He gestured him to take a seat.

'I've had a letter this morning,' he said. 'As you know, Keith Park wrote to the Air Ministry to see if we could let Frank Trent's family know about his death. I'm afraid that they point blank refused as they didn't want to upset Anglo-American relations. They believe there'd be hell to pay if Washington found out that an American had been fighting for us.'

Harry shook his head wearily. He always suspected this would be the case.

Bouchier gave Harry a letter from Park reporting the decision. It was short and curt. Harry could sense the Air Vice Marshal's anger at the Ministry's response.

'Are you asking me to write to his family?' Harry said. 'It's what commanding officers normally do. I could send it secretly, perhaps.'

'Good lord, no. That would be very foolish. You'd end up working as a mechanic again. If you ever got out of jail.'

Harry sighed. So Frank's sacrifice would never be known, except to his friends.

'Luckily,' Bouchier continued, 'there's no need for such desperate measures.' He passed Harry a second letter. 'This has just arrived.'

Harry glanced at the letter. 'It's from Churchill.' He looked at Bouchier in amazement.

'Yes. And it's to President Roosevelt.'

Harry read the letter quickly. Churchill had written briefly about Frank's record, including the number of German planes he had shot down.

Then he wrote at more length about how he had died, how he had selflessly crashed his plane to save the lives of little children. He asked Roosevelt if Frank's commanding officer could let his family know exactly how he'd died. Tell them about his courage and his sacrifice.

Churchill finished by acknowledging that this might put Roosevelt in a difficult position but hoped that he would agree to the request in honour of the solidarity that Frank had shown the people of Britain.

Harry felt a lump fill his throat. When he spoke it was in a choked tone.

'Do you think the President will agree?'

'Do you think Churchill would have let us see the letter if Roosevelt hadn't already done so?'

He passed a short memo from Air Chief Marshal Dowding. It read: 'President Roosevelt agrees we can inform Flight Lieutenant Trent's family of his death and the manner of it. The letter is to be given, in confidence, to Mrs Evelyn Nash who is going back to America to advocate on our behalf.'

'Get the letter written today,' Bouchier said. 'Let me see it and then fly across to Uxbridge to give it to Air Vice Marshal Park personally.'

He glanced out of the window. 'The weather looks bad until Monday. Take a few days leave, Harry. Spend it somewhere nice. A country pub or hotel perhaps.'

He gave a smile. 'And give my regards to your lady friend.'

'You won't be able to stay here,' Betty told Flo. 'In fact, you won't be able to stay in the WAAF.'

Her eyes filled with tears but she blinked them away. She didn't want to make Flo feel upset on her behalf. But she would miss her terribly when she was gone.

'I suppose not,' Flo said. She ran her fingers through her hair. Her whole world seemed to be disintegrating around her.

'Will you go home?' Betty asked. 'To your mum and dad.'

'There's no home left to go to, not since the bombing. My folks are all crowded into Uncle Ted's pub. There's no room for me there.' Or the baby, she thought, suddenly.

She leaned back in the bed. From now on, she realised, she had someone to worry about. The little person growing inside her. Her baby. And Frank's.

'So where will you go?'

'I don't know. The whole world's gone topsy-turvy.'

The room fell quiet, the only sound the rain rattling on the window panes.

Betty gasped. 'You could go to my mum and dad's. My bedroom's empty. They'd be glad to have you. Honestly.'

Flo gazed at her. The use of the word honestly made her doubt Betty's sense of certainty.

'Are you sure they would, Betty? They don't know me. I'm a bit of a rough diamond, not nice and refined like you. And...'

'And what?'

'And there's the baby. How will they take to a baby yelling her head off all the day?'

'They'll love it. And they'll help you. When you're tired. Or with your shopping.' Betty smiled. 'I see you've decided it's a girl.'

Flo nodded. 'And I'll call her Betty, after you.'

Betty blushed with embarrassment and delight.

She took Flo's hand. 'Say you'll go. There's no bombs where my parents live. It's so quiet and peaceful.'

Flo blinked. She had always dreamed of living in the country away from all the noise and soot. And now, here it was, given to her on a plate. She wondered exactly where Somerset was. A long way she thought. Nice and safe.

'It will be a lovely place to bring up the baby,' Betty said.

Flo took her hand. 'You mean baby Betty.'

Betty giggled.

Flo leaned back in the bed, pondering this offer, trying not to feel overwhelmed by it.

'Okay,' she said at last. 'If you're sure your mum and dad will want it, then go ahead and ask.'

Betty clapped her hands. 'This is wonderful.'

Flo looked at her askance. For you, she thought. I'm not sure if it is for me.

But then her hand went to her stomach and her heart softened. There's a bit of Frank with me, she thought. Now and forever. A gentle mist filled her eyes. She remembered that he had sacrificed his life for the sake of little children. Now, she would give him a gift of a child of his own.

Harry landed his plane at Uxbridge, climbed out and asked a corporal the way to the operations room. He pushed his cap on more firmly, took a deep breath and made his way towards it.

His stomach was doing loop the loop. The thought of seeing Claire was as nerve wracking as scrambling to fight the Jerries.

He was surprised at the sight of the operations room. It was almost identical to the ones at the stations he had been in but on a far bigger scale.

'Can I help you?' a silver haired Flight Lieutenant asked.

'I'm looking for Air Vice Marshal Park.'

'He's out visiting airfields.'

'He's just landed, Johnny,' a woman said, coming towards them. She had a pronounced American accent.

'Are you Mrs Nash?' Harry asked.

'Who's asking?'

'My name's Harry. I served with your husband. He was a good man.'

Her face wobbled a little and tears came to her eyes. 'Thank you.'

'I've got a letter,' he continued. 'It's for you to take to Washington. Although I'm to give it to Air Vice Marshal Park first.'

'Oh,' Evelyn said. You must be Harry Smith.'

He coloured. 'You've heard of me.'

'A little bit.' She smiled did not elaborate.

Johnny Longley chuckled and gave him a huge wink. He coloured even more.

The people in the room straightened up as a figure in a white flying suit entered. He noticed Harry after a moment and walked towards him.

'The young firebrand,' he said. 'I gather you have a letter for me.'

He took the letter and read it carefully. 'That seems just the ticket to me. But I'll check with Sir Hugh.'

He picked up a telephone, spoke for a few minutes and then began to read the letter quietly over the phone. Finally, he put the telephone down and returned to Harry.

'The Air Chief Marshal is happy with it. Except he thinks you should say something more about how well Trent got on with the rest of the squadron. And how much they liked him.' He gave a questioning look.

'Oh, it's true, all right,' Harry said, comprehending Park's expression. 'Frank was very popular. I just didn't think I needed to —'

'Spell it out?'

'Yes sir.'

'Well you do. Outsiders, especially family, don't really appreciate the brotherhood that combat forges. Tell them that. They deserve to know.' He pointed to an empty desk. 'Do it now.'

Harry sat and picked up a pen. He had left a space at the bottom of the letter for he hadn't been sure who should sign it. He added a paragraph about Frank's relations with the rest of the squadron.

And then, without giving it a moment of thought, he wrote more. About how much he liked, admired and loved Frank. And how he would remember him for all his days.

Park read the letter carefully. 'This is very good, Smith,' he said 'You need to sign it.'

'I wasn't sure.' Harry paused. 'Shall I put my rank?'

'You were his squadron leader weren't you? Of course you should.'

He put his hand on Harry's arm. 'I'm sorry that you lost your friend.'

Harry signed the letter and sealed it in an envelope. He gave Evelyn the letter and hoped she would have a good trip home. Then he noticed Johnny Longley gesturing to the far side of the room.

He turned and saw her.

He felt sick inside. What would Claire think now that he was here?

'I've got a couple of days leave,' he told Claire as they drank a cup of tea in the corner of the room. He swallowed the lump in his throat. 'So I thought perhaps I could see you. Tomorrow or the next day.'

She stared at her cup, swirled it as if she were about to up end it and read the tea leaves.

'I'm due some time off,' she said at last. 'Perhaps I could see you tonight.'

'For dinner?' he said. 'Marvellous.' His heart hammered with relief and excitement.

She did not answer for a long while. 'For dinner. And for breakfast.'

He nodded enthusiastically, although he wondered where they might go for breakfast. The canteen here, he supposed.

She was looking down at the ground and suddenly looked up and gazed into his eyes.

With a jolt, he realised what she was suggesting.

'You mean....?'

Claire nodded. 'There's a little hotel on the Great West Road that's very nice.' She smiled. 'We'll have to sign in as Mr and Mrs Smith.

'I'll borrow a ring from my friend Jacqueline, she continued.

His mouth opened and then shut. For once he could find nothing to say.

But then, suddenly, something came to him.

'Maybe, not now, but maybe when the war's over we can really be … really become Mr and Mrs Smith.' His face turned crimson.

Claire smiled. 'One step at a time, Harry.'

She went across to Park and asked for time off. He gave it without a second's thought.

Then she whispered to Johnny Longley. 'Do you think Jacqueline will be able to run us over to the White Hart Hotel?'

'She'd love to.' He glanced at the clock. 'She'll be finished in a little while.'

'Good. Ask her to meet me at the gate. I don't want any prying eyes.' She walked away but then came back. 'And Johnny, please, keep this under your hat.'

He grinned. 'I don't even know what you're talking about.'

She hurried off to her room to pack her bag.

Johnny spoke into the telephone, gave Harry the thumbs up and came to join him.

'Come on lad, I'll walk you to the gate.'

They spoke exclusively about the war as they strolled to the gate. But when they got there Johnny turned and gave him a stern look. 'Claire's a lovely girl. I've grown very fond of her. So, see that you treat her well.'

'Of course I will.'

'I'm just saying.'

They fell silent once again. Dusk began to settle over the base, blurring and softening its hard edges. Bird song began to sound, a few calls at first, then a growing chorus which seemed to fill the sky.

Claire appeared in the distance with a small bag in her hand.

'I don't suppose you were expecting this,' Johnny said to Harry.

'Not in a million years. I didn't even know if I'd see her.'

'Then have something for the weekend.' He pressed a packet of contraceptives into his hand.

'Thank you,' Harry stuttered. 'I hadn't thought. How much do I owe —'

'Don't be such an idiot. Just remember what I said about treating her right.'

A car screeched up just as Claire reached them. Jacqueline wound down her window.

'Did someone order a taxi?'

Claire smiled and climbed in the back. Johnny almost had to push Harry in beside her.

The car drove off, with Jacqueline casting curious glances in the rear-view mirror.

Claire put her hand in Harry's. They were going to make the best of the weekend. Any more plans would have to wait until the end of the war.

END OF BATTLE

November 1940

The German raids lessened as October wore on. The attacks on the airfields ceased and towards the end of the month came the last major strike on London. Over forty bombers were detected and Park called upon 12 Group for assistance. It took twenty minutes for them to form their Big Wing and during this time many of the bombers had been dispersed by Park's squadrons. A number of them got through to the capital to drop their bombs. By the time the Big Wing arrived the Germans were back over the Channel and heading for France.

The next two weeks there were very few raids and Harry was able to come over to Uxbridge and take her out for tea at a Lyons Corner House.

They finished their meal and went to the cinema, choosing the end seats of the back row. They did not see much of the film.

'How are Flo and Betty?' Claire asked as they strolled back to the base.

'Betty's been made a sergeant,' Harry said. 'And Flo's left already. She's gone to Betty's parents in Suffolk or Norfolk or somewhere like that. Apparently, she decided it would be best if she left before the baby began to show.'

Claire laughed. 'I thought she might have brazened it out until the last possible moment.'

Harry shook his head. 'I gather she's changed a lot. Quietened down. Grown up, I suppose.'

'It will be awful for her, bringing up a baby alone.'

'And awful having lost the love of her life.'

He squeezed her hand. Claire's heart pounded harder.

She dreaded that Harry would suffer the same fate as his friend, Frank. She was tormented by the thought. And she didn't for the life of her know whether to try to cool their relationship for fear of losing him. But then, she argued to herself, if she did, she would lose him for certain.

'How will you get home?' she asked suddenly. 'Surely it's too late to fly back.'

He gaped. 'I hadn't thought of that.' He looked crestfallen.

She stopped and stared into his face. She shook her head ruefully.

'I know you can fly, Harry Smith,' she said. 'But how good are you at climbing up drainpipes?'

He looked confused. 'I've no idea. Why do you ask?'

She gave a sigh and took his hand. 'Because there's a drainpipe just below my bedroom window.' She kissed him fondly. 'But you'll have to be on your way before daylight.'

She could not believe that she was running such a risk.

Harry landed back at Hornchurch at 07.00 hours the next morning. An hour later he was summoned to the Station Commander's office. He groaned. Bouchier must have heard that he had spent the night in the WAAF quarters.

His fears increased when he saw that Wentworth was also in the office.

'Come in, Smith,' Bouchier said, pointing to a chair.

Wentworth frowned at Harry. 'Something wrong?' He looked a little concerned.

'Not at all, sir,' Harry said.

'Good,' Bouchier said. 'I thought your lady friend might have given you the brush off.'

'Not at all, sir.' He tried and failed to keep a smug smile from his face.

Bouchier raised an eyebrow and then held up a letter. 'The King is visiting the station tomorrow.'

Harry had no idea how he was meant to take this news. He had no interest in the King or any of his doings. If he had his way, he'd be kicked out and replaced by a President.

Then his eyes narrowed. He hoped that Bouchier didn't want him to escort the King around.

'You'll be seeing the King yourself,' Bouchier said.

He caught the look of dismay in Harry's face. 'Don't worry your rebellious head, Smith, you'll not spend much time with His Majesty. Just enough for him to pin a medal on your chest.'

'A medal?'

'A DFC.' He saw Harry's uncertain look. 'A Distinguished Flying Cross.'

'But why?'

'Because I bloody recommended you.' Bouchier wagged a finger at him. 'Don't think you can try to argue, Harry. You've done a first-rate job. Off you go, lad. Get some breakfast.'

Harry got to his feet and saluted. He was very well aware that he would have only been eligible for a Distinguished Flying Medal if he'd remained a sergeant. Rank outweighed courage in the awarding of medals it seemed. And Frank, of course, would not have been eligible for anything.

'And invite your lady friend along to watch,' Bouchier said.

'Yes, sir.' He went out and then popped his head back in. 'And thank you, sir.'

The next day he stood in line as King George VI made his slow progress with Air Chief Marshal Dowding, Air Vice Marshal Park and Bouchier behind him.

Claire was in the front of the spectators opposite. She gave a little wave, her face beaming with delight.

Then the King was standing in front of him.

'Squadron Leader Smith, Your Majesty,' Bouchier said.

The King said a few words which Harry didn't take in and pinned the medal on his chest.

Then he moved on to the next man.

'Well done, firebrand,' Park said, clapping him on the shoulder. Harry smiled. It felt a far better commendation than the piece of metal on his chest.

Harry peered down at the medal. It's not just for me, he thought. It's for everyone else as well. Bob Wright, Carter, Tomasz, Jack White. Even Buckingham.

But most of all, he thought, it was for his friend Frank.

Characters in Wings of Fire

(those in bold are historical figures)

Claire Lamb Squadron Officer WAAF
Harry Smith RAF Pilot
Frank Trent, American pilot
Betty Jones, WAAF
Flo Summers, WAAF
Johnny Longley, Flight Lieutenant, RAF
Jacqueline Longley, Sergeant, WAAF
Tony Nash Squadron Leader RAF
Evelyn Nash, his wife
Rupert Buckingham RAF pilot
Tomasz Kaczmarczyk, Polish Major, RAF Flight Lieutenant
Leading Aircraftmen Jack White
Air Chief Marshal Sir Hugh Dowding
Air Vice Marshal Keith Park
Air Vice Marshal Trafford Leigh-Mallory
Wing Commander Willoughby de Broke, Senior Controller
11 Group
Wing Commander Miles Wentworth
Squadron Leader Stephen Maisfield
Wing Commander Cecil 'Boy' Bouchier, Head of Hornchurch
Sector Station Airfield

Air Vice Marshal William Sholto Douglas
Sir Kingsley Wood, Minister for Air
Oberleutnant Jurgen Diederichson
Group Commander Enid Bowles, Amazon Defence Corps
Sir Archibald Sinclair, Minister for Air
Winston Churchill, Prime Minister of Great Britain
Clemmie Churchill, his wife
Squadron Leader Anthony Norman, RAF Kenley
Henry Lamb, Claire's father
Gladys Lamb, her mother
Jimmy Lamb, her brother
Charlie Smith, Harry's father
Dora Smith, his mother
George Summers, Flo's father
Maggie Summers, her mother
Raymond and Sidney Summers, her brothers
Ted Summers, her uncle
Connie Summers, her cousin
Walter Trent, Frank's father
Mildred Trent, Frank's stepmother
Paul Bennett, Frank's cousin
Laurence Buckingham, Rupert's father
Georgina Buckingham, Rupert's mother
Violet Buckingham, Rupert's sister
Reverend Stanley Nash, Tony's father
Winifred Nash, Tony's mother
Pilot Officer Bob Wright
Wing Officer Barlow, RAF Kenley
Squadron Leader Jerrold, RAF Kenley
Sheriff Grover, Smith County, Kansas
Henry Sutton, airfield owner

Flight Lieutenant Armstrong, Hornchurch Intelligence Officer
Squadron Leader Digby, Hornchurch Senior Controller
Squadron Leader Michael Green, recruitment officer,
Regina, Saskatchewan
Peter Gaunt, owner of training field
Dick Delaney, his deputy
Oscar Rawson, recruiter of American pilots

THANKS AND ACKNOWLEDGEMENTS

Thank you for buying Wings of Fire. I hoped you enjoyed it,

No book is solely the work of the writer. It needs inspiration and nurturing, as does, often, the writer.

In the writing of this book I have had the unstinting support of my wife, Janine, who also read it and gave me many points and suggestions. I am ever grateful for all she does.

Some members of my writing group were also kind enough to read early drafts of the novel and make suggestions, improvement and point out errors I had missed. So, a big thank-you to Shirley Medhurst, Charlie Baddeley and Phil Baddeley. Any mistakes still remaining after this are solely down to me.

I would also like to thank Kevin Jausseran who spent the whole of one Friday evening locating and saving twenty thousand words of my novel which had inexplicably gone missing. He rescued me from my worst nightmare.

Finally, I must pay tribute to all the people who fought and suffered in the Second World War. Various estimates say that between fifty and a hundred million people died in the war but countless millions of other were injured, traumatised or had their lives turned upside down. Some of them figure in this book, others are fictional and can only represent the millions of others engulfed in the catastrophe.

I have chosen to focus on the Battle of Britain, one of the most important of the conflict. If the RAF had lost the battle then it is likely that Nazi Germany would have invaded and conquered Britain. The consequences for the rest of the world are unimaginable.

While I focus on the British effort in the war, we do well to remember that there is another side of the story. The pilots of the Luftwaffe were young men like the British and they suffered the same fears and exaltations, the same deaths and injuries. May everyone involved in that terrible war rest in a peace which was denied them in the years that it raged.

The recommendations and comments of readers make all the difference to the success of a book. I would be very grateful if you could spread the word about the book amongst your friends.

It would also be a great help if you could spend a few moments writing a review and posting it on the site where you purchased the book, Goodreads or any other forum you are active in.

To post a review on Amazon please click, tap or paste here: viewauthor.at/MartinLake

OTHER BOOKS BY MARTIN LAKE

Here are some other books which you may wish to take a look at.

Cry of the Heart. Viviane Renaud is a young mother living on the French Riviera in the Second World War. Times are hard but she is not the sort to be dismayed by circumstances. One day her life changes forever. A young Jewish woman, fleeing from the authorities, begs her to take care of her four-year-old boy, David. Almost without thinking, Viviane agrees.

Viviane's life is never the same again. She fabricates a story to explain how David came to be with her and must tip-toe around the suspicions of her neighbours, her friends and most of all her mother and sister. She and her husband, Alain, find allies in unlikely places, particularly an American woman, Dorothy Pine.

But then, the world crashes around them. Threatened by Allied military success, Hitler sends the German army to occupy the south of France. With them come the SS and the Gestapo. The peril for Jews and for those, like Viviane, who hide them, appears overwhelming. The challenge for them now is to survive.

A Love Most Dangerous. Her beauty was a blessing…and a dangerous burden, As a Maid of Honor at the Court of King Henry VIII, beautiful Alice Petherton receives her share of admirers.

But when the powerful, philandering Sir Richard Rich attempts to seduce her, she knows she cannot thwart his advances for long. She turns to the most powerful man in England for protection: the King himself.

Very Like a Queen. The King's favor was her sanctuary—until his desire turned dangerous. Alice Petherton is well practiced at using her beauty and wits to survive in the Court of King Henry VIII. As the King's favorite, she enjoys his protection, but after seeing the downfall of three of his wives, she's determined to avoid the same fate. Alice must walk a fine line between mistress and wife.

The Viking Chronicles:

Wolves of War. Leif Ormson lived a pleasant and uneventful life. Until the sons of Ragnar Lothbrok threw him into a storm of war, danger and destruction.

To the Death. The Viking army, with Leif a reluctant leader, does battle against the kingdom of Wessex.

The Saxon Chronicles:

Land of Blood and Water. Warfare and warriors mean nothing to Brand and his family. But then King Alfred of Wessex chooses their home for his last-ditch defence against the Vikings.

Blood Enemy. Ulf, son of Brand, has risen high in the service of King Alfred. But when he shows himself a berserker he loses everything. Can he redeem himself and return to favour?

The Lost King Books:

The Flame of Resistance. The battle of Hastings is over. The battle for England is about to begin.

Triumph and Catastrophe. Can a 17 year old boy with an ill-equipped army challenge William the Conqueror for his birth-right, the throne of England?

Blood of Ironside. Betrayed by friends and family, Edgar Atheling refuses to submit and vows to take the battle to the Conqueror's homeland.

In Search of Glory. Edgar grows accustomed to Norman rule, although he berates himself for his failures. Then events occur which cause him to continue the fight.

Outcasts: Crusades Book 1. Jerusalem has fallen to Saladin. Three newly knighted men journey through a perilous, bitter world to rescue a captive wife and family.

The Artful Dodger. The adventures of the Artful Dodger in Australia and London.

For King and Country. Three short stories set in the First World War.

Nuggets. Fast fiction for quiet moments.

Mr Toad's Wedding. First prize winner in the competition to write a sequel story to The Wind in the Willows.

Mr Toad to the Rescue. After losing his betrothed to his cousin, Mr Toad and his friends are called upon to rescue her from an even bigger rascal.

The Big School. Three light-hearted short stories about a boy's experience of growing up.

You can find my books easily by clicking here: viewauthor.at/ MartinLake

I have a mailing list with my new release, news and exclusive stories. To be the first to hear about new releases, please sign up below. I promise I won't fill up your mailbox with lots of emails. I won't share your email with anybody.

If you would like to subscribe please click here:

http://eepurl.com/DTnhb

You can read more about my approach to writing on my blog: http://martinlakewriting.wordpress.com

Or on Facebook at https://www.facebook.com/MartinLakeWriting

Or you can follow me on Twitter @martinlake14

Printed in Great Britain
by Amazon

76802270R00224